SOMEONE'S OUT TO SILENCE JUSTIS

"Another murder with magical connections. Tell me more about Regina Witcombe."

"She's president and CEO of a major financial corporation, she has more money than God, she's smart and combative and ruthless. She also opposes just about every important piece of consumer protection legislation relating to the banking industry that comes before Congress or the state legislature. I'm torn, because it's kind of nice to see a woman leading a huge multinational finance company: breaking the glass ceiling and all of that. But I really hate everything she stands for."

"Have you ever heard any whispers about her being odd around the full moon?"

Her mouth fell open. "You think she's a weremyste?" she asked, leaning in over the table.

"I have a source who says she is."

"Holy crap!"

I saw a gleam in her eyes that I knew all too well. "We're still off the record, remember?"

"Damn it! How can you tell me something like that off the record? That's not fair."

A quip leaped to mind, something that would make her laugh—I loved the way she laughed. I opened my mouth to speak.

A tingle of magic crawled over my skin, locking the words in my throat, making the hairs on my arms and neck stand on end. I saw no color, but I felt it building. Again I was reminded of the way desert air turned electric in the instant before lightning struck.

"Shit," I whispered.

"Justis?"

And in that moment, the world exploded.

Books by David B. Coe

The Case Files of Justis Fearsson
Spell Blind
His Father's Eyes
Shadow's Blade (forthcoming)

The LonTobyn Chronicle
Children of Amarid
The Outlanders
Eagle-Sage

Winds of the Forelands series
Rules of Ascension
Seeds of Betrayal
Bonds of Vengeance
Shapers of Darkness
Weavers of War

Blood of the Southlands series
The Sorcerers' Plague
The Horsemen's Gambit
The Dark-Eyes' War

Robin Hood (novelization)

As D. B. Jackson

The Thieftaker series
Thieftaker
Thieves' Quarry
A Plunder of Souls
Dead Man's Reach

HIS FATHER'S EYES

DAVID B. COE

HIS FATHER'S EYES

This is a work of fiction. All the characters and events portrayed in this book are fictional, and any resemblance to real people or incidents is purely coincidental.

A Baen Book

Baen Publishing Enterprises
P.O. Box 1403
Riverdale, NY 10471
www.baen.com

ISBN: 978-1-4767-8144-0

Cover art by Alan Pollack

First Baen Paperback printing, April 2016

Distributed by Simon & Schuster
1230 Avenue of the Americas
New York, NY 10020

Library of Congress Cataloging-in-Publication Data:
   2015018854

Printed in the United States of America

10 9 8 7 6 5 4 3 2 1

Dedication

* * *

For my father,
Whose eyes were bright blue,
and who taught me to look at the world
with humor and passion.
I miss him every day.

HIS FATHER'S EYES

CHAPTER 1

It burns and burns and burns, a pain he can't salve, a fire he can't extinguish. White, yellow, red, orange. Shades of pale blue sometimes, but then white again. Always white. White hot. Pure white. White for wedding gowns and babies' diapers and clean sheets on a crib. White. Like blank paper. And then it burns. Brown giving way to black, which comes from the yellow and orange and red and pale blue; flame creeping like spilled blood, spreading like a stain.

The land rolls downward from his chair, baked and dry, empty. But also full, if only one knows how to look at it. The rising swirls of red dirt. Red-tailed hawks wheeling on splayed wings. Jackrabbits and coyotes, watchful and tense, death and survival hanging between them.

The sky is too clear—not a cloud, nothing to break the monotony of blue so bright it makes his eyes tear. Except low, to the east, where the blue mingles with brown, like dirty, worn jeans.

That's how he is. Muddied. Clouded. Enveloped in a

haze. He feels the hot wind moving over his skin, and he waits for it to clear the air around him. But it never does; instead, dust stings his eyes, and grit crunches between his teeth like slivers of glass. He wants a cup of water, but his legs feel leaden and the trailer seems so far. So he sits, shielding his eyes with a shaking hand, listening to the flapping of the tarp over his head.

She winks into view before him, wearing a simple dress. One of his favorites. Cornflower blue, as soft as the sky is hard. She flashes that familiar crooked grin, cocking her head to the side, honey brown hair dancing around her face. The boy is there, too. Suddenly. Dropped into the scene as if by sleight of hand. Shorts and an ASU t-shirt, his hair the same color as hers, but wild with curls and the wind, so young, so oblivious to it all: the phasings that await him, the dark sadness that lurks behind his mother's smile, the betrayal masked in those gorgeous blue eyes. He's wept for her until the tears run dry, like a desert river in late summer. But he can still cry for the boy; the boy who has become a man so much like his father that it breaks the old man's heart.

Ghosts. Both of them, though only the one is dead. He shifts his gaze, follows the flight of a plane as it carves across the sky, leaving a stark white scar. He refuses to blink, until his eyes ache with the effort. When at last he checks again, the woman and child are gone.

But if he closes his eyes they're back, the images seared onto his mind, like blotches of light after he has stared too long at the sun. They were never here, of course. Not on this land. He knows that. The trailer, the tarp, the chair—all are new.

New. The boy would laugh at that. None of it is new. But she never saw any of it.

He opens his eyes again, shakes his head, sits up straighter. One of those days. The haze. The confusion. The hallucinations. He's had it all before. The secret is not giving in to it, fighting the pull. But when it gets this bad it's like climbing a mountain of sand; with every step up, he feels himself sliding backwards. Sometimes it's the visions. Violent, bloody, horrible images, so vivid, so familiar. They might be echoes of old phasings or they could be things he really saw and did. He can't remember anymore. Other times it's no more or less than the relic of younger emotions—love, jealousy, rage, grief—as vague as the scent of sage riding the desert wind, as sharp as a razor. And on some days, like today, it's all of those, and it's none of them. It defies description or understanding, and he's left to stumble alone, as though lost within that muddy cloud draped over the Phoenix skyline.

There are pills. He's supposed to take them if it gets too bad. The boy has left them out on the counter, where he'll see them. But they don't help: not enough. They bring clarity of a sort. They wake him up, like a dousing with ice water. It's not him, though; it's not anyone he recognizes. He's spent hours staring at that grizzled, slack face in the mirror, peering into those eyes, pale gray, like his own, but flat and dead and nothing like the eyes he remembers from his youth, or those he sees now in the boy. That's the drugs. As opposed to the Drug, the one the doctor won't talk about in front of him.

He laughs at the distinction, startling himself with the sound.

They give him these drugs—their drugs—to fight off the damage he did by refusing to take the other, by clinging to his magic and subjecting himself to the cruel moon. They whisper about it to the boy, not wanting him to hear, fearing that it will awaken the old visions, or send him into a fit of rage, like in old movies. As if their whispers can guard him from the memory, as if he doesn't curse his magic every goddamned day of his life, as if it isn't already too late for him.

No, he might be screwed up, but he's not that screwed up. He's not completely beyond reality. Even on those days when he can't put together a coherent thought, when the boy sits beside him, concern etched on his face, which is so like his mother's that it makes the old man's chest ache. Even when it seems that he's too far gone to see or hear or understand anything, he knows who and what he's become. That might be the worst part. If he was so far gone that he didn't remember it all—if dementia carried with it the comforting numbness that everyone thinks they see in him - then they could whisper and conceal, and smile their false reassuring smiles, and he wouldn't care. But he knows. *He knows.*

That's the slow death. That's the torment. That's the price he pays for ancient sins. Better to have nothing left. But when did the moon ever care what was better for him?

He sees the boy wrestling with the same demons, and he prays for him. Yes, he prays. He hasn't prayed for anything else in almost fifty years, not since he was a kid. Not even when he was on the job, going into Maryvale or the worst beats of South Mountain or Cactus Park with nothing more than an old service revolver in his hand and his partner watching his back; not even that time when a kid so jacked up on dust that he seemed to be doing everything with his eyes closed put four bullets in him; not even when he found her dead beside her lover, his pain an amalgam of humiliation and heartache and debilitating grief.

Even then he didn't turn to God. The Great Unbeliever. A cop to the core. A man of reason and evidence and laws. Utterly earthbound.

But for his boy, he prays. Not that it'll do a damn bit of good.

The moon is a goddess unto herself. She's as merciless as time, as unforgiving as memory. She laughs at prayers. No, the boy has to fight this battle on his own. The old man can only hope that the kid has more of his mother's strength than his father's weakness.

He wonders if the boy will be coming today, until he remembers that he was here yesterday, or maybe the day before. It's hard to keep track sometimes. The days all blend. Hot, sunny, slow. When things are good, and he keeps busy, he can follow the progression. But not in recent days. Or weeks. It's hard to keep track of time.

It's this burning. A new kind of invasion, an assault on his mind that even the phasings couldn't match. The sorrow and remorse and shame and loss are melted together into some glowing alloy that flows in his veins, scalding him throughout. Everything hurts. The sunlight scorches his eyes. The wind stings his skin. Every breath is agony. Every movement makes him wince.

And he knows that this means something. He is a

scrying glass. Shining, smooth—a blank surface on which others might glimpse the future. For years, the powers of the world have ignored him, seeing in him no more than is there: a disgraced former cop, an empty, burned-out old sorcerer. But now, for some reason, they've taken notice of him again. With all the crafting he used to do, scrying was the one type of magic he truly hated. There was too little certainty, too little control. But this is different. Others are doing the crafting now. He can't see them. He doesn't know who they are, or what they want of him. But they're all around him. Setting him ablaze, flaying his body with their power, watching him for signs of what is to come.

If he sees her, if he sees the boy, do these others see them, too? Are his visions his own or someone else's? Why would they care about her? The boy is one thing. He has power of his own now. He matters. But what is she, beyond a memory that warms him and plagues him and leaves him longing for something he no longer believes was real? Why should his torment interest these others?

He has no answers. Questions lay siege to his mind, assailing him from all sides. And he has nothing to offer in response. He sits, watches the sky, frowns at the brown haze, envies the grace of the hawk, waits for the coyote to make his move. The wind blows, an occasional cloud slides past, the sun tracks a slow circle above him, shadows grow longer, gold suffuses the light, the air cools a little.

He can feel their eyes upon him; he senses their impatience. They want portents, but he has nothing to offer. He is glass, or perhaps stone. Fate is reflected off his life. Or so they seem to believe. He doesn't know if they're right, or if they imagine in him more than is there. He just sits.

And still it burns and burns and burns.

CHAPTER 2

The image flickered in my scrying stone, like a candle guttering in the wind, before becoming more fixed, more substantial. I hadn't been sure the spell would work, but there he was—"he" being Mark Darby, an employee at Custom Electronics, in Mesa, who had been stealing computers, phones, stereo equipment, and pretty much anything else you could think of. He was by the loading dock at the rear of the store, shoving boxes into the back of a beat-up old Subaru wagon.

"Gotchya," I whispered, still peering down at the stone.

Darby's bosses had known for some time that someone on their staff was robbing them, but they didn't know who; only that he or she had been clever enough to avoid detection for the better part of four months.

Until now.

Not that the magical vision I'd summoned to the stone was proof, at least not the kind that I could use in any court of law.

"No, Your Honor, I don't have any surveillance tape. But I cast a seeing spell and saw him in this shiny piece of agate . . ."

Right.

But now that I knew for certain who the thief was, I had no intention of letting him get away.

I got out of the Z-ster, my silver 1977 280Z, which was parked along a side street near the store, closed the door with the care of a burglar, and began to limp toward the loading dock.

If someone had told me a year ago that getting shot could be a good thing, I would have said that person was nuts. And I know nuts. I'm a weremyste, which means that for three nights out of every month—the night of the full moon, and the nights immediately before and after—I lose control of my mind and my magic. It also means that eventually, the cumulative wear-and-tear of those monthly phasings will leave me permanently insane. As they have my dad.

But this is about the risks of my profession, as opposed to the dangers of my runecrafting. I'm a private investigator, owner and president of Justis Fearsson Investigations. And not so long ago I was shot—twice, as it happens—by a powerful sorcerer named Etienne de Cahors, who was known here in Phoenix as the Blind Angel Killer. He didn't survive our encounter, mostly because I had help from Kona Shaw, my old partner on the Phoenix police force.

Bringing down the bastard responsible for the Blind Angel murders, a killing spree that had terrorized the Phoenix area for the better part of three years, was enough to make me a hero. Ending up with a couple of bullets in me was icing on the cake, and it got me in the headlines. Business, which was slow before then, had been booming ever since. Except that for the first several weeks I had one arm in a sling and my leg bandaged from hip to knee, and so I couldn't do much more than sit on the couch in my home and answer the phone. People were lining up to hire me, and I was every bit as eager to get to work. But for more than a month I had no choice but to decline more jobs than I had worked in the previous year.

I still miss being a cop—losing my badge about killed me—but if I can't be on the force, working as a PI is the next best thing. Despite the reward money I'd collected for killing Cahors, I didn't want to sit on my butt catching up on the latest in daytime drama; I wanted to do my job. So about ten days ago, when I was cleared by the doctors and my physical therapist to start working again, I took the first offer that came my way. The doctors and PT told me to take it easy, and I really have tried to be good. But it's not like there are volume settings for investigative work. You're on or you're off. Despite my limp, and the lingering twinge in my arm, I was on again, and I was glad.

I reached the back of the building and peeked around the corner to get some sense of how far I was from the loading dock. Pretty far, it turned out. Custom Electronics was one of those huge warehouse stores that seem to go on for miles, and so I was still at least one hundred yards from Darby and his wagon. But the old floodlights shining high over the loading area were strong enough for me to see him. They would also be strong enough for him to see me when I stepped around the corner.

I ducked back out of sight and hesitated, unsure as to whether I could pull off the spell I had in mind.

I had spent a good deal of my recovery time honing my casting—my runecrafting, as Namid would call it. There was nothing like almost dying at the hands of a renegade runemyste to motivate a person. Namid, who oversaw my magical training, had taught me a number of new spells, including the variation on a standard seeing spell I had used to track Darby. Two nights ago, we had worked on camouflage spells, which, in theory anyway, would make me virtually invisible to the man. I'd practiced such spells before, and I was growing more comfortable with them. Problem was, I had never used one out on the street, when it really mattered, and I had no confidence that I could pull it off on my own, without Namid instructing me each step of the way.

Then again, I didn't have any better options. If I could have made myself fly, or given myself superhuman speed, I would have. But magic doesn't work that way, at least not for weremystes who still have way too much to learn about runecrafting. I had my .40 Glock 22 in a shoulder holster beneath my bomber jacket, but I didn't think Darby was armed, and I wasn't aiming to hurt the guy. My goal was to catch him in the act with enough clear evidence to convince his employers of his guilt. Those employers had impressed upon me that they didn't want to involve the police in any way, for fear of embarrassing the company.

The most simple of the spells I cast required three

elements; this one would require more. Seven probably. Certain numbers carried more power than others: three, seven, eleven. I'd never managed to cast a spell with eleven elements; I had trouble keeping track of all of them. But I could handle seven.

Darby, me, the wall of the building, the dim light of those floods, the cement under my feet, the chain-link fence and bushes behind me, and Darby again. Seven elements. The truth was, it didn't matter what those elements were, so long as I could keep them fixed in my mind long enough to cast the spell.

I recited the litany to myself six times, and on the seventh go-round I released the magic that had been building inside me. I felt the spell settle over me, as light as mist, as reassuring as a blanket.

I took a long breath, and then I eased around the corner, keeping my back to the building wall, and placing each step as softly as I could. Darby didn't notice me. I sidled toward him, wondering as I did what spell I ought to try next. Mark was bigger than I had thought—maybe six foot four, and nearly as wide as he was tall. He was soft around the middle, and with his shaggy curls and thick features he bore more resemblance to a pastry chef than to a linebacker, but still he had at least six inches and sixty pounds on me.

Most times I might have been able to take him anyway. I was wiry, and I kept myself in shape. But my muscles had atrophied a bit in the past few weeks. For this evening at least, I was hoping to rely on magic rather than brute force. That said, I was doing all right. My physical therapist had warned me that my leg might start to hurt if I tried to do too much, but for the moment it felt good. Too good.

Overconfidence in a sorcerer—or in an investigator for that matter—can be deadly. In this case it wasn't that bad; it was just stupid. As I drew closer to Darby and the car, I slid my lead foot into an empty bottle that had been left by the side of the building. It fell over with a clinking sound, rolled in a circle and bumped up against the building.

Darby spun. "Who's there?"

He sounded scared, and his eyes were wide. But he was looking bigger by the moment, and in the time it took him to whirl in my direction, he had pulled out a .380—in that light I couldn't tell what brand. Not that it mattered.

He was staring at the bottle, and still had given no indication that he could see me. But I didn't like the way he was holding his weapon; I half expected him to fire off a few rounds in my general direction, to be on the safe side.

I cast another spell, three elements this time. My fist, his jaw, and an impact that would rattle his teeth. It was a simpler conjuring, and I didn't have time to wait for the magic to build. I cast, and an instant later, he reeled. I charged him, the leg that had been shot going from "fine" to "crap that hurts!" in about two strides. If I survived the night, my PT was going to kill me.

Darby must have heard my footsteps, even though he still couldn't see me. He straightened, aimed his weapon—straight at my chest as dumb luck would have it. I knew I wouldn't reach him in time. I wasn't moving well and the distance was too great. I tried to recite that same three-part spell again, desperate to do anything I could to knock him off balance.

But I didn't have time even for that. I saw his finger move. An image flashed through my mind: me lying on the filthy pavement, still shrouded in my camouflage spell, bleeding out because no one could see me. Until I died, at which point my casting would cease as well. Spells die with the sorcerer; it's one of the fundamental rules of magic.

I'm a dead man.

Flame belched from the muzzle of his weapon, three times. The reports roared, echoing off the building. And in that scintilla of an instant—not even the blink of an eye—I thought I sensed a frisson of power ripple the air around me.

Then it was gone.

All three shots should have hit me. The distance between us wasn't great, and Darby appeared to know how to handle a firearm.

But he missed. Somehow, incredibly, he missed.

He stared, not really at me, since I remained camouflaged, but at the spot where he'd been aiming. Then he glanced down at his pistol.

For a moment, I could do little more than gape myself, amazed at the mere fact that I was upright and breathing. But he was still armed, and I didn't feel like trusting to good fortune a second time.

I went back to the fist spell, staggering him again. And before he could recover, I closed the distance between us, hammered a real fist into his gut, and knocked him to the ground with another blow that struck high on his temple. The pistol clattered on the pavement and I kicked it beyond his reach.

He stirred, but before he could push himself up, I planted a foot between his shoulder blades, forcing him back down to the ground. For good measure, I pulled out my Glock and pressed it against the nape of his neck.

"Don't move, Mark."

He stiffened.

"I'm feeling twitchy, and I'm a little pissed at you for taking shots at me. So I'd suggest you do exactly what I tell you to."

"Who the hell are you?"

I pushed harder with the pistol. "Shut up."

He gave a quick nod.

"Now, I want you to put your hands out to the sides where I can see them. Slowly."

He stretched his arms wide. He had turned his head to the side, and I could tell he was trying to get a look at me.

Casting the camouflage spell had been complicated; getting rid of it was easy. Three elements: Darby, me, and my appearance, warts and all. Not that I have warts . . . As I said, there's nothing inherently magical about the elements themselves; more than anything, having them in my head, reciting them a few times, helps me focus my conjuring. Other conjurers might have used other techniques, but this one worked for me.

One second he couldn't see me, the next he could.

"Whoa," he said, breathing the word. "How'd you do that?"

"Do what? Kick your ass? It wasn't that hard."

"No, I mean—"

"You're going to answer some questions for me." I pulled a small digital recorder from the pocket of my bomber.

"The hell I am. I know my rights."

"I'm not a cop, and you have no rights."

"If you're not a cop—"

"I'm a PI. I was hired by Nathan Felder to find out who's been robbing his stores." I switched on the recorder. "What's your name?"

No answer. I smacked the top of his head with the butt of my pistol—just hard enough to get his attention—and then pressed the barrel against his neck again.

"What's your name?"

"Mark Darby," he said, his voice low enough that I wasn't entirely confident the recorder would pick it up.

"How long have you been stealing goods from Custom Electronics?"

"I don't know what—"

I smacked him again.

"Ow! About four months."

That matched what Felder said when he hired me.

"Who are you working with?"

He clamped his mouth shut.

Before I could ask him again, I heard a siren wail from not too far away. I listened for a few seconds, long enough to know that it was coming in this direction. Felder would not be happy.

"That's your fault, Mark. If you hadn't shot at me, no one would have called the cops."

"I guess I have rights now, don't I?"

"Yeah, smart ass, you have the right to go to jail. Felder would have been happy to fire you and be done with it. But you took shots at me, which makes this armed robbery. You'll probably wind up doing ten years at Lewis or Florence."

"Shit," he said in a whisper.

"No kidding. Of course, if you tell me who you've been working with, maybe Felder will decide not to press charges. And maybe I'll be willing to forget about those shots you fired off."

The police car came around the corner with a squeal of rubber on pavement, the siren dying away. Doors opened on either side of the car and two uniformed officers got out, both holding shotguns, both using their doors for cover.

"Drop your weapon!" one of them shouted.

I placed my Glock on the pavement where Darby couldn't reach it.

"Now lie down and put your hands on the back of your head."

"Your word against mine, PI," Darby said as I followed their instructions.

I couldn't see his face, but I knew he was grinning.

"Not quite, asshole. I didn't fire any shots. You did, and the lab can confirm that. And that's your car filled to the ceiling with stolen goods."

"Quiet, both of you."

By now the cops stood over us, their shotguns no doubt aimed at our heads.

"What's going on here?"

"My name is Jay Fearsson," I said, before Darby could answer. "I'm a private investigator, and I used to be on the job. My license is in my wallet. I was hired by the owner of Custom Electronics to find the employee who's been stealing from them since February. That would be the moron lying next to me: Mark Darby. I caught him in the act, and he fired three shots at me. Missed all three times. His weapon is on the ground, a few feet to the left of him. And that's his Subaru pulled up to the loading dock."

One of the officers, a short, barrel-chested white guy, bent and picked up my Glock. "Did you fire your weapon?"

"No."

I heard him sniff at the barrel. He retrieved the other weapon and sniffed at that one as well. I couldn't see him well in the darkness, but I thought I saw him nod once to his partner.

"All right, Fearsson," this second cop said. "You can get up."

I climbed to my feet and pulled out my wallet. The other cop checked my ID before handing me my pistol and walking over to the wagon.

The second officer, a young, light-skinned African-American man, kept his shotgun aimed at Darby, but he was watching me. "You're the guy who caught the Blind Angel Killer, aren't you?" At my nod, he said, "That was nice work."

"Thank you."

"And now you're back doing grunt work like this?"

I grinned. "That's the job, right? I still need to earn a living."

"I hear that."

The other cop, who was still by Darby's car, let out a low whistle. "There must be twenty grand worth of stuff in here. Maybe more."

I walked over to Darby. "Your word against mine, eh?"

He raised his head fractionally. "Screw you."

They cuffed Darby and read him his Miranda rights, and then they took a statement from me. I made sure to mention my suspicion that Mark was working with at least one of his fellow salesmen. While I was still answering questions, a second police cruiser showed up. A few minutes later, so did Mister Felder, driving a BMW, dressed in a suit I couldn't possibly afford and flinging himself out of his car very much like a man who had been called away from a social occasion he didn't want to leave.

One of the cops explained to him what had happened. Felder eyed the loading dock and Darby's car as the cop spoke to him, but when they were finished talking, he walked straight over to me.

He shook my hand, a tight smile on his tanned, round face, but there could be no mistaking his tone as he said, "I thought we agreed that we were going to handle this matter without involving the police."

"Yes, sir," I said, not flinching at all from what I heard in his tone. "But then Darby took a few shots at me with a .380. Someone heard the shooting and called it in. It wasn't my decision."

"He shot at you?"

"Yes, sir."

Felder huffed. "Then I suppose it couldn't be helped." A pause, and then. "You're all right?"

"Thanks for asking. Yes, I'm fine."

Even as I spoke the words, though, a memory stirred. Not of the shooting itself; I'd have nightmares about that—the flare of flame from the muzzle, the deafening *pop! pop! pop!* of the shots.

Rather, I recalled—as I should have long before—that fraction of a moment during which I felt magic all around me, charging the air like an impending lightning strike.

"Mister Fearsson?"

I roused myself with a small shake of my head and faced Felder again. He was watching me, expectant; I assumed he'd asked me a question.

"I'm sorry, sir. What did you say?"

"I asked if Darby did all this alone."

"No, I don't think he did. The police showed up before I could get a name out of him. But I have some experience with these things: He won't hold up long under questioning. If he had a partner, you'll know it soon enough."

"Fearsson!"

I turned. The African-American officer was striding our way.

"Sorry to bother you, man, but Darby is claiming that you assaulted him. He says you hit him with your weapon."

I glanced off to the side, exhaled.

"Did you?"

"It was hardly an assault," I said. "I was asking him some questions, and he was having trouble remembering stuff. I was trying to jar the memories loose."

The cop laughed; even Felder allowed himself a chuckle.

"But officially," I said, "I never hit him."

"Good enough for me," the cop said. "You can go. If we need you for anything else, we'll let you know."

"Hey, wait a minute!" Darby called from the back of one of the squad cars.

"His word against yours, Darby," the officer said. He gave me a wink.

Darby swore loudly.

"Come by tomorrow, Mister Fearsson," Felder said. "I'll cut you a check."

"I will. Thank you."

I walked back to the Z-ster, favoring my bad leg, conscious as well of a dull ache in my arm. I guess this is what the doctors had in mind when they warned me about trying to do too much.

Still, I was pleased. Sure, the police had shown up, but Felder hadn't been too angry. And given how the evening could have ended—with me in a body bag—I couldn't have asked for a better outcome.

Again, I thought of that frisson of magic. I hadn't cast a spell, and I was certain that Darby was incapable of casting. Had I imagined it? Everything had happened in such a rush—it could have been a sensation born of panic and desperation. But how else could I explain the fact that Darby had missed me?

I needed to have a conversation with Namid'skemu of the K'ya'na-Kwe clan, the Zuni shaman who had been my runemyste for the past seven years, and who had been dead for close to eight centuries.

CHAPTER 3

The runemystes were created by the Runeclave centuries ago, their collective sacrifice an act so courageous, so selfless that it boggles the mind. Essentially, they were once weremystes, like me—sorcerers who had devoted their lives to the mastery of runecrafting. Thirty-nine of them were sacrificed by the Runeclave, the governing body of their kind, their spirits granted eternal life so that they could be guardians of magic in our world. They were essentially ensorcelled ghosts, although I'd learned over the years that they didn't like to be referred to as such.

As I understood it, Namid and others like him were tasked with training new generations of weremystes and keeping watch on those who might turn to the darker elements of runecrafting. In all but the most extreme circumstances, they were forbidden from acting directly on our world, but through their instruction and training of weremystes, they could help to keep wielders of dark magic from doing harm to either the magical community or the non-magical population. The renegade-turned-serial-killer I mentioned, Cahors, was one of the original thirty-nine. But he chafed at the limits placed on his powers by his fellow runemystes, and he found a way to escape their controls and assume corporeal form once again. More, by committing murders each month on the night of the first quarter moon, he was able to keep himself young and powerful. If Kona and I hadn't killed him, he would have gone on murdering for as long as he wished to live.

But Cahors was dead, and the runemystes now numbered thirty-eight. In the weeks since we'd killed him, I'd often wondered if Cahors had been training runemystes the way Namid did. Were there sorcerers out there who for years had been learning the darkest secrets of our craft?

I could have asked Namid about this, but he tended to be tight-lipped when it came to answering questions about the runemystes. To be honest, he was that way about everything, which at times made him an exasperating teacher. And tonight I had other questions that were more urgent.

I drove to my home in Chandler. It was a drive of no more than eight miles, and at this hour it took only a few minutes. At rush hour, which these days in the Phoenix-Scottsdale area stretched from dawn to dusk, it might have taken me three-quarters of an hour.

It had been a scorching day—July in Phoenix; go figure—and it was still hot in the house. The night had cooled off considerably, as nights in the desert often did, but still I turned on the air conditioner and changed into gym shorts and a T-shirt.

"Namid," I said, pitching my voice to carry over some distance. I probably could have whispered it and he would have shown up just as soon, but I liked to maintain the illusion that I had some small measure of privacy.

Within seconds, he began to materialize before me, shimmering with the light of my reading lamps like the surface of a mountain lake reflecting the moon.

In life, Namid had belonged to the K'ya'na-Kwe clan of the A'shiwi or Zuni nation—the water people, as they were known. His clan was extinct now, and had been for centuries. I didn't know if Namid's appearance was his way of honoring their memory, or if it was simply the natural, or perhaps magical, manifestation of his tribal heritage. Whatever its origins, Namid always appeared to me as a being made entirely of water. He had the build of a warrior: tall, broad-shouldered, lean, muscular. On this night he was as clear as a woodland stream and as smooth as the ocean at dawn, but one could read his moods in the texture of his liquid form the way a ship's captain might gauge the weather by watching the sea. His eyes were the single exception: They always glowed, like white flames within his luminous waters. I would never have said as much to him—I didn't want to give him the satisfaction—but he was the most beautiful creature I had ever seen.

"Ohanko. It is late. You should be asleep, and I should not be summoned at such an hour."

He was also the most infuriating.

He'd been calling me "Ohanko," which, as far as I could tell, meant "reckless one," for so long that I couldn't remember when he had started. And he had been talking to me as if he were my mother, telling me when to sleep and what to eat, for even longer.

"I'm sorry I called for you," I said, "But I can't sleep yet. I need some answers first."

He regarded me for the span of a heartbeat before sinking to the floor and staring up at me, those gleaming eyes seeming to ask why the hell I was still standing. I sat opposite him.

"You conjured tonight."

"Yes, I did. But that's not—"

"What spells did you cast?"

Did I mention that he could be infuriating?

"I used a seeing spell—"

"Using the techniques we have discussed?"

"Yes, and—"

"Did it work?"

"Yes, it worked fine."

"Good. What else?"

"I cast a couple of . . . well, I call them fist spells."

His watery brow furrowed. "Fist spells," he repeated, his voice a low rumble, like the rush of distant headwaters.

"They act like a punch, but I can cast them from a distance."

He nodded. "Crude, but effective. What else?"

"A camouflage spell," I said. As impatient as I was to discuss other matters, I couldn't keep a hint of pride from creeping into my voice.

Namid's eyebrows—such as they were—went up a fraction of an inch. "That is high magic, Ohanko. Your casting was successful."

"Yeah, it worked great. That is, until I tripped over an empty beer bottle."

His expression flattened. "Have I not told you that you must tread like the fox, that you must act at all times with great care?"

"You've told me," I said. "And I try. This time . . ." I shrugged. "What can I say? I screwed up."

"You are fortunate that your carelessness did not carry a greater cost."

I'm a grown man—thirty-three years old. My mom has been dead for close to twenty years, and my dad has been crazy for almost as long. In many ways, Namid was the closest thing to a parent that I had, and his scoldings still stung like cold rain. But at that moment, his disapproval was the least of my concerns.

"So you weren't aware of all this," I said. "You didn't see me cast the spell, or knock over the bottle. You weren't there for what happened next."

Namid had a way of going still; it almost seemed like he turned from water to ice, and most of the time I thought it was very cool. Not now. Seeing his face harden, his body tense, I shivered, as from a winter wind.

"Tell me," he said.

"I'm not sure exactly what happened. I was trying to sneak up on a guy, and when I kicked over the bottle he raised his weapon and fired at me. Three times. I couldn't have been more than ten feet from him, and though he couldn't see me, he aimed right at my chest. I . . ." I took a breath. "I should be dead."

"Why are you not?"

"I don't know. But in the instant that his finger moved,

I was almost sure I felt a spell. I—I thought that maybe you had intervened."

"You know that I cannot."

"You did, not that long ago."

"The circumstances were different. Cahors was our . . . screwup." The phrase sounded odd coming from him. "I cannot keep you safe in the normal course of your life. My responsibilities lie elsewhere."

I would have liked to ask him about that, too. Another time.

"Maybe I imagined it, then."

"Is it possible that you cast without intending, without even knowing that you did it?"

I grinned. "I'm not sure how to answer that."

"I am not sure how you could, either," the myste said, his tone wry. "But you understand the point I am making."

"Yes. But I don't think that's what happened. I was scrambling to cast a different sort of spell. I should have cast a warding, but it all happened so fast." I shook my head. "Maybe he missed, plain and simple, though I don't see how he could have. Is it possible that another of your kind has taken an interest in me?"

"Another of my kind?"

"Another runemyste."

"I have told you, Ohanko: It is against the laws that govern my kind to interfere in your world. Another of my kind would be bound by the same prohibitions that bind me. And where you are concerned, another runemyste would not chafe at those prohibitions nearly as much as I do."

I made no effort to mask my surprise; he wasn't

usually prone to such kindnesses. "Thank you, Namid. That might be the nicest thing you've ever said to me."

His translucent hand flicked out in annoyance. "I mean simply that others have not invested so much time and energy in your training. They would not be inconvenienced by your death the way I would."

That was more like the Namid I had come to know over the years.

"Still, I'm touched."

Namid frowned, but I could tell that my questions had piqued his curiosity. Or maybe it was more than that. Maybe he was scared.

"If it was someone else," I said, "a weremyste or a runemyste who's less bound than you are by arbitrary rules, it's all right. He or she saved my life. It's like I have a guardian angel."

This deepened the myste's scowl. "There are no guardian angels, Ohanko. There are sorcerers and mystes, and they rarely act out of altruism."

"So you believe that someone wants me alive for a specific reason?"

"I do not know what to believe. I will have to think on this at greater length." He started to fade from view. "Tread like the fox, Ohanko. Do not screw up anymore."

I chuckled. "Thanks, ghost."

I heard another rumble, like the whisper of approaching thunder. A moment later he was gone.

I stood, stretched my back, and crossed to the answering machine, which was a relic from a time when devices like this used tiny little cassette tapes. I had several messages, most of them from prospective clients.

One was from Billie Castle, who was, for lack of a better term, my girlfriend.

"Hey, Fearsson, it's me." I couldn't help the dumb grin that spread across my face every time I heard her voice. "I know you're working, and I know we have plans for Friday, but I was wondering if you had time for lunch tomorrow. Nothing fancy—I was thinking the burrito place on Main, near the mall. Call me in the morning."

I made a note to call her, and jotted down numbers and names from the other messages. Then I dragged myself back to my room and fell into bed, too tired even to bother pulling down the shades.

I woke with the sun, went for a run and showered, and then called Billie to confirm our plans. After grabbing a bite to eat, I got in the Z-ster and drove out to Wofford, west of the city, where my dad lives in an old trailer.

I go out to see him most Tuesdays. I bring him groceries and other supplies. Sometimes I cook for him. Sometimes I do no more than sit with him and listen to him ramble on and on about God knows what. Every once in a while—maybe one week in five, if I'm lucky—I catch him on a good day and we sit for hours talking about baseball and stuff in the news and police work; he was a cop, too, until his mind quit on him and he lost his job.

Today was Thursday, but I hadn't liked the way he looked or sounded a couple of days ago, and I wanted to check in on him again. It was a slow drive out of the city— there weren't any quick drives left in Phoenix—but by nine o'clock I was on US 60, following a lonely stretch of road past sun-baked telephone poles and dry, windswept desert. Reaching the rutted dirt road to my father's place,

I turned and steered the Z-ster past the stunted sage, a plume of pale red dust billowing behind me.

I could tell before I reached him that Dad was no better off today than he had been the last time I saw him. He sat slumped in the lawn chair outside his trailer, beneath the plastic tarp I had set up for him a couple of years before. He had his eyes trained on the horizon, and his old Leica binoculars rested in his lap. He wore dirty jeans and a threadbare white T-shirt; they might have been the same clothes he'd been wearing on Tuesday. His sneakers were untied; he didn't have on socks.

The same way I could judge Namid's moods by how roiled his waters were, I could tell what state my father was in by the care with which he dressed. When he didn't change his clothes or bother with socks or shoelaces, it meant he was out of it, and had been for a while. I hoped he'd been eating. Hell, I hoped he had slept in his bed rather than in that old chair.

I parked and got out, squinting against the glare and the dust.

"Hey, Dad," I called, raising a hand.

He didn't respond, or even turn my way. I could see that he was muttering to himself. Every few seconds he seemed to wince, as if he were in pain. He hadn't shaved since the last time I saw him; his slack cheeks were grizzled, making him appear even more haggard than usual. His white hair, unkempt and probably in a need of a washing, stirred in the desert wind.

I walked to where he sat and kissed his forehead. He stank of sweat, and his breath was rank. His gaze found mine for a second or two but then slid back to the horizon and the mountain ranges that fell away in layers until they were lost in the brown haze hanging over the city.

"How are you doing, Dad?"

He didn't take his eyes off the desert, but he shook his head. "Not so good," he said, his voice strained, the words clipped.

As interactions with my dad went, this was better than it could have been; at least he had responded to my question, which meant that he was communicative and aware of my presence. Sometimes I didn't even get that much from him.

I pulled out a second lawn chair and placed it beside his. Sitting, I leaned forward, peering into his eyes. Like mine, they were a soft, smoky gray, and today they appeared glazed, sunken.

"What's wrong?" I asked him. "Tell me what you're feeling."

"It Tuesday already?"

"No, it's Thursday. But I was worried about you when I left the other day, so I thought I'd come back."

He answered with a slow nod, his gaze following the flight of a hawk.

"What's wrong?"

"It's this burning," he said, whispering the words. "It's . . . The burning. I can't make it stop."

I laid the back of my hand against his forehead, checking for fever. His skin felt cool and dry.

"What burning?"

"They're burning me, like brands, searing my skin, marking me as theirs." He shook his head. "I don't know why, but look at me. Look!" He held out his arms, the undersides bared to the sky, his hands trembling. "Look!" he said again. A tear slipped from his eye and wound a crooked course down his lined face. "So many burns!"

Hallucinations like this one were a common element of my father's psychosis. A doctor would have told me not to be too concerned: This would pass, and this state was as normal for him as any other. Hell, doctors had told me exactly that on other occasions when his behavior bordered on the bizarre and unsettling.

But as relieved as I was by his lack of fever, and the absence of wounds on his arms, I couldn't help feeling that this particular delusion was taking a greater toll than others I'd seen him endure.

"Who's doing this to you? Who's burning you?"

"I don't know," he said, the words thick with tears, his eyes still fixed on the slack, unmarred skin of his forearms. "They think I matter still. Again. They think I matter, but I don't." He swiveled toward me. "You do. You matter. You be careful, boy. They'll come for you before long. But me . . ." He shook his head again. "I don't know what they want, or why they think I matter. But they're here, and I want them to go. I don't like this."

"You do matter."

"No!" he said with sudden ferocity. "This isn't the time for sentimental shit! I. Don't. Matter. But they don't know it! They don't! They don't! They're searing me with their brands and their torches. They're poking and prodding and hurting and pushing just to see how far they can take me, just to . . . Just because."

"When was the last time you ate?"

"I . . ." He closed his eyes, still wincing every few seconds. "A long time," he said. "I'm hungry."

"Good. What can I fix for you?"

"Ice cream."

"Dad—" I stopped myself. The doctors would have told me that when my father was like this, getting calories in him was the most important thing. He was sixty-four. He didn't have to eat his peas and carrots before he had dessert. "Sure," I said. "I'll get you some."

No response.

I stood, stepped into the trailer. Usually, with my father in such a state, I'd expect to find his kitchen an utter disaster. But it wasn't. It was worse: It remained exactly as I had left it Tuesday afternoon. I would have bet every dollar in my pocket that he hadn't eaten since the lunch we'd shared then.

I packed a bowl with mint chocolate chip—his current favorite—and got him a tall glass of ice water as well. Returning to his side, I gave him the water first.

He took it, glanced up at me, eyed the water again. He took a sip, closed his eyes once more. Then he tipped the glass back and drained it in about six seconds.

"You want me to get you more?"

He nodded.

I handed him the ice cream and went back inside. I was out again in mere moments, and already the bowl was mostly empty. He still flinched again and again; whatever was bothering him hadn't gone away. But in these few minutes his color had improved and his eyes had grown clearer.

"They don't like this," he said, pointing at the bowl

with his spoon, a knowing grin lifting the corners of his mouth. "Not even a little."

"Who don't?"

"They can't burn me as easily when I have this in me. And the water. That, too. They like that even less."

"Who's burning you, Dad? Can you tell me now?"

He sobered and shook his head, his gaze holding mine as he took another mouthful of ice cream.

He finished that first bowl a few minutes later, and I went back and got him a second. And when he finished that one, I brought him half a sandwich, which he bolted down as well.

Sometimes, getting some food into my dad brought him around a bit, helped him reconnect with reality. Not this time. He continued that odd wincing, and he went on and on about being prodded and burned. I'd been with him through a lot of different hallucinations, but again I couldn't shake the feeling that this one was different.

His skin had lost that sallow quality, though, and once he'd had enough to eat, I managed to convince him to shower, shave, brush his teeth, and put on fresh clothes. By the time I was ready to leave, he was back in his chair, staring at the horizon. I could tell he was hurting still, but I didn't know what else to do for him.

"I have to go for a while. But I'll come back later, all right?"

He didn't so much as glance at me.

"Dad—"

"If you're here, they'll know where to find you, and then you'll be in trouble, too."

"I'll take my chances. I'll see you in a few hours."

He didn't argue the point further. I kissed his forehead, got in my car, and headed back into the city to keep my lunch date with Billie. She would have understood if I had asked her for a rain check, but I wanted to see her, and I also wanted to get my payment from Nathan Felder.

Once I was back on the road and close enough to Phoenix to get a decent signal on my ancient cell phone, I called my dad's doctor to ask him about what I had seen and heard. He didn't have much to say, at least not much that was helpful. But he did end our conversation with this gem:

"The truth is, Jay, your dad is getting older, his condition is worsening, and it will continue to worsen. Trying to define what's 'normal'"—I could hear the air quotes—"is almost pointless, because normal for him is always changing; it's always deteriorating. What you've described for me is no worse than what I might expect for any patient with his history. I'm sorry, but that's the unvarnished truth."

And because you're a sorcerer like your old man, and because you go through the insanity of the phasings month in and month out, full moon after full moon, this is your future as well.

He didn't have to say that last; we both knew he was thinking it.

I thanked him and ended the call.

The moonrise was still hours away—tonight's moon would be a waxing gibbous. We were four nights from the full, three from the first night of July's phasing. And already I felt the moon tugging at my mind, as insistent as a needy child, as unrelenting as the tide.

In another few days, even before night descended and the moon rose to begin the phasing, it would start to dull my thoughts and influence my mood. Right now it was a distraction and not too much more. But at the mere thought of those nights to come, I shuddered.

I wasn't insane yet; Namid still held out some hope that with time, and with hard work, I could learn enough about casting to mitigate the effect of the phasings and perhaps put off what I had always assumed was my inevitable descent into madness. But flirting with lunacy, even if just for a few nights, still terrified me. I spent those nights alone. Always.

I wanted to believe that I had no choice in the matter. Even as a weremyste loses control of his mind, he also loses control of his magic, the power of which is augmented by the phasing. In other words, at those times when I'm least able to rein in my runecrafting, it's most likely to boil over, endangering anyone who's near me. Still, during our years together on the force, Kona had offered many times to stay with me and keep me from hurting myself or others. Last month, Billie had done the same; it occurred to me that she might have intended to again this month. For all I knew, that was why she wanted to see me.

I would tell her exactly what I had told Kona repeatedly: "I'm afraid I'll hurt you."

But both Kona and Billie were too smart to be fooled by that, even if I was content to go on deceiving myself.

What I really should have said to them was, "I'm ashamed to let you see me this way."

I had seen my father at his worst, on days when he was far, far less lucid than he had been today. I knew what moon-induced madness looked like; it was ugly, messy, humiliating. I didn't want to share it with anyone. I could barely stand to see it in my old man, much less in myself.

So I drove back into Mesa, to Solana's, the little burrito place Billie and I had gone to so many times that it was fast becoming "our place." And along the way, I tried to find the words to refuse the offer I knew was coming.

She was already seated when I got there. The lunch rush had started, but I assumed she had ordered for me; I always got the same thing: chicken and black beans, extra guac and pico, no sour cream.

Reaching the table, I stooped and kissed her lightly on the lips. Then I sat.

"You ordered?"

She nodded. "And paid. That's two in a row. You owe me."

In spite of everything, I smiled, glad to see her, happy to be distracted from my dad.

Billie and I had met less than two months ago, while I was working on the Blind Angel murder case, and we hadn't exactly hit it off at first. She was a journalist, the owner of a blog site called Castle's Village. As a cop, I had developed a healthy distrust of journalists, and the first time or two we spoke I had Billie pegged as a typical reporter: nosy, ruthless, interested in nothing but the story, and completely unconcerned with those who got in her way as she went after it.

I was wrong. She was smart as hell, and, yes, she could

be relentless in her pursuit of a story. But she cared more about getting it right than getting it first, and I had seen her go to incredible lengths to double and triple-check her facts before posting an article to her site. She was also warm, funny, and caring. She had these amazing emerald green eyes, and ringlets of brown hair that cascaded over her shoulders and back. And, most remarkably, she seemed to like me every bit as much as I liked her, which was quite a lot.

Watching me watch her, she took my hand, concern furrowing her brow.

"What's the matter?"

"What makes you think something's the matter?"

She gave me her "Are you really that stupid?" look. "You have a lousy poker face, Fearsson. I've told you that." She leaned in, her arms resting on the table. "Is it something with your case?" she asked in a conspiratorial whisper.

That was another thing I liked about Billie: She considered my work exotic and exciting, even when I was doing nothing more than tracking down the Mark Darbys of the world.

"No. The case is solved. In fact, I need to get my check from Mister Felder when we're done with lunch."

"Wow, Fearsson. That took you all of one week. I'm impressed."

"It was ten days," I told her. "And that matters because I get paid by the day." I waved off the compliment. "Anyway, I wasn't exactly dealing with a criminal mastermind." I took a long breath, my gaze dropping to our interlaced fingers. "It's my dad. He's not doing so well."

She frowned. "I'm sorry. Something specific or . . . ?"

She trailed off, allowed herself a small self-conscious smile, even as her brow remained creased. "I'm not sure how to ask the question."

"I know what you mean. And I don't really have an answer. It seems different to me. Worse than it's been. But the doctors tell me it's part of the normal downward spiral."

She winced, reminding me of my dad. "Not what you want to hear."

"Not at all."

Before I could say more, my phone buzzed. I pulled it from the pocket of my bomber and checked the incoming number. Kona, at 620, which is what we called Phoenix Police headquarters in downtown Phoenix.

I flipped open the phone—yes, I still have a flip phone. "Hey, partner. What's up?"

"Justis, I am having a day. You busy right now?"

"I'm having lunch with Billie."

"Tell her 'Hi' from me. How soon can you get away?"

"Seriously?" I said. "You want me to tell her 'Hi,' and then you want to know how quickly I can ditch her?"

"Pretty much," Kona said, seeming to find little humor in the situation. "I've got a dead body here, and I think I need for you to take a look at it, if you know what I mean."

"You think he was killed with magic?" I asked, my voice dropping to a whisper.

"Yup. So how soon can you be here?"

"Where are you?"

"I'm at the airport, terminal three. And that's the other thing you ought to know. We think there was a bomb on this guy's plane."

CHAPTER 4

Billie and I had decided early on in our relationship that
we were permanently off the record as far as her reporting
was concerned. She wouldn't try to get stories out of any
of my investigations. It was an easy agreement to reach,
because few of my usual cases—really none of them—
involved anything that would interest her readers.

But our arrangement became a bit more complicated
when I was called in to help out the Phoenix Police
Department. Those investigations were far more intriguing,
and thus just the sort of thing she would want to cover.
We had met during one such case, and it had involved
sorcery, one of the state's most prominent politicians, and
a serial killer whose crimes were as sensational as they
were gruesome. Now the PPD needed my help again, and
the case appeared to involve magic, murder, and perhaps
an attempted act of terrorism.

Billie studied me as I finished my call with Kona,
green eyes narrowing, the expression on her lovely face
shrewd, knowing.

"What was that?" she asked, as I put away my phone.

"Kona needs my help."

"I gathered that much. With what?"

I sighed, holding her gaze, a smile creeping over my face.

"What?" she demanded, her voice rising, though she was trying not to laugh.

"We should get our food to go," I said. "I need to get to the airport, and I would suggest you do the same, though obviously we have to drive separately."

Her eyes widened. "Fearsson, are you giving me a tip?"

"I'm doing no such thing. I'm simply saying that you might find it useful to make your way to the airport."

She grabbed her computer bag. "I'm going now. I'll eat later."

"If you go now, Kona will know how you found out and I won't ever be able to help you out again."

She twisted her mouth, and for an instant I could imagine her as a kid, pondering some scheme that was going to land her in big trouble. She must have been cute as a button. A handful, but cute as a button.

"At least wait for the food," I said.

"All right." She hung the bag over the back of her chair again. "What did Kona tell you?"

"This dessert menu has some interesting things on it," I said, reaching for one of the folded cardboard menus sitting on the table by the salt and pepper shakers and bottles of hot sauce. "We should come here for dinner one night."

"Fine," she said, her expression sharpening. "I'll find out on my own."

"I don't doubt it."

"Tell me about your case. The one you solved."

"There's not that much to tell," I said, still reading about the desserts. "Though it did end strangely. The guy I caught took a couple of shots at me. He should have hit me, but he didn't. It almost seemed like someone cast a spell to save my life."

When she didn't respond, I set the menu aside. She was staring at me, her face as white as our napkins. I guess it should have occurred to me sooner that I might be better off keeping those details to myself.

"You almost got shot again?"

Crap.

"Yeah. But I'm fine. Like I said, someone was watching out for me."

"Someone, but not you."

I'd long imagined that it would be nice to have someone in my life who cared about what happened to me, who wanted to be certain each evening that I was safe at home. Turns out, the imagined version is easier to deal with than the real thing. It's not that I didn't appreciate Billie's concern, but I also didn't want her worrying about me all the time.

"I'd taken all the precautions I could, but I . . . messed up. It was an accident, the kind of thing that happens once in a blue moon. I stumbled over something and let the guy know I was there before I was ready to disarm him."

"And he shot at you."

"He missed."

The waitress arrived with our food.

"I'm very sorry," I said to her. "Something's come up, and we need these to go."

She forced a smile, muttered a less-than-heartfelt "No problem," and took the plates away again.

Billie continued to stare at me, her cheeks ashen except for bright red spots high on each one.

"Fearsson—"

"Billie, this is what I do. If I was still a cop, I'd be on the streets every day, taking more chances than I do now."

"If you were still a cop, you'd have a partner watching out for you. You wouldn't have been alone with this guy."

The problem with getting involved with someone smart was that she was right more often than not, and way more often than I was. I shrugged, conceding the point.

"You say that magic saved you?" she asked, lowering her voice.

I nodded, wishing I'd had the good sense to keep quiet when the chance presented itself.

"But not your own."

"That's right."

"Was it Namid?"

We hadn't been together for long, and at the beginning I had tried to keep from her the fact that I could cast spells, the fact that I was subject to the phasings and was slowly going mad. And even after I told her, she was slow to believe it all and slower still to accept that she could be part of my strange life. But she had come around far sooner than I'd had any right to hope. Her ability to make that simple leap, to guess that Namid had been the one to save me, was evidence of how far she and I had come in little more than two months.

"That was my first thought, too. But no, it wasn't him. I don't know who it was."

"That frightens me even more than someone shooting at you."

I thought about asking her why, but realized I didn't have to. Some nameless magical entity or entities keeping me alive for reasons unknown? Yeah, I didn't like the sound of that either. If they could save my life, they could take it, and since I didn't know why they'd intervened in the first place, there was always the danger that I would disappoint them, or piss them off in some way.

The waitress came back with a couple of take-out boxes, which she placed on the table.

"Anything else?"

"No, thank you," I said.

She walked away. Billie ignored the food.

"I'll be careful," I told her. At her raised eyebrow, I added, "More careful than I've been."

"I like you, Fearsson. I'd rather you didn't get yourself killed."

I heard in what she said an odd echo of Namid's words from the previous night, and another shudder went through me. I covered it with a shrug and a nod. "I appreciate that."

We both stood, and I followed her out into the street. Once we were outside, she planted herself in front of me, and I thought she might say more. But instead she kissed me, her forehead furrowing as it had before.

"Call me later, okay? I want to know you're all right."

"I will."

I watched her hurry off toward her car and then walked back to the Z-ster.

I was on the western edge of Mesa, a few blocks from where it gave way to Tempe. Sky Harbor Airport wasn't far, and I made good time getting there. Once in the airport loops, however, the nightmares began. Navigating any airport can be a headache, but add in a murder and a bomb threat and all hell breaks loose. It took me close to forty-five minutes to get from the east entrance to the Terminal Three parking garage, and once there I had to argue with a uniformed cop for another ten minutes before I convinced him to call Kona so that she could authorize him to let me park and join her in the terminal.

Once inside, I saw that the place was crawling with cops, FBI, bomb-squad guys, TSA officers, and a few suits from Homeland Security. Kona met me in the food court and escorted me through the north security checkpoint. It was the first and no doubt the last time I would ever get my Glock through there without a question or even a quirked eyebrow.

"You took your time getting here," she said, keeping her voice low. "I've had a helluva time putting off the guys from the coroner's office, not to mention the Federal boys."

"Sorry. You wouldn't believe the traffic around the terminal."

"Actually, I would." She cast a glance my way. "Everything okay with Billie?"

"We'll talk about that later."

She led me toward the end of the gate area, past

clusters of cops and agents. And as we walked, people paused in their conversations to stare at us.

Usually, Kona by herself was enough to draw gazes. She was tall and willowy, with dark eyes, the cheekbones of a fashion model, and short, tightly curled black hair. Her skin was the color of coffee, and she had a thousand-watt smile, though it wasn't in evidence today. But as many people were watching me as her; fallout, no doubt, from the Blind Angel case.

"You're a celebrity," she said.

"I'm a curiosity. The disgraced cop who solved one last case."

She gave a low snort of laughter.

"Hold it, Shaw!"

I knew that voice. We both stopped. Cole Hibbard, the commander of the police department's Violent Crimes Bureau, was striding in our direction, his face ruddy beneath a shock of white hair. To say that Cole and I hated each other did an injustice to the depth of our animosity. He had once been my father's best friend, a colleague in the department. When my dad's mind went, Cole was the first to turn on him. When my mother and her lover were found dead, he was at the fore of those accusing my father of the murders. And years later, when I was on the force, struggling with the phasings and their effects on me, he was the one who pushed to have me fired and then forced me to resign in order to avoid that final disgrace.

"Who authorized you to call *him* in?" Hibbard asked, gesturing toward me but refusing even to glance in my direction.

"Sergeant Arroyo, sir."

"Well, he didn't clear it with me."

"I'm sure he meant to, sir."

"I don't care what he meant to do—"

"Commander," I broke in, "can I talk to you for a moment?"

Kona laid a hand on my arm. "Justis . . ."

"It's all right," I told her.

I faced Hibbard again. He stared daggers at me, appearing unsure as to whether he should be pissed or amazed at my audacity.

"I won't keep you long," I said.

I thought he'd refuse, but after a few seconds he gave a single jerky nod, pivoted on his heel, and walked to a bank of windows nearby.

"This is a bad idea, Justis."

"Maybe. It wouldn't be my first."

I joined Hibbard by the window and gazed out over the apron and runways. Planes had been pushed back from all of the terminal three gates. They sat on the sun-baked concrete, motionless, abandoned, heat waves rising from their fuselages. The other terminals hummed with activity, and even as I stood there a jet raced down the nearest runway, its nose angling upward.

"What the hell do you want?" Hibbard asked in a snarl.

"Believe it or not, Commander, I didn't come here to embarrass you or cause problems." I kept my voice low, even, the way I would if I were trying to calm a cornered dog. "I came to help."

"We don't need your help," he said.

"The head of your lead homicide unit and your best homicide detective disagree with you."

"Screw you."

"You can send me away; we both know you have that authority. But for better or worse, I'm famous now—the former cop who brought down the Blind Angel Killer. If I leave, it's going to raise questions. You'll give your answers, I'll give mine. How do you think that's going to play?"

He said nothing. I had him, and we both knew that, too. In the weeks since I'd killed Cahors, a lot of people in Phoenix had been asking why I'd been forced to leave the department in the first place. More than a few had suggested that if they'd let me stay, the case might have been solved sooner and lives might have been saved, including that of Claudia Deegan, the daughter of Arizona's senior U.S. Senator, and the Blind Angel's final victim.

If Cole demanded that I leave the airport, and this case dragged on for more than a few days, he'd have real problems.

The truth was, I found the talk about me and my firing more embarrassing than gratifying. I took no satisfaction in seeing my former colleagues on the force second-guessed in this way, especially Kona. But I had slept better at night over the last month or two knowing that Cole had to have been squirming a little bit.

"Fine," he said, the word wrung out of him. "Just stay the hell out of my way."

"Yes, sir."

He was striding away before I got the words out. I watched him go, then walked back to where Kona still stood.

"What did you say to him?"

"I asked him how he was going to explain to the press and his superiors why he had chased away from a crime scene the guy who killed Arizona's most notorious serial murderer."

"You are a piece of work, Justis." She raised a hand to keep me from answering. "I'm not saying he doesn't deserve it," she went on, voice dropping, "but these days I have to confess to feeling a little sorry for Cole. With all that's on our plate right now?" She shook her head in a way that told me there was more going on in the homicide unit than I knew.

"Something else I should be helping you with?" I asked.

"I don't think so. But just because you and I got rid of one wack-job, doesn't mean there wasn't another one waiting to take his place. Know what I mean?"

The one wack-job would have been Cahors. "You've got another serial killer?"

"That surprises you?"

"Not really."

"We're keeping it quiet," she said, whispering now. "The patterns aren't clear yet, and it may not be one guy. But inside 620, the pressure's pretty high. And Hibbard bears the brunt of it. I'm not saying you should buy the guy a beer, but as much as he might hate you and your dad, he's also dealing with some shit right now. You know?"

I nodded. "If I see him again, and he doesn't shoot me on sight, I'll give him a break."

"That's all I'm saying. Come on," she said, leading me

toward a men's room that had already been cordoned off with yellow police tape. "Our victim's in here."

We stepped into the restroom, the noise from the terminal fading to an echoey background buzz. A toilet in one of the far stalls flushed repeatedly, its automatic mechanism obviously malfunctioning, but otherwise no sound came from within the tiled space.

A body, covered with a white cloth, lay by a row of sinks.

I hesitated, but at Kona's nod of encouragement I squatted beside the corpse and pulled back the sheet, revealing the body of a young man, his head shaved to blond stubble, his face pock-marked as if he'd had bad acne. He was dressed in jeans and a black T-shirt with the words "America for Americans" printed in block letters across the chest.

I didn't need to search for evidence of what had killed him; it was right there in front of me, a shimmering blur slashed across his chest.

All spells left a residue, a glow tinged with color that no one but another weremyste could see. Each sorcerer's magic was a different color, a different shade, and each faded at its own pace. The more vibrant the color, the more powerful the sorcerer.

But this residue was unlike any I had seen before. Most of the time, magic in this form reminded me of wet paint. It was brilliant and it gleamed, but it was opaque. Even the glow left behind by the spells of Etienne de Cahors, who was the most powerful conjurer I'd ever encountered, had those same basic qualities.

Not this spell.

Whoever had killed the kid lying in front of me had left behind a flare of power that had more in common with Namid's sparkling clear waters than with the residue I was used to seeing. It had color—a deep, rich green that reminded me of early spring leaves—but I could see through the glow to the dead man's shirt. More, the residue seemed to be alive; it shifted and swirled, like a sheen of oil on top of a puddle.

"Talk to me, Justis," Kona said after I'd stared at the kid for a good minute or two. "Was I right? Was he killed with magic?"

"Yeah," I said. "But this magic is . . . it's weird. I've never seen anything like it."

"Well, that's what I want to hear right now."

I tore my eyes away from the swirling glow to scan the rest of his body. I saw no blood, no other wounds or bruising. Of course he had a lot of tattoos, including at least half a dozen swastikas on his neck and arms, which made bruising a bit harder to find. But I was sure that the spell to his chest had killed him.

"A spell hit him here," I said, tracing a line across his heart with my finger, but taking care not to touch him. "Aside from that I don't see any magic on him. We could turn him over to check for signs of a second conjuring, but I don't think there's much point."

"Do you recognize the color?"

I shook my head. "I don't even recognize the kind of magic that was used against him. It doesn't look like any spell I could cast."

"Is that because of the spell, or the guy who cast it?"

This was one of the things that made Kona such a

great cop—the best I'd known. She would have been the first to admit that she was out of her depth; she knew next to nothing about magic. But she had asked the perfect question, one that cut to the very core of the matter. One that I couldn't yet answer. First Billie, now Kona. It seemed that I was giving my friends a free education in magic: "Runecasting 101."

"I'm not sure," I said. "In the past I've only used magical residue like this to find the conjurer. Someone who knows more about this stuff than I do might be able to tell us what kind of spell was used against him, but I can't."

I scrutinized the glow for another few seconds, trying to commit to memory the color and quality of the residue. I covered the body again, and straightened.

"What do you know so far?" I asked.

Kona pulled out the small spiral notepad she kept in her blazer pocket. "We know more than we usually do this early in an investigation, but so far we haven't been able to make much sense of it." Opening the notebook, she went on. "The victim's name is James Robert Howell." She glanced up, her eyes meeting mine. "I swear, Justis, I think he went by Jimmy Bob. As you can tell from his hair style and the lovely artwork he's wearing, he was a skinhead, I'm guessing with ties to a bunch of white supremacist groups. We pulled his luggage and found that it held a bomb with an altitude-sensitive trigger. The bomb-squad guys aren't sure yet when it was set to detonate, but the way these things work is that you reach that level, the air pressure changes enough to trip the mechanism, and *boom*, no more plane."

"How do you even get a bomb onto a plane these days? I would have thought that the TSA could find any explosives in a checked bag."

"Usually they can. This was a pretty sophisticated device. They're still trying to figure out exactly where the system broke down."

"Who else was on board? For that matter, where was the plane going?"

"Both good questions. This was American flight 595, a non-stop to Washington Reagan. And the passenger list included Mando Rafael Vargas and several of his aides."

I let out a low whistle. "So you think that Mister White Supremacist here had it in mind to assassinate one of the most prominent Latino leaders in the country."

"That's what I'm thinking. That's what the Feds are thinking."

"Sounds about right. The FBI guys are letting you play in their sandbox?"

"It's my sandbox," she said. "I've made it clear to them that this is my goddamned sandbox. But yeah, for now at least they're playing nice and they're eager for any help we can give them."

"How soon was the plane supposed to take off?"

Kona nodded, an eyebrow going up. "Well, that's where all of this starts to get very interesting. Flight 595 was supposed to take off a little before nine o'clock this morning."

"What?" I bent down again, uncovered Howell's body a second time. "So how did he end up in here? Why isn't every person on that plane dead already?"

"The plane had mechanical problems. It pulled back

from the gate, a red light came on in the cockpit, and it wound up sitting on the tarmac for about two and half hours while mechanics tried to find the problem. At that point they gave up, rolled it to the gate again, and had everyone deplane, intending to move them to a new aircraft. While they were waiting, someone killed Howell. We found the bomb in his luggage a short time later."

"That's some coincidence," I said.

"Exactly what I'm thinking. I need you to put your magic eyes on a few more things for me, and maybe a few people, too."

"People?"

"I want to know if our murderer was on the plane, and I know you can tell from looking if someone's a conjurer."

"Just because a conjurer is on the plane, that doesn't mean he or she is the killer."

She frowned. "I know that. You know I know that. But it would be a place to start, right?"

I couldn't argue. "I'll 'put my magic eyes' on whoever you want me to." I shifted my attention back to Jimmy Bob. "What do you suppose Pete Forsythe is going to say was the cause of death?" Forsythe was the Medical Examiner in Phoenix, and had been since way before I joined the police force.

Kona shrugged. "I don't know. Why?"

"From what I'm seeing, I'd guess that the magic slashed through him—I don't know if it simply stopped his heart or caused a heart attack, or a rupture of some sort."

"Does it matter?"

For some reason I felt that it did, though I couldn't say why. "It's not the kind of spell I would cast."

"Well, I'd hope not."

I grunted a laugh but then grew serious again. "No, I mean that if I was going to murder someone, and if I intended to attack his heart, I'd seize it with a spell, make sure it would appear to anyone who cared that he'd died of a heart attack. And maybe this sorcerer did that, but a spell like this . . . It seems odd." I covered him again, stood.

Kona was watching me. "Go ahead and say it."

"Say what?"

"Whatever it is you're thinking right now."

I rubbed the back of my neck. "All right. It's almost like whoever killed him didn't care how it would look."

"Except that they did it with magic, which most of us can't see."

"True. But that's all the more reason to make it seem like a natural death—why would you draw attention to what you'd done by flaunting the spell?"

"I can't help you there, partner," she said. "I think all of you weremystes are crazy."

"Or at least headed that way, right?"

"At least. Come on. Let's go see the rest of it."

I followed her out of the men's room to the nearest of the gates. A TSA official swiped a card and pulled open the gate door, allowing us to walk down the jet bridge. Halfway between the gate and the open end of the bridge, the heat hit us, a fist of stifling air. I pulled off my bomber. We exited onto a stairway that led down to the apron, and climbed into what was essentially a golf cart. Kona released the brake and steered us out of the apron and onto a roadway that ran parallel to the runways and led toward an open area near the western edge of the airport.

"Where are we going?" I asked, raising my voice so that she would hear me over the rush of hot wind and the constant roar of aircraft.

"To check out a bomb."

I nodded. "You know how to show a guy a good time."

She grinned. "Don't tell Margarite. She'll be jealous."

CHAPTER 5

I hadn't seen the PPD's bomb squad in action since leaving the force, and even as a cop I dealt with them no more than three or four times in six years. They weren't called upon all that often, but when we needed them, we sure were glad to have them.

Kona pulled up next to several police cruisers and the bomb-squad truck, and we both climbed out of the cart. Kevin Glass, Kona's new partner, stood near the cars, watching as the bomb-disposal robot picked through the contents of a duffel bag some fifty yards away.

Nearby, a cop was in the process of removing his disposal suit: more than eighty pounds of Kevlar, ballistic plastic, and steel plating. The helmet, which reminded me of something an astronaut would wear, had a fan inside of it, but that was small consolation under a desert sun in this kind of heat. The cop was soaked with sweat, his hair plastered to his head. But he was grinning, which I took to mean that whatever danger there had been was past.

"What's the story?" Kona asked Kevin. "Was the bomb real?"

"Oh, it was real," Glass said. "Hey there, Jay."

"Hi, Kevin."

I still referred to Kevin as Kona's "new" partner, but the fact was, she'd been with him for over a year. He was only "new" in that he wasn't me, a fact that still rankled. Not that it was his fault. Kevin was a good guy and, from all that I had seen, a good cop, too. He'd shaved his head, which made him look older than his years. His eyes were dark, his skin a rich, warm brown. He had an easy smile and the build of an athlete. I wanted to like him, and I wanted him to like me. But we remained wary of each other. For my part, the mistrust was born of foolishness: I was off the force; Kona needed a partner. I had no right to be resentful, but I was.

Kevin was younger than I was and had been a detective in Homicide for maybe three years. He probably felt that I was judging him, and that Kona was constantly measuring his performance against mine. I doubt that she was, but I could understand why he might feel that way.

Basically it was mess, and it would remain that way until I found some way to bridge the gap between us.

"It was designed to work on a plane," he went on, speaking to both Kona and me. "The guys say it would have gone off at about twenty-five thousand feet, and that there was enough explosive to blow a huge hole in the fuselage. We got lucky."

Kona and I shared a quick glance, and Kevin's expression grew guarded. This was the other reason he hadn't warmed to me yet. Kona and I had a way of communicating that came from years of friendship and professional rapport. She didn't have that yet with him, and he was as aware of this as I was.

"They haven't found anything else in the suitcase?" Kona asked.

"Not yet."

"Can we see the bomb?"

Kevin nodded and started toward a small device that lay on the concrete, also some fifty yards from where the cars were parked, though in a different direction. Kona and I followed.

"They wanted to detonate it," Kevin said, over his shoulder. "But I held them off until Jay could see it, like you asked."

Kona nodded once. "Thanks."

"Is it safe?" I asked, slowing.

"Should be. They clipped the wires, and even if they hadn't, it's not like we're at altitude. The bomb guys said it would be really unusual for it to go off under these conditions."

"That's reassuring," I muttered, falling in step with Kona again.

"You an expert in bombs, Jay?"

I shot another glance Kona's way. She was staring straight ahead, her lips pursed. She had been telling me for months now that the best way to improve my relationship with Kevin would be to end all the secrecy that surrounded my conversations with her, conversations that almost always revolved around spells and magic. I knew she was right.

"Not really, no."

"So then what are you looking for?"

"Magic."

He stopped; so did Kona and I.

"What?"

"I'm looking for signs of magic."

Kevin turned to Kona, some quip on his lips. But her expression didn't change, and his smile wilted. "The two of you are jerking me around."

"I left the force because I'm a weremyste," I said. "I go through something called the phasing every month on the full moon."

"I've heard of phasings, but I never . . ." He blew out a breath. "This is for real?" he asked Kona.

"Listen to the man," she said.

"Kona's known for years, and over time she's learned to recognize the signs of a magical crime. When she sees something she can't explain, or when she's certain that spells were used in a murder, she calls me."

"The Blind Angel killings," he said, breathing the words.

"That's right. I'm sorry I didn't tell you sooner. Leaving the force was—"

He held up a hand, stopping me. "No apologies necessary. So you think there was some kind of mojo involved in all of this today?"

"The guy in the men's room was killed with a spell," Kona said. "I knew it as soon as I saw him."

"How?" Kevin asked. "There wasn't a mark . . ." He trailed off, shaking his head slowly. A small laugh escaped him. "Magic. Damn." He faced me again. "So, what do you look for?"

"Stuff that you can't see—the residue of spells. A flare of color that's left after a conjurer casts. Although," I said to Kona, "coming out here might have been a waste of time. If Howell was a sorcerer and he used magic on anything there'd be no sign of it now. Magic dies with the runecrafter. Besides, a conjurer doesn't need a bomb to bring down a plane."

"Check it anyway," she said. "Just in case."

I did, and as I expected there was no magic at all on the bomb. A few minutes later, the bomb-squad guys gave us the all clear and we walked to the duffel bag and examined that as well. Again, there was no residue on it. But while we were searching through Howell's stuff, an idea came to me. I picked a loose sock out of the bag and held it up for Kona to see.

"Can I take this?"

"Oh, sure, Justis. I mean it's evidence in a murder and terrorism investigation, but we always like to give souvenirs to the tourists who join us for bomb searches, so help yourself."

I stared back at her.

"You're serious?"

"I know it could get you in trouble," I said. "Though it's not as though the evidence guys will be counting socks. But it might allow me to see what Howell saw in the final moments of his life."

"You'll return it?"

"I'll give it back to you. You'll return it."

Kevin was watching us, a small frown on his face. "You two always like this?"

She nodded. "It's not pretty, is it?" Her attention on

me once more, she narrowed her eyes. "Sure, take the sock, but for God's sake, keep it out of sight and get it back to me before we leave the airport."

I slipped it into my pocket, and the three of us headed back toward the cart.

Considering what I had seen out here, and what I had found on Howell's corpse, I was convinced that our skinhead was nothing more than he appeared: a jackass domestic terrorist who had been killed by a conjurer. There had been no sign in the restroom of a magical battle, and the killing spell had hit Howell in the chest, suggesting that the conjurer who killed him hadn't bothered to sneak up on him. Howell was no weremyste. But then why was he murdered with magic?

Kona drove us back to the apron, where the plane originally designated for flight 595 still sat, sunlight gleaming off of its wings and tail. We got out and started to walk back toward the jet bridge and terminal. As we did my eyes were drawn again and again to the aircraft.

I halted. "Did they ever figure out what was wrong with the plane?"

Kona shook her head. "I don't think so. Just some warning message on the console that wouldn't go off— something about the hydraulics maybe? I don't . . ." Comprehension hit her at last, widening her eyes. "Shit."

"What now?" Kevin asked. "What are you guys talking about?"

"There wasn't any sign of magic on the bomb or Howell's bag," I said. "But I'd bet good money that there is on the plane itself. That's why it never took off."

"Magic can keep a plane on the ground?"

"Magic can foul up the instrumentation or the hydraulics, or pretty much anything else you can think of." To Kona I said, "What was the exact warning light? Do you know?"

She flipped open her small pad again and scanned her notes, frowning. "I'm not sure I wrote it down."

"The message was 'F/CTL Flaps Fault,'" Kevin said. When both of us stared over at him, he lifted a shoulder. "What? I remember stuff like that. I can't help it."

"He's handy to have around," I said to Kona.

"He is."

"I think I need to see the plane."

I should have known that it would be crawling with mechanics. We walked around the exterior and found two guys working on the left wing. They had the flaps propped up and were examining the hydraulics inside.

"Can I come up and take a look?" I called to them.

They paused in what they were doing to stare down at me.

"You know anything about planes?" one of them asked.

"A little bit." I lied.

They shared a glance and one of them shrugged. "Sure, come on up."

I climbed the ladder and stepped onto the wing, taking care to avoid the spots marked "no step." I knew that much, at least.

I peered down into the guts of the wing, amazed that these guys could make sense of the wires and mechanisms. I certainly couldn't. But I wasn't trying to; I was searching for the glow of magic, and to my disappointment, I saw none.

I examined the flaps as well; nothing on them either.

"These are the flaps that weren't working before?" I asked.

Another glance passed between the men. "These are the flaps," one of them said, pointing to several different panels. He pointed to a few other surfaces. "These are the spoilers and the ailerons. You want me to show you the tabs and slats, too?" So much for convincing them that I knew anything about planes.

"No, that's all right."

"To answer your question, yeah, these are the ones that aren't working."

"Except there's nothing wrong with them," his friend chimed in. "Least nothing I can see."

"We could probably figure out the problem if we were in the hangar," the first guy said, "but the police wanted the bird to stay right here."

I nodded, squinting against the glare coming off the wing. It was possible that in this light I simply couldn't see whatever magic was there. "But so far you've found no problems."

"Nope. The crew reported a cockpit warning about the flaps, and you don't mess around with that. And when they tried to test the hydraulics before taxiing to the runway, nothing happened. You sure as shit don't mess with that. Now though . . ." He shook his head. "Now everything seems okay."

"Gremlins," the second guy said, flashing a toothy grin.

The first one nodded. "Yeah, gremlins. That's the best I've got."

"All right, guys," I said, climbing back down off the wing. "Thanks." Once on the ground again, I asked Kona if she could get me inside the cockpit to see the console.

"I don't know, Justis. The federal boys weren't exactly eager to give us access to Howell's body. But they were downright possessive when it came to the plane. At one point I thought they were going to pull down their zippers and start marking territory. You know what I mean?"

"So you don't think you can convince them to let me take a quick look?"

"I'm not sure I can get myself inside, much less you. This is the FBI we're talking about. The only people they like less than local cops are local PIs. But let's give it a try. The worst they can do is say no."

We walked around to the side of the plane, where the boarding stairs had been rolled up to the cabin door. There was no one guarding the stairway, so Kona and I climbed them, both of us trying to act like we weren't doing anything wrong.

Before we reached the top of the stairs, though, we heard voices coming from inside.

"This isn't going to work," Kona whispered.

"I'm going to try something. Don't freak out, all right?"

"This isn't the time for you to try something."

"It's the perfect time. Stay calm."

I scanned the apron; aside from Kevin, who was trying to pretend he didn't know us, there was no one nearby. Convinced that the coast was relatively clear, I mumbled another camouflage spell. Seven elements again: the FBI guys, me, the interior of the plane, the dim light of the cabin, the bright daylight, the boarding stairs, and the FBI guys again. I hadn't seen the interior of this plane, but I could make out the color of the carpeting from where we stood on the stairs, and I had been in plenty of passenger jets over the years; they all looked pretty much the same.

As with the spell I'd cast the night before, I repeated the elements to myself six times. On the seventh, I released the spell.

"Justis, what are you doing?"

"Can you still see me?"

She eyed me like I was nuts. "Uhhh, yeah. Why?"

"Because if I did the spell right, the guys on the plane won't be able to."

"Did I lose track of the days? Is tonight the full moon?"

"I'm not hallucinating. I cast what's called a camouflage spell. Weremystes can't make themselves invisible, at least I can't. But with this magic, I can hide myself from specific people. Those guys in there shouldn't be able to see me. Trust me on this." I felt like crossing my fingers, or knocking on wood. Because really, I wouldn't know for certain that the spell had worked until I entered the plane. But I was operating under the assumption that it had.

"So what do you want me to do?"

"Talk to them, distract them. I can't be seen, but I can be heard."

"All right," she said, sounding like she still thought I was crazy.

And maybe I was. We were about to find out.

We climbed the rest of the stairs, and I followed Kona into the plane.

"Hello, gentlemen," Kona said, flashing those gorgeous pearly whites of hers. "I wanted to see if you all needed anything."

Three agents were clustered around a bank of seats about two-thirds of the way back; I assumed that was where Howell had been sitting. Two of the men glanced up, but then went back to examining the seats. A third man, tall, with dark hair and a smile as electric as hers, made a show of checking her out, head to toe.

"Hey there, beautiful. What are you offering?"

None of the men spared me a glance. Kona did look back at me, but only long enough to shoot me a "you owe me for this" glare.

While she pretended to flirt with Tall, Dark, and Handsome, I stepped into the cockpit, making sure that I didn't touch anything.

I spotted the magic right away. It would have been hard to miss, as it covered the instrumentation, though it was concentrated on the screens above the windshield, where the warning signals would have appeared. Whoever had cast the spell wanted to be certain that this plane wasn't going anywhere.

It was the same magic I had seen on Howell: a deep shimmering green, brilliant but translucent. The skinhead's murderer had also seen to it that this plane didn't get off the ground.

I left the cockpit and walked down the aisle toward Kona and the Feds, which, I decided in that moment, was a great name for a band. Kona sent an anxious glance my way, but none of the men reacted to my presence. A few feet short of where Kona stood, I slipped out of the aisle and into a row. I didn't go so far as to lower myself into a seat; doing so would have made too much noise. Instead, I pulled out the sock I had taken from Howell's bag and my scrying stone, a slice of sea-green agate that I always carry with me.

In the weeks since I had been shot, Namid had been teaching me all sorts of seeing spells. I disliked scrying magic; always had. Often scrying spells offered little more than portents, hints at the future that could be interpreted any number of ways. They tended to obscure as much as they revealed. But seeing spells of this sort were a little different; I wasn't trying to divine the future so much as I was searching for clues about the past. And Namid seemed to think that the more I could discover with magic, the less likely I was to place myself in danger. I wasn't sure I shared his confidence, but I had to admit that the seeing spell I'd used the previous night had made catching Mark Darby a good deal easier than it otherwise might have been.

The seeing spell I planned to use now was one I had learned a few months ago, and had used to see Etienne de Cahors for the first time. I wanted to see and hear what Howell had seen and heard when he was on this plane, and this casting allowed me to do that. It was specific to place and person. I would only experience what he had experienced on this plane; to see his killer, I would have to go back to the place where he had died. And I could only see the events in question through his eyes.

I folded the sock and held it beneath the scrying stone.

This was a powerful spell, and elegant in its simplicity. Three elements: Howell, the plane, and my stone.

After a few seconds, the sinuous white and blue lines in the agate appeared to vanish, leaving an image of a seat back, a pair of hands—the skin around the wrists tattooed—and jean-clad legs, one of which bounced incessantly. He was jittery. He toyed with his seat belt, rolling the slack into a tight cylinder, letting it unravel, and then rolling it again.

He glanced up after a few minutes, in time to catch the eye of a flight attendant as she walked by. She checked to see that his belt was buckled. He turned to stare out the window. I could tell that he was in the middle seat, but he took little notice of the passengers sitting on either side of him.

There was no fast-forward button on a scrying stone, but after a few minutes of gazing at the image I had summoned, I realized that I wasn't going to learn much more of value here on the plane. Howell was trapped in his seat, and with each passing minute he seemed to grow more uneasy. He must have been a wreck after two hours of this, and that would have made it easier for the conjurer to pick him out of the crowd of passengers once they deplaned. Howell never had a chance. It was almost enough to make me feel sorry for him.

I raised my eyes from the scrying stone and found that Kona was watching me, even as the FBI agent continued to chat her up. I was tempted to whisper in his ear that she was gay, just to see the reaction I'd get. But I was good. I nodded once to Kona, eased back into the aisle, and walked with care to the cabin door.

"Well, I'm glad things are going well here," I heard her say behind me. "I'll see you boys later."

"Aw, but you don't have to go."

"I'm afraid I do. But this is going to be a long investigation, and we'll have a chance to talk again."

"Good," he said, in a tone that made me want to smack him.

"Yeah. We can have a beer. You, and me, and my lover, Margarite. You'll like her, too. Good day, gentlemen."

There was a brief silence, broken only by the sound of Kona's footsteps. Then the other two agents burst out laughing. It was all I could do not to join them.

"Now, that was fun," she said in a low voice as we exited the plane. "What did you learn? Something I hope. I'd rather not find out I went through all that for nothing."

"There was magic all over the cockpit," I said, my voice low. "The same color and quality as what was on Howell. Whoever killed him also kept the plane from taking off."

"From the cockpit?" she asked. "Does that mean it was a member of the crew?"

"Or a weremyste who managed to get in there. You've seen what a camouflage spell can do."

"Yeah, nice work, by the way. That would be a handy spell when Hibbard's around."

"Why haven't I ever thought of that?"

"So what now, partner?"

"Now we take Howell's sock back to the men's room where he was found and try a seeing spell there."

"And we couldn't do this before because . . . ?"

"Because I didn't want to touch the body and mess up your crime scene."

"Right. I appreciate that."

We went back to the terminal and made our way to the restroom once more. By now, there were several cops with the body, as well as a photographer from the ME's office. This wasn't a casting I could do in front of others without drawing attention to myself, which meant another camouflage spell. I retreated to the gate area, cast the spell so that it would work in the restroom—why couldn't the guy have been murdered in a bar, or one of those lounges designed for wealthy business travelers?—and went back in.

As on the plane, no one noticed that I was there, not even Kona, since she was in the restroom when I cast the spell. I took up a position near the entrance, pulled out the sock and stone again, and cast the seeing spell.

Once more, I saw in the stone what Howell had seen. He walked into the men's room, took a piss, and then went to the sink to wash his hands. Several other men were in here already. They gave Howell a wide berth. I assumed they had taken note of his appearance: the tattoos, the T-shirt, the shaved head. No one spoke to him or even dared make eye contact.

He braced his hands on the sink and closed his eyes, taking a long, rattling breath. Then he bent over and splashed water on his face. Seeing hand blowers but no paper-towel dispensers, he muttered a curse and pulled up his shirt hem to dry his face. Leaning on the sink again he stared at himself in the mirror. A man crossed behind him and appeared to leave the restroom.

At this point, Howell gave no indication that he had noticed anything unusual. But viewing the scene through his eyes, knowing to watch for it, I did.

No one had entered the men's room since Howell's entrance, and now it seemed that those who walked in with him, and those who had already been here, were gone. Howell was alone, or at least alone with his eventual killer. I don't know how the sorcerer managed this, but I didn't doubt for an instant that he had.

Howell straightened, then swiveled his head left and right, his brow creasing. He checked the stalls, all of which were empty, before starting toward the restroom door. After two steps, he halted.

Anyone in here? he said.

His voice echoed off the tiles, but no one answered him.

He took another step, stopped again. Without warning, he whirled, an audible gasp torn from his chest.

What the f—? Who's there?

He sounded more scared than angry, though I could tell he was trying for the latter.

Again, his question was met with silence. He was edging toward the door now, his back to the sinks. This was where he was going to die, and I didn't see anyone. Not a soul.

He spun a second time, practically jumping out of his skin, swiping at something on his shoulder, something I couldn't see. His killer seemed to be toying with him now. Was he camouflaged? Had he found some other spell to make himself invisible to Howell, and thus to me?

By this time, Howell was terrified; I could tell from his

labored breathing, the tremor in his hands. He took a single purposeful stride toward the door and bounded off of something unseen, the way he would if he had walked into a wall.

Fucking hell! he said, the words choked, like a sob.

A blinding flash of green light made me squint and turn away, even as I heard Howell's truncated scream in my head. When I peered at the stone again, it was nothing more than sea-green agate.

"Damn it," I muttered, forgetting that I was camouflaged myself. My oath drew a frown from an older gentleman who was walking past me. He kept going, though, and I ground my teeth together, vowing to keep silent from now on.

I left the men's room and positioned myself in a corner of the gate area. There I cast the seeing spell again, hoping that Howell might have seen something—anything—between the gate and the men's room that would tell me more about his killer. But he walked straight from the plane to the restroom, interacting with no one, his gaze sweeping over the crowded airport but settling on nothing in particular. Considering all the trouble I had gone through to cast the seeing spells I had little to show for my effort.

I walked to a deserted spot where I could remove the camouflage spell, and then found Kona again. She was speaking with another detective from the PPD. I hung back until she was finished with him.

"What have you got for me?" she asked.

"A sock." I slipped her the sock, which she stuffed in her blazer pocket.

"Seriously, Justis."

"Seriously, that's about all I've got."

"You mean, after all that mojo you were going to do, you didn't find out anything?"

"Just that our killer casts a mean camouflage spell and can move around a men's room without making much noise."

"So you didn't see him."

I shook my head. "I saw what Howell saw, which was nothing at all. The guy snuck up on him, toyed with him for a few seconds, and then killed him with a spell."

"The killer could still be here, then," she said. "He could be watching everything we do, and we wouldn't know it."

"Or she. And yeah, that's exactly right."

She scanned the gate area, her expression curdling. "Honestly, I don't know how you live every day with this magic shit. It would drive me up a wall."

"Who says it doesn't do the same to me?" I surveyed the airport as well. "But let me try something." It wasn't a spell I had attempted before, but Namid would have been the first to tell me that such things didn't matter. If I could hold the elements in my head, I could cast it. It seemed easy enough, though I couldn't figure out how to do it with only three elements; I'd need seven: me, the other sorcerer, his camouflage spell, my eyes, the gate area, his current location, and the removal of his spell. There were a few unknowns in that list, but I hoped I could conjure around those. I repeated the elements six times and released the magic on the seventh.

Nothing happened.

"Are you all right?" Kona asked, watching me, the corners of her mouth drawn down in mild disapproval.

"I was trying a spell. I hoped I might be able to strip away whatever magic our killer is using to hide himself. If he's still here."

"I take it the spell didn't work."

"Or he's long gone."

"Right. Look, Justis—"

"You have work to do," I said, keenly aware in that moment of the fact that she was still a cop, and I wasn't. Not that I'd needed the reminder. "I'll get out of your hair."

"I appreciate you coming all this way."

"No problem. I think I can help you with this, if you want me to keep working on it."

"I do. And with your new-found notoriety, the higher-ups are more willing to have you around."

"Except Hibbard."

"Yeah," she said. "And nobody likes him anyway."

We both grinned, though for no more than a second or two.

"I'll ask around a bit," I said, sobering. "See if any of my kind have heard people talking about a new player in town. Or about why the old players might take a new interest in domestic terrorists."

CHAPTER 6

I left Kona there and ran the gauntlet of police, FBI, and TSA check points until I was out of the terminal and back in my car. The drive out of the airport loop proved to be a good deal easier and quicker than the drive in. Afternoon traffic on the interstates, however, was hideous.

I sat in my car, idling alongside about ten thousand of my best friends, the Z-ster's air conditioner working overtime and the sun glaring off the cars in front of me, and I thought about James Howell. To be more precise, I thought about the final minutes of his life, and possible reasons for his murder.

It was too easy to assume that he was killed because he tried to blow up the plane. How would a weremyste know that, and if somehow his killer was aware of the bomb, why would he or she resort to murder rather than simply alert the police or the FBI? And if this sorcerer knew about the bomb, why would he or she bother with grounding the plane first? That made no sense. The bomb was in Howell's luggage; it wasn't in the plane's cabin or cockpit or cargo area. Disabling the plane wasn't going to save any lives. That was why Howell was antsy, but not panicked. If Howell hadn't been murdered, the passengers and their luggage would have been moved to a different aircraft, and *that* plane would have been destroyed.

The more I pondered this, the less sense it made.

I don't usually use my phone when I drive, and I'm intolerant to the point of abusiveness of drivers who do. But we weren't going anywhere, and it occurred to me that I needed more information. I pulled out my phone and punched in Kona's number.

"Miss me already, huh?" she said upon answering.

"Can you get me the passenger list for Flight 595?"

"Sure. I'll e-mail it to you. Why?"

"I know a good number of the sorcerers here in Phoenix, and I'd like to see if any of them were on board."

"I'll send it right away."

"Thanks, Kona."

I switched off the phone and tossed it on my jacket. A few seconds later, the cars around me started to inch forward.

I drove the rest of the way to my office in a fog. I knew I was missing something, a logical, or at least magical, explanation for the sequence of events that ended in Howell's death. But I couldn't see it. I kept coming back to the same conclusion: Whoever had killed the man had made his crime more complicated than it needed to be.

It wasn't that I thought criminals always behaved rationally. Far from it. I'd been a cop for too long to think anything of the sort. But this was . . . odd. That was the best word for it.

What did a dead skinhead, a Latino political leader, and a disabled 757 have in common? Well, for one thing, they were all messing with my head.

Because my day hadn't had enough surprises already, when I got to my office, Namid was already there. Waiting for me. That had never happened before.

From the way he greeted me you would have thought it was the most natural thing in the world, like I was getting home from work, and he was waiting for me in the kitchen, fixing dinner.

"What are you doing here?" I asked, tossing my car keys and bomber jacket on my desk.

"You need to train. We have not worked on your craft in some time."

"It's been two days."

"And that is long enough."

I no longer resisted Namid's attempts to help me hone my craft. I still feared the powers I possessed, knowing where they would lead me. And if ever I forgot, all I needed to do was spend a few minutes with my dad. But I also understood that as my runecrafting skills improved, so would my ability to hold off the worst symptoms of the phasings, thus slowing their cumulative effect on my mind.

On an already weird day, though, his presence in my office was too weird for me to let pass.

"You've been waiting here so that we can train? That's it? That's what you want me to believe?"

"Have I ever lied to you, Ohanko?"

That brought me up short. "No," I said without hesitation.

"Then why would you doubt me now?"

It didn't take long for my thoughts to catch up with the conversation. "You haven't lied to me," I said, ignoring the second question. "But when you're concerned about my safety, you start behaving strangely. You show up at odd times. And you avoid direct questions by asking questions of your own. So why don't you tell me what you're doing here?"

"First we train. Then you may ask your questions."

It was like arguing with a kid. A seven-hundred-year-old, watery, magic-wielding kid.

He lowered himself to the floor, gazing up at me with those endlessly patient glowing eyes. I heaved a sigh and sat as well.

"Clear yourself," he said with a low rumble, like a river in flood.

I closed my eyes and summoned an image from my youth: a golden eagle circling over the desert floor in the Superstition Wilderness, its enormous wings held perfectly still, its tail twisting as it turned. I'd been no more than nine years old when I saw it; my parents and I were on one of our many camping trips, and it was one of the happiest and most memorable moments from my childhood.

Clearing was something runecrafters did to empty their minds of distractions so that they could cast spells more efficiently and effectively. Long ago, when Namid first began to teach me the rudiments of crafting spells, he led me to this memory—there's really no other way to put it—and told me to focus on it whenever I needed to clear myself for a spell. At first, clearing took me several minutes. Now, years later, I could do it in seconds.

I opened my eyes again, indicated to the runemyste with a curt nod that I was ready.

"Defend yourself," he said.

We had started these sessions when I was pursuing Cahors, and ever since then, Namid had found new and excruciating ways to test my magical defenses. Today he started me off with a spell that made me feel as though he had driven a spike through my forehead. I gasped at the pain, resisting an urge to cradle my head in my hands.

Three elements: me, the pain, and a sheath of power surrounding me. I had to repeat them to myself several times—the agony clouded my thoughts. But at last it vanished, leaving me breathless, my face damp with sweat.

"Your spell was too slow," Namid said. "In the time it took you to cast, an enemy would have killed you."

The problem with having a teacher who was just this side of all-powerful and all-knowing was that I couldn't argue with him.

"I know," I said. "It hurt. It was hard to concentrate."

"That is why you clear yourself, Ohanko. If you do so properly, you should be able to cast despite the pain."

"You understand that I can't walk down the street clearing myself all the time, right? Sometimes I have to do other stuff, like drive and interact with people."

He stared at me, his face as still as ice, not allowing me the satisfaction of drawing even the hint of a smile. "Clearing is a technique for the most inexperienced of runecrafters," he said after a weighty pause. "When you can cast at will, with the immediacy of thought, without having to pause to clear, then you will have mastered what you call magic. Right now, when it comes to runecrafting, you are little more than a child."

That stung.

"Defend yourself."

The assailing spell crashed down on me, its weight palpable. I felt as though I had been encased in glass. I couldn't move. Not to cry out, or to fight free of the invisible prison he had conjured. Not even to breathe. Panic rose in me like a tide, though even as it did, I had time to think, in a distant corner of my mind, that he must have been saving this one for a time when he was really ticked at me.

I couldn't use either of the two most common and rudimentary warding spells—reflection or deflection—nor could I rely on the sheathing spell I had cast. Those were my standbys, the spells I went to whenever possible. Namid knew this, of course. He wanted to push me away from the magic with which I was most comfortable, and for good reason. The most comfortable spells were also the easiest, and the most readily defeated by other weremystes.

My lungs were starting to burn, and my panic was about to tip over into desperation.

An idea came to me. It was ridiculous to the point of foolishness. But magic didn't always make sense, and I had no other ideas.

I'd envisioned Namid's attack spell as a prison of glass. So why not three elements: me, the glass, and a giant hammer?

Power surged through me as if I'd stuck my finger in an electrical outlet. My body jerked, and an instant later I could breathe again.

Namid canted his head to the side, surprise and—dare I think it?—a touch of pride on his crystal clear features. "That was well done, Ohanko. What spell did you cast?"

"What spell did *you* cast?"

"It was a binding, a crafting intended to paralyze you."

I shook my head. "Then my spell shouldn't have worked. It felt like you had encased me in glass—that was the first image that came to mind. And so I imagined a hammer shattering it, and somehow that worked."

"And why should it not?"

"I don't know," I said, shrugging. "Your spell had nothing to do with glass."

"That matters not. I have told you many times before that runecrafting is an act of will. The images or words you use do not matter."

"I know that. But . . ."

"You know it, but you have not understood it until now. Not really."

He was right. He was always right. But this once it didn't bother me so much. Because even as I had told myself again and again that the words of a spell didn't matter, I always assumed that my wardings needed to be matched in some way to the intent of the assailing spells they were meant to block. I was starting to understand that they didn't. They needed to match my *perception* of those attacks, which was totally different, and much easier.

I said as much to Namid, and he nodded, the smile

lingering. "It has taken longer than I would have liked, but you are learning. Defend yourself."

He threw attack after attack at me, some of them torturous, others merely terrifying. But the last one was the worst. He managed to mess with my mind so that with no warning I found myself in the middle of what felt like a phasing. Disorientation, paranoia, delusion. All I could think was that it was too early, that the sun couldn't possibly be down yet. And so with the last shred of rational thought I could muster, I grasped at three elements: me, the phasing, and sunlight.

When my thoughts cleared and I remembered where I was, I sat up—somehow I had collapsed onto my back. Namid was watching me, in a way that made me vaguely uncomfortable.

"What?"

"You have come far," he said. "Today alone, I sense the progress you have made. It may be that we are ready for a new kind of training."

"I'm not sure I like the sound of that."

"We will not begin today. You have cast enough. But soon." He nodded, more to himself than to me. "Yes, I think soon."

I stood, stretched my back. My shirt was soaked with sweat, the way it would be after a workout at the gym. But I felt good; I could tell that I was getting stronger, quicker with my spells.

"When was the last time you saw Leander Fearsson?"

I turned. Namid was standing as well, his eyes gleaming in the late afternoon light.

"Today. Why?"

"How is he?"

I stared at the myste.

"Ohanko?"

"Did you really just ask me how my father is doing?"

"Do your friends not do this? Does not Kona Shaw, and the woman, Billie?"

"Well, yeah, of course they do, but they're . . . ? What is this about, Namid? You've never asked about him before."

"If it makes you uncomfortable, I will not do so again."

"It's not that—I'm not uncomfortable. But you don't ask questions casually. So why don't you tell me what this is about?"

"I am sorry if I have disturbed you, Ohanko. I will leave you now."

He started to dissipate.

"No!" I said.

His form solidified once more.

"I don't want you to go. I was . . . You surprised me with the question. The truth is, he's not doing well at all. He's more incoherent than usual. He's not taking care of himself. And worst of all, he seems to be in pain, though I can't tell if what he's feeling is imagined or real."

Namid's waters roughened, like the surface of a lake under a gust of wind. "What kind of pain?"

"He talks about burning, and about somebody testing him, prodding him. I don't understand half of it, but as delusions go, it strikes me as worse than usual."

"I am sorry to hear this."

Something in the way Namid spoke the words caught my attention. "Does any of that mean something to you?"

"Tell me more of what he said."

I frowned, thinking back on the conversation I'd had with my dad that morning—if I could even call it that. "He said *they* were burning him, and something about brands. He thought he was being marked, like whoever was doing this owned him. I tried to get him to tell me who had hurt him, but he wouldn't."

As enigmatic as Namid could be, it was pretty easy to tell when he was troubled. Moments before he had been as clear as mountain water. Now his face and body were turbid, muddied, like the waters of a churning river. "What else?"

"That was all—" I stopped, the memory washing over me. "No, there was one other thing. He said that they think he matters, but he doesn't. And then he told me that I did matter—he was pretty emphatic about it—and he said that if I spent too much time with him, they'd find me and they'd hurt me, too."

The myste was as roiled as I'd ever seen him, as roiled as he was when Cahors attacked me in my home.

"Does all of that mean something to you, Namid?"

"I do not know," he said. "Perhaps. There are old powers in the world, nearly as old as my kind. Scrying their purpose can be difficult."

"You mean someone might actually be doing these things to him? He's not just delusional?"

"The moontimes were not kind to him. You know this. All that he said to you may well be the product of his moon sickness. But it is also possible that there is a kernel of truth beneath the layers of delusion. I must go, Ohanko."

"I'm not going to keep away from him," I said before

the runemyste could leave. "Even if it's all true, and these bastards who are hurting him might come after me, too."

"I would expect no less. Tread like the fox."

I nodded and watched him fade from view.

I stretched again, crossed to my desk, and fired up the computer. It was so old it might as well have been steam-powered, but it still worked, and within a few minutes I was wading through the junk in my e-mail inbox, looking for the message from Kona with the passenger-manifest attachment. I opened the file and printed it, preferring to work with a paper copy. It was two pages long, and several of the names had only a first initial. But I had no trouble finding Mando Vargas and James Howell. Howell was a party of one, but Mando had five travel companions—aides, no doubt. If Howell had managed to blow up the plane and kill all of them, it would have been front-page news across the country, which was probably what he and his fellow skinheads were counting on.

He was going to be front page news all right, but not the way he and his buddies expected.

I read through the list a second time, and stumbled on a familiar name. At least it might have been familiar. "P. Hesslan-Fine."

Pausing over it, I felt my stomach tightening with long-buried emotions. Rage, humiliation, and ultimately, deepest grief. Something cold crept through me, chilling me to the marrow, making my breath catch in my chest. I remembered this feeling; I would have been glad to go the rest of my life without experiencing it again. But here it was, as raw as ever. It might as well have been days instead of years.

I was all of thirteen when my mother died in a scandal that, for the worst fifteen minutes any fame-seeker could imagine, consumed all of Phoenix and splashed the Fearsson family name across the headlines of every newspaper in the state. She was found dead beside the body of her lover, a man named Elliott Hesslan. Some claimed it was a double murder and tried to pin the blame on my father. Others called it a double suicide, and still others were certain that it was a murder-suicide, though they couldn't decide which of the pair had killed the other.

All I knew was that my dad went on a bender that lasted months, and I had to go to school each day and try to ignore the stares and whispers of classmates and teachers alike. The people who could have understood what I was going through were the very ones I wanted no part of. Elliott's widow, Mary, and their children, Michael and Patricia. Michael, I knew, killed himself a few years later—that made it into the papers, too. I had long since lost track of Patricia.

There weren't that many Hesslans in Phoenix, and with the name hyphenated, I assumed that this passenger was a woman. Could that have been Patty Hesslan?

I forced myself to read on, but I saw no other names that rang a bell, and I kept going back to that single line. "P. Hesslan-Fine, party of one."

There wasn't always a lot of overlap between the attributes I associated with being a cop and those that were rooted in my being a weremyste. But one big one was a healthy skepticism about coincidence. My father was suffering, Namid was worried, a guy who tried to blow up a plane was killed by magic, and the daughter of my mother's boyfriend was on the plane in question. That was a lot to dismiss as happenstance.

I sat down at the computer again and punched "Patricia Hesslan" into a search engine. I didn't get a lot of relevant hits: a few old news stories that related back to the deaths of her father and my mother, a site that listed her as a licensed real estate agent for Sonoran Winds Realty, and a wedding announcement with the headline, "Hesslan weds Fine."

The accompanying photo was grainy, but I recognized her as soon as I saw it. We'd met one time—an unfortunate chance meeting at the funeral home mere days after the bodies were found—but hers wasn't a face I was likely to forget. She and Gerald Fine were married several years ago. He was a partner at a law firm here in town. A search of his name didn't dredge up much else. It seemed they both kept low profiles.

I typed in "Dara Fearsson" to see what a search of my mother's name would produce, but wisely deleted it rather than hit "enter." The sense of dread that had returned when I read Patty's name hadn't left me; if anything it had gotten worse the deeper I'd delved into her life. But for months after my mother's death, I had been both repulsed and fascinated by every new newspaper article about her and Elliott. I couldn't get enough of them, and yet each time I read one I wound up nauseous and in tears. Twenty years later, I wasn't as overwrought—not by a long shot. But that perverse fascination remained.

I forced myself to switch off the computer. Then I left

the office, intending to go back to my house, change out of my sweaty clothes, and track down a few of my weremyste friends to find out what they knew about new sorcerers in the Phoenix area.

My office wasn't far from my home, and I was able to take back streets, thus avoiding the worst of the late afternoon traffic. As I pulled into the driveway, I noticed a strange car parked across the street from my house. Strange as in unfamiliar, but also strange as in out of place in my quiet neighborhood. It was a black vintage Chevy Impala lowrider, probably from around the mid-1960s. It was in great shape: a gleaming new paint job, white-wall tires, polished chrome. There was something familiar about it, but I couldn't place it right away.

I retrieved the mail, walked to my door, and let myself in, my attention on the bills I'd pulled from the mailbox. Which was why I about jumped out of my skin when a voice said, "Fearsson."

I dropped the envelopes, reached for my shoulder holster.

"I wouldn't do that," the same voice warned.

I froze.

CHAPTER 7

All three of the men in my living room were Latino. They were very well dressed; two of them—the ones standing— were NFL huge, dark-haired, dark-eyed. I probably should have checked more closely for distinguishing marks—scars, tattoos, that sort of thing. But my eyes were drawn to the black SIG Sauer P220s they both had aimed at my chest.

The third man sat on the couch, his legs crossed, his arms draped casually over the back cushions. Him I recognized.

Luis Paredes was a weremyste whom I had known for years. He was short, barrel-chested, with a beard and mustache that he had trimmed since the last time I saw him, and black eyes that always made me think of the flat, disk-like eyes of a shark. Once, when I was still a cop working in narcotics, I had busted Luis for possession of pot with intent to sell. Later, after I lost my badge and became a PI, I helped him out with an employee who had been stealing from his bar. I never would have called us friends, but neither would I have expected him to show up in my house with a couple of armed goons.

He was an accomplished weremyste, powerful enough that his features were blurred. All weremystes appeared that way when I first met them—smeared, so that it seemed someone had rubbed an eraser across their faces. The effect lessened with time, or maybe the more time I spent with a runecrafter, the easier it was for me to compensate. But that initial impression was unmistakable; whenever I met another runemyste, particularly a powerful one, I knew it right away. Looking more closely, I realized that his friends were sorcerers, too, though the blurring effect wasn't as strong with them. In a battle of spells, Luis would be the most dangerous of the three. Of course the other two guys could simply shoot me.

One of them stepped around my coffee table, his .45 still leveled at my heart. He didn't say anything, but he reached into my bomber, pulled my Glock from the shoulder holster, and handed it back to the other goon. I heard the metallic ring of the round being unchambered and then the slide and click of the magazine clearing the grip. I didn't figure I'd be getting that mag back. The guy in front of me grabbed my shoulder, spun me around, pushed me against the wall, and frisked me. When he was done, he turned me back the way I'd been, flashed a smile that could have frozen the tap water in my pipes, and crossed back to where he'd been standing.

"Why don't you have a seat, Jay?" Luis said, his tone too smug by half for my taste.

"Why don't you get the hell out of my house, Luis? And you can take your attack dogs with you."

He frowned. I'm not sure his goons even blinked. They were well-trained.

"I think maybe we should try that again. Why don't you sit down, Jay?" His eyes had the flat, sharky quality again, and his tone was more pointed this time. "Be smart, *mi amigo*. We're three weremystes, you're one." He gave a little shrug. "We've got three guns now, you've got none. And Rolon and Paco here have biceps that are about as big around as your thigh. So how do you intend to make us leave?"

It was a fair question. I walked to the armchair that sat across from the sofa and dropped myself into it, my eyes never leaving Luis's face.

He opened his hands and grinned. "There, isn't that better?"

"What are you doing here, Luis? Why would you break into my place?"

"A friend wants to talk to you," he said, leaning forward. "You know that I run the Moon, but I have another job. Something I do on the side."

The New Moon was a bar in Gilbert that catered to weremystes and myste-wannabes—people who had no magical abilities but, for whatever reason, liked to act as though they did. I often went there when I needed information about Phoenix's weremystes; in fact, that was one of the places I'd been planning to go to ask about the murder at the airport. I'll admit as well that sometimes I went to the Moon for no reason other than to be with other mystes, to know that I could talk about the next phasing, or the one I'd just been through, with people who understood and put up with the same crap I did month to month. Sure, it was a dive, but it was a comfortable dive.

Luis had been running the place for as long as I could remember, and I always assumed that he owned it. But if he was working a second job, I might have been wrong, which left me wondering who the owner might be.

"Is this second job legal?" I asked.

"You a cop again?" There was no hint of humor in the question.

I laughed, high and harsh. "What do you want from me? You break into my house with a couple of guys who look like they're itching to shoot me, or kick the crap out of me, or set my hair on fire, and you start telling me your employment history. Why the hell are you here? Who's this friend of yours?"

"I'll tell you on the way."

I started to object, but he continued, talking over me. "And before you start another fucking speech, keep in mind that I could have grabbed you, let my boys knock you around a bit, and thrown you in the back of my car." He paused, rubbed a hand over his face. "But the fact is, you were right about the Blind Angel Killer being a myste, and I was wrong. I feel I owe you one."

"Thanks," I said, and meant it. Killing Cahors was pretty much the beginning, middle, and end of my résumé these days; but it was a big deal, and no one understood that better than another weremyste.

Luis stood. "Come on."

"Can I change? I've been . . . working out."

I didn't have it in mind to run, or to call the police; I

really did want to change. But Luis wasn't ready to trust me that much.

"I'm not taking you out on a date. Now, get up."

I stood, and let the three men escort me out of the house. Luis paused to let me lock the door, and then led me over to the lowrider.

"Yours?" I asked.

He shook his head. "I drive an Audi. This is Paco's."

The behemoth who had taken my pistol grinned again.

I sat in back with Rolon, who still had his weapon in hand. I had no idea where we were going, of course, but I had assumed that we would be headed into Gilbert. Instead we got on the 101 northbound. We sped through Tempe and crossed over the Salt River.

"You going to tell me where we're going?" I said, breaking a lengthy silence.

"To see my friend," Luis answered.

"That's helpful."

Nothing.

We exited the freeway in North Scottsdale and followed the side streets into one of the wealthier neighborhoods of a town known for its wealth. Before long, Paco steered us into a gated subdivision called Ocotillo Winds Estates. The uniformed old man in the guardhouse waved the car through on sight; although he didn't appear to be too happy about it. Beyond the guardhouse was a round lawn that probably demanded more water in a week than the entire state got in rainfall each year. And to make the display that much more ostentatious, a huge fountain danced in the middle of the expanse, its waters misting in the wind.

"You're moving up in the world, Luis."

"You ever heard of Jacinto Amaya?"

I opened my mouth to answer, then closed it again. I'd been on edge from the moment Luis said my name and made me drop the mail. But for the first time this evening, I felt truly afraid.

"Jason Amaya? Are you screwing with me?"

"Jason is a name he uses to make Anglos feel at ease. If you want to get on his good side you'll refer to him as Jacinto. And you'll call him Mister Amaya."

"That's who we're going to see? That's the guy you're working for?"

Luis stared back at me, his silence all the confirmation I needed.

"I thought we were friends."

"What does that have to do with anything?"

"Everything! I worked in Narcotics for eighteen months, and then I was in Homicide for over five years. And I spent a significant part of that time trying to nail Amaya for one crime or another. This man hates me; I'm pretty sure he wants me dead!"

Luis rolled his eyes. "Do I need to remind you again that you're not a cop?"

I stared out the window, watching mansion after mansion slip by as we crawled through the lanes of the subdivision. All of them were vaguely similar: manicured lawns, acacia trees in the front yards, sprawling Spanish mission-style houses behind faux-adobe walls and wrought-iron gates.

"It's not my memory I'm worried about," I muttered.

"Believe it or not, I am your friend, Jay. Jacinto doesn't

want to kill you. Not today. If he did, do you really think he'd have me bring you to his home?"

I exhaled, not realizing until then that I'd been holding my breath. Luis was right, though that did little to improve my mood. Jacinto Amaya was one of the Phoenix area's most prominent crime lords. He ran a drug trade that distributed to much of the American Southwest, and he was reputed to traffic in people as well. Some said that he helped undocumented workers reach the States and then set them up with employers, taking a finder's fee as well as a cut of the pay the laborers received. He also had a stake in Phoenix's prostitution industry, from street-level hookers to thousand-dollar-per-night call girls. And, naturally, he controlled several legitimate businesses as well, most prominently the Chofi Luxury Hotels, which, as I understood, he had named for his eldest daughter and which had strong ties to Arizona's growing tribal casino business.

I'm sure there were other components to his criminal empire that I was forgetting. But the drug trade was the most important by far; it brought in the lion's share of his cash, and it accounted for the most brutal of his crimes. He had been implicated in more killings than I cared to count, most of them so clean, so professional, that we'd never been able to prove a thing, and most of them so brutal that no one was likely to come forward with evidence against him.

Paco steered us onto a cul-de-sac and followed it to the end, stopping before a broad pair of gates and another guard house. Amaya's guards were a lot younger and a lot bigger than the guy who'd let us into the subdivision. They wore ballistic vests over their uniforms, which must have been stifling, even with the sun down, and they carried modified MP5s with laser sights.

One of the men came to the car and peered inside.

"*Hola*," he said, grinning at Luis. "*Quien es el gringo?*"

"Fearsson," Luis said. "*Jacinto nos espera.*"

"*Sí.*"

The guard straightened and waved to the uniformed man. A moment later the gates began to swing open.

"*Hasta luego,*" the guard called as he tapped a hand on the roof of the car.

Paco eased the car forward into the brick courtyard that served as Amaya's driveway. We parked, and my three friends walked me into the house, passing another pair of armed and armored guards.

We passed through a foyer—tile floors, exposed beams, and a stylized crucifix that appeared to be made of ivory—into an enormous room with polished wood floors, more exposed beams, and some of the most beautiful Oaxacan folk art I'd ever seen.

A man stood at a bank of windows, which faced back toward downtown Scottsdale and encompassed a twilight sky that glowed with yellows, oranges, and pinks.

He turned at the sound of our footsteps, and I halted midstride. He was dressed in suit pants and a matching vest, a blue dress shirt and a silk tie. His hair was shot through with silver and perfectly groomed, his skin was a soft olive. I thought his eyes were brown, and I had the sense that he was smiling at me, but I couldn't be certain.

The magical blur of his features was too strong.

"Justis Fearsson," said Jacinto Amaya, his voice a deep baritone, his words untinged by any hint of an accent. "I've wanted to meet you for a long time."

He strode across the room, a hand extended. I gripped it, not yet trusting myself to speak. He put his other arm around my shoulders, leading me farther into the room. I could make out his grin now. It was unrestrained, and utterly sincere. I'd been in Amaya's presence for no more than a few seconds, and already I could see what I never would have known from a police file or a newspaper article: This was a man whom others would follow, regardless of where he led.

"Would you like a drink, Jay? It's all right if I call you Jay, isn't it?"

"Yes, thank you," I said, finding my voice and adding "Mister Amaya" as an afterthought. "Club soda, please. And Jay is fine."

He nodded and began to fix my drink, but I noticed he didn't offer to let me call him Jacinto.

"I'm sorry to have sent Luis and his friends for you, but I wasn't sure you would come if I merely requested that you do so. And I've been eager to speak with you."

"There was a time, I believe, when you were eager to kill me."

Amaya laughed, stepping away from the bar to hand me my drink. "Not really, no. You were never important enough to kill. Forgive me; I mean no offense. But I have far more dangerous enemies than detectives in the Phoenix Police Department. And once you left the force—forgive me again—but you were not someone to whom I paid much attention."

I raised my glass in salute and sipped the soda water. "You and everyone else."

"But that's changed, hasn't it?"

"I suppose."

"You suppose," he repeated with a chuckle. He put an arm around my shoulder again and steered me to a plush leather chair near the window. I sat, and he took the chair next to mine. Luis, Paco, and Rolon were still in the room, but Amaya seemed content to ignore them, and so I did the same.

"Killing Etienne de Cahors was no small thing," he said.

I looked his way, raising an eyebrow. Cahors's name had been in the papers as Stephen D. Cahors, and I'd only spoken of him by his true name to a handful of people.

My obvious surprise seemed to please him. "My resources within the magical world are as extensive as those outside of it."

"Did you know who he was before he died?" I asked.

"No," he said, without any hesitation or hint of pretense.

"What would you have done if you had?"

The smile sharpened. "An interesting question. I'm not in the habit of giving aid to the PPD. On the other hand, he was killing Latina women, and he was using dark magic to do it." He fell silent, perhaps still weighing my question. "But you have me getting ahead of myself."

"I didn't know that you were a weremyste," I said, placing my glass on the small side table next to me and meeting his gaze. "That would have been handy knowledge back when I was on the force."

He laughed again, showing perfect teeth. "Yes, I'm sure it would have been. That's not something we tend to share with the general public, though, is it?"

"No, it's not. Why am I here, Mister Amaya?"

His eyes narrowed shrewdly. "Why do you think you're here?"

It hit me like an open-handed slap to the face, and I kicked myself for not thinking of it sooner. The plane, and the attempt on the life of Mando Rafael Vargas. In that instant I would have given a whole lot of money to see the color of Jacinto Amaya's magic.

But I wasn't sure how much I ought to say. Kona had brought me in on an ongoing investigation involving not only the PPD, but also several agencies of the federal government. She had faith in me, and in my discretion. I had a pretty good idea of what she'd think of me sharing what I knew with the leading drug kingpin in Arizona.

"I'm not sure," I made myself say, realizing that his question still hung between us.

Amaya's eyebrows bunched. "You disappoint me. Of course you know, or at least you know some of it."

"Well, let's assume for a moment that I do. You must realize that I can't tell you anything about an ongoing investigation. The person who brought me in is trusting me . . ." I trailed off, because he was laughing. At me, most likely, which tended to piss me off. "Is something funny?"

"Who do you think you're dealing with?" he asked, some of the polite veneer peeling away from the words. "Do you honestly think I need a PI to tell me what's going on inside the Phoenix Police Department, or inside the FBI, for that matter?"

"Is that how you've stayed out of jail all this time?"

He went still, like a wolf on the hunt. But I heard Luis and his friends stir behind me. Amaya glanced back at them and put up a hand, probably to stop them from pulling me from the chair and beating me to a bloody pulp. When he faced me again, the pleasant veneer was back in place, though more strained than before.

"What do you think?"

"I think it's helped, though maybe not as much as being a weremyste. And being successful, and rich, and ruthless."

"You see? When you try, you can be quite smart. So again I ask you, why do you think you're here?"

Thinking about it for all of two seconds, I came to the conclusion that playing games with the guy made little sense, and could very well get me killed. By this time, news of the attempted bombing was all over the media—television and Internet—as was speculation about the intended target of the bomber. And as Amaya had made clear, he had plenty of sources to fill him in on those details that wouldn't find their way into standard news reports.

"You want to talk about the attempt on Mando Vargas's life."

"Better." He glanced at my drink. "Finish that club soda and then have a beer with me."

He stood before I could respond. I drained my soda water, and by the time I was setting it down, he was handing me a bottle of Bohemia Stout.

"Do you want a glass?" he asked.

I held up the bottle. "It's in a glass."

Amaya grinned, and we both drank. It was a good beer, heartier than most Mexican lagers.

"So, what can you tell me about the man who tried to blow up Mando's plane?"

"Mister Amaya, I was called in by a friend on the PPD—"

"Kona Shaw. Your former partner."

I masked my frown by taking another sip of beer. "Yes. She asks me to help her from time to time, because she knows that I'm discreet. I can't help her if—"

"I'm going to stop you there and make this easy for you," Amaya said. A note of impatience had crept into his tone. I'd pushed him about as far as I could. "I want you to assume, for the remainder of this conversation, that I have a gun pointed at your heart." He opened his hands and flashed another of those perfect, predatory smiles. "Now as you can see, I hold no weapon in my hands. But you're going to pretend that I do. And you're going to keep in mind as well that if by some chance you lie to me, or hide information from me, I'll learn of it before long. And I will be very displeased."

I said nothing, but after a few seconds I nodded once.

"Splendid. Now, the man with the bomb?"

"I assume you know that he was a white-supremacist," I said, with a silent apology to Kona. "As far as I could tell, he wasn't a sorcerer, but he did have access to some high-tech toys. The bomb in his luggage was sophisticated enough to get past security and onto the plane."

"You're sure he wasn't a myste?"

"Why would a weremyste need a bomb to blow up a

plane? For that matter, why would he need to sacrifice himself to do it?"

"He might use a bomb because it would raise fewer questions than would magic, and because it would make a statement on behalf of his fellow skinheads. And if he was a good enough myste, he might not have sacrificed himself."

I considered this, but after a few moments shook my head. "I used a seeing spell, and so basically saw his murder. He was harassed by a myste before he died, and he had no idea what was happening. He wasn't a sorcerer. But whoever killed him was."

I watched Amaya as I said this last, hoping that he might give something away. He didn't.

But he did ask, "Did you see the myste who killed him?"

"No. He must have had him or herself camouflaged, or concealed in some other way. Howell—the bomber—he didn't see a thing before he died."

"And the magical residue?"

"Green, vivid, fading fast. Whoever killed him is pretty powerful."

"Was it on anything other than the body?"

I laughed. "You already know everything I'm telling you. Why would you waste your own time like this?"

"I'm wasting nothing," he said, with quiet intensity. "I have an idea of what might have happened; that's all. I need for you to confirm my guesses. Now, was the magic only on the body?"

I shook my head. "No. It was on the plane as well—on the instrumentation in the cockpit."

He nodded at this, weighing it. Then, "Anything else about the magic?" It was his turn to watch me. But on this point, I could conceal what I knew with little chance of being found out. As far as I could tell, I was the lone person who had seen that transparent residue, so I assumed he wasn't going to learn anything different from one of his many sources.

"Not that I can think of. Why?"

"No reason. I'm merely being thorough. So what do you think happened?"

"I'm sorry?"

"You've given me the basic facts, sparing no detail, I'm sure. And now I'm asking you to formulate a theory. What happened to James Robert Howell? Why is he dead, and why is Mando Vargas still alive and, by now, on his way to Washington, D.C.?"

"I have no idea."

"But what do you *think*?"

I drank more of my beer, pondering the question. "Is Mando Vargas a weremyste?" I asked after some time.

"He is not," Amaya said. "But you're thinking the right way."

"Does he rely on your magic?"

He shook his head and took a drink as well. "Mando and I have been friends for a long time. He relies on me for counsel, for support, and, on occasion, for financial contributions in support of his non-profit activities. But not for magic." A smile thinned his lips. "He does not approve."

"And he does approve of the rest of what you do?"

"Have a care, Mister Fearsson," Amaya said, his

expression hardening. "The rest of what I do or don't do is beyond the purview of this conversation."

When I didn't respond or shy from his gaze, he sat forward. "You believe me to be the worst kind of villain, don't you? You think that because of how I make some of my money, I must be a monster. Mando knows better. He sees nuance where you and your police department friends do not."

"He doesn't worry that his association with you might hurt the causes he fights for?"

Amaya laughed again, and once more I sensed that he was mocking me. "How many *Anglo* politicians associate with men like me, with men worse than me? Surely you're not so naïve as to think that Mando is the only public figure with friends who have gotten rich by less than legitimate means." He didn't give me a chance to answer. "Mando knows that I have put far more money into the Latino community than I've taken out of it. He has watched me fund community centers, drug rehabilitation centers, playgrounds, housing initiatives, and take no credit at all for the work, because of the harm that would come from my name being associated with the projects." He stood, walked to the window, and stared out over the city once more, his hands buried in his pants pockets, his broad shoulders hunched. The western sky still glowed like embers in a fire, and the lights of the city seemed to be scattered at his feet, glittering like jewels in a dragon's lair. "The history of this country is littered with presidents and governors and senators who had ties to men far worse than me."

"You told me a moment ago that I was thinking the

right way," I said. "So you must have a theory of your own about today's events. Would you care to share it with me?"

He remained at the window, and for several moments he didn't answer. At last he faced me. "You haven't said yet what you think happened."

Amaya had led me to an obvious conclusion, though I wasn't sure I believed it, at least not yet. "If what you've said is true, then I would guess the murder of James Howell had nothing at all to do with saving Mando Vargas's life."

His smile this time was genuine. "Very good. And here I'd grown worried that you might let me down."

"But whoever killed Howell and disabled the plane had to have been trying to save lives. Otherwise—"

"Otherwise why bother?"

"That's right," I said. "So the question is, who else was on that plane? Who was so worth saving that James Howell had to die?"

"My question exactly," Amaya said, walking back to his chair. "A question I would like to hire you to answer."

CHAPTER 8

I wasn't sure I had heard him correctly. "You want to hire me?"

"That's right."

I craned my neck to see Luis and his friends over the high back of my chair. "Luis works for you already, and he's every bit the runecrafter I am."

"More," Luis said, and grinned.

I faced Amaya again. "You don't need me."

The crime lord's expression had darkened in a way that made my blood turn cold. "Are you refusing to work for me?"

"No. But I don't understand why you want me."

"Luis is not an investigator. No one who works for me is. And you bring certain . . . unique attributes to the job: your connections within both the local magical community and the police department, not to mention your enhanced reputation."

"You'd pay me?"

"Of course. We're both businessmen. I believe you charge two hundred and fifty dollars a day, plus expenses."

"That's right, though I was thinking of charging you more."

His eyebrows went up. "And why is that?"

"Because fairly or not, you have a reputation, too, and I'm not sure I want to associate myself with it."

Anger flickered in his dark eyes, but after a moment he inclined his head, conceding the point. "Three hundred per day."

"Done. Can you give me some idea of what you expect me to find?"

"Where's the fun in that?"

"Right. Forget that I asked." I drank the rest of my beer, set it on the table by my water glass, and stood. "I take it I'm free to leave?"

"Of course. Luis will see you back to your home, or wherever else you care to go."

I nodded, but didn't move. There was something missing, something that Amaya was holding back. We both knew it, and I think he was waiting to see if I'd let it go and leave or challenge him. If he'd known me at all, he wouldn't have wondered: I'd always had more guts than smarts.

"There's more to this than you're telling me," I said. "I'd like to know what it is."

"With what I'm paying you, I'd have thought that you could learn what you need to on your own time."

"Do you want to play games, Mister Amaya, or do you want me to find out what happened to Flight 595?"

Amusement flitted across his handsome face, though

it never touched his eyes. "What do you know about dark magic?"

"Not a lot. I know that I killed Cahors, and that he was probably the most important and most powerful dark myste this city's seen in some time."

"If that's what you believe, you know next to nothing. Only someone ignorant of the breadth and reach of Phoenix's dark magic cabal could make such a claim."

I blinked. "You're saying that there are other dark sorcerers in Phoenix who are as powerful as he was, as dangerous as he was?"

Amaya stared back at me.

"And you truly believe Howell was killed by dark magic?"

It made some sense, I suppose. Perhaps it explained the odd magical residue I'd seen on the body and the plane.

"I believe it's possible," he said, the admission seeming to come at some cost.

"There are some who would assume that a man like you, a man of your profession who's also a weremyste, would be a practitioner of dark magic."

"And they'd be wrong," he said, his voice as hard and sharp as a knife blade. "Dark magic is not . . ." He broke off, shaking his head. "Crime and dark sorcery are not the same thing. You judge my worst deeds—most people do. That's fine; I can live with that. But dark magic is something else entirely. The mystes I'm talking about engage in ritual killings, they cast blood spells, and use magic to control the thoughts and actions of others. They . . ." He gave another shake of his head and pressed his lips thin. When he began again, it was in a softer voice. "And they do much, much worse. I promise you, I'm not one of them. I want no part of them. In fact, I'm hiring you because I want to find and destroy them."

Puzzle pieces clicked into place: information from earlier in the day fitting all too well with Amaya's words. For now, though, I kept this thought to myself. I'd have time to confirm my theory tomorrow. "If these dark mystes are all that you say they are, and if there are as many of them around here as you imply, I'm not sure I want any part of this investigation. I'm not looking to be a foot soldier in a runecrafters' war."

I thought he might threaten me again, remind me of that virtual gun he had pointed at my heart. But he was more circumspect than that. At least a little.

"Nobody wants this war," he said. "I certainly don't. It may seem like my war now, but it's going to affect all of us who craft, and it's going to do so sooner than you might think. You can't avoid it forever, and we can't rely on an all-volunteer army, as it were."

"So you're drafting me?"

"I'm hiring you, which is a good deal more than the other side is apt to do."

"Why am I just hearing of this war now?"

"I don't know. Perhaps your sources within the magical world aren't as informed as mine, or perhaps they aren't as willing to tell you what they know."

I was thinking of Namid, of course. I wasn't about to reveal to Amaya that I was being trained by a runemyste. There were thirty-eight of them left in the world, and the fact that one had taken such an interest in my life and my casting marked me as a runecrafter of some importance. Admitting as much to Amaya struck me as potentially dangerous, though at that moment I couldn't say whether I was more afraid that he might see me as a rival or as a prize to be taken.

But I didn't believe that anyone Amaya knew could be better informed about the magical world than Namid. On the other hand, I could imagine with ease the runemyste telling me a fraction of what he knew. Abruptly, my recent conversations with the myste, including those about my dad, took on added meaning. I needed to ask Namid some pointed questions.

"Who?" I asked Amaya. "Give me a name."

"Are you going to work for me?"

"Yes. With most jobs I take two days' pay up front, but you can start me off with an even thousand."

I was starting to like Amaya's laugh. It was the most sincere thing about him. "You're bold, Fearsson. I like that. Will you take a check?" When I hesitated, he said, "It would be drawn on the Chofi account; my name will be on the signature line, but nobody can read my scrawl anyway."

"Sure, a check is fine. The name?" I pulled out my spiral notepad and pen.

"Regina Witcombe," Amaya said, dropping his voice.

"Regina Witcombe," I repeated. "I know that name."

"I would have been surprised if you didn't. She's a woman of some importance in this town."

"No, it's not—"

"She owns Witcombe Financial, which she inherited when her husband died. And she's on the board of directors of several institutions here in Phoenix: a hospital, one of the local universities, the business roundtable, the arts council." His mouth twitched. "She's everything I'm not. They'll probably make her Phoenix's Woman of the Year. But trust me, she's a weremyste, like you and me, and she's up to her neck in dark crafting."

I had heard of her, though I didn't know as much about her as Amaya did. But I also knew that it wasn't her financial career or her community activities that I'd been thinking of. I had encountered her name recently, within the last day.

"The plane," I whispered. Then louder, "She was on the passenger manifest."

"Well, of course," Amaya said. "I told you this was all about dark magic."

"Which means that you already know the answer to your question. You don't need me. Regina Witcombe was the person worth saving. She's the reason Howell is dead."

"But why was she worth saving? And who saved her?"

"Maybe she saved herself."

"Perhaps, in which case this will be the easiest money you've earned in a long time. But I think there's more going on here than just Regina keeping herself from being blown up. I want to know what it is. I want to know why she was headed to Washington."

It wasn't the sort of investigation I usually took on. But I suspected that Amaya wouldn't take kindly to my telling him as much. And truth be told, if this woman really was using dark magic, I wanted to know about it. Amaya was right: Dark crafting was nothing to sneeze at. The lingering twinges of pain in my arm and leg, mementos of my confrontation with Cahors, were all the reminders I needed of that.

He cut me a check on the spot: a thousand dollars, as I'd asked. There were benefits to working for the rich and infamous. But even after he signed it, he didn't hand it to me right away.

"You're going to want to ask around about Regina Witcombe," he said. "I know that. But understand this: You are strictly forbidden to tell anyone that I told you she's a weremyste and that she has a history of using dark magic."

I wasn't used to being forbidden to do anything, and I wasn't sure I liked it, but I understood what he meant.

"I have no intention of telling anyone."

"That includes your reporter friend."

My hackles went up. He was talking about Billie. Who the hell was he to be dragging my personal life into our professional arrangement?

"My friend is none of your damn business," I said, none too wisely. "And when I say I won't tell anyone, I mean just that. Discretion is part of my job, and I'm here because you know how good I am at what I do."

"Your confidence pleases me, Jay," Amaya said, looking and sounding more pissed than pleased. "Because I'm counting on you to get me the information I want. I'm paying you a good deal of money, and I expect results from that investment. As Luis will tell you, I don't take disappointment well."

"Are you threatening me?"

"Not you alone. Your father, your girlfriend, your ex-partner."

At least he was honest.

"On the other hand, if you meet or, better yet, exceed my expectations, you'll find that I can be a valuable friend."

I held out my hand. He stared back at me, holding my gaze for several seconds before setting the check on my palm. I folded it and tucked it in my wallet.

"Anything else?"

"I'd like regular progress reports."

"I'll be in touch when I have information for you."

His smile was reflexive. "Fine." He pulled a business card from his shirt pocket and wrote a number on the back of it. "That's my private cell number. You can always reach me that way."

I slipped the card into my wallet beside the check and crossed the room back toward the front door. "Thanks for the beer," I said over my shoulder.

Luis, Rolon, and Paco scrambled to their feet as I passed them and followed me to the door.

I didn't say a word until we were back in the lowrider and pulling out of the driveway.

"He's a piece of work, Luis."

He swiveled in the front seat with a rustle of cloth on leather. "And you're fucking *loco* talking to him like that. You think you're invincible or something? You think you're fucking superman?"

"I didn't say anything that would make him want to kill me," I said, hoping it was true. "But he's got some nerve threatening Billie and my dad that way. And threatening a cop? That's pretty *loco*, too, don't you think?"

"It's only *loco* if you can't back it up."

It was a point worth considering.

"Seriously, Jay. Amaya went easy on you today, and he's not the evil bastard that he's made out to be in the media. But he'll kill you if you cross him. He does business with the Mexican and Colombian cartels. All of them. You don't screw around with somebody like that."

I nodded and stared out the window. Luis was right. I needed to be more careful, for Billie and my dad if not for myself.

"You ever played around with dark magic?" I asked.

Luis glanced at Paco and then at Rolon before turning his dark eyes back on me. "Yeah, a little. A long time ago. You?"

I shook my head. "I was always afraid to. Watching my dad go nuts was bad enough; I always figured that the dark stuff would send me over the edge sooner."

Luis gave a small shrug. "I don't know. Seems to me that part of the attraction is that some of the rules don't hold for the darker stuff. It might be that they can find a way around the phasings, and keep themselves sane."

"Jacinto wouldn't like that you were talking that way, *mi amigo*," Paco said.

"Well, Jacinto isn't going to hear, is he?"

Paco grinned.

They dropped me back at my place a short time later, and to my surprise gave me back both my Glock and the magazine they'd taken from it. The fire on the western horizon had nearly burned itself out, and the first stars shone brightly in a velvet sky.

I still planned to go out to Wofford again. I couldn't remember the last time I had arrived at my father's trailer so late in the evening, but I had promised him that I would be back, and on the off chance that he remembered, I didn't want to worry him. More to the point, I wanted to make sure he was all right, especially now after speaking to Amaya.

I grabbed a change of clothes and some toiletries, hopped in the Z-ster, and started out toward his trailer. Along the way, I called Billie, so that she wouldn't worry either.

"You're alive," she said upon answering.

"So far."

"It sounds like you're driving."

"I am. I'll be spending the night at my dad's. But if you've got time tomorrow, I'd like to see you. We can try lunch again, maybe."

"I'd like that," she said, her voice warming.

We made our plans and said good-night, and I drove the rest of the way to the trailer in silence, thinking about Jacinto Amaya, Mando Rafael Vargas, and Regina Witcombe, and wondering what the hell I'd gotten myself into. A part of me would have liked the chance to question Vargas. I didn't expect that he knew much about dark magic, but I was an admirer of his work, and I knew that Billie would be impressed. I also knew, though, that the Feds and the PPD were not about to let a PI anywhere near the man. And Amaya would have told me to concentrate on Witcombe.

Upon reaching my father's place, these other thoughts fled my mind. My dad was still outside, sitting where I'd left him, his damn binoculars still resting in his lap. The trailer was dark; the only light came from the dull orange glow of the distant city lights and the gibbous moon hanging in the eastern sky.

As soon as I got out of the car, I heard him muttering to himself. I was able to see his outline in the dim light, but not his face. I could tell, though, that he was still flinching.

"Dad?"

No answer.

I walked to where he sat and kissed his forehead. His skin was as cool as the desert night air. He fell silent and looked up at me.

"It's me. Justis."

"I told you if you came you'd make it easier for them to find you."

"Yeah, I remember. You should be inside." I took hold of his arm, intending to help him up. But he jerked it out of my grasp with a motion that was quicker and more powerful than I would have thought possible.

"I don't want to go inside. It's too damn hot in there. It's cooler out here. The burning doesn't bother me so much. The rest is as bad. But it's cool."

"All right," I said. I grabbed the other chair, unfolded it, and set it next to his. "Do you want anything?" I asked before sitting. "Are you hungry?"

"Ice cream."

I laughed. "You had ice cream for lunch. You need some real food."

A smile crossed his face, and I knew a moment of relief so profound it brought tears to my eyes.

"Did I really?" Recognition glimmered in his eyes. "You were here today."

"Right. That was when you warned me not to come back."

He nodded, the smile slipping. "I remember. It's not Tuesday."

"No. What can I fix you? Are those steaks still in there? The ones I brought the other day?"

"Steak sounds good."

The increasingly rare moments when my dad was cogent were to be treasured. These past few weeks had made that much clear to me. I needed to treat each lucid moment as if it might be the last; I was glad I'd made the drive out here this evening.

I went inside and pulled from the refrigerator the New York strips I'd brought him on Tuesday. I rubbed them with salt, pepper, and garlic and poured some Worcestershire over them, then stuck them in the broiler. I also sliced up a tomato and put salt and pepper on that. I brought the tomato out to him, along with a beer, and settled down next to him.

He ate the tomato in about a minute—I managed to salvage one slice for myself. He didn't argue when I took the plate and went back inside to slice another for him. Whatever was going on with him was making him ravenous. Either that, or he was eating so infrequently that he was starving himself. After a few minutes I flipped the steaks. When I came back out, he was sipping his beer.

"Can you tell me more about what's been happening to you?" I asked him, sitting once more.

"It's the damn brands. Burning, burning, burning, burning, burning, burning. So many burns." He held out his arms again, spilling a little beer, wincing once, twice, a third time. "They won't stop. And then they do, but they start up again, and I can't make them go away. They won't listen when I tell them that I don't matter."

I let out a breath through my teeth, taking care to do it silently, so that he wouldn't hear. Two clear minutes. And now he was gone again.

I got up without a word and went back in to check on the steaks again. Even inside, I could hear him, and I could make out what he was muttering to himself.

". . . You're wasting time with me, damnit. I'm nothing. Ow. I'm not a stone or a mirror or clear water for you to see your goddamned portents. I'm nothing. I'm husk.

"You leave her alone, you hear me? Just leave her be. She did nothing to you. And the boy is not for you either, no matter what you might think. So go away. Ow. Go! Go, damn you! You can take me down to the cottonwoods, and you can light every damn one of them on fire, and you can leave me in the middle of it, let me burn until my skin peels away, but it's not going to do you a damn bit of good. You won't have her or him, and you won't kill me. You won't. Ow! Shit! No, you goddamn will not!" He paused, and after a few seconds I heard the beer bottle clink lightly on his chair. "You don't like that, do you, you little fuckers? Well, good. I'm not as helpless as you thought, and I'm not here for you to play your little games. I might not matter, but I'm not helpless, not yet."

He went on and on in the same vein, while I pulled out the steaks, cut into one, and seeing that it was done, shut off the oven. I cut up my dad's steak for him, something I only did when he was in bad shape, and filled two glasses with ice water, which had seemed to help him earlier in the day.

"They don't like this," he had said about the ice cream and the water.

Who didn't?

Returning to my Dad, I put the plate with his steak on his lap and handed him the water glass. He took a long drink.

It had been a strange day, and it had seemed endless. Which may be why my mind was making connections it wouldn't have otherwise.

"Are they dark sorcerers, Dad? Is that who's doing this to you?"

He considered me, a spark of recognition in his pale eyes.

"I don't know. Could be."

Except for the fact that there were no weremystes here. I was sure of that. But to set my mind at ease, I cast a spell similar to the one I'd attempted in the airport. This time, though, I tried to keep it simple. Three elements instead of seven: me, a concealed myste, and my eyes.

Nothing.

"What was that?"

"You felt it?" I asked him.

"You cast a spell."

"Yeah, I did."

"What kind?"

"I wanted to see if there was a weremyste here, someone camouflaged, who might be doing these things to you."

He shook his head. "There isn't. These are powers that go far beyond you and me and other weres."

"You're talking to me again."

"Did I stop?" He glanced down at the plate and frowned. "You just started those."

"No," I said, laying a hand on his shoulder. "You've been muttering to yourself for fifteen minutes."

"Damn."

"What else can you tell me? Before you slip away again."

"I don't know what they are. They're hurting me, testing me, trying to craft their way past my wardings."

"I heard you say something about 'her,' and you also mentioned a boy."

He nodded, his face falling. "The boy is you," he said, voice thick. "They want you for something. And . . . and sometimes they make me see your mother. She looks so fine, so much like . . . like she did. Young and beautiful. Before all the rest, when it went bad. It's Dara as I like to remember her." He shook his head. There were tears on his face.

I gripped his arm, not knowing what else to do. "I'm sorry."

He cleared his throat, swiped at the tears. "I try to stop them. But that's what they want. That's the test."

"You mentioned wardings a minute ago. Have you been warding yourself?"

He frowned again, squeezed his eyes shut. "No. Not the way you mean. But I try to make them go away, and I think they learn from that."

"I don't understand."

"I know. I'm in and out. I'll be here, and then . . ." He shook his head and drank the rest of his water. "I know what it seems like. I mean, I know. *I know!* But it's not— There's something real here. You've been good to . . . You take care of me. And you've seen . . . I know what you see when you look at me, what you're afraid of. But this is real. It's . . ." He winced. "Damnit! They're hurting me again. I'm slipping, burning." His eyes closed, and he shuddered. "Listen to me." His voice had fallen to a whisper. "Justis?"

"I'm here."

"This is real. Okay? This is real."

"I believe you."

"No, you don't. But when belief is gone, all that's left is trust. And I need you to trust me."

"All right. I do."

He flinched. "Brands. Burning, damnit. I hate you bastards."

I took the empty glass from him, ran inside to fill it, and brought it back out to him. He drank deeply, and after a while he ate a few pieces of steak. But he was mumbling to himself again—more about burning and not mattering and the rest—and all the while flinching and whimpering in pain. I listened for more mentions of my mother and me, and heard what might have been a few. But there was little coherence to what he said, and I couldn't make much sense of it.

His doctor had prescribed sleeping pills for those really bad nights when the delusions kept him up. After a while I got him to take one—no small feat—and then sat with him until he fell asleep in his chair. Once he had

been out for a few minutes, I lifted him and carried him
to his bed.

I sat up with him for a while, watching him as he lay
there. He seemed to have aged ten years in the past few
days; he looked like an old man, which scared the crap out
of me. It shouldn't have; he *was* old, and the phasings and
his drinking had taken a toll on his body, so that he was
older than his years. But sitting beside his bed, seeing the
way he continued to flinch, even in a deep sleep, I realized
that in the greater scheme of things, I didn't have much
time left with him. Who knew how many years he'd stick
around? Tears welled, and before I knew it I was crying
like a little kid, terrified by the simple truth that my father
was mortal, and his mortality was exposed to me now in
ways it never had been before.

After a little while, I pulled myself together, but I
remained by his bed, thinking about the last thing he had
said to me that made any sense. *When belief is gone, all
that's left is trust. . . .* There was a time, in the years after
my mom died—I was an angry, lonely teenager, and he was
a drunk well on his way to losing his job on the force—when
I hadn't trusted him at all, when I would sooner have
trusted a stranger than my own father. But those days were
long gone. Crazy as he was, I did trust him. He flinched
again, confirming my faith. What kind of hallucination
would have followed him into a medication-induced sleep?
Strange as it seemed, I was forced to consider the possibility
that something or someone really was hurting him. Except
that I had no idea how it was possible. I sensed no magic in
the room, no ripple of power in the air around me. Maybe
it was one of those "old powers" Namid mentioned earlier.

Dad cried out, and on instinct I grabbed his hand. At my touch, he appeared to relax, the tension draining from his haggard face.

"I'm here," I said.

He shifted, began to snore.

After another fifteen minutes or so, satisfied that he was doing a little better, I pulled a spare blanket and pillow from his linen closet and lay on the floor next to his bed. There wasn't a lot of room, but I didn't expect that I'd sleep much no matter where I bedded down.

I surprised myself. My head had barely hit the pillow before I woke up to a bright morning and the song of a cactus wren drifting in through the open window. I sat up and peered over the edge of my dad's bed. He was still asleep, soundly, peacefully. No flinching that I could see.

Relieved, I gathered up the blanket and pillow and padded out of the room, making as little noise as possible. I hated to leave him alone after the night he'd had, but I had work to do, and my dad's trailer didn't even have Internet. I hoped that he would remember to eat today, and I wrote him a quick note promising to come back in the next day or two. I had no idea if he would find it or read it or be able to make sense of it. But I put it on the counter in his small kitchen, where it was most likely to catch his eye.

I went out to my car and opened the door to climb in. But then I paused, gazing back at the trailer. I'd learned a long time ago to trust my magical instincts. And they told me that there was a common thread running through all that had happened in recent days: My dad's pain, the killing of James Howell and the disabling of Flight 595, even the odd burst of magic that had saved my life the night I confronted Mark Darby. I couldn't make sense of it, not yet. But I was sure it was right there in front of me. All I needed to do was connect the dots.

I got in the car and started back toward the city, a cloud of dust rising behind me, blood red in the early morning sun.

CHAPTER 9

I stopped at home to put on fresh clothes before going to my office and firing up the computer and my seven-hundred-dollar Saeco espresso machine. What can I say? I really, really like coffee, especially Sumatran. I'll eat cold pizza for breakfast and store-brand ice cream instead of the fancy kinds that come in pint containers costing seven bucks a pop; but try to sneak cheap coffee by me and I'll know it from the smell.

Once I had a bit of caffeine in me, I searched online for everything I could find on Regina Witcombe. Most of what I read focused on her philanthropic activities; finding detailed information about her business dealings proved frustrating. Apparently, she didn't like to shine a spotlight on that part of her life. But I kept digging and over the next hour managed to piece together a rough portrait of her rise to corporate power.

Her husband, Michael, had died while yachting—alone—off the Malibu coast about ten years before. She had been in Belize, traveling with friends. The story was he drank a bit too much wine and wasn't prepared when his vessel encountered high winds and rough seas. The Coast Guard believed that he fell off the boat and drowned; the yacht, the *Regina*, of course, was discovered a day later, drifting near Santa Catalina Island. Regina and her two daughters inherited everything, and after a brief power struggle with the corporate board of Witcombe Financial, she was named its new CEO. She possessed a business degree from the Wharton School, and a degree in law from Georgetown, and she had been active in the company as a vice-president and in-house counsel. It wasn't like she was unqualified, but she leap-frogged several senior execs to take the position, and a few of them were pretty unhappy about it. In the wake of her elevation to CEO, three of Witcombe's top executives left the company.

The controversy didn't last long, however, because the board of directors and the rest of her executive team closed ranks behind her, and because the company continued to do well under her leadership.

Nevertheless, reading about Michael Witcombe's death and all that followed set off alarm bells in my head. A tragic accident, a perfect alibi, an inheritance worth more than a billion dollars. It all struck me as too convenient, too easy. Add in rumors of dark magic, and I was ready to call Kona and tell her to have the case reopened. Never mind that it was a few hundred miles outside her jurisdiction.

There was no shortage of photographs of her online. She was an attractive woman: auburn hair, blue eyes, brilliant smile, always impeccably dressed. She had been in her early forties when Michael died, and so was in her early fifties now, but you wouldn't have known it to look at her. I found a video of her as well, speaking to stockholders at Witcombe's annual meeting. She spoke in a warm alto, her manner easy, charming even. But I couldn't tell for certain, from either the clip I watched or the photos I found, whether she was really a weremyste. The blurring of features that I experienced when face-to-face with another sorcerer didn't translate to these media. I had no idea how I might get close enough to this woman to see for myself if she was a myste. And I wasn't yet ready to take Jacinto Amaya's word for it.

My perusal of the roster of Witcombe's corporate officers didn't produce much, although I jotted down the names of the highest ranking executives to run by Kona and Billie.

I kept digging, collecting tidbits about Regina Witcombe's life like a mouse hoarding crumbs. It seemed that two years ago she had sold her estate in Scottsdale and bought a place in Paradise Valley for a cool eleven million and change. Must be nice to have options like that.

Something in my mind clicked again. I picked up the phone and called a friend of mine, an ex-girlfriend as it happened, who had helped me find the office in which I was sitting.

"This is Sally Peters."

"Hey, Sally. It's Jay Fearsson."

"Hey there, stranger. How's the PI biz?"

"It's keeping me busy, paying some bills."

"Getting you in the paper, too. I saw that you got shot."

"Yeah, I'm better now."

"Well, good. Wanna take me out for dinner? Maybe get lucky?"

"I thought you were engaged."

"I was," she said. "Not anymore."

"I'm sorry to hear that, Sal. But I'm going to have to pass on the getting lucky thing."

"Jay Fearsson, do you have a girlfriend?"

A big, fat, stupid grin split my face. Billie and I had been together for a couple of months, but the novelty of being in a serious relationship hadn't worn off yet. "Yep. Pretty crazy, right?"

"Wow, yeah. Pretty crazy. So if you're not calling me for a night on the town, are you calling for business?"

"Sort of. I need a little information. If a house was sold a couple of years ago, can you still pull up the listing on your system, maybe tell me some of the details?"

"Hmmm," she said. "A couple of years? I dunno. But I can try. Where was the house?"

"Scottsdale. It belonged to Regina Witcombe."

She laughed. "The Witcombe estate? I don't have to do a search. Every agent in the greater Phoenix area was drooling over those commissions—one agency got both the sale of the Scottsdale house and the purchase of the mansion in Paradise Valley. Both were handled by Sonoran Winds Realty."

Bingo.

"You don't happen to know who the listing agent was, do you?"

"For which one?"

I wasn't sure it mattered, but I said, "The Scottsdale

sale." I held my breath, hoping against hope that she would remember that name as well.

"Oh God. I should remember. She was the toast of the town for weeks afterward."

"It was a woman."

"Yes. Both agents were; that much I'm sure of. Hold on, Jay." It sounded like she put her hand over the receiver, though I could still hear her voice as she said, "Hey, do any of you remember the name of the listing agent for Regina Witcombe's house in Scottsdale?"

Someone answered her, but I couldn't make out the name.

"No," Sally said. "She handled the sale in Paradise Valley."

"Who did, Sal?" I asked. I don't think she heard me.

She and her colleagues batted around a couple of other names before she removed her hand from the receiver.

"We're drawing a blank on the Scottsdale agent, Jay. Sorry."

"Who was the agent on the one in Paradise Valley?"

"What was the first name again?" Sally asked her coworkers. "Right, right." To me she said, "Patricia Hesslan-Fine."

"That's the name I was hoping to hear, Sal. Thank you."

"Seriously?"

"Seriously, I owe you one."

"Cool. If this thing with your new girlfriend works out, and you need to find a new place, you'll come to me, right?"

"I promise. Gotta go."

We hung up, but for a moment I remained frozen in place, staring at my computer and the image of Regina Witcombe that lingered on the screen.

Patty Hesslan had been Regina Witcombe's real estate agent, or at least one of them. And yesterday they had been traveling together. Sort of. Patty had been listed as a party of one. Checking the list again, I saw that Regina was listed the same way. Random chance? It was possible. But in the past day and a half I had encountered enough coincidences to last a lifetime, and this last one was a doozy.

I had few leads and no idea where to start digging around for more. This one, as tenuous as it was, seemed like my best bet. And I'll admit as well that a part of me was curious about Patty Hesslan and what she remembered about the horrible events that had bound our families together for a few months when we were teenagers.

I knew that both Regina Witcombe and Patty were out of town; I needed to know when they would be back, and I chose to start with Patty.

I found the Sonoran Winds Realty website and wrote down the address and phone number. Their main office was located back in North Scottsdale. I'm sure they would offer to give me her cell number, but I didn't want to speak to her over the phone; for something like this, I needed to be in the room with her, seeing her reactions to my questions about Regina Witcombe.

I called and told the receptionist that I was in Phoenix for a job interview that would last several days. I wanted to meet with an agent and see a few houses.

"A friend recommended that I ask for Patty," I said.

"Patty?" she repeated. "Might your friend have said Patricia?"

"Yes, my mistake. My sister is also named Patricia, but we call her Patty. I just assumed. I wrote it down . . . Here it is. Patricia Hesslan-Fine."

"Well, Mister . . . ?"

"Jay," I said.

"Mister Jay. Patricia is out of town at the moment. But I assure you that all of our agents offer the highest level of service. Any one of them can help you. Would you like to come by this morning?"

I didn't correct her misinterpretation of my name; for now it would do nicely. "Well," I said, "this friend felt very strongly that I should speak with Patricia. But she mentioned a few other names as well, so if she's not available, I'm sure I can contact those other realtors."

"Well, there's no need for that. How long did you say you were in town?"

"Through the weekend."

"Patricia gets back late today, and often does a few showings on Saturday mornings. I'm sure she would be happy to meet with you. Can you meet her here at 10:30 tomorrow?"

I assured her I could, thanked her, and hung up. My stomach felt tight and empty; even with a one-day reprieve, the prospect of speaking with Patty Hesslan filled me with as much dread as curiosity. But she was the sole connection I had to Regina Witcombe, and I hoped that over the next twenty-four hours the idea would grow on me. I wasn't holding my breath.

❧ ❧ ❧

The previous night, while talking to Amaya, I'd had a kind of epiphany. I needed to confirm it.

More than eighteen months had passed since I was forced to give up my badge, but the wound remained raw and tender. I could handle talking to Kona about police work, barely. But going to police headquarters in downtown Phoenix was still a bit like running into an old girlfriend who had broken my heart. Every now and then I needed to see the place, and as soon as I did I regretted making the trip. In this case, though, I had questions for Kona, and I was hoping she might be able to show me some evidence.

I drove to the heart of the city, parked in a lot a couple of blocks from the building, and made my way to 620 on foot. With every step that brought me closer, my blood seemed to thicken, until my heart was laboring with each beat. But I kept my head down and my hands in my pockets.

When I stepped inside, I took a long breath. The smell of a police station is almost impossible to describe to someone who hasn't experienced it day in and day out for years at a time. It's a blend of sweat and old paint, fear and adrenaline, overlaid with a suggestion of nitrocellulose and the acid pungency of stale coffee. Breathing it in, I felt like an ex-smoker who still craves a cigarette when someone nearby lights up.

Carla Jarosa, who had been the front-desk officer at 620 since before I became a cop, greeted me with a big hello and a visitor's badge. I put the badge on and took the stairs up to the third floor, where the homicide unit was located.

I had been hoping that the detectives' room would be empty except for Kona, but it wasn't. Not by a long shot. Kona was there, talking with Kevin, who sat at the desk next to hers. And there were about seven other guys in the room as well, two of them on the phone, another typing in classic hunt-and-peck style, and a cluster of four standing just inside the door, chatting and laughing. They fell silent when I stepped in. One of them had been here when I was still on the job; the other three I didn't know. But they stared at me; they all seemed to know who I was.

"Hey, Larry," I said to the guy I knew.

"Jay."

That was about all we had to say to each other. I nodded to the others and walked past them to Kona's desk. She and Kevin had stopped talking as well and were marking my approach.

"Social visit?" she asked, her tone dry.

"We need to talk." My gaze flicked to Kevin. In the past, I would have expected Kona to make some excuse so that the two of us could speak in private, but I'd confided in Kevin at the airport and I saw no reason to stop now. "The three of us."

He didn't quite smile, but his shoulders dropped fractionally, as if he had been on edge, and I'd set his mind at ease. "Stairwell?" he asked.

I shook my head. "Sound travels too much."

Kona stood and gestured for us to follow. We went back to the lunch room, which was empty for the moment. She closed the door and faced me, leaning against it.

"What's this about, Justis? You may be a hero now, but

that doesn't mean Hibbard won't give us all kinds of crap if he finds out you've been here."

"I know. I'm sorry. But yesterday you mentioned to me that you were working on another serial murder case. I need to know whatever you can tell me about it."

The two of them exchanged looks. After a moment, Kona shrugged. "I see a pattern," she told Kevin. "I know you're not convinced, but I am."

"Am I missing something?" I asked.

They faced me again.

"Kevin doesn't believe the killings I mentioned to you are related. That's why I told you that the patterns hadn't completely emerged yet."

"But you think they're pretty clear."

Another shrug. "Yeah, I suppose I do."

"There have been three killings," Kevin said. "One about a month ago, another three weeks later, and the last about five days ago. The bodies were found in different parts of the city; the first guy had his throat slit, the second had been stabbed in the heart, and the third also had a neck wound, though not as clean as the first."

"The victims?" I asked.

"A homeless man in his fifties, who was found in Maryvale; a nineteen-year-old hooker, who died in west Central City, and an elderly woman who lived in a duplex up in Cactus Park." He held up a fist. "No pattern to the timing or locale," he said and raised a finger. "Different wounds." He raised another finger. "Nothing to link the victims." He put up a third finger. "'O' for three. No pattern."

"They all bled to death," Kona said, glancing Kevin's

way before turning her attention to me. "Although we couldn't—"

A knock at the door stopped her. She opened it a crack. "Give us a few minutes, will you guys?"

Someone mumbled a response.

"Thanks," Kona said, and shut the door. Facing me again, she went on. "Despite the fact that they bled to death, there didn't seem to be that much blood at any of the crime scenes. You get that? With all three victims, we couldn't account for all of the blood." Kevin started to say something, but she talked over him. "All of the victims were alone in one sense or another: a homeless guy, a prostitute, and an old woman who lived by herself." Her eyes darted Kevin's way again. "I'm not saying it was one guy necessarily. But to me it sounds like it might be some kind of weird cult thing."

"A cult?" Kevin said. "Really?"

Kona's expression soured. "Anyway, the circumstances are odd enough, and similar enough, that I'm not ready to rule out a connection."

If I hadn't spoken to Jacinto Amaya the night before, I might have agreed with Kevin; at first glance, the evidence linking the murders seemed pretty thin. But that was one of the reasons Kona was such a good cop: She saw things that others missed.

"What's your interest in this, Jay?" Kevin asked.

"You're not going to like it. I talked last night to a weremyste here in the city who's worried about dark magic and the people who use it. This person mentioned blood spells and ritual killings, which sounds a lot like what you're both describing."

Kona closed her eyes for a second. "What are blood spells?" she asked, her voice flat. "And why the hell haven't you mentioned them to me before?"

"They're what they sound like: spells cast with blood to enhance the magic. I didn't mention them because they're forbidden, and I didn't think people still used them. That's the sort of thing Namid and his kind are supposed to prevent."

Kevin glanced from me to Kona. "Who's Namid?"

"A runemyste, sort of a magical ghost who helps me train."

I could almost hear Namid growling, *I am not a ghost*.

"Never mind that," Kona said. "How does this blood spell thing work?"

"I've never cast one, so I don't know for certain, but I'd imagine that a myste would simply incorporate the blood as an element in the spell, and the result would be the same as usual, but a good deal stronger."

"So you came here because you thought maybe the murders I mentioned were committed by some of your kind who aren't playing by the rules."

"Something like that."

"If you're right, how do we prove it?"

"Kevin, you said the last murder was committed five days ago?"

"Yeah. Autopsy's been done, and the body has been cremated."

I expected as much, and I wasn't sure that there would have been much to see on the corpse anyway. If the victim's blood was used to fuel a spell, chances were the spell wasn't directed at her, which meant that there would be no residue left on the body.

"Was there anything unusual about any of the crime scenes?"

Kevin deferred to Kona, appearing far less sure of himself than he had moments before. I felt bad for him. He was too new to the whole magic thing, and he was still playing catch-up.

"Nothing that I saw," Kona said. "But we can show you the photos."

"Without getting yourselves in trouble?"

"We'll worry about that."

We returned to the detectives' room, and while Kevin pulled the files, Kona and I sat at her desk.

"He's taking the magic stuff pretty well," I said in a whisper.

"He's a good cop. He's freaking out on the inside, but he won't let you see it—he might not even let me see it— and he damn sure won't let it get in the way of him doing his job."

Kevin came back with the files and handed the first one to me. It was that of the elderly woman, Muriel Carey. She bore a jagged wound that ran from the base of her ear to the middle point of her jawline, cutting right across the carotid artery. She was a mess, her face frozen in a rictus of fear, blood splattered across her skin and clothes. But I could tell that Kona was right: A wound like that on a victim who bled to death would have produced a great deal of blood, more than most people would expect, more than I could see in any of these photographs.

But nothing else caught my eye. The same was true of

the photos of the other two victims. No surprises, not as much blood as I would have expected, although in fairness, some blood might have pooled within the body of the young woman who was stabbed in the heart.

"No footprints," Kona said, as I peered more closely at the photos.

I had, in fact, been checking for them. I scrutinized the pictures for another few minutes, then closed the files and handed them back to Kevin. "Thanks."

"Anything?" Kona asked.

"No, but I didn't really expect to see much. I would have needed to be on the scene." For Kevin's sake I added, "Magical residue doesn't show up on film, or in pixels."

"That's inconvenient."

"Hang around with Justis for any time at all, and you'll realize that magic is almost always inconvenient." She toyed with one of her long gold earrings, her forehead furrowed in thought. The earrings weren't regulation, but none of her superiors had the guts to tell her that she needed to get rid of them. It was one of the perks of being a really good cop. "I suppose we'll have to call you in next time. If there is a next time," she added with a glance Kevin's way. "Hibbard's going to love that. Along with the murder of James Howell, these killings are the biggest ongoing investigations we've got, and you're in on both of them."

"I'm not convinced yet," Kevin said.

We both eyed him, and I nodded. "That's all right. I'm not entirely sure I am either. Having opposing theories is a good thing."

"He's right," Kona said.

Kevin nodded. "Okay."

I stood. "I'll be in touch if I hear more. You'll do the same?"

"Of course."

I started toward the door, but Kona called my name. I walked back to her desk.

"Who was your source on the dark magic thing? Was it Q?"

I kept my expression neutral, but on the inside I cringed. I hated keeping secrets from Kona. Long ago, my father had taught me ten rules of being a good cop—things like "Never lend your weapon to anyone" and "Don't put off your paperwork." Rule seven was "Never keep secrets from your partner." In my early days on the force, I had come within a hair's breadth of destroying my career by violating this rule. I was a weremyste, suffering through the phasings every month, and rather than confide in Kona, I tried to hide it from her. I vowed never to do that again, and I remained true to that vow until the day I resigned.

I didn't want to lie to her now. We were working together, and keeping secrets from her promised to complicate our investigation. But we weren't partners anymore; I didn't have a partner. And if I was to tell her that I was working for Jacinto Amaya, the most notorious drug dealer in Phoenix, she might never speak to me again.

"I can't say," I told her. "It wasn't Q, but I can't tell you more than that."

She pursed her lips for a moment, which she did when

she was unhappy. After a moment, she gave a shrug that conveyed more annoyance than acquiescence. "All right," she said, her tone clipped. "I'll talk to you soon."

"Right."

I walked away again, and as I did, her phone rang. I heard her pick up, and then a moment later scribble something on a note pad. "Hold on a minute," she said into the receiver. "Justis!"

I stopped, turned.

"You can't go yet. We've got a new victim who you need to see." With a sidelong look Kevin's way, she added, "Bled to death."

CHAPTER 10

The body had been found in Sweetwater Park, adjacent to the Paradise Valley Mall. I called Billie and asked if we could meet a bit later than we had planned. Then I followed Kona and Kevin out to Paradise Valley.

Upon reaching the park, we found squad cars everywhere, a frenzy of flashing blue lights. The cops on the scene had set up a perimeter starting about a block from the park and were directing traffic away from it and away from the mall as well, which couldn't have been making the shop owners happy. But Kona must have said something to them, because they waved me through without asking me for ID. We drove to the edge of the park and got out to walk the rest of the distance.

The body had been found among a line of trees that formed a boundary between the park and Paradise Village Parkway, which ran around the mall. According to the detective who met us a few yards shy of the trees, no one had touched it. Kona and Kevin stayed with the detective, learning what they could about the person who found the body. I eased closer, peering into the shadows, taking in each new detail as my eyes adjusted to the dim light beneath the trees.

"Hey, what's he doing?" the detective said.

"He's all right," Kona told the guy. "We'll join him in a minute."

I'd have to remember later to thank her.

The body was that of an older man, late fifties, maybe early sixties. He was white, with wild gray hair and a rough beard. He wore baggy pants that were held up with a frayed canvas belt, and a pale green T-shirt, stained and torn. His shoes were bound together with silver duct tape.

He had been tied to a small tree. Or rather, he had been forced to wrap his arms around the narrow trunk, and then his hands had been bound together with those plastic cable ties that electricians use. His wrists had been slashed so deeply that his hands hung from his arms at an angle, as if they might fall to the ground at any moment. Dried blood stained his palms and fingers, as well as the earth beneath them. I couldn't say for certain whether any blood was missing, but I didn't doubt it for a moment. This was a ritual killing. I could tell from the distorted grimace frozen on the man's face that he had died in fear and in pain. Tearing my eyes from him, I turned a slow circle in the cool shade, searching for any sign of magic, any glow of a sorcerer's spell. I saw nothing.

Checking on Kona and the others—they were still talking, though the third detective kept an eye on me—I walked around to the far side of the tree so that I could see the wounds on the victims wrists more clearly. At least that was how it would seem to Kona's friend.

I squatted down in front of the corpse, bracing my hand on the dirt for balance. I didn't see much on the wounds beyond what any other cop would see—there was no magic here, either. But as I stood again, I took a pinch of blood-darkened earth between my fingers.

I walked away from the body, deeper into the shadows, and pulled my scrying stone from my pocket. Holding it in my hand, with that bloodied dirt beneath it, I spoke the words of a seeing spell in my head.

The dappled light that had been reflected off the smooth surface of the stone vanished, taking with it those familiar sinuous bands of blue and white, and leaving what appeared at first to be impenetrable darkness. But I heard voices in my head, voices the dead man had heard; at first they were vague, muted. I couldn't make out their words. Within a few seconds though, they gelled, became more real.

. . . *Coming around.*

It's about time. We can't stay here forever.

Relax, the first voice said. A man, authoritative and used to having people do as he instructed. *No one's going to find us. We have all the time in the world.*

Faint light appeared in the stone, vanished, appeared again. In the seeing I had summoned, the dead man was waking up, his eyes fluttering open. He tried to straighten up, but the tree was in his way, his arms were already bound. Despite the darkness, I could see his hands and wrists, which remained whole, at least for now.

A face loomed before him. Dark eyes, a straight nose,

and trim beard, all beneath a shock of straight dark hair. A cruel smile played at the man's lips, dimpling his cheeks.

Wake up, sleepy-head. It's a beautiful night in the neighborhood.

Who-who are you? the bound man asked. *Why are my hands tied?* He sounded terrified, and he spoke with a slight lisp.

What's your name?

J-Jeff.

Well, Jeff, we need your help, and we want to make sure you cooperate. Here, let me give you a hand.

It seemed that Dimples helped him stand straighter. A moment later the victim's perspective shifted. He could look around with greater ease. He spotted the second man, who stood several feet away. He was taller and broader than Dimples, looming like a bear in the gloom, but I couldn't make out the details of his face.

Is that better? Dimples asked. When Jeff nodded, he smiled again and said, *Good, I'm so glad. Now . . .* He brandished a knife, waving the blade in front of the bound man's eyes. *We need to take a bit of blood from you. Is that all right?*

Are you fucking nuts? No it's not all right. Lemme go!

Dimples winced, his brow furrowing. *I'm sorry. I should have phrased that differently. We're going to take your blood. That's why you're here and tied to that tree. I didn't mean to imply that you had any choice in the matter. Forgive me.*

Stop fucking around, Bear said from the shadows.

Shut up. I know what I'm doing. To Jeff, he said, *This*

will hurt a bit; quite a lot, really. But with any luck we'll leave a bit of blood for you. That's the plan anyway.

The bastard. Fear increased the amount of epinephrine in the blood, and I would have bet every dollar I had that the stronger the fear, the stronger the magical enhancement in a blood spell. Dimples was scaring the guy to make his spell more effective.

Come here, Dimples said.

Bear lumbered toward him.

Please don't do this, Jeff said, his lisp growing more pronounced. I could see him struggling to free his arms, but the ties held him tight.

Dimples didn't answer. He'd done what was necessary to make his victim's fight-or-flight response kick in. But after a moment, he did say, *Hold him steady.*

Arms appeared in the periphery and took hold of Jeff. Bear was behind him, pinning him to the tree, gripping his forearms to keep the bound man from flinching or thrashing.

Dimples stood in front of them both and glanced past the bound man. His knife flashed in the darkness, gleaming with reflected light, perhaps from a streetlamp.

No! Jeff cried out. Then darkness, and a skirling scream like that of an animal being torn apart by a predator. On and on it went, spiraling into the night.

Shut him up, I heard Dimples say, the command nearly lost within the bound man's agony.

The screaming was muffled abruptly, though it didn't stop. I assumed bear had wrapped a hand over Jeff's mouth.

Dimples cursed and muttered something under his

breath. At that point, Jeff's screams did stop. Moments later, his eyes opened again, his gaze fixing on the gaping wounds at his wrists and the crimson stains on his hands.

Bear stepped out from behind him and moved to stand beside Dimples.

Ready? Dimples asked.

Bear nodded.

Dimples closed his eyes and held out his own hands toward those of the bound man, though he seemed to take care not to touch him. He said nothing; his lips didn't even move. But seconds later golden light burst from Jeff's wrists, arcing through the darkness and slamming into Bear's chest. The big man grunted and staggered back several steps, so that Jeff could no longer see him. Whatever spell Dimples had cast stopped the flow of blood from Jeff's wrists, but not for long. Moments later, the torrent began again. Jeff's eyelids drooped—blood loss, terror, pain.

Strange sounds reached him from where Bear had been. Groans, a sharp intake of breath, and a scream of agony much like Jeff's own. Jeff's head lolled to that side, his eyes opening once more. Bear was on the ground on all fours, looking like he might be ill. His back arched, his head snapping upward to reveal a bearded face locked in a feral grimace.

Before I could see more, Jeff's eyes closed again. Seconds later, Bear's screams faded. I saw nothing else in the stone, heard no more from Jeff or his killers.

Taking a long breath, I slipped the scrying stone back into my pocket and brushed the dirt from my hand. Catching Kona's eye, I gave a single nod.

She, Kevin, and the other detective spoke for a few moments more before she said, loud enough for me to hear, "Let's see what we've got."

They walked to where I was standing, the third detective eyeing me once more.

"She says you're some kind of expert in serial killers," he said, jerking a thumb in Kona's direction. "That right?"

"I have some experience with them."

"Like the Blind Angel."

"Like that," I said.

"So what do you see here?"

I didn't like the guy's attitude, and I didn't feel like proving to him that I had the chops to work his case.

"There were two guys here," I said, talking to Kona and Kevin, and all but ignoring their jerk friend. "One was about my size, the other bigger, heavier. They . . . took some of the victim's blood, though obviously not all of it."

"What do you mean took?" the detective asked. "And how do you know how big they were?"

"I told you," Kona said, "he sees stuff the rest of us miss." To me, she said, "Do you know what they used the blood for?"

My gaze flicked in the detective's direction. "Not yet. But I think I know where to start looking."

"Good. You'll call when you have more for me?"

I grinned. "Don't I always?"

She nodded. Kevin winked at me. I headed back to the Z-ster, knowing that our exchange would leave the other detective scratching his head, and not caring one bit.

❦ ❦ ❦

I drove back to Mesa, the seeing spell replaying in my head like a SportsCenter highlight reel. I'd have no trouble remembering the color of Dimples's magic, but what had he done to Bear? And what was that scream at the end? It had all the qualities of a magical attack, and yet Dimples had asked if Bear was ready and the big man had signaled that he was. It didn't make sense.

With midday traffic building throughout the city, I barely made it on time to my rescheduled lunch date with Billie. She was already in the restaurant at our usual table. I kissed her and took the seat opposite hers. Her smile faded as she read my expression.

"Rough day?"

"So far."

"Your dad?"

It took me a minute to remember my trip out to Wofford; that's how preoccupied I was with what I'd seen in my scrying stone.

"Yeah, it was a rough night with my dad. And today . . ." I shook my head.

"You said something about Kona needing you, which I'm figuring out never means anything good."

"It's not her fault," I said, hearing the weariness in my voice. "She needed help with a crime scene."

Billie frowned. "Another one?"

"Yeah. You order yet?"

She studied me for another few seconds before shaking her head.

"Right. I guess it's my turn to pay, isn't it?"

Concern lingered in her green eyes.

"I'm all right," I said, taking her hand. "There's a lot

going on right now, and I'm trying to figure out how much of it is related, and how much is just random crap coming down on me at once." I fixed a smile on my lips, hoping it would be at least somewhat convincing. "How are you?"

"I'm good," she said. "Thanks to a tip I got from a certain private eye, I'm the toast of the Internet."

"Well, good. Then order to your heart's content."

Her eyes danced. "You sure? I'm thinking about the seafood fajitas."

I considered the check Amaya had given me the previous night, and the other one I was supposed to retrieve from Nathan Felder. "A fine choice," I said. "I'm feeling flush right now."

"Good! Then I'm getting a margarita, too."

"Don't you have work to do, Miss Castle?"

She canted her head to the side, her smile turning coy. "I've already finished for the day. I was hoping you might have the afternoon free."

Before I could respond, a waitress came by to take our orders—my usual with a Coke, Billie's fajitas and margarita.

"So?" she asked when the waitress had gone. "Do you have some time today?"

I exhaled, and her face fell.

"You don't, do you?"

"I can knock off a little early, but with all I have going on right now, I can't afford to do more than that."

"Tell me."

I couldn't confide in her as much as I would have liked. I didn't think she would be any happier about me working for Amaya than Kona would have been. "Well," I said, "to be honest, I have some questions for you. Off the record."

"Questions for me?" She grinned, appearing genuinely pleased. "I get to help you with an investigation?"

"I hope so. What do you know about Regina Witcombe?"

She blinked. "Witcombe? I know quite a bit about her. I thought everyone did."

"Did you know she was on the plane yesterday? In first class, no doubt."

Billie frowned and shook her head. "She has her own jet, Fearsson. A Gulfstream; and she has a stable of pilots, one of whom is always on call. I think you've got your information wrong."

"She's listed on the passenger manifest."

"Maybe it's a different Regina Witcombe."

I raised an eyebrow.

"You asked me for information about her; I'm telling you what I know. She has a private jet. She might even have more than one."

Add one more oddity to an already odd investigation.

"On the other hand," Billie went on after a brief pause, the creases in her forehead deepening, "I did read somewhere that she was in Washington today."

"Doing what?"

"I think she was appearing before the Senate Finance Committee, to testify against the banking bill."

"Maybe her plane wasn't working," I said. As soon as I spoke the words, they echoed back at me. Could another magically induced mechanical problem have put her on Flight 595?

"Why did Kona ask you to join her at the airport?" Billie asked in a whisper, her hands resting on the table as she leaned toward me.

I stared back at her.

"That's what I thought. Was the dead guy a weremyste?"

"No," I said, my voice low. "He was killed with a spell. Kona's learned to recognize the signs of murder by magic."

"And today?"

My hesitation didn't last long. "Another murder with magical connections. Tell me more about Regina Witcombe."

She shrugged, her cheeks going pale at the mention of the second killing. "She's president and CEO of a major financial corporation, she has more money than God, she's smart and combative and ruthless. She also opposes just about every important piece of consumer protection legislation relating to the banking industry that comes before Congress or the state legislature. I'm torn, because it's kind of nice to see a woman leading a huge multinational finance company: breaking the glass ceiling and all of that. But I really hate everything she stands for."

"Have you ever heard any whispers about her being odd around the full moon?"

Her mouth fell open. "You think she's a weremyste?" she asked, leaning in over the table.

"I have a source who says she is."

"Holy crap!"

I saw a gleam in her eyes that I knew all too well. "We're still off the record, remember?"

"Damn it! How can you tell me something like that off the record? That's not fair."

A quip leaped to mind, something that would make her laugh—I loved the way she laughed. I opened my mouth to speak.

A tingle of magic crawled over my skin, locking the words in my throat, making the hairs on my arms and neck stand on end. I saw no color, but I felt it building. Again I was reminded of the way desert air turned electric in the instant before lightning struck.

"Shit," I whispered.

"Fearsson?"

And in that moment, the world exploded.

The blast came from out on the street—or at least it seemed to, was *meant* to seem like it did. Somehow I knew that, understood what the sorcerer intended. Light flashed, blinding, the color of the midday sun. I didn't have time to shield my eyes before the concussion hit, so loud it swallowed every other sound, so powerful it flung both of us against the restaurant's back wall, along with our table and chairs. Debris rained down on us: glass from the streetside window, other tables and chairs, other people, plaster from the walls, menus, salt and pepper shakers, bottles of hot sauce.

People screamed in the distance. No. They were screaming in the restaurant, and out on the street in front. But my ears were shot.

"Billie?" I called, unable to see for the dust and smoke.

Magic still danced along my skin. My untouched skin. I realized that I wasn't in pain. Nothing hurt. No broken bones, no cuts or scrapes or burns. I was fine.

"Billie?" I said again, heart hammering.

And a voice in my head whispered, "A warning. Do not push too hard."

"Who the hell?"

I didn't pursue the thought further. Because that was when I saw Billie. A table lay on top of her chest. Blood poured from a cut across her brow. The brow that wrinkled when she was confused, or worried about me, or angry.

"Billie." I crawled to her, checked her pulse, her breathing. She was alive. A dry sob escaped me. I pushed the table off of her and almost gagged at the sight of her arm. I'd seen compound fractures before, but not on someone I loved.

A warning.

Screw you, whoever the hell you are.

My ears still rang with the force of whatever had hit the restaurant, but I could make out the voices of others crying for help, of moans and sobs. There were people injured throughout what was left of the building. I should have been trying to reach them, giving what aid I could. I was an ex-cop. I knew how to help people, how to keep them calm in the midst of a crisis. I stayed where I was, refusing to leave Billie's side.

I checked her for other wounds, but saw none. That meant nothing. She could have been bleeding internally. Her breathing seemed okay, maybe somewhat labored. She might have had a collapsed lung.

This is your fault.

The voice was my own this time, inside my head, berating me—I didn't even know what for. I had no idea what I had done. But it was me and my magic. That was why Billie lay there, covered with blood and plaster dust and shards of glass.

She stirred, winced. "Fearsson?"

As far as I could tell, my name came out as little more than a breath of air. But seeing it on her lips, knowing that she was conscious, struck me as nothing short of miraculous. For the second time in as many days, relief brought tears to my eyes. First my dad, now Billie. That was important in some way. I'd need to figure out how. Later.

"Wha' happened?" I thought I heard her say.

"Hold still. There'll be ambulances here soon."

I knew some healing spells, but not for injuries as severe as hers, and not for wounds I couldn't see. She said something I couldn't hear. I made her repeat it.

"My arm hurts. And my head." Her eyes remained closed, but at least she was making sense.

"I know. Don't try to move."

I watched her lips, saw her say, "Felt like a bomb."

"It did."

"Are you all right?" She opened her eyes, but then squeezed them shut again. A moment later, she rolled over onto her side and vomited. Concussion.

"My head."

"I know. You need to stay awake, all right? Keep talking to me." I listened for sirens, but heard none, not that my hearing was worth a damn yet. I was thinking in slow motion. I pulled out my phone and dialed nine-one-one.

When the dispatcher came on, her voice paper thin to

my ringing ears, I told her where we were, and that there had been an explosion.

"We have responders on our way to you already, sir. Are you hurt?"

"I'm not, but my friend is. A head wound and a compound fracture. And there are others injured as well. Lots."

"Ambulances are on their way."

"Good, thank you."

"I'm going to keep you on the line until they arrive."

"Yes, I understand."

"Fearsson?"

"I'm right here, Billie."

"What happened?" I saw her ask again.

"I'm not sure." A version of the truth. I said nothing about magic, telling myself that I didn't want to worry her. But I was scared—scared that I had gotten her hurt, scared that I couldn't protect her if whoever had attacked us decided he or she wanted to do more than make threats.

I heard the words again—*A warning. Do not push too hard*—and realized for the first time that they had been spoken in a woman's voice. Low, gravelly; it might have been sexy, if not for the words and circumstances. She'd had an accent as well: not quite British. Irish maybe, or Scottish? *Who the hell?*

"Was it a bomb?" She was repeating herself, sounding disoriented. That was the head wound, and also the fact that she was probably going into shock. Her skin was clammy, her breathing shallow.

"I don't know. It might have been. Have you been

near a bombing before?" I was babbling, keeping her talking.

"No."

I heard sirens at last. "The ambulances are here," I told her.

"Okay."

I repeated this into the phone to the dispatcher. She wished me good luck and ended the call.

Several ambulances pulled up to Solana's with a squeal of brakes and the dying wail of sirens. Moments later, EMTs entered the wrecked building and fanned out with a crackle of walkie-talkies. My hearing was improving. It took several minutes more before one of the responders finally reached Billie and me. He was no more than a kid—probably a student at ASU. I couldn't have cared less.

"Who do we have here?" he asked me, kneeling beside her.

"Her name's Billie. She has a compound fracture of the right ulna, and I'm pretty sure she has a concussion as well."

"All right. What about you?"

"I'm fine."

He paused, eyed me from head to toe. "Damn. You were lucky."

"I guess."

"Okay, then," he said, attention on Billie once more. "We'll take care of her." He called over one of his fellow EMTs and didn't say another word to me.

I backed away, giving the two of them room to work, listening as they talked to Billie, asking her questions about her medical history and who they should put down as her next of kin.

At that, she opened her eyes and pointed at me.

I couldn't help but smile, even as my throat constricted to the point where I could barely breathe. I gave them my name, cell number, and home number.

Over the next several minutes, working with quiet efficiency, they immobilized her arm and strapped her onto a stretcher with her head and neck braced, in case she had a spinal injury.

"Fearsson?" she called as they raised the stretcher and began to wheel her out.

"I'm here," I said. I asked the EMT, "Where are you taking her?"

"Banner Desert."

I nodded. "I'll see you soon, Billie. All right? Do whatever the doctors tell you to."

"Fearsson? You'll come see me?" She looked pale, small, afraid.

"Of course I will."

She held tight to my hand even as they started again to lead her away.

"I promise," I said. "You'll see me before you know it."

She let go of me, our fingers brushing as they wheeled her beyond my grasp. She'd be in surgery for a while and would probably sleep for some time after that. I had a few hours before I needed to be at Banner Desert Medical Center. And until then, I had work to do.

The previous night, I'd told Jacinto Amaya that I wanted no part of his magical war. Well, I was in it now, up to my eyeballs. And whoever had done this to Billie was going to be sorry they had come at me with nothing more than a warning and a magical bomb.

CHAPTER 11

I picked my way through the rest of the clutter and stumbled out onto the sidewalk, fragments of glass crunching beneath my feet. There were more injured here, men and women, and even a small child. They lay on the bloodstained cement, as they would after a true bombing. Collateral damage: a cold phrase meaning people who had gotten between me and the weremyste who had issued that threat.

I turned so I could see the front of the restaurant and drew a sharp breath through my teeth. Magic clung to the shattered brick and splintered wood, glistening in the sunlight: as green as spring grass, as clear as dew, save for the faint oil-like sheen I had first noticed at the airport.

"Sir, can you tell me what happened here?"

I wheeled at the sound of the voice. A reporter, young, blonde, pretty, held a microphone inches from my face. A cameraman stood at her shoulder, lens trained on me like a weapon, white light shining in my eyes.

"Were you inside the restaurant when the bomb went off?"

"I don't know what happened," I said, blinking in the glare.

"You're covered with dust and bits of wood and glass. Were you inside?"

"Yes."

"Is that blood on your shirt?"

I dropped my gaze. There was blood on my T-shirt and some on my jeans as well. "It's not mine. It's my . . . it came from a friend."

"Is she all right?"

I shook my head.

The reporter's eyes had narrowed. "I know you. You're that private detective, aren't you? Jay Fearsson?"

"I have to go," I said.

I pushed past her and the cameraman. I should have known it wouldn't be that easy to get away.

"Were you here investigating another crime? Another killing?"

A crowd had gathered, and I couldn't plow my way free.

"Do you think the bomb was directed at you?"

I couldn't help myself: I rounded at that, glared at her, then tried again to get away.

"Mister Fearsson, do you have anything to say to whoever is responsible for what happened today?"

I should have kept going. I should have ignored the question and bulled through the mass of people. But I was thinking about Billie, and about all the other people who had been hurt because some weremyste wanted to send me a message.

I whirled, glared right into the camera. "Yeah. Watch your ass, because I'm coming for you."

This time when I tried to leave, people stepped out of my way. Maybe they had heard me; maybe they saw the rage on my face and decided they'd be better off letting me leave. I stalked off, knowing that I had screwed up and that there wasn't a damn thing I could do now to take the words back. I could imagine the way it would look on television. Kona would be pissed at me, and Hibbard's head would explode. But at least the woman who had whispered in my mind would know what I thought of her warning.

I avoided the other reporters who were converging on the place, and slipped away from the crowded block before too many more police arrived and made any quick exit impossible.

When I first reached Mesa, I'd been annoyed that all the good parking spots were gone, but now that worked to my advantage. The Z-ster was far enough from the restaurant that I had no trouble putting some distance between myself and the scene on the street.

I needed more information about dark magic and its practitioners here in Phoenix. The night before I'd as much as told Amaya that Etienne de Cahors was the only dark sorcerer of consequence the city had seen in years. Less than twenty-four hours later, I could almost laugh at how naïve I had been. Almost. The ringing in my ears, and the fine white dust coating my clothes and skin kept me from seeing the humor. That, and Billie's blood.

As a cop, I'd had a network of informants on whom I relied for information when other sources dried up. Some of them were lost to me now that I was no longer on the job. But I was still plugged into the magical community. At times in the past I had taken my questions to Luis Paredes, but given his ties to Amaya, I knew I couldn't trust him now. Instead, I drove into Phoenix's Maryvale precinct.

Maryvale's neighborhoods included some of the roughest beats in all of Phoenix. It was a relatively small precinct, but it accounted for a disproportionate share of the city's violent crime. It was home to gangs, small-time drug dealers, prostitutes, and one Orestes Quinley.

Orestes, who went by the name Brother Q, owned a small shop that specialized in what the non-magical world would call "the occult." In fact, he had named his place Brother Q's Shop of the Occult, which might have been the worst name for a business I'd ever heard. He sold herbs, oils, crystals, talismans, books on witchcraft and magic, and a host of other goods that a weremyste might need. He was a myste himself, and while he might not have been as skilled as I was, I sensed that he had more power than he cared to admit. I'd busted him long ago, when Kona and I still worked in Narcotics. He did a little time, though probably not as much as he should have, and soon was back on the streets. Any time Kona and I encountered something we couldn't explain during an investigation, I went to Orestes, at first because Kona and I figured he must have been working with whoever we were after. With time, though, he became a trusted informant, and even now, a year and a half removed from my resignation from the force, I still turned to him when I encountered a name I didn't know or a residue of magic I didn't recognize.

I could have used any number of words to describe Q: quirky, eccentric, weird; Kona called him certifiable. But I liked him, and more than that, I trusted him. Despite the fact that I was the one cop who had busted him and made the charges stick—or maybe because of it—Q and I were good friends.

But yeah, he was pretty weird.

I pulled up to his place in the 813 beat, which was as rough a neighborhood as you could find in Maryvale, and found him sitting out front on a folding chair. Orestes claimed to have been born in Haiti. He spoke with a West Indian accent and wore his hair in long dreadlocks. He had on a pair of baggy, torn denim shorts, a tie-dyed Bob Marley T-shirt, beat-up sandals, and a pair of sunglasses with tiny round lenses that couldn't have done a damn bit of good against the desert sun. He was slouched in the chair, accentuating his paunch, and his chest rose and fell slowly. It took me a minute to realize that he was sleeping.

I opened the car door and got out without making a sound. And then I slammed the door shut.

Q started, straightened up. When he saw me, a big smile lit his face. "Brother Jay, Brother Jay, Brother Jay. What brings you to Q this lazy summer day?"

Like I said: weird. Q often referred to himself in the third person, which was strange by itself, but on occasion, for no discernable reason, he also spoke in verse. I didn't know why or when he had started doing this, but I wasn't sure he even noticed anymore. I didn't think he could stop if he tried.

I walked toward him, and he peered at me over the narrow rims of his glasses, his smile melting. After a few moments, he pulled off his shades altogether. "What the hell happened to you?"

"You'll hear about it on the news. Suffice it to say, I've had a crappy day, and I'm not in a mood to screw around."

"Fair enough."

I blew out a long breath. None of this was Q's fault. "I'm sorry. How're you feeling, Q?" I asked.

When Etienne de Cahors went on his final killing spree a couple of months ago, he did serious damage to Q's shop, and the one-room apartment above it, and came close to killing Orestes in the process. The shop still needed repairs, but Q looked better.

"Brother Q is feelin' fine. How are you doin'? Q sees you got those casts off your arm and leg."

"Yeah, I'm better, thanks." I reached for the extra chair Q kept by the shop entrance and paused, waiting for his permission.

He nodded. I sat.

"Q assumes this isn't a social visit," he said, setting his glasses back in place.

I reached for my wallet, pulled out a twenty, and held it up for him to see. But I didn't give it to him. Not yet.

"What do you know about dark magic?"

He regarded me again, his gaze lingering on the blood stains, his lips pressed thin. "Enough to understand you shouldn't be askin' about it out on the street." He pushed himself out of his chair and stomped into the shop. I followed, half expecting him to shut and lock the door in my face. He didn't.

"What the hell, Jay?" he asked, as soon as I was inside with the door shut. "You come around here, lookin' like you been through a war, and you ask Q about dark magic out where everybody can see and hear. That's crazy." He shook his head. "Q's not even sure it's safe to talk about it inside."

I wanted to ask him who he thought would be listening, but he stopped me before I could get the first word out. A moment later, magic buzzed the air. Q glanced around the shop, the walls of which now glimmered with orange light.

"Wardin' spell Q came up with," he said, pride coloring his voice. "It should muffle our voices a little."

"Who are you hiding from? Who do think might be listening to us?"

He shook his head. "Q don't know."

"You never know, until I pay you."

"This time Q really isn't sure. There's strange things happenin'. People are talkin' about new powers. Not new mystes, mind you, but new powers. Q ain't never heard that before. He's not even sure what it means. Mysties are scared, though. Q's sure of that."

"I don't doubt it. What can you tell me about Regina Witcombe?"

Q's eyes narrowed. "Who've you been talkin' to, Jay?"

I shook my head. "I can't tell you that."

He frowned. "You do that a lot," he said with quiet intensity. "You come here askin' Q all sorts of questions, and expectin' answers. Today especially, covered in dust and blood, and refusin' to explain yourself. And then Q asks a question of his own, and suddenly you're all secretive and shit. That can bother a man, make him feel used."

"First of all," I said, "you're not paying me for answers."

Q's gaze slid away, but he chuckled, deep in his chest. "Well, that's true. And second of all?"

"Second, if I tell you, it could get both of us killed. And no, I'm not exaggerating." I paused to gesture at myself. "All of this, the blood, the dust—it's because there was a magical attack on a restaurant I was at. When you hear about it on the news, they'll call it a bombing, but I know better. It was directed at me."

"You look all right. A mess, but all right." He nodded toward the blood. "Unless that's yours."

"It's not. It's from the woman I love."

"Shit, Jay. Q's sorry. She gonna be all right?"

"I hope."

"How do you know this magic bomb was for you?"

"Because a voice told me it was. She said it was a warning."

"She?"

I nodded.

"Well, all right then. Regina Witcombe is that rich woman, right? The one whose husband died on a boat?"

"That's right."

"Thought so," he said. "Yeah, there's some who say she's into the dark stuff. Q's heard no proof—rumor, nothin' more. But it comes from sources Q trusts."

I found this oddly comforting. As much as I didn't want to be caught up in anything having to do with dark magic, that ship was already way, way out to sea. And I found it reassuring that Jacinto Amaya had been straight with me.

"What do they want, Q? Whoever is using this dark magic, what are they after?"

"Well, that's the question, ain't it? Used to be, they was happy to cast their spells and make themselves more powerful with blood and such. But they're changin' now. There's talk of mystes makin' war on each other."

Jacinto had mentioned that, as well.

"A war for what?" I asked.

"Q don't know. But there's rules, things mystes ain't supposed to do. You know that as well as Q does. Dark mystes don't like those rules. Someone with money, power—like that woman you're askin' about—she'd be someone Q would want on his side, when the fightin' started. You know?"

I wasn't sure what a war between mystes would be like but I had a feeling that I'd seen a preview of it today at Solana's. I felt queasy.

"All right, Q," I said, handing him the twenty. "Thanks." I stepped to the door.

"Brother Jay."

I stopped, expecting his standard parting line: *Brother Q has one favor that he'd ask of you; Please don't tell a soul that you heard it from Q.*

But when I faced him again, his expression was still as grim as it had been.

"A couple of months ago, you mentioned to Q that you had a runemyste who was trainin' you."

"I remember."

"You need to ask him about this stuff. Q only knows so much, but a runemyste—he might be able to help you."

I wanted to tell Q that Namid didn't respond well to

pointed questions, and that the laws of his kind prohibited him from interacting with our world in a meaningful way. But I kept these things to myself.

"I'll give that some thought," I said instead, and left.

I went back to my house and changed my clothes, faltering with my shirt in my hands, my eyes drawn to the blood. I was going to toss it in the hamper, but I reconsidered. The blood had set; it wasn't coming out, and I never wanted to wear that shirt again. I threw it in the trash.

Before putting on another, I crossed to my mirror and examined my arms, my back, my chest. Not a single mark. I wasn't even sore. I thought again of my confrontation with Mark Darby at the loading dock behind Custom Electronics. Twice now, a magical spell of unknown origin had kept me from harm. This second time, the sorcerer who protected me was the same one who had saved the passengers aboard Flight 595, and who had killed James Howell.

Why would a weremyste who used dark magic care about saving my life? Yes, she had conveyed a warning as well, but had she also blocked the bullets from Mark Darby's pistol? Were she and her friends tormenting my dad? Were they behind the killings Kona and Kevin had been investigating?

I pulled on a clean shirt and called out, "Namid!"

He didn't like to be summoned, and usually I would have respected his wishes, but I had too many questions, and Q was right: If anyone could help me, it was the runemyste.

But he didn't materialize. I called for him again. Nothing. I hadn't expected that.

Unsure of what else to do, I drove to Banner Desert Medical Center and after getting the runaround for some time found out where Billie was—still in surgery—and where she would be when they were finished with her—probably the trauma center in Tower A on the second floor.

The receptionist had nearly as many questions for me as I did for her, and it didn't take me long to realize that no one was going to let me anywhere near Billie unless I was family. So, I lied, told her we were married, but that Billie kept her maiden name for professional reasons. At some point she and I would laugh about it. Or she'd be royally ticked off.

The receptionist gave me a clipboard with enough paperwork on it to make me feel like I was back on the police force, and sent me on my way.

I went up to surgical waiting, with its bright lights, plastic plants, and rows of patterned chairs, and found the room overflowing with people who looked as worried as I felt. There were no seats available, no windows to look out, nothing to do but lean against a wall, fill out forms, and wait. Eventually I must have closed my eyes, because some time later I jerked awake, and almost toppled over.

"Mister Fearsson?"

Hearing the nurse say my name, I realized this wasn't the first time she'd called for me.

"Yes," I said, straightening and stepping away from the wall.

"You're Miz Castle's husband?"

"That's right."

The nurse nodded once, but eyed me doubtfully. Or maybe I was imagining it. I'd never been a very good liar.

"Can you come with me, please?"

I followed her out of the waiting area and past a sign that said Pardon Our Appearance and described a bunch of renovations taking place in the Intensive Care Departments. We walked through a series of corridors, all of them lined with heavy plastic tarps. At intervals I saw stepladders lying on their sides or propped against walls, and gaps in the ceiling where panels had been removed. I saw a few workers and heard others above me, crawling around in the space overhead. At last we came to a pair of twin wooden doors marked Intensive Care Unit.

The nurse halted outside the doors and asked me to wait there.

She went into the ICU and reemerged a few moments later with a doctor, an Indian woman who appeared to be about my age.

"Mister Fearsson?" she said, her accent light.

I nodded. My mouth had gone dry.

"I am Doctor Khanna. I am the hospitalist here. Miz Castle, she is your wife?"

"Yes," I said, lying yet again. At some point I was going to pay for this. I held up the clipboard. "Still doing the paperwork."

"Do you have identification?"

I dug out my wallet and flipped it to my driver's license. "She kept her name," I said, as the doctor peered at my picture. "She's a blogger and has a big following. She couldn't afford to change it."

"Of course," she said. She met my gaze again. I slipped the wallet back into my pocket, feeling guilty.

"Your wife hasn't woken up yet. If all goes well, she should begin to come around soon, but with head wounds and concussions, things are sometimes slower. Don't be worried if she takes a bit of time to wake up. Because of her head injury, the surgical and anesthesia teams took every precaution with her anesthesia. You should also know that even after she does wake up, she's going to be woozy for a time, and a little disoriented. In fact, it isn't uncommon for patients with brain injuries to exhibit some short-term memory loss."

"Of course." I was struggling to keep up, but belatedly that got my attention. "Wait. Brain injury? Is she all right?"

"All things considered, she is doing well. She has a concussion, some stitches in her scalp for superficial lacerations, and of course the broken arm. The orthopedist put a plate in to set the bone properly, but he was able to do all the hardware internally, so no external fixator or screws. This should mean a faster healing time and less chance of infection.

"She also has two broken ribs. One of them punctured her lung, causing a pneumothorax—a collapsed lung—which could have been much more problematic. Fortunately, it was only a partial collapse, and we were able to treat it in time. We inserted a chest tube, and she's already breathing on her own, so I believe she's going to make a full recovery. But between the pneumothorax and the concussion, she's a had a rough time of it. She's going to be staying with us for a little while."

"I understand. Thank you, Doctor."

"You're welcome. If you have questions, or if she does once she's fully conscious, have the nurses call for me."

"We will. Again, thank you."

The doctor nodded to the nurse, who said, "This way," and led me into the ICU area.

It had been a while since my last trip to an intensive care area in any hospital, and things had changed. We walked between rows of beds, each one in its own glass cubicle, each one surrounded by banks of monitoring equipment. Within some of the glass enclosures, curtains had been drawn. The nurse stopped at one of these, opened the door and pulled the curtain aside, and gestured for me to enter.

I stepped through, and stopped, swaying, my knees almost buckling.

Billie lay on a bed that made her appear tiny. Her head was wrapped in a light gauze that was stained with patches of blood. Her arm, which rested on several pillows, was in a double splint and swathed heavily in what looked like the sticky purple bandaging usually used for sports injuries. A plastic tube snaked from an oxygen tank to a nasal cannula that had been looped behind her head, around her ears, and under her nose.

The nurse placed a gentle hand on my back.

"It's always hard the first time you see someone like this. But she's better off than she was when they brought her in." She steered me to a chair. "Let her know you're here, hon. Talk to her."

I nodded, swallowed. But I had no idea what to say. *I'm sorry I got you blown up. I'm sorry we can't even have a lunch date without one of us almost getting killed.*

"Billie," I said, my voice shaky. "I'm right here, and I'll be here when you wake up. Okay?"

The nurse patted my shoulder. "That's good, hon. That's good." She left me there, closing the curtain and glass door behind her, and giving Billie and me what in a hospital passed for privacy.

I sat and stared at Billie, waiting for her to wake up, turning questions over in my head, and feeling rage at my own impotence build like steam in a kettle. Why would the same weremyste who killed James Howell go to such lengths to keep me alive? What did Dimples and Bear do with the homeless man's blood? What was happening to my father? What did all of this have to do with Regina Witcombe and Jacinto Amaya, and why were so many mystes suddenly so interested in me? I tried again and again to piece it all together, but each time the result reminded me of a modern art sculpture gone wrong; everything seemed to jut in random directions. There was no coherence, no story line.

All the while, as my thoughts churned, Billie remained as she was. Despite the doctor's warning that she might not wake for some time, I began to wonder if something was wrong, and if I ought to call the nurse back to check on her. When at long last she stirred, her eyelids moving ever so slightly and her uninjured hand shifting, I whispered a quick "Thank God" and sat forward in my chair.

"Billie? Can you hear me?"

She shifted her head maybe an inch and winced even at that. "Fearsson?" It came out as a croak, but it sounded like music to me.

"Yeah, it's me."

"'M thirsty."

I hesitated. "Let me get a nurse." I slipped out of the cubicle and hurried to the nursing station. The woman who had brought me in was there with a couple of other nurses. "She's awake," I said. "She says she's thirsty."

"I'll bet she is," the nurse said, walking with me back to Billie's bed.

It turned out there was a large plastic carafe bearing Banner Desert's logo and a long flexible straw sitting near the bed, already filled with ice water. I hadn't noticed. The nurse told me to let Billie have some. "But slowly at first," she said. "Not too much." She turned and checked the monitors.

Billie took a small sip and slipped her tongue over her dried, cracked lips.

"How do you feel?" A stupid question, I know, but it was all I could come up with.

"Like I got blown up."

"Sounds about right."

Her eyes slitted open at that. "Are you okay?"

I wondered how much she remembered from the restaurant, but we'd have plenty of opportunity later to talk about that. "Yes," I said. "I'm fine. Are you in a lot of pain?"

"No. Drugs, I think. Where are we? Wha' hospital?"

"You're in intensive care at Banner Desert Medical Center. You have a concussion, a broken arm, a couple of broken ribs, and you even had a collapsed lung."

"Holy crap," she mumbled.

"No kidding. You've been out for a while. But the doctor says you're going to be okay."

"Guess it's a good thing I have insurance."

I laughed. "Yeah, I guess."

"Where did you say we are?"

I glanced at the nurse.

"That's normal," she mouthed.

"Banner Desert."

"Tha's right."

That was how our conversation went for the next several minutes. We talked about nothing at all. She asked me to list her injuries again, and she wanted to know how long she had been unconscious. The more we talked, the more lucid she grew. Her eyes opened wider, her speech cleared. She sipped more water but told the nurse in no uncertain terms that she wanted nothing to do with food, at least not yet.

The nurse still eyed the instrumentation by her bed, which monitored her blood pressure, heart rate, temperature, and a host of other things I didn't pretend to understand. She didn't seem too alarmed by anything she saw, but after a time she told me, "She needs some quiet time. I don't want her getting too tired."

"I understand. I have . . . a few places I have to go."

"We'll take good care of her. Oh, and Mister Castle, don't worry if her bed is empty when you get back here. We need to test her lung capacity, and also do some further scans: neurological—we want to see how she's doing with the concussion."

"Of course." To Billie I said, "I have to leave for a little while. I have things to do. As soon as they let me come back, I will. All right?"

"I'll be here."

I smiled, stood.

"Fearsson?"

"Yeah."

She made a little motion with her hand, beckoning to me. I bent closer to her.

"Did she just call you Mister Castle?" she asked, her voice as soft as a spring breeze.

I nodded, my cheeks burning. "Yeah. That's a long story."

"Okay. Then tell me this: How is it possible that you're not hurt at all?"

I looked her in the eye, not wanting to scare her, but also unwilling to lie to her. I'd had to keep things from her early on—stuff about magic and the phasings and Namid—and that had almost ended our relationship before it got started.

"You already know the answer," I whispered.

"Magic?"

"Magic."

"But—"

"That's all I know right now. But I'm going to find out. I promise." I kissed an unbandaged spot on her forehead. "I'll see you soon."

CHAPTER 12

I swept out of the ICU and took the stairs down to the ground floor, unwilling to wait for an elevator. Billie's questions had set my thoughts churning again. I still had questions of my own, of course, but I wasn't thinking about them now. I was unhurt because someone had decided to protect me. Billie was lying in a hospital bed looking like she had been run over by a truck because that same someone wanted to send me a message. My dad was suffering in ways he never had before, and though I couldn't prove it yet, and didn't understand what was being done to him, I no longer had any doubt that he was a victim in all of this, too.

Some goddamned sorcerer was screwing with me and the people I loved. I was scared and pissed off, and I'd had enough.

Nothing else could explain the decision I made in that moment. Because it was pretty stupid.

I drove back into North Scottsdale, to Ocotillo Winds

Estates. When the guy at the guardhouse asked me who I was and who I was there to see, I told him. He called ahead to the mansion and after a brief delay raised the barrier that blocked the gate and waved me through. I hadn't been paying as much attention as I should have to the route we followed the previous night, but after taking a few wrong turns, I made it to Amaya's place.

The guys with the MP5s were waiting for me, their expressions far less welcoming than they had been when I showed up with Luis, Paco, and Rolon. They surrounded the Z-ster, weapons held ready, faces like stone.

"Get out," one of them said. "And keep your hands where we can see them."

I unlatched the door, pushed it open with my foot, and climbed out, my hands raised.

"I have a Glock in the shoulder holster under my left arm," I said.

"What else?"

"That's it."

The man gestured in my direction with his head. "*Revísen le.*" Search him.

One of his friends strode toward me, grabbed me by the arm, spun me around, and shoved me against my car. Pressing the muzzle of his submachine gun against the back of my neck, he pulled the Glock from my holster and frisked me. He was thorough and none too gentle; it was probably a good thing I hadn't lied about having a second weapon. When he was finished, he gave me one last shove and backed away.

"Turn around," the other man said.

When I faced him again, he pointed toward the front

door of the mansion. Two more guards waited for me there, both of them also holding MP5s. I almost asked if they'd bought the family pack, but decided I'd be better off keeping my mouth shut.

"Go on. Jacinto is waiting for you."

"Thanks."

I walked to the door, my hands lowered but plainly visible. The guards let me pass, saying not a word, but eyeing me in a way that made the back of my head itch. I could almost feel the sight beams tickling my scalp.

Amaya was in the living room, sitting in one of those plush chairs, one arm resting casually over the back of it, the other hand holding a tumbler filled with ice and what might have been tequila.

"Hello, Jay."

I glanced around the room. It was empty except for Amaya and me. It really did seem that he had been expecting me, even before the call from the guardhouse.

"I saw you on television today. Tough words. I guess you're going into battle with me after all, eh?"

"What happened today? What was that?"

His eyebrows went up, an expression of innocence I wasn't sure I trusted. "You were there, not me. Why don't you tell me what you think it was?"

"It was magic."

"The media is calling it a bombing, though they don't seem to know what kind of bomb could do that kind of damage without burning the place to the ground."

"It was a spell, and it came with a warning."

He sat forward, interested now. "Someone spoke to you."

"Yeah. A woman. She said not to push too hard, whatever that means."

"Fascinating. I suppose it means you're already making progress."

"Maybe. But a friend of mine is in the hospital, and I want to know what the hell is going on."

"I told you last night—"

"You told me shit last night! You gave me Regina Witcombe, but I've since learned that I could have gotten her name from any number of people."

"And yet you didn't," Amaya said, ice in his tone. "You knew nothing about her except that she was rich. So don't tell me that I gave you nothing."

"How do I know it's not you?" I said. Probably not the smartest road to go down, but I wasn't thinking all that clearly. "You send me out to find dark sorcerers, talking like you're trying to make the world safe for the rest of us. But how do I know this isn't anything more than a turf war, an attempt by one dark myste to get the jump on another?"

He glared back at me, his eyes as black and hard as obsidian. "Did you see the magic?"

"What?"

"On the restaurant. Did you see it?"

"Yeah," I said. "It was—"

A blow to the gut doubled me over, stole my breath. I almost retched. Amaya hadn't moved.

Before I could straighten up, something hit me again. The jaw this time. It felt like a cross between a fist and a cinder block. I was catapulted backward, my feet might even have left the floor. I landed hard on my back, the breath pounded out of my lungs.

Amaya sipped his drink, still comfortably ensconced in his chair.

"There's magic on your shirt where I hit you," he said. "Also on your face. What color is it?"

I raised a hand to the side of my face, dabbed at the corner of my mouth. My hand came away bloody. The residue of his spell shone on my stomach. It was dark purple, the color of desert mountains at dusk, and it was as opaque and glossy as wet paint.

"What color?" Amaya asked again, his voice like a hammer.

"Purple," I said.

"And what color did you see at the restaurant?"

"Green. I owe you an apology."

"You certainly do."

I climbed to my feet, crossed to the bar and filled a glass with ice and water. Then I walked to the chair next to his and dropped myself into it. "The magic on the restaurant was transparent as well; it was like looking through the glass of a wine bottle. Does that mean anything to you?"

"No," Amaya said. "You're sure it wasn't a trick of the light?"

"Pretty sure. I saw the same thing at the airport, on James Howell and on the cockpit panels."

He glared. "So, you lied to me yesterday."

I said nothing, but stared back at him.

He flashed a grin, though it faded as quickly as it appeared. "The same myste who struck at the airport issued this warning to you."

"Apparently."

"Very interesting indeed."

"I need more information, Mister Amaya. You said last night that the dark mystes were capable of doing some terrible things. I'd like to know what you meant."

Amaya regarded me for another moment before getting up and walking to the bar. He unstoppered a glass decanter and poured himself more tequila. "Some things are not mine to tell," he said. "But I can give you another name." He smiled back at me over this shoulder. "Someone a bit more accessible than Regina Witcombe."

I pulled out my pad and pen, drawing another grin.

"You know, they have devices now, things that you can use for taking notes, taking pictures, even making phone calls."

"Well, maybe after you've paid me for this job, I'll be able to afford one."

"His name is Gary Hacker. He lives outside the city, on a small plot of land on the outskirts of Buckeye." He gave me the address. "He won't want to speak with you. Tell him I sent you."

"What should I talk to him about?"

"Like I said, it's not my story to tell. But he's a were, and I think you'll find what he has to say pretty illuminating."

"All right."

"Don't take a lot of time with this. You've only got two more days until the phasing starts."

"Do you really think I need you to tell me that?"

A small laugh escaped him. "Probably not."

I drank the rest of my water and stood. "Thank you for the name." I patted my gut. "And for the lesson in magic."

"Your friend, is she all right?"

"How'd you know it was a she?"

Amaya grinned. "I saw you on the news, remember? You were angry, ready to take on an entire army of weremystes. And I saw as well the way you came charging in here, despite my guards, despite my reputation. We do those things for the ones we love, and I happen to know you are in love with the blogger Billie Castle."

I didn't like that he knew her name, that he had found it so easy to learn so much about me, but I probably shouldn't have been surprised.

"She's alive," I said. "But she's not in great shape."

"I'm sorry to hear that. Truly. I know what it's like to have your enemies strike at loved ones."

Pain lurked behind the words; I wondered what had been done to him. "Thank you," I said, unnerved by the sympathy I felt.

I walked toward his front door, curious about this new name he had given me and belatedly aware of how lucky I was to be leaving his home alive.

It seemed he was thinking along the same lines. "Jay."

I halted, faced him.

"I don't care who's in the hospital or how many times you've been blown up. Don't ever come to me in anger again."

Another warning. This one I was likely to heed. I nodded and let myself out of the house.

I returned to the hospital and managed to get in to see Billie for a few minutes. She looked better than she had; she had more color in her cheeks, and she admitted to me that she had eaten a bit.

She begged me to bring her something from Solana's, until I reminded her that it had been destroyed by the explosion.

"Then anyplace. I want fajitas, Fearsson, not braised beef tips." She made a face, and I laughed.

"I'll do what I can."

"I also want to know why all the nurses keep referring to you as my husband."

I winced, rubbed the back of my neck. "It was the only way I could get in to see you. They don't allow just anyone in this part of the hospital, and I wasn't willing to wait until they moved you. So . . ." I shrugged.

"So you claimed you were my husband?"

"Yeah. I don't know your Social Security number, by the way. That really is information you should share with the man you marry."

Her laughter was like the sweetest music.

"I think Kona would say that you're a piece of work."

I nodded. "Yeah, she would."

Before we could say much more, her nurse—a different one—shooed me away, telling me I was welcome to come back in the morning during regular visiting hours.

I would have liked more time with Billie, but at least I knew that her condition was improving and that she was being taken care of, even if it was by Nurse Ratched.

I went by Nathan Felder's house, where I picked up my check, and then made my way home. I only stayed long enough to grab a change of clothes before driving out to my dad's. I would have to make the trip back into town first thing the following morning to keep my appointment with Patty Hesslan, but I didn't feel comfortable leaving him alone for too long.

When I got to Wofford, he was out in his chair, sitting in the dark, wearing the same clothes he'd had on the day before and smelling a bit ripe. I saw no evidence that he had eaten anything.

I fixed him a bowl of cereal, filled a glass with ice water, and sat with him as he ate and drank, listening to him rant about the burning and the pain and how he didn't matter. He mentioned my mom again, and told them to stay the hell away from "the boy." I smiled at this; I couldn't help it. It wasn't that I found it amusing in any way. Far from it. But I was touched that in the deepest throes of his madness or his suffering—whatever this was—he took it upon himself to protect me.

The rest of it sounded like so much nonsense, of course. It was the same stuff I'd heard the day before, and two days before that. He was flinching again, but the food and water seemed to help, and I took some comfort in the fact that he appeared to be no worse than he'd been yesterday.

I didn't like to overuse his sleeping medication—the doctors had warned me that, given his history as an alcoholic, he could develop an addiction to the pills. But he wasn't going to sleep in this state without some help.

Once the pill took effect, I put him to bed. I showered and shaved, lingering in front of the mirror to scrutinize the deepening bruise along my jaw, the purple under my skin blending into the fading purple glow of Amaya's spell. At last, exhausted, I settled down on the floor of my dad's room, as I had the previous night. Weary as I was, though,

I lay awake for a long time, reliving the explosion at Solana's and thinking about the spell I'd felt prickling my skin. There had been two spells, of course, one working at cross-purposes to the other. The first blew up the restaurant; the second protected me from injury, despite the potency of that first casting. I couldn't imagine the power and skill necessary to weave two such spells together, although I thought it possible that Etienne de Cahors might have pulled it off, had he still been alive.

Which begged the question: Had the spells been cast by one myste or two, or even several? If both spells had come from the same "person"—and I used the term loosely—I might well have been dealing with a being who had more in common with Namid than with me. If they had come from two or more sorcerers, I was facing some sort of conspiracy. Lying in the dark, listening to my father's snoring, I wasn't sure which possibility frightened me more.

I slept later than I had intended, and woke to find my dad stirring as well. He sat up in bed, pushed both hands through his white hair. At the sight of me on his floor, he frowned.

"You're here."

"I didn't want you to be alone all night."

"I'm alone every night."

I shrugged, peered up at the sky through the window. It was another clear, sunny day in the desert; it was going to be hot as hell. "You haven't been yourself lately."

I chanced a glance in his direction and saw him nod.

"You stayed the night before, too, didn't you?"

"It seemed like a good idea at the time."

"Thanks."

"How are you feeling?"

"Better. I don't expect it'll last, but right now I'm okay." He narrowed his eyes at my jaw. "You don't look so good."

I raised a hand to the bruise. It was tender, a little swollen. "I'm all right."

"I should see the other guy, right?"

"Actually I never touched the other guy. I deserved this—needed to learn a lesson."

"Okay."

I got up, gathered the blanket and pillow. "I'm sorry to run, but I need to go see Billie, and then I have a meeting."

Dad's face brightened. "How is Billie? When are you going to bring her out here again?"

I didn't want to burden him with bad news, but Billie was something of a local celebrity, and if he switched on the TV he would hear about the explosion and her injuries. "She's not so good," I said, and proceeded to tell him about the attack on the restaurant as I put the bedding away and got dressed.

"So the rest of the world thinks it was a bomb, but you know it was magic," he said when I was done.

"Well, that's . . . yeah. Billie knows the truth."

"And your partner from the force? The black woman?"

"Kona. She doesn't know yet."

"Right, Kona. You need to tell her. They're looking for a bombing suspect."

He was right. "I'll call her," I said. "But right now I have to—"

"Go." He waved a hand toward the trailer door. "Get out, vamoose, skedaddle."

I grinned, and so did he. It was nice to have a conversation with him, rather than just listen to one of his incoherent monologues.

"Dad, did you . . . ?" I stopped myself. I had intended to ask him whether he had ever spoken to Mary Hesslan, Elliott's widow. But I feared his response; he seemed fine now, but I knew his mental state was fragile. Talking about anything having to do with my mom might set him off again, especially if she was part of the hallucinations or dark magic attacks that had been troubling him in recent days. And the truth was, I didn't think I was ready for the conversation my question might provoke.

He was watching me, eyes narrowed again. "Did I what?"

"Did you eat anything at all yesterday?"

His gaze lost some of its focus, and he shrugged. "Honestly, Justis, I don't remember."

"Well, try to have something today, all right?"

"I will."

I hugged him and let myself out of the trailer. I had barely enough time to get to the hospital and check on Billie before my meeting at Sonoran Winds Realty. It being Saturday, I hoped that I would have smooth sailing all the way back into the city. An accident on the Phoenix-Wickenburg Highway killed that dream. By the time I was through the worst of the traffic, I was too late to get to the medical center and a bit too early to go straight to my meeting. I stopped for coffee, stalling.

I'd been unsure yesterday about whether I ought to

follow through on my plan to speak with Patty, and the intervening day had done little to convince me that this was a good idea. At this point, though, I figured it was too late to back out. I walked back to my car and drove the rest of the way to North Scottsdale.

I had to remind myself that to the folks at the realty office, I was Mister Jay. And, I realized, that gave me an out: I didn't have to tell her that I was Dara Fearsson's son. I could ask her questions about Regina Witcombe and leave without her ever knowing the truth. Provided she didn't examine my PI license too closely. I blew out a breath, my dread deepening by the moment.

Before I knew it, I was parking the Z-Ster in front of the building, my hands sweating, my mouth dry. You'd have thought I was here for a first date rather than an interview with a potential lead. I wiped my hands on my jeans, got out, and walked to the door.

The place exuded class, as you might expect from a realty company that routinely handled the sales of million-dollar homes. Glossy photos of enormous estates hung in the windows, along with fashion-model-quality portraits of the various agents who worked there. I recognized Patty's photo right away. She was rather plain, as she had been in high school, with light brown hair, brown eyes, and a sprinkling of freckles across the bridge of her nose. I took a breath and stepped inside.

Predictably enough, the office had been decorated in the geometric patterns and earth tones associated with the Southwest—warm browns that shaded toward red, pale ochres and beiges, and the lapis-like blue of a high desert sky. A pretty blond receptionist sat at a large desk near the door, wearing a white blouse and tan jacket that blended perfectly with the office color scheme. She was on the phone, jotting down notes on a pad. I waited in front of the desk.

After a few more minutes, she hung up, put the note she had written in one of several shallow boxes on her desk, and fixed her attention on me. Blue eyes raked over my bomber jacket, T-shirt, and jeans in a way that left me thinking I ought to go back home and change. I'm sure the bruise on my jaw didn't help with this first impression. At last, her gaze met mine again and her features resolved into a thin smile that said, *You can't possibly afford anything we have listed. Why are you wasting my time*?

"Can I help you?"

"I called yesterday morning to make an appointment with Miz Hesslan-Fine."

Her look of disdain gave way to one of disappointment. "Mister Jay?" No doubt she had hoped I would be wearing an Armani suit.

I glanced at my watch. "I'm a few minutes early," I said, still avoiding a direct lie about my name. "If she's not ready for me, I can wait." I waved a hand at the plush couch that sat near the desk, in between a matching pair of glass end tables. I should have known that would get me in faster; receptionist Barbie didn't want me sitting out here, scaring away her rich clientele.

"No, I believe she's free right now." She reached for the phone, punched in an extension number, and after waiting a few seconds said, "Patricia, your ten-thirty is here." She hung up again and smiled up at me, lowering the temperature in the foyer. "She'll be right out." Which I took to mean, *Don't even think about sitting on that sofa.*

I remained where I was, standing in awkward silence, admiring the photographs that hung on the walls: the Grand Canyon, Lake Powell, Petrified Forest, and several desert scenes that could have been taken in the Superstition Wilderness or Sonoran Desert National Monument.

The door along the back wall behind the receptionist's desk opened. I turned, and felt the world drop away beneath my feet, making my stomach swoop.

I was sure that the woman walking through the door was Patricia Hesslan-Fine. The receptionist wouldn't have called for the wrong agent. But at first glance I could barely be certain. Because the woman's face was obscured by a blur of magical power.

I opened my mouth to say something, a thousand questions rushing into my mind. You're a myste? Was your mother a myste? Or was it your father? Did my mother cheat on my dad with another weremyste? Is this why Regina Witcombe chose to work with you? But every one of those questions died on my lips. Some of them I couldn't ask yet, not where anyone else could hear. Others . . . others I wasn't sure I wanted to have answered.

Upon spotting me, Patty slowed, no doubt seeing the same blur across my face, although obviously without understanding its implications for the history she didn't yet know we shared. In the next instant she recovered, striding forward, a hand extended.

"Mister Jay, how nice to meet you. I understand you were referred to us."

I shook her hand; she had a firm grip. "That's right. A friend recommended your agency, and you in particular."

"Can you tell me who? I'd like to thank this person."

"Actually, it was another real estate agent who, for obvious reasons, would prefer to remain anonymous."

Patty's smile tightened. "Well, there's nothing more gratifying than the respect of a rival." She gestured toward the door she'd come through. "Won't you join me in my office?"

I nodded to the receptionist, pulled open the door, and followed the corridor toward the back of the building. Patty walked behind me, her steps muffled by the thick carpeting, her blazer and skirt rustling softly. The décor remained much the same, but the photos of natural landscapes gave way to aerial photos of more huge estates and sprawling Spanish mission homes.

"Second door on the left," she said, her voice low.

I entered her office and turned to face her as she came in behind me and shut the door.

"Please," she said, gesturing toward an armchair. She stepped around her desk, settled into her black leather desk chair. "Can I have April bring you anything? Coffee, tea, a soft drink?"

I sat. "No, thank you."

"Well, then, why don't you tell me what you're after?"

I couldn't tell if she was talking about real estate or had assumed, because I was a myste, that I had come for a different purpose.

"I understand that you handled the purchase of Regina Witcombe's home in Paradise Valley," I said, unsure of how else to break the ice.

"That's right. Is that your price range?"

I laughed. "No. I don't have that kind of money. She must have been pleased with the work you did for her."

Another tight smile settled on her face, though it failed to reach her eyes. "If you need further references, I can provide them, Mister Jay."

Yeah, this wasn't working.

"My name isn't Jay," I told her. "At least not my last name."

"I don't understand," she said, though clearly she did. "If you're not—"

"April misinterpreted something I said. My name is Jay. Jay Fearsson."

She couldn't have looked more surprised if I had told her I was from Mars. But it didn't take her long to recover.

"You're a private investigator. I read about you online a couple of months ago. And I assume you're seeking information about Regina."

Fame wasn't all it was cracked up to be, especially when exacerbated by my own overly aggressive questions.

"Guilty as charged. But I'll admit that I was curious about you as well. Your friendship with Missus Witcombe gave me an excuse to come here."

"We're not friends."

I faltered. "My mistake. I didn't know you were a weremyste. Do you take after your mother or your father?"

Her gaze dropped. "I'm not sure I want to talk about that, either. I think you should go."

"Mine came from my father. That's why I ask. I'm wondering if my mother left my father for another myste, or if she found in your father someone who was—"

"I don't want to talk about it!" She stood. "You should leave."

I didn't flinch from what I saw in her eyes, nor did I move. "I'm curious: If you're not friends with Regina Witcombe, why were both of you on Flight 595 on Thursday? Did you go to Washington with her?"

She stared back at me; after a few seconds she lowered herself into the chair once more, perching on the edge of it. "It was a coincidence," she said. "She was as surprised to see me as I was to see her."

"You were in Washington on business?"

"Yes. Is your father still alive, Jay?"

I nodded. "Your mother?"

"Yes. She lives in Tucson now."

"I was sorry to hear about your brother."

She toyed with her wedding ring. "Michael was always very . . . sensitive."

The way she said it made me think she meant to call him weak, but thought better of it.

"You must have been surprised the first time you met Missus Witcombe. I can't imagine that many of your clients are mystes."

"Yes, it was quite a coincidence—another one; both of us were surprised. Just as you and I were today." Her voice had a hard edge to it. Despite the words, she assumed I hadn't been surprised. I said nothing to convince her otherwise.

I wanted to ask her if she had ever seen Regina Witcombe do any dark spells, but I couldn't bring myself to pose the question, and I trusted the instinct that kept me from doing so. I didn't believe for a moment that mere chance had put the two of them on that plane. If Regina was working with other dark sorcerers, so was Patty, and I didn't want to draw any more attention from their kind. Not yet, at least. But I was there, and Patty would be wondering why. Fortunately, I had the perfect excuse.

"On Thursday, after your aircraft rolled back to the gate and all of you were asked to deplane, where did you and Missus Witcombe go?"

"Are you working with the police again?"

"Yes."

"Like you did on the Blind Angel killings."

"That's right."

She nodded. "We stayed in the gate area. That's what the gate agents told us to do."

"Did either of you leave the area for any reason?"

She shook her head. "Not until the police showed up. At that point, Regina took me to the airline's club lounge. We knew it would be hours before we took off, so we asked the detectives. They had a few questions for us, but then they allowed us to go."

"So you didn't even leave to use the rest room?"

"No."

That didn't mean one of them hadn't killed James Howell, but it did make proving it more difficult.

"Can you tell me why Regina Witcombe would fly on a commercial jetliner? I understand that she owns a jet of her own."

"She owns two. And her daughters currently have them both, one in Belize, where the Witcombe family has a second home, the other in Anchorage."

"Leaving poor Mom to fly with the masses."

Patty's expression brightened. "Precisely." She stood once more and smoothed her skirt with an open hand. "Now, I really do think you should go. I'm not going to answer any more questions about someone who was once a client, and may well be again. I've probably already said more than I should."

This time I stood as well. "Thank you for speaking to me. My apologies for surprising you the way I did. It wasn't really fair of me."

"No, it wasn't. But I understand why you did it. Our families . . . well, let's just say that some bonds can't be broken, no matter how much we want them to be."

I held out my hand, which she took. "Thank you," I said. "Don't be too hard on April. She made a simple mistake and I twisted it into a lie."

"You're sweet to be concerned for her. Don't worry. Our punishments here at Sonoran Winds aren't too extravagant." She said it with humor, but I had to resist the urge to shudder. I wondered how many more of the agents here were weremystes, and how many of them engaged in dark castings.

She led me out to the reception area, shook my hand once more, and wished me a good day. I pushed through the entry and walked back to my car, trying to act casual, and all the while expecting to feel a fire spell hit me between the shoulder blades. I was sure Patty was watching me, and I was equally certain that she would be on the phone to Regina Witcombe as soon as I pulled away from the curb.

That was fine. There was someone I needed to speak with as well: Amaya's friend out in Buckeye.

CHAPTER 13

I first went to see Billie, stopping along the way to pick up an order of fajitas. She was better today, though it sounded as though she'd had a rough night.

The last of the anesthetics from her surgery had worn off during the evening, leaving her in a good deal of pain. The doctors were still trying to figure out the right dosages, but already she said that she was more comfortable. And seeing that I had brought her food improved her mood significantly.

She didn't look happy when I told her that I couldn't stay long, and she asked the nurses to leave us for a while. They obliged, closing the curtains and glass door as they left.

"Where did you get that bruise?" she asked, once we were alone.

"Lost a fight."

I expected some expression of concern, but it seemed her thoughts were taking her in another direction.

"I don't know if I imagined this or if it really happened." Her voice had dropped to a whisper. "Did you tell me that the explosion at Solana's was caused by magic?"

I nodded.

"And that's why you weren't hurt."

"Right."

"Damn. And so you're leaving now because . . . ?"

"Because I'm trying to find out who did it. I have a couple of leads. Nothing solid, and there's a lot I can't explain right now. But I'm working on it."

She took hold of my collar with her good hand, pulled me closer, and kissed me on the lips. "Well, be careful. If they can blow up a restaurant and keep you from getting hurt, they must be pretty good at this magic stuff."

Smart woman.

"I was thinking the same thing last night. I'll try not to do anything too stupid."

"Good." She kissed me again, then smiled. "Thank you for my fajitas."

"Enjoy. I'll be back later."

I took I-10 west through the Phoenix suburbs out to Buckeye, a middle-class town that had seen unbelievable growth in the past decade and a half as the city and its satellite towns continued to sprawl across the desert. It wasn't the most scenic town in Arizona, and most of the land around it was pretty flat, some might even say desolate. The notable exception was Skyline Regional Park to the north of the city, which was a nice place to hike.

Amaya's friend, Gary Hacker, lived about as far from the park as a resident of Buckeye could manage, in a rundown single-wide on the southern fringe of the town. The land near his home made my father's place seem lush by comparison. The wind had kicked up, blowing clouds of pale dust across the gravel road. Sun-bleached "no trespassing" signs were mounted on posts lining the drive, and the yard around the single-wide was littered with old tires, plumbing fixtures, empty jugs of motor oil and antifreeze, scraps of wood, and just about every other form of trash I could imagine. A beat up Dodge pick-up sat next to the single-wide.

I pulled in behind the truck and climbed out of the car, squinting against the glare and the dust. An air conditioner mounted on one end of the single-wide rattled like an old train and dripped water on the dusty ground. Yellow jackets swarmed over the moistened dirt.

I pulled off my sunglasses and glanced around, thinking—hoping—that maybe I was in the wrong place. Before I had time to do more, the door of the mobile home banged open, revealing a tall, rangy man who held what looked like a worn Savage 110 bolt rifle at shoulder level.

"I think you'd better get back in your car, mister."

It was like I'd fallen into a bad Western.

I put up my hands, playing my role. "I'm not looking for any trouble. Are you Gary Hacker?"

"Who the hell are you?"

"My name's Jay Fearsson. Jacinto Amaya suggested I come and talk to you."

He'd been squinting into the sights of his rifle,

prepared, I was sure, to blow my head off. But upon hearing Amaya's name, he straightened, his eyes narrowing. "Amaya sent you?"

"Yeah. Would you mind lowering that rifle?"

"Remains to be seen. Why would he send you out here?"

"I'm a weremyste," I said, assuming that explained everything.

"I can see that. Why'd he send you?"

I regarded the man, shading my eyes with one raised hand. Apparently Hacker could see the blur on my features, which was odd, because I saw none at all on his. Amaya had said he was a myste, too.

Or had he? *He's a were,* Jacinto told me. Not a myste, or a weremyste, but a were. I knew weres lived in the Phoenix area, as they did throughout the country, but weremystes usually had little use for them. Were magic was very specific. Just as weremystes went through the phasings, weres changed form on the full moon, and on the nights before and after. But that was all. Weres couldn't cast spells; they weren't runecrafters, as Namid would have put it.

Hollywood portrayals notwithstanding, weres weren't monsters; they didn't go around biting people, infecting them with a taint that made the innocent into creatures like themselves. But they did have dual natures; they shared their bodies with a totem beast that took control during the nights of the phasing. A werewolf transformed into a wolf, a werelion turned into a mountain lion—or perhaps an African lion in that part of the world. And in their animal forms, they behaved as would any other creature of that species. If Hacker was a were, he would be able to see my magic, but since he possessed none himself, he didn't appear to me to be anything more or less than a normal person.

"I don't know why he sent me," I said after some time. "Maybe you can tell me that. But he did suggest that I come out here; you can call him to confirm that if you want. I have a cell . . ."

"I don't need your phone. This place might not look like much, but I do have a landline, and an iPhone."

I grinned. "My mistake."

He frowned, but after another moment or two, he lowered his weapon. "All right, come on in." He shuffled back into the single-wide, leaving the door ajar.

The small stairway leading to his door was nothing more than piled cinder blocks, and I expected that the interior would be as trashed as the yard. Inside though, Hacker's place was far nicer than I ever would have guessed. The carpeting was spotless, and the front room was furnished with a plush couch, a couple of upholstered chairs, and a low wooden coffee table.

Hacker stepped into the kitchen, which was about as big as a coat closet, but tidy.

"You want anythin'?" he asked, his tone conveying that he had little to offer.

"I'm fine, thank you."

He nodded, came back out into the living room, and sat in one of the chairs, gazing up at me with an expectant air that reminded me oddly of Namid. He had a long, crooked nose and small, dark eyes. His hair was light brown, shading to gray, and his three-day beard was more white than anything else. Deep lines were etched in the skin around his eyes and mouth. Forced to guess, I would have said that he was in his late forties or early fifties, but I wouldn't have wanted to bet money on it.

"Why are you here? Why would Jacinto send you to me?"

"How well do you know Amaya?" I asked, stalling, unsure of where to begin.

He shrugged. "Well enough, I suppose. I know about the drug stuff, if that's what you're askin'. And I also know that he's a crafter."

I glanced around the mobile home again.

"You gonna sit down?" he asked. "It's a little weird, you standin' and me sittin'."

I ignored that for the moment. "I'm trying to figure out how someone like Jacinto Amaya would have ended up being friends . . ."

"With someone like me?"

"I'm sorry. That didn't come out—"

"It's all right. It's a good question really. Sit down, would ya?"

I took a seat on the couch, opposite his chair.

"I met him about three years ago," Hacker said. "I was livin' in the streets in Phoenix." He stared at his hands, which were thick, powerful, but incongruously short-fingered. "I was a meth addict at the time."

"I'm sorry."

"Ain't nobody's fault but my own." He sat a bit straighter, still not meeting my gaze. "Anyway, I was in the streets, and I heard that Jacinto was openin' one of his new drug treatment places nearby. I went over to see the ceremony, and to ask him a question, and the police tried to shoo me away, like I didn't belong, ya know? But I belonged more than anybody.

"Jacinto saw them tryin' to get rid of me and came over to say that I could stick around. And I called to him, asked my question."

"Which was?"

Hacker's cheeks reddened. "Seems sorta stupid now, but at the time it didn't. I wanted to know if his treatment centers were just for Mexicans, or if a white guy could get in, too.

"While we were talkin' I said somethin' about him bein' a myste. I guess that wasn't so smart, though I didn't know it then. I was in bad shape and I'm not all that smart to begin with. But he didn't get too mad, like he shoulda. He wanted to know how I knew, and I told him I'm a were." He shrugged again. "He told me to stick around, and after the ceremony we talked for a while. He got me into the center; paid for everythin'. He had lots of questions, too. Wanted to know what kind of animal I was." Hacker paused, his eyes narrowing. "You're wonderin' yourself, aren't ya?"

"A little bit."

"I'm coyote." He said this with pride, pronouncing it *KI-yoat*. "Wily, quick, strong. I like bein' coyote."

"I don't doubt it," I said. "But I'm still not sure why Amaya would have sent me here."

"You know many weres?"

I shook my head. "Very few." I hesitated, unsure of how much Amaya would want me to say. "He and I were talking about dark magic, and the weremystes who use it."

Hacker's eyes went flinty. "Yeah, that would be it." He rubbed the stubble on his jaw, his mouth open wide enough that I could see his blackened, broken teeth, a product of his meth habit, no doubt. "You and Jacinto workin' together?"

"I'm working for him," I said. "I'm a private investigator. Amaya hired me to look into a few things."

I thought he'd ask for details, but he didn't. He nodded once, still rubbing his jaw.

"Well," he said, "I owe everythin' to him. This place, my job, my god-damned life. So if he wants me to talk, I'll talk." He sat forward. "But you can't tell a soul about me. You understand?"

"You have my word, Mister Hacker."

He nodded again, stood, and began to pace. "How much do you know about weres?"

"I know that you go through phasings, like weremystes do, but that during yours you take the form of your animal. So I suppose you turn into a coyote three nights out of the month."

"That's right. And that's all. At least that's supposed to be all. But when I was still an addict, I needed money all the time. And I met a guy." He continued to pace, scratching the back of his head so hard he reminded me of a dog with fleas. I winced at the thought, realizing this might not be so far from the truth.

"He was a myste, like you," Hacker went on. "I saw that right away. He said he could help me, and that far from havin' to pay him he'd go ahead and pay me on top of what he could do for me. How could I say no?

"He wanted to do a spell. He said he was

experimentin' with some new magic. If it worked it would make things better for me; and if it didn't I'd be no worse off than I was already."

"Better for you how?"

"He didn't say at first. But eventually it comes out that he wants to . . . 'to free me from the moon.' Those were his words."

"So that you wouldn't change at all?"

Hacker shook his head. "That was what I thought, too. And I told him I didn't want that." He lifted a shoulder. "I know some weres would leap at the chance. No more phasin's? Some folks would love that. But like I said, I enjoy bein' coyote. I don't mind the change so much. I mean, sure, it hurts. But I can live with the pain."

Something stirred in the back of my mind, grasses rustling in a light wind. A memory, though I couldn't place it.

"Anyway, this guy says that I've got it all wrong. He doesn't want to make the phasin's stop. He wants to make it so that I can change anytime I want."

"What did you say?"

"I said sure. I thought it would be great to have that kind of freedom. To control when I changed? And get paid to boot? Why the hell would I say no?"

"So you let him cast the spell."

"Yeah," he said, his voice dropping. "I let him. They used blood. A lot of it. Killed some poor kid. I was too out of it to really understand at the time. But now . . ." He shook his head. "They killed some kid. I still think about that."

"They?"

"A man and a woman. The woman was nobody I'd met before or seen since. She didn't do much. But obviously he wanted her there."

"And the spell worked."

He laughed, short and bitter. "It worked just the way they wanted it to. I don't need to wait for the moons to become coyote. And I can change into him anytime I want. Changin' back is . . . well, that's more complicated. Sometimes it's quick, sometimes it takes a day or more. But all of that is beside the point. Always was, as it happens.

"They can change me. They can make me into coyote night or day. It doesn't matter what the moon's doin'. And what's worse, while I'm coyote they can control me, make me do stuff. I don't remember much of what happens when I'm turned. The memories are mostly images, you know? Like stream of consciousness, but blurred and almost too fast to keep track of. But there are times when I see people with me, and I know they're mystes, dark ones. And sometimes I can piece stuff together. They've had me attack people. They've sent me into places where they would never send a person."

He lifted his T-shirt and pointed at a crater-like scar on his side, beneath his left arm.

"You see that?"

I nodded.

"I was shot by a guard at some air force installation down near Tucson. I don't even know which one, or what I was doin' there. But they had me runnin' along the fence line and some guard took a shot at me. I coulda been killed."

So much had clicked into place for me while Hacker talked. That memory—it was from the seeing spell I'd cast in Sweetwater Park. This is what Dimples and Bear had been doing with the blood from the homeless man. Dimples's spell made it possible for Bear, who must have been a were, to change anytime Dimples wanted him to. The roar of pain I had heard before their victim lost consciousness was Bear turning. For all I knew, he really was part bear.

Weres like Hacker and Bear had been made into servants of the dark sorcerers who changed them; wereslaves, in a manner of speaking. Being a were still carried a stigma, in some ways even more so than being a weremyste. At least we kept our human form. Our phasings were misunderstood, as was the more permanent psychological damage they caused. But some people valued the spells we could cast, and few ever questioned our humanity.

Weres, however, had been portrayed in movies and on television as monsters, and from all that I had heard—I'd never seen it for myself—their transformation to and from animal form could be terrifying for the uninitiated. Others in Hacker's position had no recourse. Hacker could talk to Amaya, though clearly Jacinto had not been able to do much for him. But others like him would be reluctant to admit to anyone what they were, much less that they had been stripped of their freedom in this way. And having no magic of their own, they couldn't fight back, not against a sorcerer.

But their plight also begged a question that chilled me to my core: If this could be done to weres, could it also be done to weremystes? Could a myste who was powerful enough cast a similar spell on me, so that he or she could induce in me at will the insanity and enhanced power of the phasings? Sure, I had access to spells, too. I could defend myself. To a point. But what if the myste in question was more skilled than I was, more powerful? Could I be used as a magical slave as well? Could my dad? Could a myste, or a cabal of them, create an entire army of ensorcelled magical warriors, beyond reason, wielding spells too powerful for those not in the midst of a magically induced phasing to withstand?

The attack on Solana's had convinced me that Amaya's talk of a magical war had some basis in fact. But until now, I hadn't understood fully how dangerous such a conflict might be.

Hacker had pulled his shirt back down and was watching me, wary, perhaps wondering if he had told me too much.

"You promised you wouldn't tell no one about me."

"I remember," I said. "You don't have to worry about that. The man who did this to you, have you seen him since?"

He didn't answer right away. "Yeah. Like I said before, I don't remember everythin' from when I'm turned. But I remember him. Not every time, but enough that I know he's still out there, still controllin' me."

I wanted to ask him for a description of the man, though I was pretty sure he'd tell me the myste had dark eyes, a trim beard, and a thatch of straight dark hair. Dimples.

But I didn't get the chance to ask.

Hacker's eyes went wide. "Aw, shit!"

"What is it?" I asked.

Even as the words crossed my lips, I felt it. Magic, as gentle as an exhaled breath, but unmistakable.

"Get out!" Hacker said. "Now!"

I had no intention of leaving. Instead I tried a warding, something big enough to protect both of us. The touch of the spell had reminded me of a soft breeze, and so I envisioned a glass dome dropping over the single-wide. The dome, the spell, the mobile home.

The flow of power didn't slacken in the least. Either my spell didn't work, or the other runecrafter was too powerful for me to oppose. Guess which one I was betting on.

I cast again: less ambitious this time. A sheath of power around the two of us. Nothing.

Hacker bellowed, his face contorted. He dropped to the floor, landing on all fours. An instant later, he reared back on his knees and tore off his T-shirt. Another roar of agony was ripped from his throat, and he collapsed back down onto his elbows.

The skin on his back rippled. He was hairy to begin with and as I watched, the hair thickened, lightened in color. He cried out, more wail than roar this time. I heard bone snap. His fists clenched and his limbs bent at odd angles. My stomach gave a queasy lurch.

In a distant corner of my mind I thought that for all the nonsense that comes out of Hollywood, this—the turning of a were—they had about right. The mangling of the body, the rapid sprouting of hair, brightening of the eyes, and above all, the agony the transformation induced.

It took less than a minute for Hacker to shift into his coyote; I had no doubt it had seemed far longer to him. He was a good deal bigger than most coyotes I'd seen in the wild. It seemed to me that he resembled a dire wolf more than he did a coyote. But that could have been a function of proximity and closed space.

The animal shook itself loose of Hacker's jeans and then rounded on me, ears flattened, lips drawn back in a fierce snarl. His human teeth might have been a wreck, but the coyote's were just fine, thank you very much: white as bone, and sharp enough to make me back away. He padded closer, stalking me, yellow eyes locked on mine.

I reached for my Glock, but then thought better of it. I didn't want to hurt Hacker any more than I had to. I had a feeling that his runecrafting masters would have been happy to see me kill him; it didn't escape my notice that he hadn't shifted until my questions began to touch on those who controlled him. So if they wanted him dead, I'd do what I could to keep him alive.

But that didn't include allowing him to snack on me.

He growled, deep in his chest, his hackles standing on end. And then he leaped at me, teeth snapping. I lashed out, trying to bat him aside with my forearm. In theory it should have worked, but theory doesn't amount to much while fighting a wild dog in a single-wide.

His jaws clamped down on my arm, vise-strong. If I hadn't been wearing my bomber, he would have ripped through my flesh. As it was, his canines punctured the leather and stabbed into my skin.

I gritted my teeth against the pain. But while he had

hold of my arm, I threw a punch, hitting him hard on the snout.

The coyote let go of me, backed away, snarling again, teeth still bared.

Before he could charge me a second time, I began to recite a spell in my mind. The coyote, me, and a stone wall between us. Simple, and effective. I hoped.

I watched the animal, waiting for the right moment, not wanting to cast too soon and thus tip off its masters, who, I assumed, were watching our fight somehow.

The coyote launched himself at me. And I released the spell.

He went for my neck. But before he reached me, he collided with something solid and completely invisible. The coyote dropped to the floor at my feet, dazed.

Before he could attack again, I tried to think of some other spell I could cast, one that would keep him from attacking again without hurting him. I considered using a transporting spell, a casting that would put him elsewhere, out of harm's way and far from me. Most transporting spells were complicated craftings, requiring many elements and some forethought. I wasn't sure I had time for either. More to the point, I didn't know where to send the creature. I couldn't send him very far; I didn't know how. And if I put him somewhere else in the mobile home—say, in another room that happened to have a window—he could escape and hurt himself or others. I wanted him incapacitated, and perfectly safe.

The coyote growled again and got to its feet. I took another step back, and met a wall.

I thought once more of the spell I'd cast when training

with Namid, of the imaginary hammer I'd used to shatter his binding. Again I was thinking too literally, not allowing my crafting to do all that it was capable of doing. Three elements: the coyote, the floor of the living room, and leather straps holding the animal down. I recited the elements in my head three times as quickly as I could, and let go of the spell just as the coyote sprang for me.

Magic charged the air in the room, and Hacker in his coyote form gave a fearsome yowl: rage, confusion, terror. But the were didn't leap at me; he didn't seem to be able to move at all.

I eased away from him, my heart racing, my hands shaking. The coyote snarled and bared his teeth, his feral gaze following my every move. But he remained where he was. I backed away and made a quick search of the single-wide. It didn't take me long to find exactly what I was looking for: The bathroom had a small vent high on the back wall, but no window.

I returned to the living room, walking slowly. The were eyed me and growled, but my casting held. He didn't move. I removed my bomber, and, still moving with the stealth of a hunter, I approached the creature. His growls grew more urgent, and he scrabbled at the carpeting with his back claws, trying to break free of the bonds I'd conjured, tearing the fabric. Reaching him, I threw my jacket over the coyote's head and upper body. He yowled. I didn't give him time to do more.

Gathering the jacket tightly around him, I lifted him. His back paws scraped my chest and arms, peeling away my skin. I hissed through my teeth, but held tight and strode back to the bathroom. There I managed to pull away my jacket and toss the coyote into the plastic, faux-tile bathtub, all in one less-than-smooth motion. The coyote clawed at the tub, desperate to gain purchase. I jumped back into the corridor and yanked the door shut as the animal made a dash for freedom. He crashed into the door and then threw himself at it again and again, shaking the entire single-wide. I held fast to the doorknob, unsure of whether the coyote could find a way to pull it open, unwilling to risk letting go, and without a clue as to what I should do next.

CHAPTER 14

The coyote's snarls and the snapping of his teeth reached me clearly in the hallway, reminding me—as if I could have forgotten—how flimsy the bathroom door was. The single-wide quaked with the were's panicked attempts to escape his prison. I hoped he would exhaust himself before he broke a bone or gave himself a concussion.

I pulled out my wallet and managed to extract Jacinto Amaya's business card while maintaining my grip on the doorknob. I retrieved my flip phone from my jacket pocket and dialed the number he had scrawled on the back of the card.

He picked up after two rings.

"Amaya. Who's this?"

"It's Jay Fearsson. Your friend attacked me, and now I have him trapped in his bathroom."

"Fearsson? What the hell are you talking about? What friend?"

"Gary Hacker."

"Hacker attacked you? Is he all right? Did you hurt him?"

"I'm fine, thanks," I said, my voice rising.

"Did you hurt him?" Amaya asked again. Even through the thin connection, I could hear the steel in his tone.

"I made every effort not to."

"What happened? What did you say to him?"

"Nothing! We were talking about what had been done to him, and I asked about the man who's been controlling his changes. And at that point we both felt a pulse of magic. Next thing I know, he shifts and attacks me."

"He shifted? So he attacked you in his animal form?"

"That's right."

"Damn." I heard Amaya exhale, though the sound was nearly drowned out by the snarls and thrashing coming from the bathroom. "Where are you?"

"We're in Hacker's single-wide; I have him locked in the bathroom."

"The bathroom!" Amaya repeated, sounding angry.

"It's the one room in his place without a window," I said.

Amaya was silent for so long, I began to wonder if the call had been dropped. But then he said, "Yes, I understand. Thank you, Jay."

"I don't know what to do with him," I said. "He's trying to get out, and I'm afraid he'll hurt himself. I'm also afraid that if I leave, he'll find a way out of the single-wide. There's no telling what kind of trouble he could get into."

"Someone cast a spell to make him turn," Amaya said, still catching up with the conversation. "How did that person know what you and Hacker were talking about?"

"That's an excellent question. I have no idea. But he did. Or she. Maybe it was the same woman who spoke to me before Solana's blew up. Listen, Mister Amaya, I can't stay here all day waiting for Hacker to pass out or shift back to his human form. I don't know what to do."

"What makes you think that I have answers for you?"

"He's your friend. I could have shot him, or used an attack spell on him. I didn't. But you set up this meeting, and it's gone to hell. And you hired me to do a lot more than pet-sitting."

Another pause, and then, "I'll send a man."

"Thank you." I started to close my phone, but heard him say, "Jay."

"I'm here."

"They wouldn't have been watching Hacker. They control him. They don't see him as a threat."

A cold feeling crept down my spine, like a bead of sweat. "Which means they're watching me."

"Night and day, I'd assume."

"Right. Thanks."

I ended the call and leaned against the wall, which shuddered every time the coyote threw himself against the door. The impacts were slowing; Hacker was wearing himself out. I figured that right around the time Amaya's man arrived, I wouldn't need him anymore.

As I waited, I considered what my next move might be. I needed to speak with Namid; with all that had happened in the past two days, I was more alarmed than ever by his failure to materialize the last time I called for him. Had he refused to answer my summons because he knew that others would overhear our conversation? Had something happened to him, making it impossible for him to communicate with me? Days ago, the very idea would have seemed impossible; not anymore.

I also needed to get back to my dad. He was under attack, like I was. But why?

I could hear him in my head. *I don't matter*, he had said, so many times that the words lost their meaning. But not to him. *The boy is not for you*, he had said as well.

Did he know I was in danger before I did?

Sooner than I would have expected, I heard a car pull up outside. Of course, a few minutes before, the noise from within the bathroom had stopped. The coyote was probably sleeping soundly, harmless as a puppy.

The door to the single-wide opened, and Rolon stepped inside. He carried an oversized handgun; I didn't recognize the model. After surveying the living room, he peered down the hallway and spotted me.

"*Amigo*," he said.

"Hey, Rolon." I nodded toward the weapon he carried. "You do understand that Jacinto wants this guy protected, not shot, right?"

"It's a tranquilizer. One shot, and Hacker will be out for hours."

I frowned. "Is that safe?"

"It is if he's still a doggie. If he's human again, I shouldn't need it, right?"

It made sense.

I pushed away from the wall and walked out into the

living room. "I think he's out already," I said. "But just in case, keep that thing handy."

He grinned.

I crossed to the door, and as I pulled it open, Rolon said, "Jacinto sent a message."

I exhaled, turned. No doubt I'd broken some unspoken rule by calling his cell. "Yeah?"

"He says, 'When the time comes to fight, don't go in alone. Call and you'll have backup.'"

Better than what I was expecting. I nodded once. "Tell him, thanks."

I left the single-wide, climbed back into the Z-ster, which was oven hot, and drove out of Buckeye, intending to make my way to Wofford. There was no direct route to my dad's from Hacker's place, and the closer I got to Phoenix, the worse the traffic would be. So I took the scenic route, hoping it would prove quicker. I wound up on a lonely stretch of road known as the Sun Valley Parkway, which cuts northward through the desert from I-10 a couple of miles west of Buckeye, before heading east back toward the city on the north side of the regional park. In another ten or fifteen miles it would intersect with the Phoenix-Wickenburg Highway, which I could take to my dad's trailer. The parkway was popular with bikers of all stripes—cyclists as well as motorcycle enthusiasts—and it was one of the prettier stretches of road in the Phoenix area.

Huge saguaro cacti stood like sentinels beside clusters of palo verdes and catclaw acacias, desert creosote and brittlebush, barrel cactus and several species of chollas. Beyond the cacti and shrubs, the White Tank Mountains rose from the desert plain, their peaks and ridges like the cutting edge of a bread knife. Ravens soared overhead, black as coal against the azure sky, and a hawk circled in the distance, nearer to the mountains.

I had passed a couple of guys on fancy road bikes in the first mile or two outside of Buckeye, but after that I had the highway to myself, and once more I thought about the attack at Solana's, what was being done to my dad, and, now, my encounter with Hacker. It all came back to Flight 595. I was sure of it. But why, and how?

Maybe ten miles out from Buckeye, a car appeared in my rearview mirror, coming up on me fast. It was a silver sedan, not a make or model I recognized. And I knew every make and model there was.

The windshield glass was tinted top to bottom, which was illegal in this state. Then again, there was no plate on the front of the car, so I didn't know where it was from. All I knew was I couldn't see the driver at all, and that made me nervous.

I floored the gas and the Z-ster leaped forward. Still, the silver sedan continued to gain on me.

And then the magic hit.

Dark mystes, I'd learned when battling Cahors, liked to go for the heart. That's what this one did. It felt as though someone had reached a taloned hand into my chest, taken hold of my heart, and squeezed with all his might. This was what it must have been like to have a heart attack. I clutched at my chest and eased off the gas. My car shimmied, slowed, and drifted off the road, through the shoulder, and into the sand and rock and dry brush that lined the highway.

The sedan slowed as well, pulling onto the shoulder and halting.

I wasn't going to sit there and let them finish me. Despite the agony in my chest, I stepped on the gas again. The wheels spun, spitting up rocks and sand before finally gaining traction and fishtailing out of the desert back on to the road, a cloud of red dust in my wake.

The sedan glided after me, and whoever was gripping my heart seemed to give a good hard twist. I gasped, afraid I was on the verge of blacking out.

Namid had once told me how to block attacks like these. I grunted a warding spell. The pain, my heart, and a sheath of magic around it.

The crafting hadn't worked very well when I tried it against Cahors, but I'd gotten stronger, more skilled. As soon as I released the magic, the pain in my chest vanished. And before the bastard could attack me again, I cast a second spell, encasing the car in magical armor.

The moment I released the magic, the sedan sped up, until its front end was right on my bumper. Literally.

I'd had enough of him, too. I slowed, forcing him to do the same, and then I punched it. That sedan, whatever kind it might have been, was more than a match for the Z-ster, but I did manage to put a few yards between us. And then I cast a third time.

As simple as you please: the road, his tire, a nail.

I heard the blow-out, watched in my rearview mirror as the sedan swerved and slowed. The driver managed to stop without flipping over or going off the road, but by then I was doing one hundred and ten, with no intention of slowing down.

I chanced a grin, knowing that this one time, I'd gotten the better of these dark sorcerers who had been screwing around with me for the past several days.

"That was well done, Ohanko."

I practically jumped out of my skin. The Z-ster veered dangerously, and I slowed down.

"Damnit, Namid! You can't surprise me like that when I'm driving!"

"I am sorry. Should I leave you?"

"No! Where have you been? I tried to speak with you, and you didn't answer, not even to tell me that you don't like being summoned."

"I do not."

"I know."

"When was this?"

I hesitated. "Yesterday afternoon." Had it only been yesterday?

"Why did you summon me?"

"Because Billie and I were nearly blown up by a magical bomb."

I chanced a peek his way and found him staring back at me, his waters placid, his eyes as bright as searchlights.

"All right, she was nearly blown up. It seems I wasn't in any danger at all. Not then, at least."

"You are now."

"So I've gathered. What is this about, Namid?"

"What do you think it is about?"

If I'd thought it would do any good at all, I would have pulled out my Glock and shot him. I hated it—*hated* it— when he answered my questions with questions. He reminded me of a teacher I'd had in high school, the most annoying geometry teacher on the planet, who had responded exactly the same way to all of our questions. I couldn't stand the guy. Learned a helluva lot of geometry, though.

"I think I'm caught up in a magical war between dark sorcerers and whatever you'd call people like us."

"I am a runemyste," Namid said in a voice like a hard rain. "And you are a runecrafter. Or a weremyste, if you prefer. It is these others who should bear names of a different sort."

I glanced his way. "So you admit that there are others."

The myste frowned. "Would it not be foolish of me to do otherwise? I have said many times, have I not, that my kind guard against the use of dark magic in your world."

"Yes, you've said that, but . . ." I shook my head, the frustration of the past few days spilling over. "But you say it in a way that makes it sound like dark magic is a random occurrence, that you're here to guard against men like Cahors, who present a threat that's real, but isolated."

"And so I am."

"But it's more than that, isn't it?"

"I do not understand what you are asking."

I couldn't tell if the myste was being purposefully obtuse, or if this was simply the hazard of communicating with a centuries-old being who saw the world in a fundamentally different way. On most occasions, this would have been when I threw up my hands and surrendered. Not today.

"I'm asking why you've concealed from me the fact that your war with dark weremystes is ongoing. I'm asking why you've effectively lied to me for more than seven years."

"I do not believe I have," he said, his waters riffling as from a scything wind.

"There's a war going on."

I looked at him again, though I didn't dare take my eyes off the road for too long. I could imagine dark sorcerers coming after me in a whole fleet of those sleek silver sedans.

"Yes," he said after a long pause.

"And it didn't occur to you to mention this to me until now?"

"It occurred to me many times. I did not believe you were ready to know the entirety of this truth."

"I'm not a kid, Namid. I know I'm not as skilled as you'd like me to be, and I know that I disappoint you more often than not. But I took down Cahors, and that should have earned me some modicum of consideration, of respect."

"You have my respect, Ohanko, and have for longer than you know. Why would I expend so much time on your training if I did not respect your crafting and your mind?"

This was without a doubt the kindest thing he had ever said to me, and yet it served only to make me more angry.

"You've got a pretty twisted way of showing respect."

"I am sorry you feel that way."

We fell into a lengthy silence, until at last I said, "Well?"

"Well, what?"

"Bloody hell, ghost! Are you going to tell me what's going on or not?"

"I still am not certain you are ready to hear all of it."

"I don't give a god-damn! Somebody's trying to kill me. Someone came within a hair's breadth of killing Billie. Someone is tormenting my dad. And that doesn't even begin to get at the stuff I've been hired to find out. Whether you think I'm ready or not, I'm in it now. And I want to understand it—the risks and the stakes."

"I should have asked sooner. How is Billie?"

I felt much of the anger I'd directed at the myste sluice away. "She's better, thank you. But I almost lost her. And I'm afraid I'm losing my father. I need your help, Namid."

"And what do I get in exchange?"

He couldn't have surprised me more if he had asked to borrow money from me. In spite of everything, a small laugh escaped me. "What do you want?"

He appeared to consider the question for a few moments. "I am not a ghost," he said. "You know this, and yet you insist on referring to me as such again and again. I would prefer you did not."

I laughed again, shook my head. "Wow. Okay. I'll . . . I'll try to stop calling you a ghost."

"You will try?"

"Some habits are hard to break."

Again he weighed this before nodding. "Very well."

We lapsed once more into silence, until I wondered if he expected me to ask more questions. But eventually he began on his own.

"You know the history of the runemystes," he said, his voice as deep as a mountain lake. "How we were sacrificed by the Runeclave so that we might forever be guardians of magic in your world. Often omitted from that history is the fact that some in the Runeclave saw a different path for those skilled in runecrafting. They wished to make war on the non-magical, to become dominant. When the Runeclave created the runemystes, these dissenting weremystes sought to do something similar.

"Theirs, though, was not an act of sacrifice or self-abnegation. They used blood magic to take immortality for themselves. They became immortal as well, and their powers are similar to ours. And so some might say that there is little difference between us. But there is an inherent darkness in what they are and in their crafting. They are corrupt in the truest sense of the word. I have heard it said that they rarely appear to humans or even to ordinary weremystes, because the stench of decay clings to them still, even after so many centuries."

"So, you're telling me that there's a war between the runemystes and these other . . ."

"My kind call them necromancers: beings who have taken power from the realm of the dead. And yes that is what I am telling you. Surely you knew much of this already."

I shook my head, blew out a long breath. "I thought there were weremystes who were dabbling in dark magic. It never occurred to me that they would have allies as powerful as you." I tapped a finger on the steering wheel, thinking. "So then Cahors was one of them?"

"No. As I told you at the time, Etienne de Cahors was a runemyste, but he chafed at the limitations placed on my kind by the Runeclave." Namid paused, appearing uncomfortable. "What I did not tell you then is that he was lured into disgrace by the necromancers. He was to be their prize. He could have told them much about our craftings and how they might be overcome.

"They gave him aid at the beginning, instructing him in the uses of blood magic. But he soon tired of their control. He wished to be beholden to none, to be free of the Runeclave and also of the dark ones. But he was important for other reasons."

Something in the way Namid said this caught my ear. "What reasons?"

"They invested much in him: decades of wheedling, secrets of their evil magicking, their darkest aspirations. When he abandoned them, they were enraged. Their one consolation was that my kind were even more enraged. Their loss was great; ours was greater. We were thirty-nine. When we lost him we were thirty-eight. This pleased them, and more, it gave them a glimpse of a possible path forward from their failure. Equally important, they took note of how he died. And at whose hand."

"Mine," I said.

"Just so."

"This is why they're so interested in me. Because I killed Cahors."

"Because you are a weremyste who killed Cahors. The necromancers long were contemptuous of weremyste power. They have subordinates of your kind—weremancers, we call them. But they have never considered them more than servants to their cause. Your victory over Cahors has forced them to consider the weremancers anew, to imagine a new role for them in this war."

"And what role is that?"

The myste shook his head. "This I do not know."

I wanted to believe him, but I wasn't sure that I did. He'd kept too much from me over the years.

"Do you know who was in the car that came after me right before you showed up?"

"I know it was a weremancer, but that is all."

"So a weremyste was able to attack my heart that way?"

He shook his head. "No. I felt a second presence as well: a necromancer. It was she who attacked you. I believe the weremancer was here to . . . to finish you, as you would put it."

I found this comforting in a strange way. I couldn't have seized another person's heart with magic the way the necromancer seized mine. I didn't want to think there were other runecrafters like me out there who could. "I warded my heart from her attack. If her magic is comparable to yours, I shouldn't have been able to do that."

"You may have surprised her with your warding. Or she may still be familiarizing herself with your craft. Do not count on such spells working a second time."

I nodded at that, my mind already turning in a new direction. "It's necromancers who are hurting my father, right?"

"I do not know, Ohanko. I believe it is possible, assuming that Leander Fearsson's suffering is not— forgive me—the product of delusion."

"It's not."

"You know this?"

"I feel it," I said. "I'm going to see him now. You're welcome to stay with me and see him for yourself."

"Thank you. Perhaps I will."

We drove in silence for a minute or two. I had more questions for the myste, but I wasn't sure that I wanted to ask them, not because I thought he would refuse to respond, but because I didn't think I'd like his answers. It didn't take long for the cop in me to decide this was a piss-poor reason not to ask.

"Since the day I met you, you've been telling me that you and your fellow mystes are forbidden from interfering in our world."

"And we still are."

"Even now?"

"Our laws have not changed."

"But circumstances have. You can't expect weremystes to fight off these necromancers without help."

"Our expectations are irrelevant." I started to argue, but he held up a translucent hand, stopping me. "We are what we are. Our laws help to define us. To ignore them out of expedience diminishes us, makes us little better than those you would have us fight on your behalf. We can help you, prepare you, guide you. But we cannot intervene. To do so would compromise too much."

"You intervened with Cahors," I said, knowing what he would say.

"This I have explained to you as well. Cahors was an anomaly, one of our own who escaped our notice. He acted on your world in large part because our vigilance slackened. We did what was necessary to undo some of the damage he wrought. This is different."

Not the answer I had been hoping for, but I had to admit that there was a certain logic to what he said. That logic was likely to get me killed, but, hey, at least the runemystes were sticking to their principles.

"You're putting a lot at risk," I said. "They may be your laws, but it's our lives you're wagering."

"Not yours alone."

I frowned, looked over at him. "What do you mean?"

"Think, Ohanko. What is it the necromancers want?"

I shrugged. "Power?"

"Yes, of course. But what lies in their path to power?"

I thought about it for all of three seconds before the answer became obvious. The runemystes wouldn't intervene directly, but what other beings would the necromancers fear? Weremystes could fight them; many of us would. We didn't stand a chance, though, without the runemystes doing all that Namid had said they would: training us, preparing us, guiding us.

What did they want? They wanted to destroy Namid and his brethren.

"It's you who are at risk," I said. "I'm sorry. I should have understood. The necromancers see the thirty-eight of you as the only obstacles they have to overcome."

He nodded, solemn and slow. "That is our belief as well. You should know, however, that there are now but thirty-seven of us left."

CHAPTER 15

I gaped at him. Cahors's betrayal was one thing, but to lose another runemyste . . . I didn't know how that was possible.

"What happened? Did another of your kind . . . go over to the dark side?"

I regretted the wording as soon as I said it. Fortunately Namid rarely caught my pop culture references.

"No," he said. "As far as I know, there was no betrayal. At least not as you mean it. A runemyste was murdered."

Which was far, far worse.

"Do you know who did it? Or how?"

"We do not know. We know only that one of her weremystes was killed as well. They died together, perhaps battling a necromancer and his or her servants."

"How does one even kill a runemyste?" I asked.

Namid turned my way, his expression unreadable. "None but another runemyste can do it, and even that would be no small feat. I might slay one of my brethren, but I would have to vanquish him in what would be a great and terrible battle."

"But a necromancer has as much power as you do, right?"

"A necromancer has power to harm your world and to craft spells that would seem as powerful as mine. But the Runeclave made my kind centuries ago. We are creatures of magic, elemental. We cannot be destroyed so easily."

"And yet, one of you was."

"Yes," he said, the word coming out as flat and hard as a river stone.

By now we had reached the Phoenix-Wickenburg Highway. I hadn't seen another silver sedan or sensed the presence of the necromancer since Namid appeared in my car. He might not have been willing to act on the human world, but merely by staying with me, he was keeping me safe. I almost said something to this effect, but I didn't want him leaving, so I kept my mouth shut.

I followed the highway to Wofford and soon reached the rutted road leading into my father's place. Namid remained beside me in the passenger seat, his watery face impassive, his hands resting on his thighs.

I stopped near the trailer and switched off the engine, but I didn't open the door right away.

"When was the last time my father saw you?" I asked.

"It has been many years."

"So this might not go so well."

"I have always been fond of Leander Fearsson, and I believe he was fond of me. Even with the moon sickness, I do not believe he will be displeased to see me."

I didn't feel that I could argue the point without being

rude, and I really did want Namid to see firsthand what my Dad was going through. But I was less convinced than the myste that this would prove to be a great idea.

I climbed out of the car and closed the door, expecting Namid to do the same. But when I turned, he was already standing beside me. I jumped, hissing a curse. The passenger door had never opened.

My father sat in his chair, staring across the desert, flinching every few seconds. I could see that he was muttering to himself. He seemed to have on clean clothes, but he wasn't wearing socks. Mixed signals.

"Try not to startle him," I said, my heart still hammering as I began walking toward my dad. Namid followed.

At first my father took no notice of us. And why should he? Each time I'd come to see him, he'd been in a similar state and had largely ignored me until I spoke to him or checked his forehead for fever. But Namid and I hadn't been there for more than a minute—I'd barely had time to pull out a second lawn chair—when my dad's flinching ceased and he looked up, first at me and then at the runemyste.

"They left," he said, his gaze lingering on Namid, his voice rough with disuse. "They sensed you, and they left."

Namid frowned. "I had hoped to observe you under their influence, perhaps to learn something of their nature."

"Their nature is they're afraid of runemystes."

"How are you feeling?" I asked him, stooping to kiss his brow.

"Hungry."

"You're always hungry when I get here."

My dad grinned. "You always feed me." He canted his head in Namid's direction. "What made you bring the ghost?"

"I am not a ghost!" Namid said, in a voice like pounding surf.

I laughed.

"You Fearsson men share a most peculiar sense of humor."

"I guess that still gets him riled, doesn't it?"

"Did I learn it from you?" I asked. I was still smiling; no one enjoyed humor at the runemyste's expense more than I did. But there was something a little weird about it, too. It was like finding out that my Dad and I once had the same teacher in high school, or the same girlfriend, but without the "ick" factor. Ridiculous as I knew it would seem to the runemyste, I had long considered Namid my mentor—mine, and no one else's. I found it hard to imagine him training another weremyste, especially a younger version of my father.

"Seriously, Justis. Why'd you bring him here? Did you know it would make them leave me alone?"

I shook my head. "I'd love to tell you I'm that clever, but I'm not. He asked about you, and I told him I was on my way here. He came along."

My dad shifted his gaze to Namid. "You must have known what would happen when you showed up."

"I did not. I was not entirely certain that your suffering was anything more than delusion."

"Thanks a lot," Dad said, his tone as dry as a Sonoran wind.

"You should know that Ohanko insisted that it was real."

"Ohanko?"

"That's what he calls me," I said. "It means 'reckless one.'"

Dad narrowed his eyes. "What was it you used to call me? Lokni, right?"

The myste's waters rippled gently. "Yes. It was also a name born of frustration. You were as stubborn as your son, and even more likely to chance upon danger."

"You were also a better runecrafter," I said. I waved a hand at Namid. "He's told me so several times."

Dad looked away, following the flight of a red-tailed hawk with his eyes. "That's okay. You're stronger than I ever was. You got that from your mother."

I shared a quick glance with the myste.

"Tell me what has been done to you, Leander Fearsson."

Dad's mouth twisted sourly. "You want me to waste your time with delusions?"

"I no longer believe them to be delusions. Delusions do not flee at the arrival of a runemyste."

My father's gaze found me. After a moment he nodded and launched into a description of the psychic and physical torture to which he'd been subjected over the past couple of weeks. I had pieced together most of it from his ramblings and the few coherent minutes we'd shared during my previous visits. But hearing as a single narrative all that he had endured—the pain inflicted on his body, sometimes for days uninterrupted, and the images from his past forced into his mind—made my hands shake with rage. I wanted to turn my magic on whoever had done all of this to him.

He repeated himself some—he was relatively lucid, particularly when compared to what I'd seen recently, but he was still a burned out old weremyste. After a while I went inside the trailer to make him a sandwich. When I came back out again and handed him the plate, he was still rambling.

"There was nothing random about it," he said, as he had several minutes before. He took a bite of his sandwich and added for my benefit, "It probably seemed pretty random from the outside. They were testing me, almost like they wanted to see what hurt the most."

"You talked about the burning a lot. Was that the worst?"

"I don't know," he said, shrugging and talking around a mouthful of food. "It all hurt. The burns, knife points, bludgeoning. And then there was the emotional stuff." He faced me again. "They dredged up memories of your mother, threatened to hurt you, took me back to my worst memories of when I was on the job."

"To what end?" Namid asked. As far as I knew, it was the first thing the myste had said since my father began his story.

"I don't know."

"They threatened Ohanko. Did they say more about him?"

Dad raked fingers through his white hair, so that it stood on end. "Like I said, they talked about hurting him, because they knew that would hurt me. But the rest . . ." He shook his head. "I don't remember."

"You heard voices," I said, remembering the message I'd gotten at Solana's just as the restaurant blew up. "Male or female?"

"Both. Female mostly. One in particular. But others, too." He attempted a smile but managed only a grimace. "There have been a lot of people in my head."

I didn't know how to respond to that last, so I focused on the first thing he'd said. "The woman's voice: low, gravelly, kind of sexy even?"

"You've heard her, too?"

"I think she blew up that restaurant I was in with Billie."

His eyes widened, and I had the sense that he didn't remember me mentioning this before. "She's all right? Billie, I mean?"

"She's getting better. I'll let her know that you asked."

Dad nodded. I could tell he was overwhelmed by all of this: Namid's appearance, the news about Billie, all he had been through with the dark mystes. Maybe it had been a mistake to let him see the runemyste.

"Very well, Leander Fearsson." The myste paused, pain lurking in his glowing eyes. "I must leave you. And I fear that when I do, those who have done this to you will return."

"I'll stay with him."

"No, you won't," my dad said, growling the words. "You have work to do, don't you?"

I hesitated.

"Yeah, I thought so. And you, ghost, you have stuff to do, too. Important stuff."

"Dad—"

"Justis, you can't babysit me!" He huffed a breath and tried with little success to smooth his hair. "You can't stay here forever," he went on after a few moments, his tone less strident. "And you've already made things better."

"But for how long?"

"For all of it," he said. "I mean that. Even when they're doing their worst, I still have a shred of myself to hold on to. And knowing that you believe me, that both of you do . . . That's worth something."

I could do more good back in the city, following up on the few leads I had. I knew this. But the thought of leaving him to these bastards was more than I could handle.

He saw me struggling and managed a smile that broke my heart. "Go. I'll be all right."

"I'll be back. I'll try to come tonight; tomorrow at the latest."

"Good. Bring more ice cream."

I stood, hugged him, and put my chair back.

"Farewell, Lokni. Be well."

"Take care of him, Namid," Dad said.

"I will do what I can."

Before the myste could leave, I said, "Ride with me back to the city. I have a few more questions for you." At Namid's frown, I added, "Please."

"For a short while."

I climbed back into the Z-ster. When I glanced toward the passenger seat, the myste was already there, his waters still and clear.

I held my tongue until we were away from the trailer and back on the main road through Wofford.

"So?" I asked.

Sometimes Namid could be pretty dense, and I half expected him to act like he didn't know what I was asking. But this time at least, he answered the question.

"I believe that he has been under siege from necromancers," he said. "That is the lone explanation for what I saw and what he told us. But I do not know what they hope to gain by causing him pain. Forgive me, but he is an old man and represents neither a threat to them nor a prize to be won. You, on the other hand, are a formidable enemy and, potentially, a valuable ally."

"I'd never ally myself with necromancers."

"You and I know this to be true; they do not. And they may believe that by using your father in this way, they can manipulate you."

As much as I hated to admit it, that made a good deal of sense.

"Is there more you wish to ask me?"

A part of me simply wanted an excuse to keep Namid around. The necromancers had fled my father's mind as soon we showed up, and the rhymes-with-witch who warned me at Solana's and tried to crush my heart on the Sun Valley Parkway—the one who, as it happened, was also tormenting my father—had made herself scarce since the myste's arrival. He was like a good luck charm.

I couldn't keep him here forever, but as it happened, I did have another question for him.

"The runemyste you mentioned before, the one who was murdered—where did that happen? And when?"

It was a stab in the dark, nothing more. And yet, somehow I knew what he would tell me.

"She was killed within the last two days; we do not

know exactly when. And the body of the weremyste was found in what you would call Northern Virginia, near—"

"Washington, D.C."

The myste's gleaming eyes bored into me like lasers. "You knew this?"

"I guessed."

"Guessed," he repeated.

"An educated guess." I gave him the *Reader*'s *Digest* history of Flight 595, and, without mentioning Amaya's name, told him what little I'd learned about Regina Witcombe and Patty Hesslan-Fine.

"This could be coincidence," Namid said in a way that told me he didn't believe it was.

"It's not," I said. "I would never argue with you when it comes to crafting spells. You're the expert. But this other stuff—this is what I do. These are not coincidences. It's all connected in some way. Dark magic killed your fellow runemyste at the same time these two women were in that part of the country. And as soon as I started investigating them, a necromancer blew up my girlfriend and tried to kill me on a lonely stretch of highway."

He faced forward again, his features ice-hard. "I will make inquiries among my kind," he said.

"I'll do the same."

"If you can help us identify the dark ones responsible, you would be doing us a great service. But you must tread like the fox, Ohanko."

"Don't I always?"

He faced me again. "No, you do not. Most times you are reckless and foolish. You place yourself in danger more often than I care to consider. But you cannot be so careless with this. Necromancers hate my kind with a blinding passion; it consumes them, driving all that they do. In pursuit of victory over the Runeclave, they would think nothing of killing weremystes and humans. You must exercise more caution than usual."

"I will," I said, sobered less by his words than the gravity with which he spoke them. I didn't often see Namid frightened; it wasn't a pretty sight.

The myste nodded once, and vanished. I had to resist an urge to drive home and hide under my bed with my Glock and every magical herb I had in the house. Instead, I pulled out my phone and called Kona at home. Driving and dialing again; I hated myself a little. But I couldn't bring myself to pull over. As it was, I expected at any moment to feel that clawed hand take hold of my heart once more.

Margarite answered and after a bit of chit-chat, told me that Kona was at 620, despite it being close to four o'clock on a Saturday afternoon. I shouldn't have been surprised. Between the murder at Sky Harbor Airport, the attack on Solana's, and the murders committed by Dimples and his weremancer friends, she, Kevin, and the rest of the Phoenix Police Department had plenty to keep them busy 24/7.

I didn't bother calling her at 620 from the highway; I just drove into the city.

Somehow, I made it downtown without being killed or run off the road by a silver sedan. I parked near 620 and called Kona's number as I walked to police headquarters. She answered on the second ring.

"Shaw."

"Hey, partner."

"Well, if it isn't the television star."

It took me a minute to remember my on-air temper tantrum outside of Solana's. "Oh, right."

"That was must-see TV, Justis. Hibbard in particular gave you rave reviews."

"Billie and I were in there. She almost died."

"I know," she said, the sarcasm leaching out of her voice. "I'm sorry. How's she doing?"

"Last time I saw her she was doing okay, improving. Listen, I'm parked nearby. Can you come down? We have a lot to talk about."

"I'm pretty much slammed right now. Two terrorist attacks in less than a week, not to mention that murder in Sweetwater Park—even with the federal boys taking over the lion's share of the airport and bombing investigations, I have more than enough to keep me up nights, know what I'm saying?"

"The attack on Solana's wasn't a bombing. It was magic. I should have told you sooner, but—"

"You think?" she demanded, voice spiraling upward again. "That would have been helpful information!"

"And I'm ready to tell you everything I can. But I think we'd be better off talking about it outside of 620."

She heaved a sigh. "Should I bring Kevin?"

"Sure, why not? The more the merrier, right?"

"Where are you?"

"I'll be right across the street."

"We'll be down in five."

It didn't even take them that long. Kona was

uncharacteristically sheepish as they crossed the street and approached me.

It was Kevin who said, "She's sorry for how she was on the phone."

"He your spokesman now?"

"Probably should be," Kona said. "I am sorry. Billie was hurt, you've probably been working on this night and day since it happened. And I should have guessed from the way you were on television that it wasn't an ordinary bombing. You know better than to talk to the press. But a spell aimed at you and your woman—that would throw anyone off their game."

"Thanks." I glanced at Kevin. "Both of you."

"What can you tell us?" Kona asked.

"Not much right now. There seems to be dark magic flowing in every direction, and I don't know what to do with it all. The body at Sweetwater Park, some weird stuff happening with my father, the attack on Solana's. And those don't even cover the worst of it."

"I know I'm going to regret asking this," Kona said. "But what's the worst of it?"

"One of Namid's kind was murdered in the last day or so."

Kona's mouth fell open. "I didn't think they were mortal."

"Namid's the ghost-thing you told me about the other day, right?" Kevin asked. "The one who helps you train?"

Namid would hate the description, but I didn't see any point in correcting him.

"That's right." To Kona I said, "I didn't know they were mortal, either. Even Namid is at a loss to explain what happened. But somehow one was killed. I'm wondering if you've had any reason to investigate Regina Witcombe since I left the force."

"Witcombe," Kevin said. "Don't tell me she's into magic, too."

"Dark magic, from what I hear."

"Shit, Justis. This keeps getting better and better." Kona closed her eyes, rubbed the bridge of her nose between her thumb and forefinger. "No, I haven't had anything to do with the woman. Neither has anyone else on the force as far as I know. I've been convinced for years that she had her husband killed, but we were never—" Her hand dropped to her side. "We were never able to prove it. And now you're telling me that she's a myste, too." She shook her head. "Well, at least now I know how she got away with it."

"Any new leads on the Sweetwater Park murder?" I asked.

She shook her head. "We've got nothing. I was going to ask you the same thing. What can you tell me about what happened at Solana's?"

I gazed across the street at 620. "It was aimed at me. I heard someone speak to me after the explosion. 'A warning. Do not push too hard.' That's what she said."

"She? You think it was Witcombe?"

"No, I don't. I think Regina Witcombe is a weremyste. Like me, but richer, and into dark magic. I think Solana's was attacked by someone who's more on Namid's level."

"So it was aimed at you," Kevin said, studying me with a critical eye. "And yet your girlfriend's the one who's in the hospital."

"Kevin!" Kona said.

"He's right. That might be the weirdest part of it. Nothing happened to me. Nothing at all. I didn't so much as tear a fingernail. No cuts, no bruises, no burns." Kona glanced at my jaw. "I got the bruise elsewhere," I told her. "I'm serious: Nothing happened to me at the restaurant. Someone blew up Solana's to send me a message, and at the same time did everything in her power to keep me safe."

The words echoed in my head. Kona asked me something, but I didn't hear her. I was remembering the touch of magic dancing along my skin the instant before the explosion, and also the tickle of magic I'd felt before Mark Darby shot at me. There should have been some residue of power on me after both episodes. That there wasn't must have meant something.

"There's no residue on my dad, either," I whispered.

"What are you talking about? Are you all right?"

My gaze snapped to Kona's face. "This wasn't the first time she saved me," I said. "The night before, I was working on a case and nearly got myself shot. By all rights, I should have died. But someone cast a spell that saved my life. I still don't know who."

"So there's some weremyste out there—"

"I told you: She's not a weremyste. She's too powerful for that."

"All right. Some magical entity. And she's doing everything she can to keep you alive, while at the same time blowing up your favorite restaurant and the woman you love with it."

"Sounds a little crazy doesn't it?"

Kevin exhaled. "I'm glad you said that, and not me."

"Welcome to life with Justis," Kona said. "Crazy just follows him around."

"I need to speak with Witcombe," I said, "and I'm not sure how best to get close to her."

Kevin gave a small shake of his head. "She has a security detail. A good one. If she doesn't want to talk to you, you won't get past them."

Kona and I exchanged glances. She grinned.

It was like a light bulb went on over Kevin's head. "Unless you happen to have magic."

"You don't know her address in Paradise Valley, do you?"

"No!" Kona said. "Talking about this is one thing. Giving you an address so that you can go harass arguably the most influential woman in the city? That's something else entirely."

"She was on the plane."

For the second time in about five minutes, Kona stared at me as if I'd sprouted wings and flown over 620. "By 'the plane,' you mean . . ."

"Flight 595. For all I know, she killed Jimmy Howell. Then she flew to Washington, and within twenty-four hours of her arrival there, one of Namid's fellow runemystes was murdered in—wait for it—Northern Virginia."

She pursed her lips.

"Does that change things a little?" I asked.

"Not as much as you'd think. In case you've forgotten, the PPD doesn't investigate murders of runemystes, or, for that matter, murders that take place two thousand miles beyond the state border."

"And the plane?"

"There were lots of people on the plane. We have no evidence whatsoever—at least none that's admissible—implicating Regina Witcombe in either murder or sabotage. Add to that the fact that the FBI guys practically claw out our eyes anytime someone from the department gets near their desks, and there's really not much I can do for you."

I nodded. I could call back Sally Peters, who had access to the real estate databases, but I was sure her company would frown on her giving out private information, too.

"Of course," Kona went on a moment later, "a woman like Witcombe is probably at her office more often than she's at home, even on a Saturday. And corporate addresses are easy to find, even for a private investigator."

Kevin snorted.

I lifted an eyebrow. "I'd thought of going to her office. But I figure that's where I'm most likely to encounter that security detail Kevin mentioned. She might relax a bit at home."

Kona frowned. "I hate it when he's right."

"If I find something, you know I'll bring it to you. Wouldn't you like to beat the FBI guys at their own game?"

"Go back inside, Kevin."

Kevin's face fell. "What'd I do?"

"Nothing," Kona said, rounding on him. "I'm trying to protect your ass. If I get caught doing something wrong, I want you to be able to swear on a stack of Bibles that you knew nothing about it. Now get back to work."

His eyes narrowed a bit, and his expression hardened. But after a moment his gaze flicked in my direction. "Jay."

"See you later, Kevin."

He said nothing to Kona before walking away, crossing the street and entering 620. Once Kona couldn't see him anymore, she faced me again.

"I'll get you Witcombe's address. I'll call you with it. But I don't like this."

"For what it's worth, I don't either."

She dipped her chin. "I believe that. Twice now you've mentioned your father. What's he got to do with this?"

"I wish I knew. He's been . . . someone's been hurting him, using magic to . . . to do I-don't-even-know-what. I don't understand what's happening to him, but I'd bet everything I own that it's tied in some way to the rest of this."

Her lips pursed again, and I could tell what she was thinking.

"You're taking a lot on faith. I appreciate that."

"I was thinking that the full moon's only a couple of days away, and you get a little funny even before the phasings start."

"Is that a polite way of suggesting that I might be imagining all of this?"

"No," she said. "I'm sure that it's all happening the way you say it is. But this strikes me as a little odd—you're hearing voices, your father is suffering—"

"You mean, my father the nutcase."

"And then there's the plane, and Solana's. And even that bit about you almost getting shot. What is all this, Justis?"

I shook my head and started to answer, but she held up a hand, stopping me.

"Kevin's inside. This is just you and me. And I'm asking if there's more to this than you're saying."

I wasn't sure how to answer. If she thought the rest of it sounded over the top, how would she react when I started talking about a magical war? But I thought again of Jacinto Amaya and how I'd kept from her that he was my source on the role of dark magic in the ritual killings she and Kevin were investigating. The last thing I wanted was to alienate her further with more secrets.

"Yeah, there is," I told her. "We seem to be on the brink of . . . well, of a kind of magical civil war."

She blinked. "That doesn't sound so good."

"It's not. When runemystes start dying, you know that things are headed in a bad direction."

CHAPTER 16

My cell rang before I'd made it back to my car. Kona gave me the address, whispering so quietly I had to ask her to repeat herself twice before I could make out all of it, which probably defeated the purpose of all that whispering.

Not surprisingly, Regina Witcombe lived in one of the most exclusive neighborhoods in the entire Phoenix metropolitan area, in a mansion that was about six times the size of my place in Chandler. It also didn't come as a surprise to me to find that the house had a sophisticated security system, as well as armed guards, several of whom were accompanied by German shepherds that made Gary Hacker in coyote form look like a chihuahua.

The guards, and even the security sensors, could be fooled by a decent camouflage spell. The dogs were the problem. They could hear almost anything, and what their ears missed, their noses would find. Trying to sneak into the Witcombe estate would be idiotic, the kind of thing you might see in a movie, right before the hero is captured by his nemesis.

I decided to try a more direct approach. I drove up to the front gate and smiled at the guy in the guardhouse, who could have been a walking advertisement for a home gym.

"Can I help you?" he asked as I rolled down my window. He sported a military-style buzz cut and carried a CZ 75 nine millimeter in a shoulder holster. His navy blue uniform had to be a couple of sizes too small, but given how big his biceps were I wasn't sure they made shirts in his size.

"I'm here to see Missus Witcombe. My name is Jay Fearsson. I'm a private detective doing some work for the Phoenix Police Department. I'd like to talk to her about Flight 595."

Whatever he'd expected me to say, that wasn't it. Sometimes, nothing flummoxed a potential adversary like the unvarnished truth.

"Is she expecting you?" he asked.

"No."

He stepped back into the guardhouse, picked up the phone, and punched in a three-digit number. Seeing that I was watching him, he shut the guardhouse door and turned his back on me. I scanned the courtyard beyond the gate, taking in the Spanish mission-style house and the vast desert garden in front of it, complete with prickly pear and ocotillo, teddy-bear cholla and barrel cacti. A pair of orioles darted past, flashes of orange and black in the afternoon sun.

After a brief conversation, the guard came back out. "She's unavailable right now. She suggests that you call her office on Monday. Her attorney will be happy to answer any questions you might have."

"Could you let her know that I've already spoken with Patty Hesslan-Fine. The three of us have a good deal in common. You should tell her that, as well, and that she'll see what I mean as soon as she meets me."

Buzz-Cut glared at me, and I was sure he'd refuse. I half-expected him to pick up my car and toss it back into the street. But he stalked back into the guardhouse and made a second phone call.

This conversation went on longer than had the first. Several times he glanced back at me and at one point he laid down the receiver on his desk and came out to ask for my PI and driver's licenses. After a few minutes he hung up, handed my IDs back to me, and waved me through the gate.

I parked beside a silver Mercedes—apparently silver was the car color of choice for weremancers this year—wound my way through the garden, and approached the front door. There, two more security officers, probably the guardhouse guy's workout partners, asked me if I was carrying a weapon. I handed over my Glock and let them wand me before I stepped through a metal detector. I thought it ironic that I'd been screened more thoroughly here than I had the other day at the airport. But I kept this thought to myself.

Regina Witcombe was waiting for me inside the front door. She was wearing beige slacks and a loose-fitting black tunic that might have been silk. Her auburn hair was tied back in a ponytail. She was taller than I'd expected—almost my height. I couldn't see much of her face—the blurring of her features was every bit as strong as Patty Hesslan's had been.

"Mister Fearsson," she said in that warm alto I'd heard in her online video. She extended a hand, which I gripped. "Welcome to my home."

"Thank you for agreeing to see me, Missus Witcombe. I'm sorry to have come unannounced."

"It's my pleasure. Thank you, Andrew," she said to the guard who had my Glock.

She led me through an enormous living room and then a rec room, complete with pool table, wet bar, and a television that wouldn't have fit through my front door, to an open patio that offered a breathtaking view of Camelback Mountain. More chollas and ocotillos grew in a pebbled garden that fringed the terrace. Anna's and black-chinned hummingbirds buzzed around a pair of red glass feeders like winged, iridescent gems.

"Can I offer you something, Mister Fearsson? Wine perhaps?"

"I'm fine, thank you."

She indicated a chair with an open hand and took a seat in the one beside it.

"Patricia says you and she share some history, though she wouldn't tell me what kind."

"Yes, ma'am. Our families are connected by a tragedy. None of us likes to speak of it."

"She also said that you came to her under false pretenses. Was that why?"

A reflexive smile touched my lips. "I suppose. I used a false name. I worried that she wouldn't agree to our meeting if she knew it was me."

She tipped her head to the side; I could see her frown through the blur of magic. "And now you come to me, supposedly with questions about the flight I was on Thursday morning. I'm not entirely sure I believe that."

"I understand your skepticism. But I assure you it's true. Kona Shaw, a detective in the homicide unit, asked me to help her with the PPD's investigation into the murder of James Howell."

"The man they found in the men's room."

"Yes, ma'am. You can call Detective Shaw to verify this."

"There's no need for that. I read about you in the paper a couple of months ago. I know you've worked with the police before."

"Yes, I have." I pulled my notebook and pen from the pocket inside my bomber. "Did you know Mister Howell?"

She quirked an eyebrow, seeming to say, *Are you really asking me that*? "Yes, Mister Fearsson. He and his white supremacist friends are on my board of directors."

I smirked. "Forgive me. Let me rephrase that. Were you aware of him on the flight?"

She shook her head. "Not really. I might have seen him come through first class, after I took my seat on the plane. It's not every day one sees a man with swastika tattoos on a commercial flight."

"Did you see him deplane?"

"No. By that time I knew that Patricia was on board and I was watching for her once I was back in the terminal."

"So you and she didn't sit together."

"No, we didn't. She flies coach; I don't."

"Did you take notice of any of the other passengers?"

She frowned again. "I'm not sure I know what you mean."

"Did you notice any other weremystes?"

"Ah," she said with a sage nod. "I take it Mister Howell was killed with magic."

Kona wouldn't be happy with me, but I didn't bother to deny it. "That's right."

"Your visit makes a bit more sense to me now. To answer your question, no, I can't say that I noticed any other weremystes. That doesn't mean there weren't any, but I didn't see them. And so, allow me to anticipate your next question. Patricia and I never went near the airport men's room. We remained by the gate, and, after the body was discovered, were questioned by the police. Once they were through with us, we went to the club lounge, of which I'm a member. We stayed there—chatting, getting some work done—until our new flight finally departed late in the day."

She was pretty convincing, and her story dovetailed perfectly with Patty's. I wondered if they'd worked on it together, or if they were both telling me the truth.

"And how was your time in Washington?"

For the first time, I sensed a weak point in her armor. Her smile slipped momentarily and I thought I saw a flicker of unease in her blue eyes.

"It was fine, thank you."

"You were there on business?"

"I'm not sure how this relates to your investigation, but yes, I was."

"And so was Patty? Excuse me: Patricia."

"I don't know why she was there."

I furrowed my brow. "Really? You spent hours with her in the terminal and then in the lounge, and it never occurred to you to ask why she was going to Washington?"

"Well, I'm sure I must have. I might . . . It was a business trip; I'm sure of that. I think she must have been meeting a potential client, someone who plans to move here in the near future. I was preoccupied with my testimony. I had some last-minute work to do before I appeared before the committee."

She shifted in her chair, no doubt trying to look casual; it had the opposite effect. I'd managed to put her on edge, and I decided to push her a little harder.

"I saw you on television," I said. "It must be quite an experience to testify before a Senate committee."

Her laugh sounded tight, nervous. "It's not really very exciting."

"The last time I was in Washington, I wound up spending some time in Arlington and Alexandria. Nice area. Did you get over to Northern Virginia this visit?"

"No." It was too abrupt, too final. I didn't believe her for a minute. "Is there anything else, Mister Fearsson? My time is quite valuable."

"I didn't recognize the magic that killed James Howell," I said, ignoring her question. "I used a seeing spell to try to learn what happened in the last moments of his life, but that didn't tell me much either. And it occurred to me that there have been some odd murders committed in the Phoenix area over the past couple of months. Some in the police department have been talking about cults and ritual killings, but I'm wondering if it's something else. Do you know anything about dark magic?"

She sat bolt upright. "Are you suggesting—?"

"I'm not suggesting anything. I'm certainly not accusing you of anything. I was just wondering what you know about the darker side of what we weremystes do."

"Nothing at all. And for you to imply otherwise is . . . is as ridiculous as it is insulting." She stood, smoothed her slacks with a shaking hand. "Now, I think you should leave."

I stood as well, knowing that I couldn't stay without her permission, and reluctant to get into a fight with her security guys. Before either of us could say more, though, the cordless phone on the table by her chair rang. She glared at me for another moment, but then grabbed the phone on the second ring and switched it on.

"Yes?" Her gaze flicked in my direction like a snake's tongue. "Yes, hold on." She put a hand over the receiver. "Wait here," she said to me. Before I could respond, she stepped back into the house and closed the glass door. She crossed through the rec room and out of sight, leaving me little choice but to remain there. Several minutes passed; I started to wonder if I wasn't being a fool. If this woman was guilty of a fraction of what I suspected, I needed to get the hell out of her house. I recited a spell in my head; three elements: any magic Witcombe might try on me, a shield of power, and me at the center of it. On the third recitation, I released the spell and felt the warding settle over me like a winter coat. Wardings worked better when they were specific to the attack spell, but I wasn't sure I would have that luxury if it came to a fight. This was better than nothing. With the spell in place, I checked the door connecting the patio to the house, half expecting to find it locked.

It wasn't. But as I opened it and took a step back inside the house, Missus Witcombe appeared in the rec room doorway on the other side of the room. She still held the phone, but her conversation appeared to have ended. When she spotted me, she faltered, then strode through the room in my direction.

"Where were we, Mister Fearsson?"

"You were in the process of throwing me out of your house."

She flashed a smile that made me shiver. "An overreaction on my part. Forgive me."

I remained in the doorway. "Still, perhaps I should leave."

"There's no need for that. Come back outside with me. We'll have a drink and discuss those questions of yours."

"The ones that outraged you? The ones about dark magic?"

"As I said, I overreacted."

I shook my head. "I shouldn't have asked them, and I have someplace I need to be." A lie, but I wanted out of there.

"But you did ask them, Mister Fearsson. And I feel that I should have the chance to respond."

We stood there for a few seconds, her eyes locked on mine. Eager as I was to be on my way, I found it hard to argue with her logic, and harder still to imagine how I would get past her guards if she didn't want to let me go.

I acquiesced with a lift of my shoulder and backed out of her way. She crossed to her chair and gestured for me to do the same.

I didn't trust this change of heart, and so I chose to stay on my feet, though I wandered a bit closer to where she sat.

"Dark magic is such an odd term, don't you think?"

"I suppose," I said.

"I mean, for centuries it was all considered dark, wasn't it? The witch trials and all that."

"I had something specific in mind, Missus Witcombe, and I think you understood that when I asked the question. Now, I don't know who that was on the phone, and I don't think I want to find out. Thank you for speaking with me. I'm going to leave now."

I turned to go. But before I could take more than a step, the air around me chimed like a plucked harp. Magic. For a split second, I was glad I had warded myself. Then her spell took shape, and I realized once more the limitations of such a general-purpose shield spell. I'd protected myself from an attack. But she had cast a barrier spell on the door. I hit it and bounced back, feeling like I'd walked into brick.

I clung to that image—the brick wall—and added two more elements: a sledgehammer and me swinging it. Her barrier gave way, but by now she was on her feet.

"Andrew!" she called.

He must have been waiting for her summons, because almost as soon as she called his name, he loomed in the rec room doorway, also as solid as brick. He hadn't drawn his weapon, but that hardly mattered.

I considered another spell: an attack on him; the magical equivalent of a two-by-four to the head. But before I could cast, magic tinged the air once more.

"I wouldn't cast if I were you," Witcombe said from behind me. "Whatever you do to him will rebound."

Andrew folded his massive arms over his chest and stared at me, impassive, implacable.

"Come back outside, Mister Fearsson. Our conversation isn't finished, and you're not going anywhere."

I faced her once more, then stepped past her onto the patio.

"Stay where you can see us," she said to the guard. "If he tries to escape or does anything to me, shoot him."

"Yes, ma'am."

Witcombe shut the door and sat again. I lingered near the house.

"Oh, come now, Mister Fearsson. Sit back down. Have a drink. You're not leaving, but that doesn't mean you have to brood about it."

I returned to my chair.

"That's better," she said, purring the words.

"Why did you go to Washington?" I asked her.

"I don't think I want to tell you that."

I nodded, not at all surprised by her answer. "Then maybe you'd like to tell me how an ordinary weremyste like you managed to kill an ancient runemyste granted eternal life by the Runeclave more than seven centuries ago."

"I don't know what you're talking about."

"I think you're lying."

The smile that touched her lips must have been the

one she reserved for employees who had really pissed her off. "You'll find that I don't like being called a liar, any more than I do being called ordinary."

I opened my hands. "You're the one who told me that our conversation wasn't done, who said that you deserved a chance to answer my questions. So talk to me, Missus Witcombe. What do you know about dark magic? What dark spells have you cast recently?"

"Where did you get the idea that I was involved with such things?"

"You're famous here in Phoenix. People talk."

"Rumors," she said, dismissing them with her tone. "Gossip."

"I believe what I heard rises above that level. And my friends at the police department agreed."

The smile remained fixed on her lips, but some of the color fled her cheeks. "A false accusation. You could face serious legal consequences."

"First you'd have to prove it false. What do you know about those ritual killings I mentioned?"

"Nothing."

"I don't believe that, either."

"You don't seem to grasp how much trouble you're in, Mister Fearsson. Calling me a liar again and again is only going to make matters worse."

"What do you think you can do to me?" I asked, with more bravado than I felt. "Several of your guards saw me come in. Others saw me drive to your house. My car is still sitting in your driveway. And friends of mine at the PPD know that I was headed here. If something happens to me, or I vanish, this is the first place they'll come looking."

The door opened behind us, and a woman's voice said, "That shouldn't be a problem."

I stood. Patty Hesslan-Fine stepped out onto the patio. She wore the same business suit she'd had on for our meeting this morning.

"You haven't been very smart, have you, Jay?" She shifted her gaze to Witcombe. "Why the hell did you let him in here in the first place? I warned you about him when we spoke earlier"

"He used your name, and made it sound like you wanted me to speak with him. I assumed it was all right."

Patty shook her head. "Next time assume nothing. Speak to me first. Do you understand?"

Witcombe nodded.

"What were you doing up in Washington, Patty?" I asked. "What was your excuse for making the trip?"

She eyed me coolly. "It's Patricia. I haven't gone by Patty since I was seventeen years old. And I told you this morning: It was a business trip."

"And your jaunt over to Northern Virginia?"

Her expression didn't change. I already had the sense that, at least in matters of magic, Witcombe answered to her and not the other way around. I could see why.

"You think you're terribly clever, don't you? You were a dead man anyway, but I'm afraid the timetable has been pushed up a bit. It's your own doing."

"What do you mean?" Witcombe asked. "Pushed up to what?"

Patty continued to regard me, her brow creased. "I am interested to know how you learned about Regina. Surely you're not intelligent enough to have figured that out for yourself."

I said nothing.

"Fine." She faced Witcombe once more. "Tell the guard he can go back outside. Is your assistant still here?"

"You mean Heather?"

"Yes, Heather. Is she in the house?"

Witcombe nodded.

"Good. Get rid of the guard and then call for Heather."

"But—"

"Just do as I say."

Regina pasted a smile on her lips and walked back into the house, leaving the glass door ajar. "Everything is fine now, Andrew. Just a small misunderstanding. You can go back out front."

"Are you sure, Missus Witcombe?"

"Yes, quite."

A few moments later, I heard Witcombe calling Heather's name. I kept my eyes on Patty.

"Do you really think she's ready for this?" I asked Patty. "She seems a bit beyond her depth. And murder . . . That's a big step for someone like her."

"She's killed before," Patty said, sounding bored. "Nice try, though."

When Witcombe joined us again on the patio, her cheeks were pale and she appeared nervous. "She'll be joining us shortly. What did you mean before? What are you doing to the timetable?"

"I didn't do anything to it. Fearsson did, and so did you. But it's obvious, isn't it? After all of this, we can't let him go. You decided his fate the moment you invited him into your house."

"You know I'm standing right here, don't you?"

Patty shot me a glare that could have melted the skin off my bones. "Shut up."

"You mean we have to do it now? Here?"

"Now, yes. Not here."

Witcombe seemed relieved to hear this.

"But still," Patty went on. "We need to be sure that we control him."

Neither of them had time to say more. A young woman appeared in the doorway—petite, pretty. She couldn't have been more than twenty-five years old. I would have guessed that Witcombe hired her right out of school. The poor kid probably thought it was the opportunity of a lifetime.

"Ah, Heather," Witcombe said.

The woman hovered in the doorway, clearly unsure of herself. "Is there something I can help you with, Missus Witcombe?"

Witcombe eyed Patty, who gave a single curt nod.

"Join us for a moment, won't you?" Witcombe said, the smile on her face doing nothing to mask her fear. "I'd like you to meet some people."

Heather joined us on the patio, pulling the glass door closed behind her.

I didn't know what Witcombe and Patty had in mind for her, but I cast a warding anyway, not on me, but on Heather. The gazes of both weremancers snapped my way as soon as I released the magic.

"What was that?" Witcombe asked.

I stared back at her, defiant.

"Nothing that matters," Patty said.

"Have you met Missus Hesslan-Fine?" Witcombe asked, even as Patty walked to the edge of the patio and gazed out at the mountain.

Heather shook her head. "I don't think so."

"She's the agent who found this house for me. And she helped me sell my old one. She's lived in this area for . . . How long has it been, Patricia?"

Patty didn't answer.

"Well, a long time."

Witcombe glanced my way, swallowed. "And this is . . . this is Mister Fearsson. He's a private detective."

Heather turned in my direction. At the same time, Patty spun and lunged, covering the distance between herself and the young woman in a single, shockingly sudden motion. Sunlight gleamed off something in her hand. I opened my mouth to shout a warning, but couldn't get the words out.

I'd warded Heather against attack spells. It never occurred to me to ward her against a knife blade.

Patty's aim was uncanny. She slashed with the knife along the side of Heather's neck, sending a spray of blood across the flagstone patio and a torrent of it down over the young woman's shoulder and chest.

Heather staggered, dropped to the ground. More blood pooled around her and ran in rivulets along the grouted seams between the stones.

Witcombe stumbled back a step, gaping in horror at what Patty had done "Oh, dear God! Heather! My God, my God!"

I dropped to my knees beside the girl, blood soaking my jeans, and put my hands over the wound. "The cut, my magic, her healed flesh! The cut, my magic, her healed flesh!"

I hadn't cast many healing spells, and I was too freaked out to try to recite the spell silently. As it was, the magic I summoned felt weak, inadequate to the task.

"Don't bother," Patty said, her voice so calm it made me want to snap her neck. "She was dead before she hit the ground."

"Her blood's still flowing. She's not dead."

"But you're not weremyste enough to save her, are you?"

I repeated the spell. But Patty was right: Heather was dying, and I wasn't strong enough to do anything about it.

Witcombe continued to babble and blubber, saying "My God, my God" again and again.

"Would you shut up already?" Patty snapped.

Witcombe whirled on her, the rebuke seeming to kick her out of her panic. "Are you fucking crazy? Killing her like that, here in my home? What in God's name were you thinking?"

"We need the blood," Patty said. "And I didn't kill her; Fearsson did. That's what we'll tell the police."

Something clattered on the stone beside me. The bloodied knife.

Three elements. My hand, Patty's foot, and a good hard tug. I'd used the spell before, and it worked every time. Her foot shot out from under her, and she landed hard on her back.

I scrambled up. And was hammered back to my knees

by what felt like the kick of a mule to my temple. Magic stirred over my skin a second time, and I was hit again. This time, I sprawled onto my back, too dazed to do more than lie there.

"Quickly now," Patty said to Witcombe. "You know the spell." She got to her feet and kicked me in the jaw with her open-toe shoe. It hurt more than I would have imagined.

I tried to get up, but another spell stopped me. This one seemed to thicken the air. Magic surrounded me, clung like heavy mist to my skin, my hair, my clothes. And then it fell upon my mind with the fury and finality of an avalanche. It buried my will, my ability to act. I tried another attack spell: fire this time. Nothing happened. I tried to sit up, to roll onto my knees

I raised my eyes to Patty; I couldn't so much as lift my head. She leered down at me, and for good measure she kicked me again, digging her foot into my side this time. I felt the impact, gasped for breath. But I couldn't raise my hands to clutch the spot she'd hit. I wasn't even sure I grunted.

"Dark magic, Jay. You should try it sometime. It really is exhilarating."

If I could have turned her into a torch, or peeled back the skin from her face, I would have done it. But I could no more cast than I could speak or get up and walk away.

I tore my eyes from her face—they seemed to be the one part of my body still under my control—and looked around. Heather lay beside me, her eyes open and fixed on the sky, a bit of blood oozing from the wound. Most of the blood, though, had vanished with the spell Patty and

Witcombe cast. I would have bet that even the blood on my jeans was gone, though the spell kept me from confirming the hunch.

The conjuring had put me in mind of a landslide. I imagined a giant shovel digging me out, removing this terrible weight, freeing me. The weight of the spell, the imagined shovel, and me. Nothing.

"You can't save yourself with a spell. You're ours now."

"What are we going to do with him?" Witcombe asked.

Patty loomed over me, regarding me the way she might a newly listed property. "Just what we planned to do all along. We're going to use him to kill his runemyste."

CHAPTER 17

I thought they would have to carry me—or have the guards do it. What they did instead was infinitely worse.

"Get up," Patty said, her voice echoing in my head.

I stared at her, wanting to tell her she was nuts, that obviously I was incapable of sitting up, much less getting to my feet.

But even as these thoughts flashed through my mind, I rolled onto my hands and knees and pushed myself up. My vision swam, and I felt like I was going to pass out, but I didn't sway.

"Get it now?" Patty said. "Pick up the knife." Again, the command reverberated in my head, the power lashing at me.

God knew I didn't want to do it. Her control spell had wiped the blade free of blood, but her fingerprints were still on the hilt, and that was the only way I'd be able to prove that she, and not I, had killed Heather.

"By the hilt," she said.

I bent and picked it up.

"Grip it the way you would if you were about to stab someone."

I fought her with every ounce of strength I possessed. The effort should have been enough to make my muscles tremble, my pulse race. But I had the feeling that no one watching me would have noticed at all. I wrapped my fingers around the handle, which was made of some dark, polished wood.

Etienne de Cahors had used similar magic against me when I fought him, but somehow this was worse. Patty and Witcombe were weremystes, like me. They shouldn't have been strong enough to control me with such ease.

"Now," Patty said, voice echoing, "hold that blade to my throat."

I did as she said, laying the honed edge along her neck just below her jaw line. She showed no fear at all. Her smile, the look in her eyes: She was as sure of her power over me as she was of her own name.

"You'd like to kill me, wouldn't you?" she said, her voice low, so that only I could hear. "It wouldn't take much; a flick of your wrist, and I'd probably be dead before anyone could stop the bleeding. But you can't do it, because you belong to me, completely, utterly, without hope of reprieve. You can fight me all you like. You can try to cast spells, you can resist until your heart bursts within your chest. It won't matter. Our spell will hold you until you're dead."

Or until you are. I wanted to scream the words at her. Nothing.

"Put the knife in your pocket."

I slipped it into the inside pocket of my bomber, despising myself.

"What about her?" Witcombe asked, gawping down at Heather's body, her cheeks ashen.

Patty eyed me in a way that made my stomach clench. "Jay will carry her out to his car and put her in the back. We'll decide what to do with her later." She faced Witcombe. "But first you need to clear out your guards. Too much to explain if they see us with the girl's body."

Witcombe eyed me. "But won't—?"

"Jay's not going anywhere without my permission. We don't need the guards right now. We need privacy."

Witcombe nodded and hurried into the house.

"Hard to believe, isn't it?" Patty said, gazing after her. She waved a hand toward the view. "To the rest of world, she's a corporate giant, one of the most powerful women in the country. But as you can see, she's a bit pathetic. She's handy to have around—all that money, you know. But otherwise she isn't good for much. And before long, I'll have access to enough income that we won't even need her for that. For now, though, in our circles—yours and mine—she answers to me. Just like you do. Stay here. Don't move."

She went back into the house, and emerged a short while later with a drink. It smelled like Scotch. She sat in the chair I'd used a short while before and sipped her drink, ignoring me.

And still I fought, straining at the invisible bonds that held me, desperate to lift a hand, to grab hold of that knife again, to kill Patty and escape to my car. I felt a tickle of sweat on my temple and couldn't even wipe it away.

We're going to use him to kill his runemyste.

I had no idea how they planned to make me do this. The day before, I would have sworn that Patty was delusional, because I knew with the conviction of the ignorant that runemystes couldn't be killed.

Thanks to Namid, I now knew better. And thanks to Patty, I understood in the vaguest sense how it might be possible. What had Namid said when I asked how his fellow runemyste died?

We do not know. We know only that one of her weremystes was killed as well. They died together, perhaps battling a necromancer and his or her servants.

What if they hadn't been fighting side by side, but instead had battled each other? What if the weremyste had been controlled, just as I was now, and had been used as a weapon against the runemyste?

I wouldn't know how to kill Namid. Surely I didn't have the power to defeat him in magical combat. But he trusted me, as I trusted him. I could get close to him, enable someone who wielded as weapons my body and my runecrafting to strike a killing blow.

Is that what Patty and Witcombe had done to the runemyste in Virginia?

"You're awfully quiet," Patty said, without turning. Then she laughed. She swiveled in her chair to face me and narrowed her eyes. "Why do *you* have a runemyste? I've felt your magic now, and it doesn't strike me as being terribly powerful. And yet, from what I've been told, a runemyste has taken interest in you. He's training you. So he must see some potential that I'm missing. And you did kill Cahors, though I'd wager that was more dumb luck than anything else."

The door swung open once more and Witcombe bustled out onto the patio. "They're gone for now. The ones around the house, that is. There are still men at the guardhouse, but I assume that's all right."

Patty regarded me for a moment longer. "Yes, that should be fine. Jay and I will take his car. You'll follow us."

"Where are we going?"

"His house, I think."

"And . . . and Heather?"

"I told you, we'll work that out later. But I think that Jay's status as city hero is about to end. A messy murder-suicide with a pretty young thing like Heather should do the trick." She drained her Scotch and levered herself out of the chair. "Pick her up," she said, her voice taking on that echoing quality once more.

I lifted Heather's body into my arms and then slung her over my shoulder.

"Very good. We're heading out to your car now. You're going to follow Regina through the house, doing exactly as she says." She stepped forward and reached a hand into my jeans pocket, her eyes finding mine once more, a mocking leer on her lips. She pulled out my car keys and held them up for me to see. "Go," she said to Witcombe.

The word didn't echo as her commands did in my head, but they had the same effect. Witcombe made her way through the house, and I followed. She glanced back at me every few seconds, acting like she was afraid to have me so close to her—or perhaps afraid of the corpse I carried. My eyes scanned the furniture as we walked. Even knowing that I was helpless, I searched for something I could use as a weapon or a distraction. Not that I could take advantage of either. I followed, as dutiful as a trained puppy.

Once we were outside, Patty had me halt and wait as she opened the back hatch of the Z-ster.

"Put her in here."

I laid Heather's body down in the back, taking care not to let the little bit of blood on her neck touch the upholstery. The significance of this wasn't lost on me. Patty hadn't told me how I should position the body, and so I could put her in there any way I wanted. As loopholes went it wasn't much. But maybe I wasn't completely helpless after all.

"Get in the car." The command echoed as had the others. "And drive us back to your home, obeying all traffic rules, taking the most direct route possible, and doing nothing to draw undue attention to your car or to us."

I climbed into the car on the driver's side, sifting through her words for something—anything—that I could do, within the constraints of her instructions, to gain the upper hand. Nothing came to me. She had been specific enough to keep me on task, and general enough to leave no loopholes. I had the sense that she had done something like this several times before.

I drove back to Chandler with Regina Witcombe trailing me in her silver Mercedes. Thanks to Patty, I was the model driver, hitting the speed limits dead on, using my directionals for every lane change and every turn. Anyone who knew me well enough to have driven with me would have realized straight away that something was wrong; I wasn't *this* good a driver. But to the strangers on

Phoenix's freeways, I was just another grunt in a car, following the rules and driving in the slow lane.

As we neared my house, my cell phone rang. I couldn't reach for it, or even glance Patty's way to gauge what she wanted me to do.

On the second ring, she reached over and took the phone from my jacket pocket.

"Kona Shaw," she said.

My heart leaped.

"She was your partner when you were a cop, wasn't she?" She dropped the phone into the tray behind the stick shift. "That's a call you won't be taking."

Fine with me, I wanted to say. I *always* took Kona's calls. She'd try again, and if I didn't answer a second time, she'd come looking for me.

I felt Patty's eyes on me, and I wondered if mastering my body in this way also allowed her to read my emotions. Or maybe she was simply too smart for my own good.

"Except that you probably take her calls all the time, don't you? I've heard that partners on the force get very close. It's practically like a marriage. If she calls again, you'll have to answer."

Call again, Kona.

The sun had gone down by the time I navigated the streets of Chandler to my house. It hadn't gotten completely dark yet, but it wouldn't be long. I parked in the driveway and sat, waiting for Patty's next set of commands. Glancing at my rearview mirror, I saw Witcombe's car glide to a stop by the curb in front of my house.

Patty took my keys from the ignition. "You're going to get out, shut the car door, and walk to the door of your house acting like nothing is the matter. You'll allow me to unlock your front door. If a neighbor calls to you, you'll wave and smile before continuing to the house. Now get out."

I opened my door, climbed out of the Z-ster, and closed the car door. Patty joined me, and we walked to the house. She unlocked the door, pushed it open, and waved me inside. "Go in and stop in the middle of the first room. Keep your hands where I can see them."

I walked into the house and did as instructed. She was too good at this, too thorough. I needed help.

And as we waited for Witcombe to join us, I got it.

My cell rang again. Patty still held the phone, and she checked the incoming number, frowning. "It's Shaw."

"Who's Shaw?" Witcombe asked as she entered the house.

"Fearsson's partner on the police force. This is the second time she's called."

"Ignore it."

Patty shook her head. "She'll keep calling." She held up the phone for me to see as it rang a second time, but didn't hand it to me right away.

"You're going to talk to her, but tell her nothing about us or what I've done to you. You'll keep your tone casual, and you'll say nothing about being in trouble or needing help." A third ring. She handed me the phone. "Now answer, on speaker."

I opened it, unable to refuse. But on the inside I was doing cartwheels. Patty's commands had been rushed, because she didn't want Kona to get no answer a second time. She'd left loopholes all over the place.

"Fearsson," I said.

"Hey, partner. Where have you been?" Kona's voice sounded thin and tinny on the tiny speakers, but I'd never been so happy to hear her.

"Busy day," I said. "I've been all over."

"Did you get out to Paradise Valley?"

Patty and Witcombe shared a look.

"Yes, I did. Thanks again. Tell Hibbard thanks, too."

Kona's pause was a split second longer than it ought to have been. I wasn't sure that Patty would notice, but I certainly did. Kona knew something was wrong. "I'll tell him," she said. "He's gone for the day, but I'll tell him. Where are you now?"

"Lie to her." Patty mouthed the words, lending only enough breath to make them chime in my mind.

But I felt the compulsion; I was incapable of telling Kona I was at home. Once more, though, haste had made Patty careless.

"I'm with Billie at her place."

"Nice. Tell her 'hi' for me."

"I will."

"Listen, I just called to let you know that we've cleared the Sweetwater Park case. We won't be needing your help on that anymore."

"Good for you, Kona. Glad to hear it."

Message received. I'd told her a whopper, and she had come back at me with the same. She knew I was in trouble.

"Thanks. I guess I'll talk to you next week."

"Sounds good."

I snapped the phone shut. Patty took it out of my hand and tossed it onto my couch. "That was well done. You see how easy this is when you follow directions?"

I stared back at her, hoping that she would see rage and impotence in my glower.

"We need to hurry. In case that conversation wasn't as innocent as it sounded." Patty glanced toward the windows that faced out onto the street. "Close those blinds."

She didn't say it as a magical command, so I remained as I was. Patty glanced Witcombe's way. "Now!"

"I thought you meant him."

As Witcombe lowered the blinds, Patty said to me, "Usually we do this with weremystes who have already been turned to our cause. We don't have that kind of time with you. Not anymore. So we'll have to try a different way. Take off your jacket and your shirt, and then retrieve my knife from your jacket pocket."

I had forgotten I was carrying it. I shrugged off my bomber and pulled off my shoulder holster and T-shirt. Then I took the blade out of the jacket pocket and held it out to her.

She didn't take it from me. "Grip the knife, but don't use it against anyone. Not yet."

Half-dressed, I felt cold and vulnerable. I didn't like where this was going. I tightened my hold on the knife hilt and waited.

In my mind, though, I said, *Namid, I need help.*

"Regina are you ready to cast the spell?"

Witcombe nodded.

Ohanko. Namid didn't materialize in the house, but I heard him speak in my mind. *I am here, but you know I cannot help you.*

Can you tell me how to break her hold on me?

"I want you to listen closely to me, Jay," she said, her words echoing loudly in my head. "We need blood for this casting as well. But you can't cut too deeply. The spell takes time, and we can't have you passing out before we're ready. I want you to draw the blade . . ."

She controls you? Somehow I heard the runemyste's voice over hers, though he didn't seem to be speaking any louder than usual.

Yes. The two of them cast a blood spell. The body of their source is in my car. I can't fight them. I can't even cast.

". . . The symbols should look like this." She had drawn a circle; I didn't remember her having a pen and paper. Now, within the circle, she drew a stylized P with the loop pointy rather than rounded, like the corner of a triangle. Beside it, she drew a second symbol: a vertical line with a slash through it. And then a third: a plain vertical line.

If you cannot cast, I do not know how to help you.

I'm going to die here, Namid. You have to do something.

You must find a way to craft, Ohanko. They control your entire being, but the magic is attacking your mind. If you can shield it, you can win your freedom.

But I told you—

". . . And when I say so, you will summon him."

The world seemed to fall away beneath me. If I'd had control over my limbs, my knees would have buckled.

There was only one being I could summon: Namid.

And he was right here with me, so close he could have whispered in my ear. In my desperation to break free of their spell, I had endangered the runemyste.

Leave me, Namid. And when I summon you again, don't respond. Stay away from me.

I do not—

They'll use blood. The summoning will be powerful. You might not be able to resist it on your own. Get others to help you. Whatever you do, don't come when I call you!

Ohanko, you are—

Listen to me, ghost! They plan to use me to kill you. Just the way they killed your friend in Northern Virginia. Now, go!

"What are you doing, Jay?"

Patty had stepped closer to me, so that her face was inches from mine. An instant later, pain exploded in my chest, as if the same bomb that destroyed Solana's had gone off inside me. I let out a small huff of air, but couldn't clutch at my heart or fold in on myself as I wanted to. I could do no more than stand there, the pain making me grind my teeth.

"What are you doing, Jay?" she demanded again, biting off each word, and at the same time imbuing them with magic, so that I heard them with reverb.

"Warning Namid," I said, the words torn from my throat.

"You shouldn't have."

The air shivered with another spell, and I heard bones break. Agony. It felt like she had smashed my left hand with a brick. My stomach heaved, though I managed somehow not to throw up.

"It shouldn't matter, really. The blood compels him, so long as the spell is cast correctly. But to make it interesting, if your warnings keep him away, you'll pay a price. If, after the spell is cast, he's not here in ten seconds, I'll shatter your knee. Ten seconds after that, I'll break the other one. You don't have to be standing for any of this to work. When I'm done with your knees, I'll move on to your elbow, your femur, your tibia. And so on. Now, cut your wrist."

I turned over my mangled hand, so that I exposed the underside of my wrist. And using the knife I held in my other hand, I angled the blade so that I would hit only artery and carved through my skin with the precision of a surgeon. The pain brought tears to my eyes and drew another chuffing of breath. But all I could do was watch as blood coursed from the gash, running over the blade and down my hand, and dripping onto the pale carpet.

"That's enough," Patty said. "Not too deep, remember?" She took the blade from me. "Now, the pattern."

I dabbed a finger in the blood and drew a circle that encompassed my chest and belly. Gathering more blood, I made the stylized P, the line with the slash through it, and the second vertical line. Somehow, I drew them so that they would appear to Patty as they were meant to, though from my perspective they were upside down.

"I couldn't have done better myself." To Witcombe she said, "It's time!"

They chanted something in a language I didn't know. Once through, and then again.

"Get ready to summon him, Jay."

They began to speak the words a third time. Their incantation must have been intended to strengthen my summons, and to extend their control to Namid as well. I couldn't allow them to finish.

I'd never cast a blood spell before, but I knew in theory how it should work, and I had no time to second guess myself. I hoped the blood would allow me to overcome the control spell they'd used against me.

Patty, Witcombe, me, the spell they'd cast to control me, my mind, a shield, and the blood coursing from my wrist. Seven elements. I couldn't risk repeating it seven times. I gathered the elements in my thoughts and released the magic at the same time they completed their chanting. The hum of this spell reminded me of the crackling static electricity of rustling blankets on a winter's night. It slid along my skin, making the hair on my arms stand at attention.

"Now, Jay! Call for the myste!"

Patty shouted the words, and I heard them clearly, like the ringing of a church bell. But they were flat. There was no echo.

She must have heard this, too, because she whirled around, eyes wide. By then I'd drawn back my fist. My punch caught her square on the jaw, and she reeled, falling back into Witcombe. The second woman righted her, and I could tell that Patty was gearing up for a spell.

I cast first: a reflection spell. Her attack stirred the air an instant later, but it rebounded off of my warding. She went down in a heap, a welt appearing high on her temple.

Witcombe eyed me, rage and fear mingled on her face. Tires screeched out front.

"That'll be Kona Shaw," I said. "And she'll be armed."

"The police detective," Witcombe said. "Good luck explaining Heather to her."

Quick footsteps on the walkway, a fist pounding on the door. And then the door burst open. Kona had her weapon drawn, but she didn't get a shot off.

Witcombe and Patty vanished with a pulse of magic. A transporting spell. Seconds later, the Mercedes growled to life and sped away. Kona spun, ran back outside, but again, she didn't have time to fire off a shot.

I sank to the floor, overwhelmed by the pain in my hand, my wrist, my chest. The blood that had stained the carpet and glistened on my chest was gone, wiped away by the spell I'd cast, but fresh blood ran from the gash on my wrist and down the length of my fingers, dripping onto the carpet once more. I gripped my wrist with my good hand, my index finger pressing on the artery just above the cut, the other fingers digging into the wound itself. It hurt like hell, but at least it would slow the bleeding.

Kona came back inside. "Well, they're— Justis!" She hurried to my side and knelt next to me. "Shit! We have to bind that wrist."

"Gently," I said, breathless and weary. "My hand is broken in about twenty places."

"All right. Bandages?"

"Survival kit's in the bathroom, bottom drawer on the left."

"Bottom, left. Got it."

"And, Kona . . ."

She had gotten to her feet again to retrieve the

bandages, but she heard the urgency in my voice and stopped.

"There's a dead girl in my car. She was murdered by one of the women who did this to me. They used her blood for a spell, like with the other killings. But that's the knife that killed her." I nodded toward the weapon, which lay on the floor a few feet from me. "And my prints are all over it."

She regarded the knife, faced me again, and heaved a sigh. "Yeah, all right," she said. "Nothing's ever easy with you, is it?"

CHAPTER 18

Kona came back moments later with rolls of gauze and elastic wraps to hold the gauze in place. She knelt and reached for my bloodied wrist. At the first touch of her fingers against my hand, I recoiled, wincing and sucking air through my teeth.

"Oh, right. You have a broken bone?"

"I'd be surprised if there's still an unbroken bone in that hand."

"I'll be careful."

She was. She worked on me in silence, her motions deft, economical, gentle. One roll of gauze she kept wound, and set just over the upper part of the wound, securing it there with a wrapping of gauze from a second roll and then an elastic bandage.

Once she was convinced I wouldn't bleed to death, she made a series of phone calls on her cell: nine-one-one for an ambulance, the Medical Examiner's office for Heather, Kevin to help her work the evidence and my interview. I remained where I was, spent, light-headed from blood loss, in pain, and afraid that I would wind up spending the rest of my life in jail for a murder I didn't commit. I no longer needed to apply pressure to my wrist, but both my hands were still covered with drying blood, as were my jeans and the carpet beneath me. I wanted a shower and then a nap of about two days. I didn't think either was in my immediate future.

When she was finished on the phone, Kona walked to the back of my house again and brought a pile of towels, some dry, some damp, to where I sat.

"Are those my good ones?" I asked.

"I'll buy you more. But we should clean you up a little bit."

"I'll take care of this. You check the girl."

Her gaze met mine for the span of a heartbeat before sliding away. "Her being in your car isn't good, Justis. I don't have to tell you that."

"I didn't kill her."

"And you don't have to tell me that. I'm just saying that from a evidentiary standpoint, this is going to be tough."

"Do I need a lawyer?"

"Not yet. But yeah, you'll probably need a lawyer."

Kona went out to the car. I stared at the towels she'd left for me. At last, I picked up one of the damp ones and began to dab at the dried blood on my broken hand.

"Ohanko."

Namid appeared before me, his waters roughened, so that he seemed to have scales.

"I almost got you killed," I said.

"But you did not. You saved me, and at some cost to yourself."

"You've done the same for me."

"Is that why you protected me, because you felt beholden based upon past events?"

I couldn't keep from laughing. "No, Namid. That's not why."

"Then why did you—?"

"Can we talk about this later? I'm sorry. I'm just . . . I'm in some pain here, and I've lost a lot of blood."

He got to his knees, much as Kona had done moments before, and yet nothing like that at all. Kona was as lithe and graceful as anyone I knew. But Namid's movements were liquid and perfect. He didn't kneel so much as he flowed to the floor. And then he did something he had never done before. He reached out his hands of formed water and took hold of my mangled hand.

I winced again, in anticipation of pain. There was none. His touch was gentle and cool, like the slow wash of a spring stream.

"I can heal this," he said. "It is allowed."

"But I thought—"

"It is allowed," he said again, his bright gaze meeting mine.

"Because you say so?"

He smiled. "Yes, because I say so."

"The fracture then. Kona's called for an ambulance; they'll be expecting to see the laceration. But if you could repair the bones, I'd be grateful."

"Of course."

That sense of dipping my hand in cool water

intensified and tipped over into agony as the temperature dropped. I squeezed my eyes shut, my hand throbbing with each beat of my heart. The pain of his touch went on for a long time, the anguish radiating from the center of my hand out along my fingers. But even as it spread, it was followed by warmth that expanded in the same way, like concentric rings in a still lake. Soon, the pain began to subside.

"Is that better?" the runemyste asked, still grasping my hand.

I nodded. "Thank you."

The door opened and Kona came back in. "Well, it's pretty clear that she was dead when you put her in the car. There's no blood in your hatch."

She couldn't see Namid—only those with runecrafting blood in their veins could—and she came close to kneeling right on top of him.

"You should show yourself," I said to the myste. "It's only fair."

"What are you talking about?" she asked.

And at the same time, Namid said, "She knows of me?"

"Yes, she has for a long time."

"Justis, are you all right?"

"I'm fine. I'm talking to Namid."

"He's here?"

Before I could answer, his waters rippled, small waves spreading from the middle of his body. Kona let out a yelp and scrabbled back from him on all fours.

"Holy shit!"

"He's here."

She stared at him, her mouth hanging open, her eyes like saucers. I'd seen Kona shocked speechless more often in the last few days than in the eight years that came before.

"He is so cool looking!" she said, whispering the words.

"Thank you." His voice was like a cascade.

She smiled. "Sounds cool, too."

"I have healed the bones in Ohanko's hand."

"Ohanko?" she repeated to me.

"Long story. I'll explain later."

"Since you have called for medical assistance, he insisted that I not heal his wrist. I have repaired the damage to his blood vessel despite his wishes. We do not want him to die."

She shook her head. "No, we don't."

"You are as dear to him as any person in his life. And I am grateful to you for all that you have done for him over the years. You are a fine friend."

Kona blinked. Another smile crept over her face. "He's pretty dear to me, too."

Namid replied with a nod, apparently satisfied with their exchange. To me, he said, "Tell me what happened with the women."

I began to tell them both the entire story, from my arrival at Regina Witcombe's home to Kona's appearance at my door. The ambulance arrived before I had gotten far, and the EMTs bustled in, their radios crackling. They knelt on either side of me, and one of them examined Kona's bandage, complimenting her on how good it looked. They couldn't see Namid, which Kona found amusing.

Once they examined the wound more closely, though, they grew quiet. Eventually, one of them asked if all the blood on my clothes and the floor had come from my wrist. I hesitated. I knew they were asking because, as far as they could tell, the cut shouldn't have bled so much. Thanks to Namid, my artery was undamaged. But given that I was about to be implicated in Heather's killing, an unexplained excess of blood might ensure a murder conviction.

I chanced a peek at the runemyste, who seemed to understand. He gave me a wink—something else he had never done before—and suddenly blood was gushing from my wrist once more.

"Geez!" the other EMT said. "It must have started to clot or something, and then . . . Geez!"

The other guy grabbed for the gauze and bandage. "Put this back on, quick!"

They stanched the bleeding, rewrapped my arm and got me on a stretcher. I would have preferred to avoid a hospital stay, but that was no longer a possibility. The EMTs told Kona that they would be taking me to Chandler Regional Medical Center.

"I'll see you there," Kona said as they wheeled me outside and to the ambulance.

"Lock up my house, all right?"

She frowned. "I was going to have a garage sale."

I laughed and waved as they closed the ambulance doors.

The next several hours were a blur. An arterial laceration required surgery and, usually, general anesthesia. I had to argue with the ER surgeon and anesthesiologist for several minutes before I convinced them to numb my arm and give me a mild general to blunt the pain.

Still, by the time I came round again I sensed that hours had passed. I wouldn't be getting out to my father's place tonight, nor would I see Billie. Kona was sitting beside my bed in recovery, and, to my surprise, Namid was there as well, standing as still as ice at her shoulder.

"Hey stranger," Kona said, sitting forward. "How are you feeling?"

"Hung over."

Namid said nothing.

"He been here the whole time?"

She glanced up at him, scowling. It seemed the novelty of having him around had worn off. "Yep. He won't leave. And he doesn't say much. To be perfectly honest, it's been a little awkward."

"Welcome to my world. What time is it?"

"A little after eleven."

I closed my eyes to stop the room from spinning. "Damn."

A nurse come in, checked my vitals, asked how I was feeling, and told Kona in no uncertain terms that she would have to leave in another five minutes.

Once the nurse was gone, I said, "Namid, I need you to check on my father. I had intended to go out there again tonight, but clearly that's not happening."

"You fear for him."

"Very much."

"I will go to him now."

An instant later, he winked out of sight.

Kona exhaled and shook her head. "He is a piece of work, Justis. How do you put up with him? I mean, he's amazing to look at, and he obviously cares about you a lot. But . . . Wow."

"I know. Tell me about Heather."

Her expression grew more guarded. "Are you sure you're up to this right now?"

"No. But I need to hear it anyway."

She pulled out her notepad. "Heather Royce, twenty-four. Graduated two years ago from ASU with a degree in Finance. Her parents live in Yuma. As far as we can tell, she's been working for Regina Witcombe for about a year."

"Has anyone from the department talked to Witcombe yet?"

"No. Kevin and I will tomorrow."

"She knows your name, Kona, and she knows that we were partners. You should send Kevin with someone else."

She frowned. "What do you think she's going to do to me?"

"I don't know. I—"

The nurse threw the curtain open and glared at Kona. "You have to go now."

"She'll go in a minute."

"Mister Fearsson, you've been—"

"She'll go in a minute!"

The woman looked from one of us to the other and then withdrew, closing the curtain once more and muttering to herself.

"It's dangerous for you to go there," I said, once I was

sure the nurse was out of earshot. I kept my voice to a whisper.

"What if I can get her to come to 620?"

"That might be all right. She'd have a lawyer with her, so she probably wouldn't try anything. And in that case it's possible that your involvement with the investigation will make her think twice about some of the lies she's going to have to tell."

"That's what I'm thinking. The girl died at Witcombe's house, right?"

"Yes, but all the blood vanished when Witcombe and Patty cast their spell."

"Right. Tell me more about Patty."

I gave her all the background: the ties between the Hesslans and the Fearssons, everything I'd learned about Patty from my online search, and the details of our conversation at the realty office. At one point, the nurse came in again, glowered at us both, and left without saying a word.

As I finished, Namid returned.

"He seems well, Ohanko. He sits outside, asleep in his chair. But I do not believe he is in pain, and I sensed no necromancers or weremancers near him."

"All right. Thank you."

He answered with a solemn nod. Then he folded his arms over his broad chest and went still. Apparently, he had no intention of leaving.

After a brief silence, Kona said, "So this Hesslan-Fine woman killed the girl and used her blood for a spell. And Witcombe let it happen. Is that right?"

"Yes. Witcombe called the girl out onto the patio, but

I don't think she knew that Patty intended to kill her. She was pretty upset when it happened."

"All right, that could help." She closed her notepad. "I have more questions for you, but I think your nurse's head is about to explode. I'll be back in the morning."

"Does Hibbard know about all of this?" I asked before she could leave.

Kona cringed, nodded. "Kind of hard to keep it from him. To be honest, though, he doesn't seem as giddy as you might think. As much as he'd like to throw you in jail for the rest of your life, I don't think he believes you'd kill a girl like that."

"I suppose I should be flattered."

"I suppose. Get some sleep."

She let herself out through the curtain, and a moment later my nurse came back to check all my numbers again. "Are you hungry?" she asked. "It's late, but I can get you something."

I wasn't, but I also knew that I hadn't eaten in hours, and I had lost a lot of blood. "Yes, thank you. And I'm sorry about before. It's been quite a day, and I needed to tell Detective Shaw as much about it as I could."

She smiled, which was probably more than I deserved. "It's okay. I'll get you some dinner."

As soon as she was gone, Namid stepped closer to my bed. "Tell me about the crafting these women did."

And so I began yet another soliloquy. I started by describing the spell Patty and Witcombe used against me at Witcombe's house, but I skimmed over those details. "The more important spell was the one they didn't cast," I said. "The one they intended to use against you. They used blood again, and they had me mark myself with what I think were runes."

His waters grew turbid. "What kind of runes?"

I described each one in the order in which Patty had me draw them: the odd P, the line with the slash through it, and the simple vertical.

"That is the order they were in?"

"Yes. Left to right. Do you know what they mean?"

"I am familiar with each on its own. The first is *wynn*, which is often a fortuitous symbol. It can mean 'joy' or 'welcome,' or can imply a granting of wishes. I believe, though, that in this case 'welcome' is the intended meaning. It is meant to serve as a lure, a means of entrapment. And I know this because it is followed by *nyd*, which is a rune of constraint, of need, and *is*, which is a rune of impedance and control."

"So the runes don't spell out a word?" I said, my voice low.

"Not as you think of words, no. It is common for modern mystes and those who pretend to be crafters to treat runic patterns as one might an alphabet. But runes are more. Each is imbued with meaning and power, and they can be used in different ways by different runecrafters. This particular use of runes, in a triad, is one with which I am familiar. They are placed in this way so that each will fulfill a certain role in the casting. In this case, the first rune invites." As Namid said this, he made the shape of the first rune in the air with his finger, leaving a trace of silvery blue light before him. "The second establishes purpose." He drew the second rune as he had the first, so that both now hovered between us. "And the third binds." He drew the single vertical beside the other two. When this one was complete, the three letters changed color, darkening from silver to smoke grey and then to black, before vanishing completely.

"So they would have trapped you?" I asked.

"If you had summoned me as they instructed, and the casting was completed with those runes drawn in blood, then yes, I would have been imprisoned in whatever vessel they chose for me."

My stomach did a slow, unnerving somersault. "Vessel," I repeated. "What do you mean?"

"Just what I have said, Ohanko. The two women sought to imprison me, and would have needed a vessel to do so."

"Crap." I breathed the word. "I know how they killed your fellow runemyste in Northern Virginia. I know how they were going to kill you."

Namid didn't appear surprised; no doubt he had reasoned it out for himself. He knew a lot more about this stuff than I did. But he said, "Tell me."

"I was to be the vessel. The runes were drawn on me. I'm guessing that you would have been trapped inside me. And when they killed me, they would have taken both our lives."

"I fear that you are right, although I do not believe that they would have killed us. That final act they would have left to the necromancer who is instructing them in the ways of dark magic."

Something in the way he said this . . . "Why do I get the feeling that you know who this necromancer is?"

"I know nothing for certain," he said, an admission of

a sort. "But yes, I have an idea of who this might be. Germanic runes and those of Old English are similar; these three are identical in the two traditions. But I believe this casting belongs to a Celt. A woman."

"A female druid?"

"A priestess. What some today would call a witch, though the term is crude at best."

"Tell me about her."

"I shall, but not this night. You have need of sleep, and I must speak with my kind. I will tell you more tomorrow."

I felt my cheeks color, and I took a sip of water from the carafe my nurse had left for me, hoping to mask my discomfort. I had assumed that Namid would stay here while I slept. I was in danger still; we both knew it. And I couldn't defend myself and rest at the same time.

The runemyste, though, knew me pretty well. "I can communicate with other runemystes and remain by your side. You have nothing to fear from the dark ones tonight."

"Thank you," I said, embarrassed but also relieved. As soon as I lay back against my pillows and closed my eyes, I felt sleep tug at my mind. I hadn't realized how exhausted I was. "At least tell me her name," I said, my voice already sounding thick with slumber.

"What did you say?"

I forced my eyes open. "The priestess. What was her name?"

He said the name twice, and still he had to spell it out for me before I caught it. Saorla of Brewood, she was called. He pronounced her name as SARE-la.

"Now sleep," the myste rumbled, reminding me of a

tumbling river. "We will speak of her at greater length in the morning."

As it happened, I didn't have to wait that long to learn more about her. I couldn't have been asleep for more than a few moments when I found myself in a dream that felt nothing like those I usually have. At first I thought it must be the painkillers, and the after effects of the anesthesia. But even allowing for all the crap in my bloodstream, this vision felt different.

It was utterly bizarre, and yet it struck me as more real, more visceral than any dream I'd ever had.

I was alone on an open grassy plain. *It is a moor*, a voice in my head corrected. A woman's voice. *The* woman's voice: low, gravelly, accented with what I now knew to be an Irish lilt. It was the voice I'd heard in Solana's after the explosion. I turned a quick circle, searching for her, but I saw no one. The grasses bowed and danced in a swirling wind, and far in the distance to the west, the setting sun reflected off a broad expanse of open water. Nearer, in the opposite direction, low hills cast rounded shadows across the moor.

"Where are you?" I called, my voice swallowed by the rush of wind and the vast landscape.

A fire burned in a small ring of stone a few paces from where I stood. I hadn't noticed it until that moment. Or perhaps it hadn't been there. A cooking spit stood over the ring with what might have been a skinned rabbit roasting in the flames.

"Perhaps you are hungry. Supper will be ready shortly."

"This is a dream. I can't eat in a dream."

"You can in this one. You can drink as well. Would you like wine?"

Two ceramic goblets rested on the ground beside the fire, a bottle made of translucent glass between them. I was sure they hadn't been there a moment before.

"Show yourself," I said, turning once more. "Let me see you."

And she did, appearing as suddenly as had the food and drink. She stood with her back to the hills, the dying sunlight illuminating her face.

She wore a simple green dress of coarse cotton, and a gray shawl hung about her shoulders, anchored against the wind by a slender but powerful hand. I couldn't have guessed her age. Her brown hair was streaked with silver, and it danced around her face, whipped to a frenzy by the gale. Her eyes, a clear, pale blue, seemed both ancient and youthful. There was wisdom there, and wit, and a hard, uncompromising intelligence. Her face was oval and very pretty—"winsome," I thought, though I didn't know why. I don't think I had ever used the word before. But that's what she was, despite the tiny lines around her mouth, at the corners of her eyes, on her brow.

I wanted to ask her name, though I thought I knew it, and I would have liked to know why she had brought me here.

But before I could speak she said, "You have your father's eyes."

Her words shocked me silent; judging from her inscrutable smile, I guessed that she had known they would.

"Yes, I have seen him. I have looked into his eyes as I

am looking into yours. I have sounded the depths of his moon sickness, explored his passions, his loves, his fears, the most precious memories he holds, and also the most daunting. I know him more intimately than you ever will."

"You've tortured him," I managed to say.

"I have tested him."

"Well, you'd better stay the hell away from him from now on."

"I have also saved your life, spared you when I did not spare others. You should show me some courtesy." This last she said in a tone that made my breath catch in my throat. I wondered if Namid could protect me here, wherever "here" was.

But even wondering this, I didn't back down. I'd always been kind of stupid that way. "You also hurt my friend."

"The woman."

"Yeah, her. Do that again, and if I have to I'll rip you apart with my bare hands."

"You have fire in you, which I can admire. But you lack discipline; you are ruled by your emotions. I could crush you where you stand, and would be justified in doing so. No one speaks to me as you have." She considered me for another moment before appearing to come to a decision. "But I think I will not. You are angry, hurt, frightened. I will even admit that you have cause—that I have given you cause. And so, you have nothing to fear from me on this night. Not because Namid'skemu protects you, but because I choose to keep you safe."

I felt like I should thank her, but I couldn't bring myself to speak the words. Instead, I said, "You're Saorla."

"I am. And you are Justis Fearsson."

"That's right."

She walked toward me and past me to the cooking fire, her hips swaying provocatively. "Come and sup with me, Justis Fearsson."

I hesitated, catching the briefest scent of something sickly as she passed. But before I could name it, it was gone, swept away by another gust of wind. A memory stirred, deep in the recesses of my slumbering mind. *The stench of decay clings to them still . . .*

"The meat is not poisoned. But it is real and will offer sustenance. You have been wounded and must heal. Food will help."

I followed her to the fire, but remained standing, even as she sat.

She picked up one of the goblets and held it out to me. I took it from her, taking care not to allow my fingers to so much as brush hers. Another smile curved her lips.

"You are cautious. That is probably wise."

She sipped from the other goblet. I glanced down into mine.

"The wine is not poisoned either," she said, sounding impatient. "Caution is one thing. Such mistrust is rude."

I drank. It was honeyed and strong. With the first sip, I felt a small rush of dizziness.

"Food will help."

"Why are you being so kind to me?" I asked. "You had intended to kill me tonight."

"Yes. And I will want you well the next time I try. Your death will serve me better if you are hale and strong."

CHAPTER 19

I laughed at her candor, even as a chill ran through my body.

She produced a knife from within the folds of her dress and began to cut pieces of meat from the rabbit. "You think I jest?" she asked as she worked.

"I know you don't."

"And yet you laugh."

She held out a strip of meat to me. I took it and bit into it without pause. It was succulent and smokey and delicious. Suddenly I was ravenous. I downed the rest of what she had given me in two bites and took another piece the moment she offered it.

"I laughed," I said, chewing on yet another mouthful, "because it's not often that someone is so up front about their intention to kill."

"Do you fear death?" she asked, tipping her head to the side and regarding me through her lashes. She really was quite beautiful.

I thought there might be a right answer to this, but I didn't know what it was. "Yes," I said. "I don't want to die. But I worked as a cop for a long time, and I've learned to manage that fear."

"So, you prefer to live." She stood and took a step toward me. Again, a hint of decay soured the air around us.

I fell back a step. "All things being equal, I'd prefer to live."

"I can arrange that," she said.

"At what cost?"

"To you? Nothing at all."

There was no such thing as a free lunch—my dad had taught me that years ago. "What about to Namid?"

"He uses you, as the runemystes all use their weremystes. You are little more than slaves to them, doing their bidding and in return receiving 'training' so that you can continue to serve their cause. Surely you see this."

"I've known Namid a long time. You're going to have to do better than that."

"You don't know him at all."

The wind died down, and once more that elusive odor reached me. "At least I know what he really looks like," I said. It was a hunch, but I'd long since learned to trust my instincts.

Her smile this time was bitter, and it made her far less attractive.

"You believe you do," she said, "but that, too, is an illusion. He appears to you as he thinks you would like him to."

"You've done the same."

"Yes, I have. Like me, he can take on any guise he wishes."

"So, let me see the real you," I said.

"The real me," she repeated. "They are all the real me." She gestured at herself. "This is as real as any form I might take. Once I appeared as you see me now. But I can be this." The figure before me wavered, as if heat waves rose from the ground before her. An instant later, she was transformed into a great, dark-pelted deer. "Or this." She morphed again, this time into a gray wolf, with bright yellow eyes and paws that were the size of my hand.

"I can be a woman." Abruptly she was herself again. "Or a man." As quickly as she had taken on that familiar form, she shifted once more, this time to a burly, bearded Scottish warrior in a plaid kilt and brown leather vest. "Or I can be someone I've never even met." This time I stumbled back, appalled and fascinated by what I saw. She was Billie, naked to the waist, her eyes and hair as I knew them, but the expression on her face too cruel, too predatory.

"Stop that," I said, my voice shaking. "After what you did to her, you have no right."

She shifted back to her original appearance. "So, you like this one after all."

"No. It's a lie; I can tell. I can smell you from here. You stink of rot, of death. This isn't how you look. I want to see the demon beneath that skin."

Her expression went stony. "You are his creature through and through. You belong to him and you do not even know it."

"I belong to no one. But Namid's my friend, and I trust him with my life. Now, let me see you."

She smiled, as thin as a blade. And when next she shifted it was to something hideous, ghoulish. Her flesh seemed to melt away, and with it her dress and shawl, leaving little more than an animated corpse, rotted, skeletal in places. Only her eyes remained even remotely the same. They gleamed in their desiccated sockets, white orbs, blue at the center. And she kept them fixed on me.

"Is this what you wanted to see?" she asked, her voice unchanged.

I could smell her now, the stench of decay so strong it made my eyes tear; it was all I could do to keep from gagging.

"Yes," I said. "This is the first form you've taken that seems genuine."

"Your precious Namid'skemu would look the same, if he were as honest with you as I am being now."

"I don't believe that," I said. "I understand more than you think I do. He was granted eternal life by the Runeclave. And in giving him that, they also gave him the form I see when he appears to me. He's a creature of magic, and that form is as elemental to him as his voice and his thoughts. But you and your kind—you took everything that you are now. It wasn't a gift, it was . . . it was plunder. And so you stink of corruption, because you are, in fact, corrupt."

"Bold words, weremyste. You dare speak them now because I have given you my word that no harm will come to you from this encounter. And despite what you think you know about me, I keep my oaths. Your runemyste is not as pure as you might like to believe, nor am I as evil as you judge. You are young and foolish and you see the world in black and white when all around you are shades of gray. You do not trust me; I understand why. But ask him, and perhaps you will glean a kernel of truth in what I am telling you."

I faltered, not wanting to put any stock in her attacks on Namid, and yet unable to deny them with any credibility. The truth was, being a cop and an investigator had taught me long ago that there were no absolutes. As she put it, everything existed in gradations of gray. Except where Namid was concerned. I had always accepted that he was an agent of unalloyed good, the same way I now assumed that this putrescent creature before me was evil incarnate. I should have known better, which meant I needed to start questioning assumptions I'd lived with for far too long.

"You are thinking about it, I can tell. It may be there is more to you than I have credited thus far." I heard surprise in her voice, and, I thought, a hint of respect as well. "Nevertheless," she said, her voice hardening once more, "I offer no assurances as to your safety when next we meet. You and I are on opposite sides in this struggle. At our next encounter I will act accordingly."

"And I'll do the same. Count on it."

She laughed, the effect in her current form chilling. "That is the third time you have threatened me," she whispered.

In the blink of an eye she had covered the distance between us so that she stood inches from me. Her fetor seemed to poison the air. I couldn't breathe, couldn't move. She raised a moldered hand, the skin dark and leathery, and she traced a line down the side of my face, her touch as gentle as that of a lover. Only then, having touched me as her true self, did she shift again, this time back to the form she had assumed when my dream first began.

"Three times, Justis Fearsson. We are enemies sworn now. The next time we meet you will have no choice but to fight me. And you will die. I assure you of that."

I jerked away from her, able to move at last. And opening my eyes, I found myself back in my hospital bed. I searched the room for a clock and spotted one on the wall behind me. Twisting around enough to read it proved more difficult than I'd imagined. It was a few minutes shy of five o'clock. Despite the dream, I'd gotten a bit of sleep and felt better for it. I wondered if I'd really eaten, and if that had helped as well. Settling back down in the bed, I realized that Namid was still with me, watching my every move, his eyes brilliant in the dim light.

"You were dreaming," he said.

"Of Saorla."

"I gathered as much."

"She fed me and gave me wine. Could that have been real?"

He frowned, but nodded. "You took a risk accepting food from her."

I started to say that I was dreaming, though I knew he wouldn't accept that as an excuse. But really, I had known it wasn't a dream, just as I had known that I could trust her on this one occasion. "I don't believe I did take a risk," I told him. "She believes that you're still keeping things from me, that you're refusing to tell me everything I should know about your history and hers. Is she right?"

"It is not that I refuse, but yes, I have yet to tell you all. Ours is a long and complicated history. I could not possibly convey all of it to you at once."

"I understand that," I said, my patience strained. "But she says that you're . . . telling me things that present your actions in the best light and hers in the worst." I wasn't explaining it well.

His waters were roiled. "She implies that I am misleading you, that if I told you all there is to tell, you might side with her."

"Exactly." I hesitated, unsure of whether I wanted to know the truth. "Is she right?"

"No, and yes."

I scowled. "That's helpful."

"We were at war, Ohanko. I fought against other weremystes. Some I wounded, others I killed. I can justify all that I did. I believed that I was doing right. But obviously my foes disagreed and felt that my allies and I were at fault. I am sure Saorla could tell you tales—all of them true—that would make my deeds sound foul, even villainous. Such is the nature of war. I am not perfect, nor have I ever claimed to be. And as a young man I made terrible mistakes that I rue to this day. But I remain a loyal servant of the Runeclave, and I remain as well your friend."

"Is that why you stayed here all night?"

A faint smile touched his face. "It is."

He still hadn't told me all. I knew that. But I knew as well that he had told me the truth as far as it went. More, now that I was awake and free of Saorla's influence, I was able the name the difference between them: Namid might not have been as forthcoming with information as I would have liked, but he never threatened or cajoled. What he shared came unvarnished; I was free to do with it what I would. And that gift of freedom was an expression of friendship that Saorla couldn't have understood.

"I must leave you for a time," the myste said. "I believe you are safe, at least for now."

"All right. Thanks for protecting me."

"I did not. That would have been an act of interference. I merely remained by your side out of concern for your health."

We both smiled. Then he raised a hand in farewell and vanished.

I closed my eyes and must have dozed off, because the next thing I knew a nurse I didn't recognize was checking my vital signs, and a tray of scrambled eggs and toast had been set by my bed. The nurse's tag read "Alicia."

"You're awake," she said. "I heard you talking before; do you talk in your sleep?"

"Sometimes," I said, fighting an urge to laugh.

"Well, if you feel up to it, someone's here to see you." She leaned closer to me. "And she's very pretty."

I tensed. Could it have been Patty? Witcombe wouldn't have come herself.

"Come on in," the nurse said, pulling the curtain open.

Margarite, Kona's partner—of the domestic sort—walked to my bedside. I gave her a big smile, my pulse slowing.

"Hey, you! I'm surprised to see you here."

She stooped to kiss my cheek, dark hair brushing my forehead. "How are you, Jay?"

"I'm good. I mean, as good as a guy in a hospital can be, you know?"

The nurse left us, although not before setting the table with the food tray on it right in front of me.

"I knew Kona would be working this morning. You didn't have to come."

Her smile tightened. "Actually, I did," she said, dropping her voice to a whisper. "You have to get out of here."

"What?"

"Kona told me to tell you that she and Kevin will be coming here to arrest you this morning. They might be on their way already. She tried to keep them from charging you, but right now the evidence is weighted against you too much."

I nodded, trying to fight off a surge of panic. I could hear my heart monitor beeping out a salsa beat, and I expected the nurse to come back at any moment to find out what the hell we were doing in here.

On cue, the curtain slid open again. "Mister Fearsson?" Alicia said, eyeing us both.

"I have to leave," I said.

"I'm afraid I can't—"

"I'll sign whatever papers are necessary releasing the hospital from any responsibility for my well-being. But . . . my father. He's taken ill. He might even have had a heart attack. He's at another hospital and I need to get to him."

As lies went, it seemed like a pretty good one.

I could tell Alicia wasn't pleased, but after a few seconds, which felt like an eon, she said, "Yes, all right. I'll start the paperwork right away."

Margarite left, telling the nurse that she needed to hurry back to "our father's" side. It took Alicia some time to gather the necessary documents, and she insisted on changing the bandage on my wrist before letting me go. My hand was still tender, despite Namid's healing magic, and I winced several times as she worked on me, prompting a lengthy scolding during which she told me in no uncertain terms that I was making a terrible mistake.

I was out of there by seven-thirty. I guessed that Kona and Kevin had done their best to get stuck in traffic; Kona wouldn't have sent Margarite to warn me if she then intended to rush over.

I had someone at the visitor's desk call a cab for me, and went outside to wait for it. As soon as I cleared the building and set foot on the pavement, it hit me: the moon. It's pull on my mind was magnetic; I could no more resist it than I could fight the passage of time. Somehow I had lost track of the days, but it came rushing back to me now. As the start of the phasing approached, the moon's effect on my thoughts and mood grew ever stronger. But the difference in magnitude between the tug of the moon approaching full and its power as the phasing began was the difference between a sip of beer and a couple of shots of tequila. The phasing would begin tonight at sundown, and already I could feel it bending my mind, leaving me muddied and grasping for clarity. Other weremystes—Q, Luis, and Amaya, and also Patty, Witcombe, and Dimples—would be experiencing much the same thing. Like the laws of nature, the laws of magic brooked no exceptions. But I doubted that the weremancers would rest today in anticipation of this evening's moonrise. If anything, they'd be working even harder in advance of it.

Considering once more that laws-of-magic thing, I wondered if there were blood spells that somehow allowed them to escape the worst of the phasings. I wasn't proud of myself for thinking along those lines, but I had to admit that if blood magic was that powerful, I'd be tempted to give it a try.

Before I could wander too much further down that path, my cab showed up. I climbed in and told the driver to take me up to Banner Desert Medical Center. It was incredibly stupid of me, but I wanted to check in on Billie.

She had been moved to a private room, which made tracking her down a bit difficult. Soon enough, though, I found her. She was asleep when I walked in, and for a few moments I stood and stared at her, rage and guilt and relief warring within me. Her color was better, though she still had enough bandages on her head and arm to qualify for mummy-hood. She was going to be fine. I was sure of that. But I also knew I could claim no credit for her survival. Not only had I failed to protect her, it was because of me that she was here in the first place, wrapped in miles of gauze and wired to those damn machines.

Even private rooms in hospitals had curtains, so that nurses and doctors could examine patients in private when they had guests. I pulled the curtain out part way and sat on the far side of it so that Billie couldn't see me. And then I spoke her name.

I had to call to her a couple of times before she woke, but at last I heard her say, "Fearsson?"

"Yeah, it's me."

"Where are you?"

"On the far side of the curtain."

"Well get over here, clown. Let me see you."

"I can't do that."

"Why not? Are you hurt? Did something happen to you?"

"No, I'm fine. I mean, yeah, something happened to me. I'll explain it all when I can. But right now you need to know that the police are trying to find me."

"Why?"

I sighed. "They think I killed someone."

Silence. After about ten seconds, which in the middle of a conversation is a lot longer than it sounds, she said, "Did you?"

"Of course not."

"Then—"

"Kona is going to come here with Kevin, her partner, and they're going to question you. They have to. Kona knows I didn't do it, but she's conducting an investigation, and she answers to people who don't like me as much as she does. The point is, I want you to be able to say with a straight face that you haven't seen me. If they ask you whether we've spoken, that's what you say: You haven't seen me, and we haven't even spoken by phone. You understand?"

"I guess. But then why did you come here? Why go to all this trouble?"

"I needed to see you. I wanted to make sure you were doing all right."

"Okay, I think I must be getting too caught up in your

twisted world, because, ridiculous as this all is, that strikes me as being incredibly sweet and romantic."

I grinned. "Good. How are you feeling?"

"I'm better. The fajitas you brought helped. You didn't happen to bring more, did you?"

"No. I was . . . I couldn't get to a restaurant."

I could almost hear her frowning. "Are you sure *you're* all right?"

No. "I'm working on it."

"Does this have anything to do with—?"

"Don't say any more, Billie. Please."

"But no one else is here."

"They don't have to be here to be listening. Get what I mean?"

"Yes," she said. She sounded scared, and more than anything I wanted to shove aside the curtain and take her hand.

"I'm sorry. I have to go. After they search for me at the other hospital and at home, this is the next place they'll come."

"You were in the hospital?"

Oops. "Just overnight. I had a . . . a cut on my wrist."

"That must have been some cut."

"It was. I'll come back as soon as I can. I promise. In the meantime, I need you to turn away so that I can pull this curtain back and leave."

A pause. Then, "All right."

I pushed the curtain away and stood. Glancing at her, I saw that Billie was watching me.

"Billie!"

"I lied," she said. "And I'll lie to Kona if I have to. But

I wanted to see you." Her gaze fell to the heavy bandaging on my wrist. "That doesn't look so good. Did you try to kill yourself?"

"Someone needed blood for a spell, and they took mine without my permission."

"And was this the same person who committed the murder Kona wants to blame on you?"

"She doesn't want to . . ." I cringed, squeezed my eyes shut for a second. I didn't have time to explain it all. "Yes. Same person."

Billie stared at my arm for another second before again finding my eyes with hers. "Your job sucks, Fearsson."

I laughed. "It certainly does this week." I stepped to the bed and kissed her on the bridge of the nose. "I have to go," I whispered.

"Okay."

I kissed her again, and slipped out of her room. I took the stairs to the ground floor, avoiding the elevators, grabbed another cab out front, and had the driver drop me off a block from my home.

I walked the rest of the way, and seeing no sign of Kona's Mustang or PPD squad cars out front, I let myself inside. I changed clothes as quickly as I could, retrieved my cell phone and bomber jacket from where I'd left them the night before—I'd lost my Glock to Regina Witcombe's security guys, and I didn't think they'd give it back, even if I asked nicely—and went back outside, intending to jump in the Z-ster. At which point I remembered that the car would have been impounded by the police. After all, there'd been a dead body in the back.

After considering the problem for all of two seconds, I walked away from the house, pulled out my cell phone, and dialed what was becoming a familiar number.

"Amaya."

"Good morning," I said. "It's Jay Fearsson."

"So it says on my phone. When I gave you this number, I didn't think you'd add me to your circle of phone friends."

"I need a car."

"Excuse me?"

"I was kidnapped last night by Regina Witcombe and a friend of hers. They controlled me with one blood spell and tried to use my blood for a second crafting that would have killed my runemyste. And in the process they framed me for murder. The police have my car, and I can't do anything until I have a replacement."

He didn't answer right away. "So I was right about her."

"Yes, you were."

"I'll have Rolon and Paco bring you a car. Any requests; I have a nice collection."

"Something understated. I don't want to be noticed. Paco's lowrider would be a bad choice." I paused, knowing I would regret this. "I could also use a firearm. A Glock 22 would be great—the .40. Failing that, any nine millimeter will do."

"All right. Where are you?"

"I'll be waiting for them in the parking lot of the Chandler Airport in half an hour."

"They'll be there," he said, and ended the call.

I didn't like relying on Amaya for help. It was bad

enough that I was working for him, and that I had to conceal our arrangement from Kona. But I didn't know where else to turn; few of my friends had extra cars lying around, not to mention extra pistols. Unfortunately, I had the sense that each time I called the man for help or a favor, I was cementing a relationship of which I really wanted no part.

But like the approach of the phasing, this couldn't be helped. I needed a car, and fast. I set out on the lengthy trek to Chandler's little municipal airport. As I walked, I tried to work out how best to use the remaining hours before the phasing began. I had much of the day left, but that didn't seem like enough time; not even close.

I wasn't ready to face Patty and Witcombe again, which left Dimples. And I'd thought of a way I might track him down.

I reached the airport in good time, and had to wait a few minutes before Paco and Rolon showed up. They pulled into the parking lot with a bit more fanfare than I would have liked, Paco's lowrider rumbling like some hotrod in a Sixties beach-party movie. Rolon trailed him, driving a cream-colored, late-model Lexus sedan. I could tell already that Amaya's loaner was going to spoil me for any car I'd ever be able to afford.

They got out of their respective cars and waited as I joined them. I eyed the Lexus.

"Nice car."

"You sure you don't want the lowrider?" Paco asked, grinning. "She's pretty fast."

"Too much car for me," I said.

He laughed.

Rolon reached into the pocket of his sports jacket, pulled out a Glock just like the one I'd lost, and held it out to me. "From Jacinto. He says to keep it."

I took the weapon from him, but shook my head. "I'll bring it back to him once I have a chance to retrieve mine or buy a new one."

Rolon turned grave. "Don't, *amigo*. He'll be insulted, and he's not a man you want to piss off, you know?" He shrugged. "Besides, it's not like he'll miss it. He's got enough to arm . . ." He glanced at Paco, grinned again. "Well, he's got plenty."

"All right," I said, slipping the weapon into my bomber pocket. "Tell him I said thanks."

"The magazine's full," Rolon said. "And it's the high capacity; seventeen rounds."

"Good to know. Again, thanks."

Rolon tossed me the fob. "Jacinto also told me I should offer my help."

I was already reaching for the door handle on the Lexus, but I stopped now. "What?"

"I can ride with you. Help you with what you're doing." He flashed the familiar grin once more, exposing a single gold tooth. "I shoot good, and I can craft a bit."

"Not to mention, you're built like a brick shithouse."

Paco laughed. After a moment Rolon did, too.

"Yeah, not to mention that."

I pulled off my bomber and held up my bandaged arm. "This may not look like much," I said, "but I nearly died last night. And the guys I'm going up against today aren't likely to be any more gentle."

"You trying to scare me, Fearsson?"

"I'm trying to be straight with you. You're not volunteering for an easy day off from whatever it is Amaya has you doing."

His grin vanished. "It's Mister Amaya. And I wasn't interested in a day off. He told me to go with you because he thinks I can help. If you don't want me riding along, say so."

I opened the driver's side door of the Lexus and slid into the seat. "Hop in. I'm driving."

He flashed another smile and said something to Paco in Spanish that I didn't catch.

A moment later he got in the car.

I was taking a moment. Leather seats that molded themselves to my body, a steering wheel that felt like an extension of my hands, an interior that was more spacious than rooms in some five-star hotels. Yeah, I never wanted to drive anything else. And I hadn't even turned the key yet.

After studying the dashboard for about three seconds, I realized there was no key. This was one of those push-button-start luxury models. I started it up, the purr of the engine as sexy as Saorla's voice. What can I say? I like nice cars.

"So where are we going?" Rolon asked as I steered us out of the airport lot.

"Back to the doggie's single-wide."

He nodded, leaned forward, and clicked on the radio. It was already set to a Latino pop station. He grinned at me and cranked the volume. It wouldn't have been my choice, but he'd brought me a car and a new Glock. I couldn't complain.

CHAPTER 20

The weremyste community in Phoenix was small compared with the general population of the metropolitan area. There might have been a thousand active mystes in all, and we tended to know each other. Not always, of course. I hadn't been aware that Regina Witcombe and Jacinto Amaya were mystes, nor had I known about Patty. But people as famous as Witcombe and Amaya were bound to be exceptions, and I assumed that those who dabbled in dark magic would have kept to the shadows as well. The rest of us, though, had at least a passing familiarity with our fellow runecrafters, be it because we hung out at the same bars, or because we saw each other every month at the Moon Market, a floating marketplace where mystes could buy herbs and oils, crystals and talismans, and just about any other goods purported to lessen the effect of the phasing.

I was hoping that the werecreature community worked the same way.

I drove us into Buckeye and down to Gary Hacker's single-wide. We parked by Hacker's truck and got out. Rolon already had his SIG Sauer in hand. I pulled out the Glock. The structure and yard looked exactly as they had the day before, and the air conditioner was still rattling. But something about the place gave me pause. Or paws. Yesterday, Hacker had appeared at the door almost as soon as I pulled up to his home. Today it was too quiet; thinking this made me feel once more like an actor in a bad movie.

Rolon and I exchanged glances. I pointed at myself and then at the door to the single-wide. He nodded and followed me, gripping his pistol with both hands.

I knocked once on the door and called, "Hacker?"

No answer. I tried the knob. The door was locked. I pounded again.

"Wha' the hell?" I heard from inside. He sounded fine. Hung over, but fine.

I glanced at Rolon again. He had lowered his weapon.

"It's Jay Fearsson. Open up."

"Go away. I'm not riskin' bein' turned again."

"I have Rolon with me, Gary, and he's perfectly willing to tear the door off your house if he has to. Now open up. We won't stay long."

I heard uneven footsteps, and then the click of a door lock. The door swung open, revealing Hacker, unshaven, puffy-eyed, and a not-so-healthy shade of green.

He pointed a shaking finger at Rolon. "You did this to me. You and that goddamned trank. I'm still sore where the dart hit me, and I feel like I've been on a six-day bender."

"Let us in, Gary."

He glared at me. "Why the hell should I? The two of you ruined my yesterday; today's goin' to be no better."

"Rolon's with me. And that means Jacinto wants you to help us."

His expression curdled, but he backed out of the doorway and waved us in.

I entered. Rolon followed me, closing the door behind him. Hacker had dropped himself onto his couch; he looked like he was about to be sick.

"So, what? More questions about the people who spelled me?"

I shook my head. "No. There's another were I need to find and I thought maybe you'd know him. He's a big guy, tall and wide. Dark curly hair, bushy beard and moustache." I closed my eyes, trying to recall the image of him I'd seen in my scrying at Sweetwater Park. "I think he may have a tattoo on his left shoulder. A hawk, or maybe an eagle." Opening my eyes again, I said, "Do you know of anyone like that?"

"A were, you say?"

"That's right."

"The tattoo is an angel, I think. But yeah, I know him. His name's Bear. Least that's what he calls himself."

I wanted to say that I'd been calling him that, too, but I kept it to myself, asking instead, "He have a last name?"

"Martell. I think his real name's Carl, but don't hold me to that."

"All right. Do you know where he lives?"

"Not too far from here. Avondale, I'm pretty sure."

"Thank you, Gary. That's helpful."

I reached for the door, ready to leave.

"That's it? That's all you wanted to know?"

"It's all I'm willing to risk asking. Someone's watching one of us—you or me. We learned that the hard way yesterday. And besides, I think I know what the guy who spelled you looks like."

"You do?" Gary asked, his eyes widening.

"Yeah. Take care."

Rolon and I left the mobile home and got back into the Lexus.

"You still have that tranquilizer gun?" I asked, as I backed up and got us turned around.

"*Sí*, it's in the trunk. Jacinto told me to bring it. Why? You expecting more doggie trouble?"

"No, I'm pretty sure this next guy shifts into a bear."

While I drove to Avondale, Rolon used his smartphone to track down an address for Carl Martell. Bear lived in a working-class neighborhood on the west side of the town. His house was small, and similar places stood shoulder to shoulder with his. Kids played in one yard; an older couple sat on a narrow porch in front of the other, eyeing us with understandable mistrust. Rolon managed to retrieve the trank gun and slip it under his jacket without drawing too much attention to himself, but still I thought the old woman was going to run inside and call the police.

Lacking a better plan, we walked to Martell's door and knocked. "I'll do the talking," I said, my voice low.

"You're the boss, *amigo*."

After a few seconds, the door swung open and Martell

stood before us in a black Nickelback T-shirt and baggy cargo shorts. "Yeah, what do you—" He stared at us, his mouth hanging open, one mammoth hand clenched. I knew he could see the magic on us; I was counting on that getting us in the door.

"What do you guys want with me now?" he asked, his gaze flitting back and forth between us.

"Just to talk, Carl."

He squinted, chewed his lip. "Do I know you?"

"No. But I know a bit about you, and we need a word."

"What about?"

"Inside," I said.

He crossed his arms over his massive chest. "What about?"

Rolon reached into his jacket, probably for his pistol, but I held out a hand, stopping him.

"About Jeff."

"Who the f—?" His face went white. "Shit," he whispered.

"Let us in."

He nodded and pushed open the screen. Rolon and I stepped into the house. Bear closed the door and faced us. Big as he was, he appeared terrified; I swear I thought he was going to cry.

His place stank of cigarette smoke and was sparsely furnished: There were a couple of chairs and a coffee table, but otherwise the living room reminded me more of a playroom. He had a nice stereo system and a good-sized flat-screen TV set on the wall between his speakers. Closer to the front door was a rack of compact discs that must have been five feet high. Martell was a music fan.

"You guys must know that it wasn't my idea to kill Jeff. I mean, I swore to Palmer that I'd do it, but I didn't know . . . I thought it was going to be different—after I mean."

I stopped surveying the room and focused on Bear. "You knew that Palmer was going to kill him."

"Well, yeah, sure. I mean, that's how blood spells work, right? You know that as well as—"

He clammed up, his eyes narrowing as the realization hit him. He even took a step toward me, but as soon as he did, Rolon drew his pistol. Bear halted.

"Who the hell are you?"

"Not who you thought we were," I said. "But I guess that's pretty clear by now, isn't it?" I gestured toward the nearest chair. "Sit down."

"Not until you tell me who the fuck you are, as if I don't know already. Cops, right?"

There were laws against lying about such a thing, and on this day in particular I wasn't in the mood to run afoul of the police. Any more than I already had. "I'm a private detective," I said. "Jay Fearsson. I'm helping the police with an investigation."

"And him?" Bear asked, eyeing Rolon.

"A concerned citizen," Amaya's man told him. "Now, sit."

He glanced again at Rolon's .45 and sat.

"How did you get hooked up with Palmer?" I asked.

Bear stared back at me and said nothing.

"I can make you talk, *cabronazo*," Rolon said. He held up his weapon. "I don't even have to use this."

"It won't come to that," I said. "Bear wants to help us,

because he realizes now that he's in over his head." He remained silent, but he wasn't glaring at me anymore. In fact, he refused to look at me at all. I pressed on. "You thought they were going to make you more powerful, didn't you? You thought you'd have control over when you shifted. You probably even imagined that tonight would be easier for you because of the spell Palmer cast. And Jeff, he was collateral damage. An old homeless guy, living alone? No one was going to miss him, and it's not like his life was that great, right?"

Still nothing.

"C'mon, Jay," Rolon said. "Let me soften him up a little. Just enough to get him talking. We're wasting time here."

I didn't know if Rolon was serious, or if he was playing a role, trying to get Bear to answer my questions. Either way, though, he was helping. Martell might have had a few pounds on the guy, but he seemed to understand that he was no match for him in a fight. He'd gone pale.

"Yeah, all right," I said.

Rolon took a step in Bear's direction. That was all it took.

"No, wait," Bear said, holding up his hands.

"Hold on."

Amaya's man glanced my way; I could tell he was disappointed.

I recited a spell in my head. The three of us, the room we were in, and a thick blanket. The idea was to mute the sound of our voices so that anyone listening in—namely Saorla—wouldn't be able to hear us. I repeated the elements three times and released the magic.

"What was that?" Rolon asked.

"A muffling spell," I said. "The last time I had a conversation like this, it reached the wrong ears. This time it won't."

Bear frowned.

"How did you meet Palmer?" I asked.

He chewed his lip for a few seconds, his gaze settling again and again on Rolon and his SIG Sauer. "He found me," he said. "I'm not entirely sure how. But he knew I was a were, and he said he wanted to help me."

"How long ago was this?"

He shrugged. "I don't know exactly. Just a few months, though. Not long."

"And what's his first name?"

Bear's brow furrowed. "What?"

"Palmer's first name: What is it?"

"That *is* his first name," Bear said, frowning at me like I was the dumbest guy on the planet. "Palmer Hain."

"All right. My mistake. Go on."

"Well, it's like you said. He made it sound like a great idea. I'd be able to control when I shifted, maybe skip a phasing or two if I wanted. That sounds pretty good. I was ready to go for it right away. But then he starts putting me off, you know? One week to the next I don't know when we're going to do the spell. I'm eager, but he's suddenly hard to reach. First he's my best friend, and then he's nowhere, right?"

"But that changed this week," I said, prompting him.

"Yeah. Last week, actually. He calls me and says he's sorry, that he's been really busy helping out other weres. But he's ready for me now, and I'm to meet him somewhere in Paradise Valley."

"Sweetwater Park?"

He nodded. "I met him there, and we just talked. He told me about the spell and what was involved. He told me then that we'd . . . well, that we'd have to kill a guy to do it. At first I was, like, 'Whoa! No way, dude!' But he promised me the guy wouldn't feel anything, that he'd spell him first. And he said it would be nobody, right? A homeless guy who didn't have a family or friends or anything to live for." He twisted his mouth and blinked a couple of times, trying not to cry. "I suppose that sounds really lame. Truth is, I wanted to do the spell. I don't like being a were, at least not most of the time. I was happy to go along with it."

"So what happened after the spell?"

"After?" he repeated, sounding surprised that I didn't want him to describe the murder itself. I didn't bother telling him that I'd seen it in my scrying stone. "Palmer turned me, and then turned me back." He grimaced. "Then he did it again, and a third time." One of his hands strayed to his chest and rubbed at his heart, perhaps remembering the way it felt when that arc of golden magic hammered into him. "You're both weremystes; I can see the magic on you. So you wouldn't know what it feels like being a were. It hurts like hell. And having someone force a shift on you a few times—that'll mess you up pretty good.

"He turned me, and after the third time he told me that I'd be hearing from him. He'd have things for me to do, he said. Stuff to repay the favor he'd done for me."

"I'm guessing that at this point it doesn't feel like much of a favor."

He shook his head.

"I'll be honest with you, Bear, I don't give a crap about you. You're not exactly a victim in all of this, but you're sure as hell not the brains of the operation either. I want Hain. If you help me get him, I'll put in a word for you with my friends at the PPD."

"I don't know, dude," he said. "I don't know you at all. And Palmer's no one to screw around with."

"Neither am I," Rolon said.

It was a nice try, but Martell hardly spared him a glance. As menacing as Rolon might have sounded, I knew that Bear was talking about a different level of threat. Amaya's man might kick the crap out of him, but Hain was an accomplished dark sorcerer. I'd take an ass-whipping over blood magic any day.

Unfortunately, Bear didn't get a chance to choose for himself.

"I could not hear what you were saying," came a voice from behind me. Saorla.

I whirled.

"And so I thought I would join your conversation, perhaps lend a bit of wisdom."

She appeared in the same form she had taken in my dream the previous night. She still wore the green dress, though without the shawl, and her hair was down. But eyeing her more closely, I realized that this form wasn't entirely the same. Her appearance was similar to what it had been, but there were subtle differences. The gray streaks had vanished from her hair. The skin around her eyes and mouth was smoother. She looked younger; her dress fit her more closely, accentuating her figure. She was here to charm, perhaps even to seduce.

"We didn't want you listening," I said. "That's why I cast the muffling spell. You really should learn to take a hint."

"And you should learn to show some respect."

"Where'd she come from?" Bear asked, trying to keep up with events. "Who are you?"

She sauntered past me into the middle of the room. Rolon caught my eye and raised an eyebrow. At the same time, he made a small gesture with the hand holding his pistol. I shook my head.

Saorla paused in front of Bear. Even sitting, he appeared huge compared to her; to the untrained eye it might have seemed that he could crush her with one hand. And yet, he seemed to dwindle beside her, becoming little more than an overgrown boy.

"You are a were," she said. "A bear, I believe. Is that right?"

"Yeah, how did you—?"

She held a slender finger to her lips. "Do not speak more than is necessary. Among the minds in this room, yours is the least worthy. You have nothing to say that I wish to hear."

He blinked, frowned. But he held his tongue.

She focused her attention to Rolon. "You should put away your firearm. It will not help you fight me. More likely than not, you will hurt yourself or one of these others."

He glanced my way again. I nodded, and he slipped the weapon back into his shoulder holster.

Facing me, Saorla smiled in a way that promised either death or a night to remember. At that moment I couldn't decide which. "I did not think we would meet again so soon, although I did hope."

"You're turning weres into slaves," I said.

"I am?" she said, her lovely face a study in innocence. "I have done no such thing."

"My pardon. The weremancers who work for you are turning them."

"Weremancers." Her smile thinned. "That sounds like a term Namid'skemu would use. I suppose to him I am a necromancer."

"Yes, you are."

"He can call me such if he wishes; I cannot stop him. Yet. If the name crosses your lips, you will die in agony."

"What would you prefer I call you?"

"I am a runemyste, just as he is."

I shook my head. "No, you're not. The runemystes were chosen by the Runeclave. You made yourself immortal using magic you should never have attempted."

"Brave words, Justis Fearsson. But you should know better than to challenge me when Namid'skemu is not here to protect you."

"What are you doing with the weres?"

"You said we are making slaves. We are not. We are making soldiers."

That brought me up short. And it made all kinds of sense.

"Soldiers?" Bear said.

Saorla ignored him, still watching me. "Think about it. With weres, weremystes, and runemystes like myself, we have an imposing army. It is like a chess set. Those of us with power can accomplish much, but we need our pawns. And the weres will serve quite well in that capacity."

Her pale eyes flicked in Martell's direction for no more than an instant. But in that scintilla of time, magic filled the room; the air practically shimmered with it.

Bear let out a roar and tipped out of his chair onto his hands and knees. I cursed, having seen this the day before in Gary Hacker's single-wide. Bear screamed again.

"Jay, what's going on?" Rolon's voice had gone up half an octave, and for the first time since we'd met, he appeared truly frightened. He had pulled out his weapon again, and had it aimed at Bear.

"No! Not the pistol. The trank."

Bones snapped, Bear's body contorted, and another ear-splitting howl of pain made the walls shake.

Rolon seemed finally to grasp what was happening. He holstered the SIG Sauer and pulled out the tranquilizer gun.

"No," Saorla said. She didn't raise her voice, but I heard her anyway.

Rolon cried out. The trank fell from his hand, its grip glowing red. As I watched, the barrel flattened, as if some giant beast had stomped on it.

"If you want to stop the were from turning," Saorla said, "you will have to kill it." She shrugged. "As I said, he is a soldier."

Martell bellowed once more. His hair was becoming fur; already he had grown larger. His T-shirt hung in tatters from his body.

"Why would you waste one of your army?"

"It is not a waste. As it is, you are wanted for murder.

And here you stand with a servant of the criminal Amaya. If you kill the bear, he will shift back into the man, and the police will pursue you with that much more rigor."

Crap. It was time to leave.

I should have known it wouldn't be so easy.

The front door opened, and a man stepped inside. Tall, lean, a trim beard and dark eyes beneath a shock of black hair. Dimples, whom Bear had called Palmer Hain. I couldn't make out the details of his face because they were blurred by his magic. He was at least as powerful as I was. In a battle of spells, Rolon wouldn't stand a chance against him.

Maybe Rolon saw this as well. For a third time, he produced his weapon. Hain's expression betrayed no hint of fear. He made a small, sharp gesture with his right hand, and Rolon went down in a heap, his eyes rolling back in his head, the pistol slipping from his fingers. I didn't know if he was dead or alive.

Nor did I have time to find out. I warded myself: Hain, me, and a sheath of power. I didn't bother warding myself against Saorla; her power was beyond me. If she wanted to kill me herself, there was precious little I could do about it.

Hain's gaze snapped to my face as I cast. He threw a spell at me. I couldn't tell what it was. The impact jarred me, made me take a step back. But my warding held, and a second later he swayed as his attack rebounded on him.

By this time, Bear's transformation was nearly complete. The good news was he had taken the form of a black bear, as opposed to a grizzly. The bad news was that he might have been the biggest black bear I'd ever seen.

His bellow had become a full ursine roar. I backed away, thought about reaching for my Glock, but reconsidered. I didn't want to kill the guy, for his sake and mine.

"I had thought to spare you, Justis Fearsson. I saved your life more than once because I thought you could help us kill Namid'skemu. But that opportunity has passed."

The bear lumbered toward me, Hain behind him and to the side. If one of them didn't kill me, the other would.

Weres, when they shifted, took on the attributes of their totem creatures, and black bears, as a rule, tended to be timid. They weren't natural killers. I cast again: a solid piece of wood, the bear's nose, and a good hard thwack. Bear howled and reared at the impact of my spell, but he broke off his advance.

I wasn't done. Hain, unlike the bear, was every bit a killer. I'd seen the look in his eyes the night he murdered the homeless man. And I was certain that he had warded himself against any direct magical assault.

I threw another spell at Bear, this one more aggressive. I heard bone snap and a deafening shriek of agony, watched as the animal toppled over, narrowly missing Hain. And as the weremancer danced out of the way of the werebear, I cast my third spell. My magic, Hain, and a hole in the floor beneath him.

He fell, though he was able to throw himself to the side and avoid being swallowed by the hole I'd conjured. Bear continued to flail and howl, and Hain had to roll away from the creature.

Hain, Bear's CD rack, and a firm shove. The rack crashed down on the weremancer with a cascade of jewel cases and discs. He groaned and tried to push the rack off of him. But by then I was in motion. I closed the distance between us in two quick strides and kicked him in the head. Hain went still.

Bear's cries had become loud whines, and his writhing had slowed. Still, I held out some hope that he would crush Hain and finish him off.

"Impressive," Saorla said from behind me.

I spun, bracing myself at the first touch of charged air on my face. But still I could do nothing to keep her spell from hammering into me. I flew across Bear's living room, slammed into a wall, and slid to the floor, dazed and sore. It was like I'd been backhanded by King Kong.

She walked to where I lay and stood over me, her mouth set in a thin, hard line.

"I am not certain what I ought to do with you. You are more than you seem, and we have invested much in preparing you for Namid'skemu's death. We learned your defenses, studied your wardings, saved your life when we had to. That took time, effort. I am loath to waste it."

"When did you do all of that?" I asked, trying to clear my head and buy myself a little time.

"We have been doing it for quite a while now. This is why we studied your father."

That got my attention. "You've been hurting my father so that you could learn about me?"

"Of course. Why else would we bother with an old man who has lost his mind? You use different warding spells, but your magic and his are similar, as is the case with all children of weremystes."

I nodded slowly, and sat up. I had noticed in the past that the blurring effect I saw with every other myste I met was absent in my dad, and I had even wondered if this was because our magic, for lack of a better analogy, operated on the same frequency. Here was proof.

"He was right, then," I said. "He kept telling me that he didn't matter, but that I did. You were testing him to get at me."

"Aye, we were. But now Namid is warned against us. He will not be so quick to answer your summons, and he will be ever more cautious. Your value to us is largely gone. I ought to kill you and be done. But you intrigue me, and you have proven yourself unusually resourceful." She glanced back at Hain, who hadn't moved since I kicked him. "He is one of my best, and you defeated him. I did not expect that."

Bear, still in animal form, continued to watch us, even as he licked gently at his broken leg.

"Well, you might as well kill me," I said to the necromancer. "Because I won't be joining your army. I'm no chess piece."

She faced me again, solemn and beautiful. "I can compel you," she said. "Not all the time, but during the phasings. And I might even be able to force you into a phasing, as we force the weres to turn."

I felt myself blanch. The phasings were bad enough three nights out of each month. But to be subject to them at someone else's whim might have been enough to convince me that I ought to take blockers, the drugs some weremystes used to suppress the phasings. I had refused in the past to take them because the relief they offered from what Namid called the moontimes came at a cost, namely my access to magic. I was willing to endure the phasings as the price of being a runecrafter. But I would give up spellmaking forever before I allowed Saorla to use me as another of her magical slaves.

"This frightens you. I can see it in your eyes."

"I'll take blockers," I said. "I'll take my own life if I have to. You will not own me in that way."

"You choose death, then."

"I choose to fight."

I cast the spell as quickly as I had ever crafted any conjuring. Namid had long wanted me to cast without hesitation, to make my magic as immediate as thought. That's what I tried to do now.

Yes, she was a creature of magic, much as Namid was. But she had taken corporeal form here in this house, and I was banking on this being her one potential weakness. I didn't go for a direct assault; she'd be expecting that. And there were no more shelves to bring down on her; I'd used that up on Hain.

But there was plenty of stuff lying around the room. I opted for something small and hard that wouldn't draw her attention. The elements flashed through my mind. Saorla, the stone ashtray on Bear's coffee table, and the distance between them. I didn't wait for the magic to build. I didn't even pause to visualize the spell in action. It was the runecrafting equivalent of grabbing the ashtray and hurling it blindly. Except far more accurate.

The ashtray spun like a Frisbee and rammed into her face, an inch below her left eye. She let out an enraged screech, even as she fell to the floor. She was on her feet again before I could cast a second spell, blood pouring from an uneven gash across her cheekbone. Pain exploded in my head—a thousand hot metal spikes piercing my skull. I clutched at my temples, screaming, unable to stop myself.

"You will pay for that, Justis Fearsson," I heard her say, so close she might as well have been breathing the words into my ear. "You will die in anguish, slowly, so that you have plenty of time—"

Gunshots blared, three of them in quick succession, and blood began to spread across the front of Saorla's dress. I glanced to my right. Rolon lay on his side, his pistol held before him, his face wan. I grabbed my Glock from my pocket and opened fire as well, squeezing off six shots. Every one found its mark. Her chest and her gut were glazed with blood. Her body convulsed with the impact of each bullet, but she didn't go down. I knew we couldn't kill her; and the next time I saw her she would be totally healed, not to mention totally pissed. But all I cared about right now was surviving this encounter.

Rolon shot her four more times, twice in the chest, once in the neck, and once in the forehead. Wailing, she changed to her ghoulish form. The bloody wounds remained. She took a step in our direction, and I shot her again, staggering her. She bared her teeth and then vanished entirely.

As soon as she was gone, Bear roared and began to change back into a human. Hain, I saw, was gone as well. I guessed that Saorla had taken him with her.

"Nice shooting," I said to Rolon.

He nodded. "You, too."

"Are you well enough to get the hell out of here?"

"Damn right."

I stood and helped him up, and we lurched to the door.

Bear was halfway through his change: He remained very hairy, and his face still had a certain ursine look to it, but his eyes were more human than bear. With his leg still broken, he wasn't going anywhere anytime soon, but I couldn't worry about that right now.

I glanced around at the mess we'd made of his living room. "Too bad about your house," I said, and left with Rolon behind me.

CHAPTER 21

Rolon was unsteady on his feet, and his face remained gray. I had no idea what kind of magic Hain had thrown at him, but I had a feeling he was lucky to be alive. I helped him into the Lexus, hurried around to the driver's side, and got us out of there as fast as I could without drawing the notice of traffic cops. Once on the freeway, I headed back to Amaya's place.

Along the way, I pulled out my phone and dialed Kona's number.

She answered on the first ring.

"You're hot, partner," she said. "Don't go home, don't go to your office."

"I won't. Thanks. You have a pencil?"

"Yeah, why?"

I gave her Bear's name and address.

"Avondale is outside my jurisdiction," she said.

"I think that falls under the heading of 'not my problem.'"

"I suppose it does," she said. "Who is he?"

"One of the Sweetwater Park killers. The other, the brains behind the killing, is a dark sorcerer named Palmer Hain. Dark hair, trim dark beard, dark eyes. He's about six feet tall, one-eighty, and he drives a late-model silver sedan of unknown make. Be careful with him. He's dangerous as hell, even for me."

"Thanks, Justis. I'm . . . I'm sorry about all this. I know you didn't kill that girl."

"You have nothing to apologize for. Hopefully I can clean up this mess before long."

"That would be good. Where are you now?"

I hesitated. "Maui," I said. "Wish you were here."

"Sorry, shouldn't have asked. Habit, you know? I swear that's all it was."

"I believe you. Gotta go."

"Right. Stay safe."

"I'm trying."

I closed the phone and glanced at Rolon, who was already watching me.

"You're in some serious trouble, aren't you?"

I wasn't crazy about the idea of sharing my problems with one of Jacinto Amaya's attack dogs, but right about now he was the best friend I had. And moments ago he'd saved my life.

"I'm wanted for a murder I didn't commit, and for the life of me I don't know how I can prove I didn't do it. So, yeah, I guess you could say I'm in some trouble."

"And still you're helping the cops. They might be able to track you with that call."

I shrugged, my eyes on the road. "Would you let dark

sorcerers get away with murder just to save your own skin?"

"I might. I'm not sure. But you didn't, and I respect that." He stared out his side window. "So will Jacinto."

We got stuck in traffic passing through Phoenix on our way to North Scottsdale, and if it hadn't been for the impending start of the phasing, I wouldn't have minded at all. This was a very, very nice car. But I begrudged every minute we lost.

When we reached Amaya's mansion, Rolon got us past the security guys without delay—maybe he sensed my impatience. He was still wobbly on his feet, and he made a show of letting me help him into the house, which I appreciated.

"What happened?" Jacinto asked, meeting us inside the door.

I explained it all as succinctly as I could: the visits to Hacker and then Bear, Saorla's appearance and Hain's arrival, and our escape.

"Your man saved my life," I said, as Rolon sat on a couch sipping club soda. "And he's lucky to be alive."

"Good thing I'm built like a brick shithouse, eh, *amigo*?"

I grinned.

Jacinto smiled, too, but soon turned grim again. "I can't help you with Saorla," he said. "She's beyond me. But this man Hain, I might be able to track him down."

"I have the police working on it," I said.

"I'm better than the police."

I didn't doubt it, but I also didn't want Hain being found dead within a day or two of me mentioning his name to Kona. "Why don't we give the police a chance first."

He nodded. "All right."

"I need the car for a while longer," I said, already eager to get going. "Is that all right?"

Jacinto opened his hands, smiling faintly. "*Mi coche es tu coche.*"

"Thanks. And also for the Glock, by the way. It came in handy."

"Where are you going next?"

I took a breath. "To be honest, I'm not sure." I checked the time. Two o'clock. Daylight was slipping away, and I didn't have much confidence in my ability to win this fight and exonerate myself before night fell and the phasing began.

"He needs a place to spend the night," Rolon said. "He can't go home."

"Is that true?" Amaya asked.

"It's true that I can't go home." As soon as I gave the matter even a moment's thought, though, I knew that I couldn't stay here, either. "But I have somewhere else I need to be."

"With the woman? Miss Castle?"

I shook my head. "The police will be looking for me there. But Saorla will be looking for me out at my father's place in Wofford. And if I'm not there, she'll hurt him."

"If you are there," Rolon said, "she'll kill you."

"She'll try."

"Where does your father live?" Amaya asked, drawing my gaze.

In his saner moments, my father would be no happier

than Kona about me working for Jacinto. He certainly wouldn't want the man on his property, even to fight on the right side of a magical battle. Twenty years after leaving the force, my dad was still a cop to the core. And I wasn't sure I gave a crap.

Long ago, as a safety precaution, I had memorized the GPS coordinates for my dad's trailer. I wrote them down for Amaya.

He glanced at the paper and met my gaze once more. "Your old man crazy?"

I bristled at the question but kept my voice under control as I said, "Most of the time."

He nodded. "Mine, too. If you let me help, I won't allow anything bad to happen to him."

"What's your interest in this, Mister Amaya? You hired me, you put me on Regina Witcombe's trail, you're being more kind to me than I have any right to expect. And for the life of me, I don't understand why. What's in it for you?"

"Isn't it possible that I do this because it's the right thing to do? Even vicious drug lords have moments of altruism."

I said nothing. I waited, watching him.

A brittle smile touched his lips. "Rolon, if you're feeling up to it, find Paco and tell him we might be heading out to Wofford later in the day."

Rolon eyed us both, then stood. "Sure thing." He left the room, his gait steadier now than it was when we reached the house.

Once we were alone, Jacinto said, "There is an element of altruism in this. You can believe that or not, but it's true. I meant what I said to you the first night you came here. Blood magic is an abomination. Even on those rare occasions when the 'donors' are volunteers, they rarely have a full understanding of what it is they're about to do. And most of them are conscripts."

I thought of Heather, and of Jeff, the man in Sweetwater Park, and I couldn't quite suppress a shudder.

Amaya took a breath. "And as it happens, in this case my altruism dovetails nicely with my business interests."

"How so?"

"Dark sorcerers are relatively new to the Phoenix area. They haven't yet established themselves here to the extent they have in, say, Los Angeles, Las Vegas, New York, even Chicago. But in those other places, they have insinuated themselves into the street culture. They deal drugs, run prostitution rings, sell weapons to gangs."

"Forgive me for saying so, Mister Amaya, but they sound a bit like you."

I thought he might take offense, but he merely raised an eyebrow, a faint grin curving his lips.

"I told you, I have a business stake in this. The last thing I want is to have my . . . enterprises competing with those of dark sorcerers." He sobered. "But it's more than that. Yes, some of the drugs I bring into the city find their way to people you and I would call kids, even if they don't see themselves that way. And some of the prostitution money that comes my way is sourced in the same age group. But when these dark crafters are hunting for blood for their spells, they almost always prey on the young, the kids living out in the streets. That might not be the pattern here yet, but it will be soon enough. It's what they do in those other cities I mentioned. They kill kids for spells. That's how dark magic works. And you in particular know this as well as I do, because it's what Etienne de Cahors did with the Blind Angel killings."

He was right. Almost every one of the Blind Angel victims, more than thirty all told, were street kids, many of them Latino or African American.

"I don't want the competition," he said, without any apparent shame. "And I don't want them killing off my clientele."

"That's hardly admirable," I said.

"I never claimed otherwise. You asked about my interest in all of this. I'm being honest."

"But not entirely."

Amaya's expression calcified. "Meaning what?"

"I think there was another reason you had me brought here that first night. For some reason you thought that Witcombe and the others might come after you. You wanted them worrying about me instead."

His mouth twitched to the side. "They were already worried about you," he said. An admission. "I think you know they were. After Cahors you were more important to them, more of a threat. I gave them one more reason to focus their energy on you."

"And in the process you took some of the heat off yourself."

"Yes," he said. "But the rest of what I told you is true. They're a danger to my livelihood, and I don't take that lightly."

"So you think that Regina Witcombe is prepared to bankroll a criminal empire to match yours?"

"No. Missus Witcombe is providing money now, to get them started. But I'm sure she'll steer well clear of the drugs and prostitution."

That made sense, too. Something Patty had said to me about Witcombe when I was under her control came back to me now. *Before long, I'll have access to enough income that we won't need her . . .* Did Patty Hesslan-Fine envision herself as a potential rival to Jacinto Amaya? Was that what Saorla had promised her, a criminal empire run from behind the unimpeachable façade of Sonoran Winds Realty? And in return, Saorla would have a veritable blood factory: thousands of kids trapped by drugs and prostitution, easy pickings for her and her weremancers. It made sense, in a twisted, terrifying way.

For now I kept this thought to myself, saying instead, "I figured out why they went to Washington, by the way, and why it is that Saorla would have been willing to kill Jimmy Howell and ground the plane to keep Witcombe and her companion safe."

"Tell me."

"They've figured out how to kill the Runeclave's runemystes."

For the first time since I'd met Amaya, I had the feeling that he had no earthly idea what to say. He stared at me, appearing stunned and more than a little frightened.

"They murdered one near Washington," I said. "That's also why they wanted me. They tried to use me to kill a runemyste I know. I was reluctant to tell you because generally speaking I don't like to announce to the world that a runemyste has taken an interest in me. But I figure that if Saorla manages to kill me in the next day or two, someone else should know."

"Does that mean you've come to trust me?"

I checked my watch again—another fifteen minutes gone. "I suppose so. Don't tell anyone, all right?"

We both grinned.

"You have a reputation to uphold."

"Exactly. Listen, I have to leave. I'm guessing that Saorla wants to find me again before the phasing begins and her weremyste friends are no longer any use to her. And that's fine with me, but I need to be prepared."

"As I've told you before, I can help you with this. I'll fight."

"I'm not sure that's such a good idea."

"Why not?"

"Because I'm still wanted by the police, and I'm not sure it would be helpful to either of us to be seen together."

"You were planning to bring in the police for a fight against dark sorcerers?"

I started to shake my head, then stopped myself. And as I did an idea came to me, a crazy idea, but one that might allow me to solve all of my problems at once. Something else occurred to me as well, and before I knew it I had the bare outlines of a plan. "All right," I said. "I'd be glad to have your help with this." I pointed at the paper on which I'd written the coordinates of my dad's trailer. "Meet me there an hour before the moonrise. And bring Paco and Rolon—Luis, too, if you can get word to him." I started toward his front door.

"Anything else?"

I heard the irony in his tone; he wasn't used to taking orders from anyone. Fortunately, he seemed more amused than offended by my manner. "Yeah," I said over my shoulder. "Make sure you ward yourselves."

I climbed back into the Lexus and drove to one of the fancy malls in Scottsdale that had a covered parking complex. Once there, I sent Kona a text message telling her to meet me on level three of the parking garage.

I knew that it would take her some time to get there, and also that she wouldn't know what car to watch for. I was fine with that. I didn't think that Kona and Kevin intended to arrest me for Heather's murder, but I preferred to go into this encounter with a few advantages, just in case. I sat in the car and waited, checking out each vehicle as it cruised onto the third level, making sure that none of the cars carried detectives.

I spotted Kona and Kevin about half an hour later, almost as soon as they drove into the lot. Still, I remained in the Lexus as they pulled into a space and turned off their car. They got out right away. I didn't. I hunkered down a bit lower and watched them for a few minutes, waiting for any sign that they had backup with them. When I was convinced that they didn't, I got out and walked toward them, my steps echoing off the low cement ceiling.

Kona spotted me right off, but she didn't move and she didn't seem to say anything to Kevin, at least not until I was close to them.

I halted about twenty feet short of where they stood, and glanced around. "Thanks for coming," I said.

Kona buried her hands in her blazer pocket. "There a reason we're here, and not in the open someplace?"

I shook my head. "Not a good one. I didn't feel like waiting for you in the sun."

She gazed past me, trying to get a glimpse of the car I'd been in. "What are you driving?"

"A loaner. Anytime the forensic guys are done with my 280Z, I'd be glad to have her back."

"I'll let them know. You doing all right?"

"Considering," I said. "It's been quite a day."

"Right," she said. "About that, your friend Martell wasn't at his place when the Avondale cops got there, but they tracked him down at the local hospital. Did you break his arm?"

"Yeah, but it was a leg when I did it."

She frowned.

"What the hell is that supposed to mean?" Kevin asked in a hard voice. I had the sense that he was less convinced than Kona of my innocence in Heather Royce's killing.

"He's a were," I said. "He attacked me in his bear form and I used a spell to break his leg. When he shifted back to human form, that leg became an arm."

He didn't say anything. I couldn't tell from the way he was watching me if he thought I was crazy or lying. Kona, for her part, seemed to be struggling not to laugh.

"Anything on Hain?" I asked.

"Not yet," she said. "He doesn't show up in any of our files, and he's not listed as being a resident of Phoenix or any of the surrounding cities."

I rubbed a hand over my face. "Yeah," I said, as much to myself as to her. "I probably should have expected that."

"We have your description, and the name. Even if it's an alias, we should be able to track him down."

"I hope so." I glanced around again, and after taking a few steps toward them, cast the same muffling spell I'd used in Bear's house. Neither Kevin nor Kona noticed, of course. But I didn't want Saorla hearing what I had to say next.

"I need to get out to see my dad. Is anyone from the PPD watching his place?"

"That's not—"

"No," Kona said, talking over Kevin and glaring at him. "Nobody's there. Your place, your office, Billie's hospital room. They're all being watched."

"Kona—"

"What part of 'he didn't do it' do you not understand?" she said, rounding on him.

"I thought we were friends, Kevin."

He stared at her for another moment before turning back to me. "We are, Jay. But you're wanted for murder, and I don't take that lightly."

"Neither do I. Neither does Kona. But these other murders you're investigating—Jimmy Howell, the killing in Sweetwater Park and the others like it—those are real, and they were all committed by weremystes. I can help you with those, and the people who framed me for Heather Royce's murder know that." To Kona I said, "My father's trailer would be a natural place for me to go to. How did you keep them from sending someone to watch it?"

She flashed her million-dollar smile. "By telling them that we'd take care of it."

I smiled back at her. "Thanks." Sobering, I said, "There's something else you should know. And you're not going to like it."

"Okay."

"When I first mentioned to you that dark magic might have played a role in the murders you're investigating, you asked me who my source was, and I wouldn't tell you."

"I remember. You're going to tell me now?"

"Only if you promise not to blow a gasket."

"I'm not promising anything."

I stared back at her, saying nothing until she rolled her eyes and said, "Fine, I promise. Who was it?"

"Jacinto Amaya."

Kevin muttered, "Shit."

Kona looked like she wanted to take a swing at me. "Jacinto freakin' Amaya?" She said, her voice surging upward and echoing so loudly I was sure Saorla would hear her, despite my spell.

"He hired me," I said. "I've violated the privacy of a client in telling you that, but I thought you should know. A lot can happen between now and tonight's moonrise, and I'm not sure I'll survive it all. I know that you have list a mile long of crimes you'd like to pin on him, but in this one respect he's on the side of the angels."

"I'm not entirely sure I care. If I can nail him for anything, I'll do it."

"Not this, Kona. I need his help. And if something happens to me, you'll need it, too."

"What's going to happen to you?" Kevin asked.

"I don't know. But I had a similar conversation with Amaya not too long ago. I have a bad feeling about tonight. There's a powerful myste out there—Namid calls her a necromancer—and she's good and pissed at me. If she gets a chance to kill me she will. And she might have help from Patty Hesslan-Fine, Regina Witcombe, Palmer Hain, and whoever they hang out with on poker night. I have a lot of enemies right now. Plus, in case you didn't know, I'm wanted for murder."

"What can we do to help?" Kona asked.

I hesitated. "Probably nothing."

"Probably?"

My gaze flicked toward Kevin. "I'm not sure how much I can ask of the two of you right now."

Kevin and Kona shared a glance before facing me again. For the moment I ignored her and watched Kevin.

"Try us," he said. "We might surprise you."

We talked for a while longer, and by the time I left the mall I felt that Kevin was on my side again. I hoped that his and Kona's faith in me would be enough.

From Scottsdale, I intended to drive out to Wofford, to see my Dad and begin to plan for tonight. But I was still in the side streets near the mall when an all-too familiar voice spoke in my mind.

Once again you have used magic to keep me from hearing a conversation that was of interest to me.

"Saorla," I said aloud, knowing she could hear me now. "Didn't anyone ever tell you that eavesdropping is rude?"

You will come to me right now and you will come alone.

"No, I don't think I will. You and I will meet again, soon enough for my taste, but right now—"

Right now I am with a friend of yours. Speak to him. Tell him that I am here.

"Fearsson?"

I don't know how the necromancer managed it, but it was like she had Billie on a magical speaker phone. I heard her voice as clearly as I heard Saorla's. Somehow I knew that she would hear me as well when I said, "Are you all right, Billie?"

"Yes." She sounded frightened. Who could blame her?

She is fine. I have not harmed her, yet. But if you refuse to come here, I will kill her.

"Is she really there with you, Billie?"

"Yes. Who is she?"

Never mind that, Saorla said. *I will be waiting for you, and I am not feeling particularly patient.*

"Leave Billie where she is and we can meet elsewhere."

I do not think so.

"I can't get into that hospital, Saorla. It's crawling with Phoenix police, and they want to arrest me for a murder committed by your friend Patricia Hesslan-Fine."

You have proven yourself resourceful, Justis Fearsson, inconveniently so. I am confident that you will find a way past the police. You have thirty minutes to get here.

"No, I need more time than that!"

Nothing.

"Saorla!"

She didn't answer. I spat a curse and sped up. The last thing I wanted was to end up as one of those classic headlines: "Murder Suspect Arrested After Routine Traffic Stop." But the threat implied in her time limit was enough to have me pushing the envelope on speed limits all the way back to Mesa.

Only when I reached Banner Medical's parking complex—with all of four minutes to spare—did I slow down. I didn't see any police cruisers, but I hadn't expected that I would. They wanted me to walk right in so that they could nab me in a controlled environment. There were probably a dozen plainclothes cops inside, clustered on Billie's floor, and a few more near each of the entrances. There was no way I could walk in.

But a transporting spell might work. I had been in Billie's room once, so I could visualize it, and I knew the magic well enough to pull off the crafting. The problem was the distance. Billie was on the second floor, and for all I knew her room was on the far side of the building. I hadn't paid much attention to its exact location when I visited earlier in the day. That uncertainty wasn't going to make this conjuring any easier.

I was down to two minutes, though. I had to cast.

Since I wasn't entirely sure where the room was, I focused on Billie, and on Saorla. I cast with seven elements this time: Billie, me, the car in which I was still sitting, the image of the room I wanted to be in, the distance between me and that room, Saorla, and Billie again, because I was doing this for her.

I repeated the elements to myself seven times, concentrating as I never had before on any crafting. On the last recitation, I released the magic.

In the past, when I'd cast transporting spells, I had experienced a wave of dizziness and a moment of intense cold. This was ten times worse. Maybe it was because of how far I was trying go. Or maybe it was because I was lost, undone by my lack of certainty as to where in the building Billie's room was located. I felt like I was spinning uncontrollably through outer space. I was bone cold, and I couldn't breathe. I began to panic, knowing that it was taking too long, that somehow the spell had failed. I wanted to call Billie's name, but I couldn't even do that.

And then my knees struck something solid. I cried out in surprise and fright. Still my head was spinning, and I tumbled onto my side, my cheek flush against a cool, smooth floor.

"Good," I heard Saorla say. "You are here. Another few seconds and I would have had to kill her."

CHAPTER 22

I was afraid to open my eyes, knowing that I would probably throw up as soon as I did. If anything, the spinning was worse now than it had been while I was still trapped in the icy between, desperate to reach Billie's room.

"A transporting spell. As I said, you are resourceful."

I forced myself to open my eyes, to sit up and face whatever it was the necromancer had in store for me. The dizziness wasn't as bad as I had expected, and I was able to climb to my feet.

Billie watched me, her eyes wide, her face as white as the sheets on which she lay. I sidled closer to her bed and took her hand.

Saorla sat in a chair near the bed, clad once more in the green dress, her face and hair as lovely as they had been at Martell's house. As far as I could tell, she had healed herself of the wounds Rolon and I inflicted upon her.

I cast a quick warding that I hoped would protect Billie and me from whatever spells she directed at us.

The necromancer quirked an eyebrow. "You believe that you can ward yourself from me?"

"I'm pretty sure I can't. But I'd be a fool not to try, don't you agree?"

"You are a fool in either case."

Even with a warding in place, I was helpless against her magic. Fortunately, at the first touch of it, I dropped Billie's hand. Saorla's spell was similar to one she had used against me in Bear's house; it swatted me off my feet, so that I rammed into the nearest wall and crumpled to the floor.

"Fearsson!"

I groaned, but forced myself up. "I'm all right," I said. "She's playing with me. If she wanted me dead, I'd be dead."

"I am glad you understand that."

The door to Billie's room rattled.

"Miss Castle?" a man's voice called from out in the corridor.

"Tell him you are all right," Saorla said, steel in her tone.

Billie glanced my way, and I nodded.

"I'm fine," she said, loud enough for the man to hear.

"Your door seems to be stuck. Can you open it from in there?"

The necromancer shook her head.

"No," Billie said. "I guess I'm locked in."

"Don't worry, we'll get you out."

"Maybe you and I should leave," I said to Saorla.

"They will not get in until I allow them to."

"Fine. What is it you want?"

"Let us begin with the conversation you just had, the one you would not let me hear. What did you discuss?"

When I didn't answer right away, she shifted her gaze to Billie. That was all, but it was like watching her aim a loaded pistol.

I moved to Billie's side again and laced my fingers through hers. "I'm making plans for this evening. I believe you intend to send your weremystes after me before the phasing begins, and I want to be ready."

"Where?" she asked.

I glowered. "My father's place," I said, my voice flat.

"What else did you talk about?"

"The police investigation into Heather Royce's murder."

"They believe you are guilty."

"The police here do. The two I spoke with know that I'm not. I told them about Patricia Hesslan-Fine. And also about Palmer Hain."

She scowled. "You should not have done that."

I shrugged. "Oops."

"What else?"

"That's all."

"I do not believe you."

"And I don't care."

The door rattled again. We could hear several men speaking on the other side of it. "Don't worry, Miss Castle, we'll have this open in a minute."

"I could let them in," Saorla said. "Several of them are detectives. I could vanish and leave you to fight them off."

"Yes, you could." I let go of Billie's hand and gave her a quick smile. "What is this about, Saorla? You didn't bring me all the way here to ask me about a conversation. If you want to kill me for shooting you earlier, then go ahead. If it's something else, then get to it. But I have more important things to do with what's left of my day. I'm not going to waste the last hours of sunlight on you."

"Once again, you speak bravely, though you have no power or skill to back up your words. I can kill you at will. I can do the same to her, or to your father."

"And yet here you stand, just talking, just like me. You need me for something. What is it?"

"You know already."

I took a breath, because I did know. And I was certain as well that she could could compel me to do pretty much anything she wanted, simply by threatening Billie, Kona, and my father. "Namid," I said.

"Precisely."

"What about Namid?" Billie asked.

"She wants me to help her kill him."

"Can you do that?"

"There are ways," Saorla said.

"Your minions tried last night. If they'd succeeded, I'd be dead, too."

"Yes, but they are limited, as you are. Working together, however, you and I can kill the runemyste and spare your life."

"How?"

She shook her head. "Do not mistake me for a fool, Justis Fearsson. I will not tell you that until I am certain that you will help me."

"I won't."

"Not even to save the lives of those you love?"

Even knowing that the threat was coming, I experienced a moment of pure terror. It seemed my heart was in that taloned grasp again; she had only to squeeze.

"Don't, Fearsson! Don't you dare let her use me that way!"

I'm not sure I'd ever loved Billie more than I did in that instant.

"I won't," I said again, to her this time. And with the words still on my lips, I lunged at Saorla and took hold of her, one hand gripping each of her shoulders. The stink of rot filled my nostrils, and I had to grind my teeth together against a wave of nausea. But I held fast to her.

She let out a small disbelieving gasp. That was all I gave her time to do. I cast again, blindly, without pause or thought. The elements flashed through my mind like flickers of lightning. The necromancer, me, my grip on her, the room where we were, the parking lot, the distance in between, and Billie, safe and alone here once we were gone.

Cold and darkness closed in on me once more. My breath caught in my throat, and we spun as if thrown from a speeding car. But I refused to let go, even as she made her skin flare like the sun. Flames seared my hands, and I howled. She let out a wail as well: shock, rage, the indignity of being touched by a mere weremyste.

We landed hard on the pavement, rolled twice before stopping with me on top of her. That lasted about a tenth of a second. I was blasted into the air, flailed as if trying to fly, and then came down hard on the hood of a sedan.

The car alarm blared. I hoped I hadn't ruined Amaya's Lexus.

She stood. I slid off the car and faced her, swaying, my body aching, a trickle of blood flowing from a scrape on my elbow. But already I could hear raised voices and approaching footsteps. My hands still tingled with the pain of touching her, but when I chanced a glance down at them I saw that they were unmarked. The skin wasn't even red.

"I could kill you now," she said, her voice a raw snarl. "You who dare to lay your hands on me. I need only form the thought."

"Then do." As I spoke the words, I cast again; two spells this time, not simple wardings, but something more focused that Namid had taught me a couple of months before, when I was about to face Cahors. And I used that small bit of blood in the casting. I felt guilty about it, but this didn't seem like the time to let qualms get in the way.

She went for my heart first, as I had known she would. I grunted at the impact of her assault. But the clawed hand could not penetrate the warding I'd placed around my heart. She tried for my mind next; the thousand-spikes attack again, I expect. That shield spell held as well. I was learning.

Saorla let out a low growl, more demon than human. But then she pointed a finger at me and shouted, "There he is! Justis Fearsson is here."

Crap! Men and women were already closing on us from several directions, and at the sound of my name, most of them broke into a run.

I glanced back at the sedan. It was a smoke gray

BMW, with a great big Fearsson-shaped indentation in the hood. Me, where I was standing, and Amaya's cream-colored Lexus.

The closest of the cops had their weapons drawn, and one of them—a tall, blond-haired guy I remembered vaguely from my last visit to 620—halted now and leveled his pistol at me. "Get your hands up, Fearsson!"

I released the spell, felt the icy air overtake me again.

An instant later, I was behind the wheel of the Lexus, about six rows away from Saorla and the cops. I had time to see the cop blink and straighten, his mouth hanging open. Then the necromancer vanished as well, and I swear I thought Blond-hair was going to piss himself.

I eased the Lexus out of the space and pulled away, driving slowly, trying to make it seem that I didn't have a care in the world.

But I checked my rearview mirror and watched as the rest of the detectives converged on the spot where Saorla and I had been. Blond-hair was gesturing wildly with the hand holding his weapon, and the other cop who had been nearest was nodding. They'd be explaining this to Hibbard and their other supervisors for the rest of the day.

You were fortunate to escape, the necromancer said in my mind.

"Maybe," I said. "I'll see you before the moonrise, and you can try again."

And what is to keep me from going back and killing the woman?

I nearly swerved off the road. Idiot! I could see that chess board before me: I had put my opponent in check, but I'd left my queen exposed.

"Nothing," I said, ashes in my mouth. "Nothing at all. But you've done enough to her, Saorla. Leave her alone."

And what do I get in return?

"What do you want?" I asked in a monotone.

I want Namid'skemu.

"I can't give him to you. I won't."

He means more to you than the woman?

"I'm not choosing between them. But I'll give you my life for hers."

Your life has no value to me.

"And hers does?"

Silence. Either she had ended our negotiation or I had stumped her.

"Saorla?" I said, trying to keep the fear out of my voice.

Very well, Justis Fearsson. I will spare the woman. But if you survive this night, you will owe me a boon. I do not know what it might be or when I will collect. But you will owe me. Is that agreeable to you?

I knew better than to think that I had gotten off easy. I was incurring a debt, and the cost of repayment would be high. There would come a day when I cursed myself for the bargain I was about to strike. But for today I had kept Billie alive, and that was all that mattered to me. For today.

"Yes, I accept those terms."

Good.

She practically purred the word. My stomach knotted.

An odd pressure withdrew from my mind—I hadn't known it was there until I felt it vanish. Saorla was gone, at least for the time being.

I steered the Lexus onto the freeway and headed out to Wofford. About five miles short of my father's place, I pulled off the highway, parked along the side of the road, and hiked a short distance into the desert. Satisfied that no one would hear me, and that I couldn't be seen from the road, I called Namid's name.

I didn't have to wait long before he appeared before me, the desert sun glimmering on his waters and shining through him so that he appeared to glow from within.

"You summoned me, Ohanko. You do this with disconcerting frequency."

"I know; I'm sorry. But I wanted to warn you, and I need your help."

"Begin with the warning."

"Saorla is still determined to kill you. She tried to force me to help her by threatening to kill Billie. I refused."

"Is Billie—?"

"No, I . . . I talked her out of it." I didn't want to admit to him that I had struck a deal with the necromancer. He wouldn't approve. Not that I thought I'd been so clever, but the last thing I needed was a lecture from Namid about how foolish I was.

"She relented?" he asked, sounding skeptical.

"Not exactly. The important thing is that Billie's safe for now; you're not."

A tight smile rippled the surface of his face. "I will tread like the fox."

"Good. As to the second thing—"

"You know that I cannot help you. It is—"

"Against the rules that govern your kind. You've told me before."

"And yet, still you ask me."

"That's right. Because in this case, those rules don't apply."

His face roughened. "Explain, please."

"Do you believe that the two women who used their magic against me the other night were responsible for the murder of the runemyste in Virginia?"

"You told me that you believe this to be so. I found the evidence you presented to that effect quite compelling."

"And do you also believe that if their spell had worked last night they would have managed to kill both of us?"

"The runes they had you draw on yourself would have made such a murder possible, yes."

"Then you must also believe that at this point you and your fellow runemystes are at war with Saorla and her fellow necromancers."

"War may be too strong a word, but I believe I see your point. Still, Ohanko, I cannot act on your world. We have laws, and even a conflict with other beings as mighty as my kind does not allow us to forget who and what we are."

"But what if Saorla is trying to act on our world so that she can gain an advantage in her fight with you?"

"I am not sure that matters."

"Doesn't matter?" I said, my voice rising.

"If the runemystes ignore the laws that created us, we betray the trust placed in us by the Runeclave. And at that point, we cease to be what we were. We become no better than the necromancers themselves."

I suppose there was something admirable about his principled dedication to the law, and at some point maybe

I'd be able to tell him as much. But just then he was really pissing me off. I realized, though, that he didn't have to act on our world. Not in a strict sense, at least.

"Surely, though," I said, "your mandate from the Runeclave involved more than abiding by the law that keeps you from interfering in our world."

He frowned at that, his brow turning choppy. "Yes. But—"

"You were tasked with protecting our world from the influence of dark magic, isn't that right?"

"I believe I see what you are getting at."

"Do you? My life depends on your understanding."

"You would argue that my oath to uphold those laws is in conflict with my oath to guard against dark magic, and that therefore I should honor the latter over the former."

"I would argue that, but I know you too well to think you wouldn't find a way to honor both." I smiled. "So I've found a way for you."

His frown deepened. "You have?"

"Yes. Are there others of your kind who can help you?"

"Others?"

"I don't trust Saorla, and I fear the blood magic of her weremancers. You should have backup."

"Backup," he repeated. Another word that sounded awkward when he said it. "I do not know what this is."

"It's a police term," I said. "It means support, help."

"Ah, yes. Perhaps . . . backup would be wise. But how does having help allow me to obey my laws and still fight for you?"

"I don't need you to fight for me, not really. I'll have

some . . . some backup as well. We'll be able to fight the weremancers. All I need for you to do is live by your laws and make certain that Saorla does the same."

"You want us to keep her from fighting against you."

"Exactly. You wouldn't be acting on our world so much as preventing her from doing so."

He gave a slow shake of his head. "I do not know, Ohanko. We are not to interfere, even if others possessing powers similar to ours do. I do not know if others of my kind will agree to your request."

"Then you've already decided," I said. "The runemystes believe that following the Runeclave's directive not to interfere is more important than combatting dark magic."

"I did not say that."

"Your actions say it. If the dark sorcerers have Saorla on their side, and she's able to do as she wants with us, I'm dead, and so are any who fight beside me. But it's up to you, Namid—you and the rest of the runemystes. If you're determined to stop the spread of dark magic in my world and, oh-by-the-way, if you're also determined to prevent further attacks on members of your little circle, you'll help us in this one way. If not . . ." I shrugged. "Well, I'm going to fight anyway."

He stared at me for a long time. I didn't know if I had ticked him off, and I sure wasn't sorry if I had.

"I will speak with the others," he finally said. "Be well."

I watched him evaporate into the desert air. Then I got back in the car and drove the rest of the way out to my father's trailer.

Sunlight angled across the desert, casting long,

twisting shadows from the bases of saguaro cacti and bathing the sand and sagebrush in gold. I pulled up near the trailer, my eyes on my dad, who was slumped in his chair as usual. He didn't appear to be twitching anymore, but there was an empty, dirty cereal bowl at his feet, and he wasn't wearing socks. He certainly wasn't at his best. I opened the car door.

Upon stepping out of the car onto the dirt and gravel drive, I felt the pull of the moon again, even more forcefully than before. My thoughts seemed to fragment and for a moment I just stood there, one hand on the door, the other braced on the roof of the Lexus. I couldn't remember what I'd been about to do.

But the phasing hadn't started quite yet, and after a few seconds I was able to clear my head enough to recall where I was and why I had come. I did a quick survey of the land around my father's place and saw nothing. That was what I had hoped for, and also what I expected. Still, I knew a moment of relief.

I shut the door and walked to where my dad sat, feeling a little unsteady on my feet. I kissed his forehead, drawing his gaze, which was clouded, unfocused.

"How are you doing, Pop?"

"Justis?"

"Yeah." I pulled out the extra chair, unfolded it, and sat. "Are you feeling all right?"

He rubbed a hand over his face and then ran both hands through his thin hair. "I don't know," he said. "I'm not . . . I'm better, I think." He eyed me again. "What are you doing here?"

"Long story."

He glanced at the bandage on my wrist. "What happened?"

"Another long story."

He nodded rather than pursue either question. "I feel the moon. What day is it?"

"The phasing begins in less than two hours."

"Crap," he whispered, reminding me of me. "Why are you here? Do you usually come for the phasings?"

"No, but this month is different."

"Different how?"

Another long story, but this one I couldn't keep from him.

"Do you remember the pain you've been experiencing the last few weeks?"

"Pain? I . . ." He stopped, pressed his lips into a hard line and dipped his chin. "The burning," he said. "Yeah, I remember."

"Dark magic. You've been under attack from what Namid calls necromancers."

"Namid." He sat up straighter. "He was here. In fact, you were with him."

"That's right."

"And these necromancers . . ."

"They're like runemystes. Their powers are similar, but they weren't created by the Runeclave. They bought their power and their immortality with blood magic."

"And they were hurting me to get at you."

I nodded. "I'm sorry. They wanted to learn about our wardings, our defenses, so that they could then use me to kill Namid."

His forehead creased. "Kill Namid? That's impossible."

"No, it's not. And at some point I'll explain to you how they intended to do it. But what matters now is that at least one of them is coming here, along with some weremystes who have been helping them. They threatened to hurt you again, and I'm here to make sure they don't. But ultimately what they want is a fight, some would say a war. And this is going to be the first real battle."

He smiled at that. "I'm not a praying man, Justis, and I haven't been to church in about a hundred years. But even I know that the first battle in this fight was fought a long, long time ago. This is the latest incarnation of the same damn war."

I lifted a shoulder, conceding the point.

"So you and I are going to fight side by side, huh? I always dreamed of that."

I grinned. "So did I. But no. You're going to stay in the trailer."

"The hell I am."

"Dad—"

"Justis."

I winced and stared out over the desert. A pair of ravens swooped and soared over the first line of hills, jet black against a deep blue sky. "I feel bad saying this, but on your best day you're not the sanest guy I know. We're right on the cusp of the phasing, and this is not going to be your best day. I can't be worrying about you at the same time I'm fighting off a bunch of dark sorcerers."

"Then don't worry," he said, the stern tone taking me back to my childhood.

I opened my mouth to say more, but closed it again.

Patty Hesslan-Fine would be coming; I was as certain of that as I was of anything I'd told him. I didn't know how he would respond to hearing her name, much less seeing her in the flesh.

"Left you speechless, eh?"

"Tell you what," I said, standing. "Let's get you some food and a change of clothes and we'll work from there."

"You humoring me?"

"No, sir. I'm trying to see how capable you are today. If you're a danger to yourself or to me, I'll lock you in the goddamned bathroom. If you're all right, we sure as hell could use the help."

He pushed himself out of his seat and stared me right in the eye. We were about the same height, and his eyes were so much like mine it was like gazing into the mirror.

"God, you look like your mother," he whispered.

"Except for my eyes."

"Right. Except for them." He broke eye contact, glancing back toward the city. "I'll eat," he said. "And I'll put on a fucking tie and jacket if you want me to. But if you try to lock me away, I'll tear this place apart."

"It's your trailer," I said. "I've got a place to sleep tonight." A lie, but that was not a conversation I wanted to have at the moment.

He smiled. "You know what I mean."

"I do."

I followed him into the trailer, pausing on the threshold to check back over my shoulder. I still saw nothing on his land; I hoped that was a good sign.

He changed clothes, which meant putting on a clean T-shirt and jeans. He even put on socks. In the meantime,

I fixed us both sandwiches and poured a couple of glasses of orange juice. I hadn't eaten since leaving the hospital that morning, which may have been why the moon was already affecting me so powerfully. I felt better after I'd downed my sandwich.

After he finished his, I cleaned up and turned to face him.

"How are you feeling?"

"Muddled," he said. "The way I always do right before a phasing. And you'd be lying if you told me you weren't feeling the same."

"You're right," I said.

"So, you going to lock me in the bathroom?"

"So that I can spend the next ten Tuesdays doing repairs? No, thanks."

He chuckled. "Good."

"But, Dad, there's something you should know. One of the dark sorcerers—"

"Car," he said, staring past me toward the door. "Coming fast."

"Damn."

He started for the door, but I stopped him.

"Wardings first," I said.

"Right."

We each cast several spells in quick succession. I put every warding I could think of on both of us, and I felt his magic settling over me like a warm rain. He had done the same.

Once finished, we went back outside. He halted a few steps from the trailer, and stared at Amaya's Lexus. "That yours?"

"One more long story."

His mere glance conveyed so much disapproval I almost laughed. But then our gazes were drawn to the two SUVs bouncing down his rutted road and raising a plume of rust-colored dust. I had hoped that Amaya and the others would arrive here before Saorla and her friends, and it seemed that this once luck was on my side.

And then it wasn't.

A figure winked into view a few yards from where we stood. Long brown hair twisting in the wind, a green dress, and a shawl around her shoulders.

Dad shot me a questioning look. But he didn't get the chance to give voice to his curiosity. Several more people appeared behind Saorla. I made a quick count; there were eight in all. Hain was there, apparently fully healed from our encounter earlier in the day. Witcombe stood near him, as did Gary Hacker and four other guys I didn't recognize. Clearly, Hacker and some of the others weren't pleased by the company they were keeping. But my dad couldn't tear his eyes away from the third woman in their group. The setting sun shone on her face, and glimmered in her warm brown eyes. I had wondered if my father would recognize her through the blur of her magic. I should have known better than to doubt.

"What is she doing here?" he whispered.

"That's what I was trying to tell you a minute ago."

"Elliott Hesslan's daughter, right? I'm not imagining this?"

"You're not imagining it."

"Justis Fearsson," Saorla said. "And Leander as well. Did you ever imagine that you would die together?"

"I know that voice," my dad said, turning his gaze to the necromancer. "Who is she?"

"She's your worst nightmare," I said. "A runemyste without a soul."

CHAPTER 23

The SUVs stopped some distance short of the trailer with a scrape of skidding tires on dirt and another billowing cloud of dust. The doors opened and several men got out. In addition to Amaya and Rolon, Paco and Luis, I thought I recognized a few of the others as well—maybe from the army of gun-toting guards I'd seen at Amaya's house. But the four I knew were the only weremystes among them. The others were there as muscle. Heavily armed muscle. Every one of them, including Amaya, held a weapon in his hand. Several had MP5s, Rolon and Paco were carrying what looked like SIG Sauer 556 SWATs, and the rest had handguns—also SIG Sauer. I wondered if Amaya owned stock in the company.

"Who are they?" my father muttered. "Where the hell are all these people coming from?"

"I know them," I said, speaking quickly, my voice low. "They're here to help us."

"They look like they're here to cause trouble."

He was right, they did.

Saorla made a sweeping gesture with her right hand and even out in the open air, I felt the frisson of magic on my skin. Amaya, Rolon, and the others went down like bowling pins. Their weapons were ripped from their hands, but rather than scattering on the desert dirt, the MP5s, SIG P220s, and SIG 556s rose into the sky, swirling as if caught in an eddy of air. Saorla raised her hand over her head and closed her fist slowly. The weapons began to gleam red, and I heard the dull, rapid *pop, pop, pop* of ammunition going off in the magazines.

She dropped her hand and the spinning weapons fell to the ground, now a circular mass of molten steel and plastic.

"I think we will not involve these firearms in our evening's activities," she said.

Those standing with her laughed.

My father rubbed his arms; I saw goosebumps on his skin. "That voice," he said again. "She's the one who spoke to me."

"She's also the one who tortured you. I hate her a lot."

My dad glanced my way, and I made myself grin. Inside, though, I was reeling. The necromancer had cast her spells with ease. We were lucky she had chosen to disarm Amaya and his men rather than kill them. I assumed she and her weremancers wanted their blood. It seemed that Namid had been unable to convince his fellow runemystes to keep Saorla in check. If the myste had even tried.

Paco and one of the guards I didn't know by name were the first of Amaya's men to get back up. They helped the others to their feet, including Jacinto. Amaya caught my eye, and I held up a hand, telling him to stay where he was. I didn't know if Saorla would allow him to join my father and me near the trailer, but I liked the idea of Patty, Witcombe and the others having to fight on two fronts, as it were.

"There is much blood here," Saorla said. "I am pleased. Thank you, Justis Fearsson, for inviting your friends to join us."

"What is it you want with us?" my dad called to her, his voice hoarse. "What the hell are you doing on my land?"

"Dad—"

"I want nothing from you, Leander Fearsson. It is your son whose aid I seek. He knows what for. But I will admit that you showed more spirit than I had guessed a mad, enfeebled man might." Her body and face rippled, like reflections in disturbed water, and a moment later she stood before us as my mother from the earliest memories I had of her. She wore a cornflower blue dress, and the crooked smile that still occasionally haunted my dreams. Honey brown hair fell in soft curls to her shoulders, and the color of her eyes had darkened from Saorla's pale blue so that it matched the dress perfectly. I had remembered my mother as beautiful, but even so, I had not remembered her like this. It was magic, I knew: Saorla's enchantment. But still I couldn't avert my eyes. She was mesmerizing.

I heard a soft sob from my father, and I put an arm around his shoulders.

"Stop it," I said, my voice as harsh as I could make it.

"Does your father want me to stop?" she asked, canting her head to the side, looking more alluring than any guy should ever see his mom look, even if she was an illusion.

I chanced a quick glance at my dad. He had closed his eyes and was muttering to himself in silence. "You know he does, Saorla. Now either take your true form, or go back to the lying hag we all know so well. But stop this."

Her form wavered a second time, and the familiar Saorla glared at me through pale eyes. "You should be careful what you ask for, Justis Fearsson."

Magic surged through the air again, and Hacker and one of the other men standing with Saorla let out sudden howls and fell to the ground, writhing, moaning.

All of us stood transfixed, watching the weres shift. Alone among us, Saorla appeared to enjoy what she saw. A faint smile played at the corners of her mouth, and she stared first at one and then at the other, a disconcerting hunger in her pale eyes. Most of the others closed their eyes or turned away. Hain and Patty watched, but even they flinched at the men's contortions and the snapping of bone.

"This can't be good," my dad said.

I didn't bother to agree. After a few moments more, Hacker had transformed into the large coyote I'd seen at his single-wide. The second man had become a mountain lion. The transitions had taken less time this evening. I attributed that to how close we were to the moonrise and the start of the phasing.

The coyote padded toward the trailer and my dad and me. The cougar slunk toward Amaya and the others.

Hacker growled low in his chest, and the big cat let out a hunting scream the likes of which I'd only heard previously deep in the Arizona wilderness.

Amaya and his men backed away. I cast the same spell I'd used in Hacker's home—dad and me on one side, the coyote on the other, and a barrier of magic in between.

The animal stopped a pace short of my conjuring and bared its teeth.

"Big dog," dad said. "I take it that spell will work."

"It should. It has before."

He nodded.

The cat let out another wail and went down in a heap. Amaya or one of others had attacked him with a spell.

"Don't hurt him!" I called, knowing I was too late.

"We don't have our weapons!" Luis hollered back at me.

Jacinto rounded on him. "He's being controlled. Just like Hacker. Protect yourself, but don't do anything more to the were."

"What about them?" Luis asked, waving a hand in the direction of Hain and the rest.

Jacinto glowered at Saorla once more, murder in his eyes. "Them you can kill."

I shouted a warning again, but not in time. I was too far away to feel the magic, but I saw Patty, Hain, Witcombe and their friends stagger and then watched as Amaya and his men were hit by the rebounding magic of their own conjurings. I didn't know who had cast or what kind of spell he had attempted. But I had assumed that the dark sorcerers would all be warded in every way imaginable, including reflection spells. Fortunately,

Amaya had followed my advice: His men were warded, too. He had even used protective magic on the men who weren't weremystes, though a couple of them were knocked to the ground by the force of the reflected attack.

We had roughly equal numbers of runecrafters on each side, some more skilled than others, of course. But we were evenly matched. Except for Saorla.

"We are stalemated," she said, a challenge in her eyes. "Is that not how it seems to you?"

It bothered me that she could give voice to what I had been thinking moments before. Was she reading my thoughts?

"Yes," I said. "So perhaps you and your friends should go."

"I do not think so." She half-turned and gave an almost imperceptible nod.

Patty stepped and spun, not toward me or Amaya and his companions, but toward one of the men standing near her. I recognized the motion, having seen it at Witcombe's place the night before, and I saw the blade in her hand colored with that rich golden sunlight. But I didn't have time to cry out a warning or cast a spell. I don't even know what sort of crafting might have stopped her. There was nothing anyone could have done.

Her knife struck true, and the man next to her went down, blood fountaining from the side of his neck.

My dad sucked in air through his teeth. "Good God."

"Cast!" Patty shouted.

Light burst from the dying man's body, from the blood on his neck and shoulders, chest and back. It was striated, gold from Hain was layered along with blue and green and red. I couldn't help but think that there was something beautiful about it, even as those rainbows of magic leaped from the body in curving bolts that crackled and hissed like lightning.

Two of them arced toward my father and me; four more surged toward Amaya, Paco, Luis, and Rolon. They struck our chests, smashing into us with the force of freight trains, battering us to the ground.

I felt like I'd grabbed hold of a live wire and then been run over by the power truck that came to fix it. My father groaned.

"Dad?"

"I'm all right," he said, sounding anything but.

In retrospect, I recognized the craftings. They had tried to control our magic, to bring on the phasing a few minutes early. That was why they had aimed the spell only at the weremystes, not bothering with Amaya's other guards.

I forced myself to my feet. "All right, Amaya?"

Jacinto was still on the ground, though he was sitting up and rubbing his neck. He raised a hand in answer to my question.

"That didn't work," I said to Patty. "I guess we'll all be going through the phasing together."

She shook her head. "We won't be going through them at all. As I told you the other day, dark magic has its advantages."

"So you killed that man for nothing."

"No. If it had worked, it would have saved us time, effort. And we want to see if we can control weremystes the way we do the weres. If not for your wardings, I think we would have succeeded."

"You're insane."

"Enough," Saorla said. "You heard her. The moon time is about to begin, and when it does, you, your father, and these others will be at the mercy of my weremystes, whom I protect from the moon. Or I can kill you all before the moon even rises."

"So in your mind you've won already," I said. "What's stopping you from doing as you please?"

"A third choice. Surrender yourselves. Remove your wardings and submit yourselves to my power. You will live, you will be spared the phasing, as you call it, and you will serve the side that is destined to prevail in this coming war."

"I'm not about to surrender to you. And I refuse to accept that my only choices are between death and betrayal of everything I believe in."

"Then you're a fool," she said, snarling the words.

"You're not the first to say so."

I visualized the spell as I spoke, and released it before Saorla could answer. I didn't know if it would work, and I didn't have time enough to recite the elements. I just cast, as Namid had taught me. After what Rolon and I did to her in Bear's house, I knew she would have warded herself against bullets. So I conjured a blade: my hand, her heart, and sharpest steel.

Saorla gasped, her eyes going wide. Blood stained the front of her dress, and she shrieked her pain and rage.

I knew I'd hurt her, and that was something. But I'd wanted to kill her, and, it seemed, I didn't have the power to do so. An instant later I was in agony. Somehow I was on the ground again, magical spikes piercing my head, my chest, my hands.

I should kill you now, her voice whispered in my mind. *You have earned a slow, agonizing death, and you shall have it. But I will have your blood and that of your father. And you will watch him die before I take your miserable life.*

The anguish ended as suddenly as it had begun, leaving me gulping for air.

"Get up!" she said, speaking aloud this time.

I didn't move.

"Get up right now or Leander Fearsson dies."

My father helped me to my feet, his eyes locked on mine.

"Any ideas?" I mouthed.

He shook his head. "I'm already feeling the moon. I've got nothing. I'm sorry."

"I'm not doing much better." I cast a look Amaya's way only to find that he was watching me. I read my own despair in his dark eyes.

We could use your help here, Namid, I said in my mind.

Saorla clapped her hands and laughed. The blood, I noticed, had vanished from her dress. For all her power, she had used her own blood to heal herself. Or to torture me. Whichever it was, I knew this was significant in some way, though I had no idea how or why.

"You have learned nothing, Justis Fearsson," she said. "I do not believe he will be coming. I have told you before, the runemystes are more concerned with their own safety and their precious rules than they are with the lives of those who serve them. I warned you of this when first we met."

"I remember. I refused to believe you then, and I still do."

"And again I tell you that you are a fool." She opened her arms wide. "Where is he? Where is your precious Namid'skemu? You have asked him to help you. You did so just now, and I have no doubt you have done so several times before. But where is he?"

"Here."

She and I turned as one. Namid stood on a low rise to the west of the trailer, sunlight shining through him as if he were made of glass. Two figures flanked him. One, a woman, had an odd, mottled appearance. It took me a moment to realize that she was made of stone, granite perhaps. She was beautiful and yet as severe and remote as a mountain top. On Namid's other side stood a slight man who appeared to waver and dance, even as he remained still. He was even less substantial than Namid in his clearest form. But somehow I knew that this was illusion. In his own way he must have been every bit as powerful as my runemyste.

"You are well, Ohanko?"

"Feeling better now."

"You cannot interfere!" Saorla said. "I know you cannot! You were punished for what you did to Cahors."

Namid's waters riffled, making the sunlight passing through him waver. "I was, because I did not have the permission of my kind to act. This time I do. At Ohanko's urging, I have convinced the other runemystes that you are a threat to us, and to the world we are sworn to protect." He indicated the two mystes standing with him. "They have sent the three of us to keep you from taking additional lives."

"I do not believe you!"

"Believe what you will. We shall not interfere with them," the runemyste said with a small gesture that somehow encompassed every human on my father's land. "But you shall not help your friends, nor will you harm mine."

She spun toward me both hands held before her. Flames leaped from her fingers. I threw my arms up in a vain attempt to protect myself. I needn't have bothered. The fire never reached me; it never even came close. Nor was it the shield I had conjured to protect my father and me from the coyote that stopped her spell. The flames simply vanished, swallowed, it seemed, by the air before me.

Saorla screeched her frustration.

Patty whispered something to Witcombe, and an instant later one of Amaya's guards was thrown into the air. He somersaulted toward the dark sorcerers and landed on his back at Patty's feet. She stabbed down with the knife, but the man managed to roll out away from the blow.

I pulled the Glock from my jacket pocket and fired off a shot. I aimed for her blade hand, but missed. She gaped at me—maybe she hadn't considered that I might still have my weapon even after Saorla had disarmed Amaya's men. And that moment's hesitation gave Amaya's man time enough to find his feet. He braced himself to throw a punch, but another spell fell upon him. His head snapped to the side, and he collapsed like a puppet whose strings had been cut. I had a feeling he was dead before he hit the ground.

Hain grinned.

I fired again, this time at Hain's head. But in the span of a few seconds between my first shot and my second the weremancers had warded themselves against gunfire. The shot ricocheted back at me, missing my dad and me by inches and gauging a hole in the side of the trailer.

That shot was like the report of a starter's gun. Abruptly spells were flying in all directions. Luis went down, as did Witcombe and Patty. But in moments all of them were up again, casting as fast they could, trying to find a spell that would overcome their opponents' wardings. Hain threw spell after spell at my father and me, each one landing like a fist. Our wardings held, but the force of his attacks was enough to leave me dazed; I couldn't image how my father stayed on his feet.

"Are you—?"

"Don't worry about me," he said through clenched teeth. "Just get the bastard."

Sometimes I thought that weremystes of all sorts were too enamored of fancy spells. Namid had taught me to think in simpler terms. I aimed two spells in quick succession at Hain. With the first I pulled his foot out from under him as I had done to Patty at Witcombe's house. And as soon as he hit the ground, I cast again.

Hain, the ground beneath him, and a large chasm in the desert dirt.

The crack opened and he let out a cry of surprise and

alarm. He teetered on the edge trying to swing himself free, and then toppled into it.

The crack, Hain, and the dirt covering him once more. The spell hummed in the air and I heard another cry, more desperate this time. His arm flailed above ground; I didn't know how much air he had down there, but for the moment at least I had other concerns.

"That was well done," Dad said.

"Thank—"

He shoved me aside and cast at the same time. At least I thought the magic came from him. It played along my skin like a summer wind and met the oncoming spell with enough force to shake the ground beneath my feet. The great coyote that had continued to growl and bare its teeth at us all this time flattened its ears and let out a soft whine.

I stared at him. "What the hell."

"I saw her cast," Dad said, pointing at Patty. "I don't know what it was, but she aimed it at you. I met it with a warding of my own, a wall spell, I used to call it."

"Seemed to work."

The ground opened again near Patty and Witcombe, and Hain scrabbled out like an insect, his clothes covered with dirt. He nodded once to Patty and they pivoted in unison toward my father and me.

"Ward yourself!" I said.

But they had learned. I felt the spell course in our direction and then pass over us. Stone shattered behind me.

"What was—"

"Crap!" my father said. "Move!" He shoved me again, this time following right on my heels.

I heard a deep metallic groan. Another spell skimmed over us, and more stone broke. Not stone, cinder block. The supports holding up the trailer.

The groan crescendoed, tipped over into a grating shriek. From within the trailer came a frenzy of shattering glass: windows, plates, glasses, picture frames. If it was fragile and my father owned it, it was smashed in those few seconds. And then the trailer fell over, crashing to the ground where my father and I had been standing seconds before.

I conjured fragments of broken cinder block into the air and hurled them at Patty, Hain, and Witcombe, hoping that their warding had been specific to bullets. Surely they hadn't anticipated that I might throw rock at them.

I think my dad must thought the same thing, because chunks of cinder block rained down on them, opening wounds on their faces and necks, battering them to the ground.

Saorla growled again, her body going rigid as she strained against the magical constraints placed upon her by Namid and his companions. For good measure, I hit her with a piece of cinder block, too.

We threw another volley of stone at the weremancers, but by now they had warded themselves. The fragments fell to the ground in front of them; a few hurtled back our way, but missed us.

My eyes flicked westward. The sun hung just above the horizon, fiery orange and enormous. Looking to the east, I saw the first glimmer of moon glow touching the sky. We had no more than a few minutes before the phasing began. If what Patty said was true, while our minds were at the mercy of the moon, hers and those of her dark sorcerer friends would remain clear. And all would be lost.

You have little time, Ohanko, I heard in my mind.

Did he really think I needed to be told?

Hain and Witcombe had aimed their spells at Jacinto, Rolon, and the others, pounding them with attack after attack. Amaya's wardings held, but they were falling back step by step. Hain and Witcombe had only to keep them occupied for a while longer.

An idea came to me, and though I didn't like it, I didn't feel that I had much choice. I'd cast with a small bit of blood in the hospital parking lot and had used the fact that I was fighting a necromancer as my excuse. I needed more now, and I didn't even bother trying to justify the spell I intended to craft. I tore the bandage from my arm, grabbed a shard of window pane from the ground and carved a gash in my arm alongside the scar from the other night. Blood welled, ran over my skin.

The expression on my father's face nearly stopped me: disapproval, fright, even disgust. "Justis, what are you doing?" But I saw no other way to stop them.

Seven elements: the glow of the moon brightening the eastern horizon, the shape and color of it as it would appear in mere seconds, the land beneath my feet, my mind, my magic, a shield against the phasing, and my blood.

Magic prickled painfully on my arms and neck and down my spine. The blood on my arm was wiped away, and a weight I hadn't known was there lifted from my mind, like haze blown away by a clean desert wind.

Everything was clearer: my vision, my thoughts, my emotions.

"Very good, Jay," Patty called to me. "You see it now, don't you? The power of blood magic. It's like nothing you've experienced before, right?"

"You think I'm one of you now." I shook my head. "You're wrong. When have you ever used your own blood for a spell? When have you accepted that the power you want demands a cost that you have to pay on your own, without taking it from others?"

More blood seeped from the cut on my arm.

My fist, her face, my blood.

The spell smashed through whatever wardings she had conjured. She staggered back, falling onto her rear. I had aimed the blow with care; didn't want her using a bloodied nose to strengthen spells of her own.

I saw Paco, Rolon, and Luis cut themselves and cast. Hain and Witcombe went down. Jacinto didn't draw blood. I couldn't read his expression, but I guessed that he felt as my dad did about what I had done. That was all right with me.

Patty clambered to her feet again. There was something in her hand, and I wondered for the span of a heartbeat if it was a pistol. Only when she mashed it down on the head of the man next to her did I understand that it was a rock. The man fell to the ground, and she followed him down, her blade flashing with the last rays of the sun.

She laid the knife blade along his throat.

"I'll kill him," she said. "You think your own blood is more powerful than someone else's. Maybe it is. But do you know how much blood I can take from one man? And do you know what I can do with it when my magic is enhanced by the pull of the moon?"

CHAPTER 24

"How many people are you going to kill, Patty?"

"As many as I have to! You think you've found some secret formula, don't you? But your spell won't last long. You think you're the first weremyste to use blood against the phasing? You're not. The spell Saorla put on us is more powerful by far than what you've done. You've bought yourself a few minutes, that's all."

I wanted to argue with her, but already I could feel the weight of the moon pressing down on me once more. She was right. I'd won a moment's reprieve. The moon wasn't even up yet and my spell was failing. I suppose a runecrafter could keep the moon at bay all night long, if he was willing to bleed himself to death.

"I can cast again," I said. "I can keep myself sane long enough to destroy you."

She shook her head. "You can't. I'll bleed this one, and then bleed your friends. I'll bleed my friends if I have to. Saorla and I have plans. Nothing else matters." Her gaze flicked in Jacinto's direction.

Saorla and I have plans. Once more I thought of Patty's comment about not needing Witcombe's money for much longer. She was the competition Amaya had been talking about at his house. I doubt that he knew this, but I was sure of it. And though I wanted to laugh away the possibility—Patty Hesslan, a crime boss? A rival to Jacinto Amaya?—seeing her holding a knife to the throat of a man who was ostensibly her ally in this fight made the possibility seem all too real.

She gave a shrill whistle. The coyote—Hacker—lifted his ears at the sound and trotted back to her.

Patty grinned. "More blood." She eyed my dad and me, and then looked over at Jacinto and the others. "Are you willing to kill him to save yourselves?"

"So you'll kill anyone you have to. Just like you killed Heather Royce."

Witcombe was on her feet again, seeming unsteady and uncertain, her gaze flicking back and forth between Patty and me.

"How do you feel about that, Missus Witcombe? Are you ready to help Patty kill again, like she killed Heather?"

"She did what she had to," Witcombe said. "You wouldn't understand."

"So you approve of what she did to Heather? It didn't seem like it that night."

"I was upset. What happened was regrettable. But . . . but I understand now."

I nodded. "You heard?" I called.

"We heard."

Witcombe whirled. Patty turned her head sharply, searching for the source of that voice.

Three elements: the camouflage spell, an end to the conjuring, and Kona and Kevin, who had been hidden by it.

They were warded already, and had been since our conversation in the parking garage. A spell from Witcombe forced them back a step, but did no damage. Kona raised her pistol and fired.

"No, Kona!"

The shot rebounded back at her but missed. She ducked belatedly.

But while Patty and Witcombe were still distracted, I cut myself and cast again.

Patty cried out, dropped the knife, which I had heated, and watched as it melted into the desert dirt.

The moon peeked over a ridge of distant mountains, blood red and huge. I felt my thoughts slipping away, slick, like they were coated in oil. I cast the shielding spell again and knew another moment of clarity. But I was more clouded than I had been, and I knew that even this moment of relative sanity wouldn't last long.

But I saw as well that Patty and Witcombe weren't doing much more than staring at that rising moon.

"What have you done?" Saorla demanded.

I thought she was talking to me, but she wasn't. She was facing Namid and the other runemystes.

"We have removed your spell," Namid said. "Blood of the innocent should not be used to help others escape the laws of magic. Your weremancers will experience the phasing as they are meant to. At least for this night. Take them and go."

"No!" I said, the word ripped from my chest.

This time they all looked at me.

"Patty and Hain and Witcombe—they're all guilty of murder. They need to . . . to . . ." I was having trouble keeping my thoughts on track. I could barely remember what I had just said. And I had cast a spell. It was supposed to help in some way. "They're murderers." I stared past the woman in the green dress, to two people who were walking toward us. Kona. One of them was Kona.

"He's right," she said. "The two women are wanted for the murder of Heather Royce, and the man is wanted in connection with a murder that took place a few nights ago in Sweetwater Park."

"I will not give them up," Saorla said. "Let me leave this place, Namid'skemu, with these three who serve me." She indicated Hain, Witcombe, and Patty. "And I will allow the Fearsson men to live."

"They're not yours to bargain away," Kona said to the runemyste, her voice so cold I wondered if Namid would ice over.

"Perhaps not," Namid said. "But with Saorla's help they are too powerful for your jails to hold."

Kona aimed her weapon at Patty. "There are ways around that."

"She's still warded," I said. "They all are."

Kona kept her weapon trained on Patty, but she pursed her lips, clearly unsure of where that left her. I hated to admit that Saorla and her weremancers had us beaten. But it was true: They were warded—against bullets, against magic, and, no doubt, against a host of other assaults as well.

But, as it happened, not against everything.

I had forgotten about Hacker. It seemed as though everyone had after Patty called for him. He remained in coyote form, his yellow eyes gleaming with moonlight, his fur tinged with red in the rich light of the setting sun. Now, with a snarl that came from deep in his chest, he leaped at Hain, who was still on his knees, and who, long ago, had spelled Hacker, robbing him of his freedom, making him little more than a slave to the moon and to magic.

Hain was in a moon-induced haze and couldn't react fast enough. The coyote went for his throat, teeth snapping, paws planted on the weremancer's chest. Hain fell back with the animal on top of him and let out a gurgling cry as the beast tore at him. Blood soaked his shirt and the ground beneath him. His eyes rolled back in his head.

Saorla made another sharp motion with her hand, and the coyote flew from him, yelping as it hit the ground a few feet away and rolled.

But I wasn't watching Hacker or Hain.

I saw Patty's lips moving. She was about to cast using Hain's blood. God knew what she would do or at whom she would aim her magic. My father, Kona and Kevin, Jacinto and the others, me—any one of us could have been her target.

And so I did the one thing I could think of. Three elements: Patty, a cylinder of magic around her, and all that blood. I cast without hesitation, without thought, without consciously putting the elements into words. I pictured what I had in mind and let the spell fly.

Magic surged through the ground and practically made the air shimmer. I couldn't have said which of us cast first. It felt as though the spells released simultaneously. The blood vanished and flames shot from her hands. Only to be blocked by the barrier I'd conjured. The fire rebounded, an assault spell fueled by blood; whatever wardings she had placed upon herself before coming here could never withstand such powerful magic. She screamed, flailing and writhing, trapped by my spell and under siege from her own.

Flames swallowed her like some ravenous beast. Her clothes and skin and hair blackened until at last she fell over, still twisting, her movements growing weaker by the moment.

Kona, Kevin, and my dad stared at her, wincing but unable to avert their eyes. Regina Witcombe had covered her mouth with trembling hands. Tears coursed down her face. Even Jacinto and his men flinched at what they saw. Alone among us, Saorla and the runemystes seemed unaffected. Namid and his companions watched Saorla, but the necromancer had her hard glare fixed on me.

"You have cost me a servant I value," she said. She cast a quick glance at Hain's body before meeting my gaze again. "Two servants. You will pay a price for that."

I ignored her. Pointing at Witcombe, I said to Namid, "What about her? She and Patty killed a runemyste, and she was an accessory to Heather Royce's murder."

"She is mine!" Saorla said. "I will not lose another."

I shook my head. "That's not for you to say."

"She cannot be held by a jail, Ohanko. You know this."

"She killed one of your kind! You'd let her go?"

"I am helpless to do otherwise."

Saorla's mouth curved into a great big shit-eating grin. I would have loved to say or do something to wipe it from her winsome face, but my thoughts were fragmenting again. It was all I could do to follow the rest of the conversation.

"What about my damn murder investigations?" Kona asked.

"I believe they are solved," Namid said. "The man who committed the murder in the park is dead, as is the woman who killed Heather Royce. Do I have all of that right?"

Kona frowned, but after a moment she nodded. "Yeah, I suppose."

Namid turned to Saorla. "We have a bargain then, you and I. You will take the Witcombe woman and go. And you will leave the Fearsson men alone."

"And the people we love," I said, thinking of Billie and of Kona.

Namid weighed this and then nodded. "And those they love."

Saorla shook her head. "Unacceptable."

"It is, for the most part, the bargain you proposed."

"I demanded all three of my servants!"

Namid's shrug was so casual that even in something of a daze, I had to keep from laughing. "Two of them are now dead, through no fault of mine." He pointed my way. "Nor of his."

"His spell killed her!"

"Ohanko's spell kept her from harming others. She was killed by her own crafting."

"I still do not—"

"You will agree to this," Namid said, his voice like ice grinding against stone, "or I will step outside of the law and wipe you from this earth right now."

I hoped that Saorla would refuse and force the runemyste to act. But I think she sensed that she'd pushed him as far she could. "Very well," she said. Her eyes found mine. "Beware, Justis Fearsson. I am not finished with you."

"Did I not make the conditions of this bargain clear?" Namid demanded.

"Of course you did, Namid'skemu. I am merely telling young Fearsson what he knows already to be true." She looked at me sidelong once more. *You still owe me a boon*, she whispered in my mind. Out loud she said, "We shall meet again."

Her disappearance was sudden enough to startle me. It took me a moment to realize that Witcombe was gone, too. The bodies of Hain and Patty Hesslan-Fine remained, as did Hacker, the werecat, and the others— dead and alive—Saorla had brought with her. I was vaguely aware of movement off to the side. Men were leading others to a pair of SUVs. That should have meant something to me, but my attention was drawn back to the watery figure before me. He was speaking to the woman—to Kona.

"They need a place to sleep," he said.

"I know. Justis can go back home now. I'll take him there myself. I'll take both of them."

"It is well. You have my thanks."

After that I lost track of the conversation and just

about everything else. I remember gazing at the moon from the desert, and later through a car window. I think Kona said stuff to me, and I suppose I tried to answer, but I remember nothing of what we talked about. I do remember, though, that my father rode with us, and that he slept.

I awoke the next morning feeling hungover, my thoughts clearer than they had been, but far from crystal. The door to my second bedroom was closed, which it never is. I was about to open it when I remembered that my dad was here with me, that his trailer had been knocked over, and that Patty Hesslan-Fine was dead. I left the door shut and dragged myself into the kitchen to fix some coffee.

I wanted to go see Billie—now that I had remembered my dad, I was recalling lots of other stuff as well—but I didn't want my father waking up alone in a strange house. He'd been in my place before, but it had been a while, and his memory wasn't always so good, particularly in the middle of the phasing.

While I was waiting for him to wake up, Kona called and asked to come by. She and Kevin showed up at my door a short time later, badges in hand.

"I take it this isn't a social visit," I said, eyeing them both.

"'Fraid not," Kona said. "We need a statement from you about Heather's murder, about your friend Martell, and about what happened last night to Hesslan-Fine and Palmer Hain."

"All right." I stood aside and waved them into the house.

Kona went right in, but Kevin faltered, his eyes lowered. "I think I owe you an apology."

"No, you really don't. You're new to this magic thing, and this week you got thrown into the deep end without water wings or anything." I grinned, and so did he. "You've handled it well," I said, "and I appreciate it."

The three of us talked for the better part of an hour. Kona and Kevin had a lot of questions, and I answered them as best I could, trying to reduce magical occurrences to explanations that wouldn't raise too many eyebrows among those who read their report. Eventually I heard my father stir in the back room and call out, "Justis?"

I excused myself and went back to see how he was doing. When I opened the door, he was sitting on the edge of the bed, his hair tousled, his T-shirt wrinkled.

"My place was destroyed, wasn't it?" he said as I walked to the bed and sat beside him.

"I think we can repair it, but yeah, it's in pretty bad shape."

"And I suppose everything else I think happened last night really did happen."

I raised an eyebrow.

"I remember a coyote killing someone and Elliott Hesslan's daughter lighting herself on fire."

"That all happened."

"Damn." He rubbed a hand over his face. "You know, I do fine with the phasings on my own. If that's your idea of a good time, you can count me out next month."

I laughed, though only for a few seconds. "How are you feeling?"

"Not too bad, considering. Hungry. You got any food?"

"Yeah. Kona and her partner are in the living room. They needed a statement on what happened last night."

He nodded and looked around the bedroom. "I don't suppose anyone thought to crawl inside my place and get me a change of clothes."

"I don't think so, no."

"Oh, well." He stood and followed me out into the living room where he greeted Kona with a hug and introduced himself to Kevin. I fixed the two of us some scrambled eggs and toast, and, as I cooked, finished my conversation with Kona and Kevin. When they left, my father and I went outside and sat on the front steps to eat our breakfast.

I expect that he felt as muddled as I did, and for a time we ate in silence.

Then Saorla popped into view in front of us, and we both dropped our forks, just about in unison.

I cast a quick warding to protect both of us. The necromancer laughed at the touch of my magic.

"You still believe that your wardings can stop me?"

"I have no idea. But as long as I can cast, I'll keep protecting myself."

She shrugged, as if she didn't care one way or another. "I did not come to kill you, though kill you I will." She smiled. "Yes, Namid'skemu protects you still as part of the bargain we struck. But with time his vigilance will slacken, and then I will have my revenge."

"Well, until then," my dad said, "why don't you leave us the hell alone?"

"I miss you, Leander Fearsson. I miss being in your mind. I miss hurting you."

"Forgive me if I don't say the feeling's mutual."

"Perhaps you would miss me more if I looked like this." Her body flickered like a dying light bulb, much as it had the night before, and she stood before us in my mother's form, her hair down, the same cornflower dress bringing out the blue in her eyes.

"Get out of here," I said. "Before I summon Namid."

"You sound like a child. You will call for Daddy if I don't leave you alone?"

She was right, that was exactly how I sounded. But I didn't have the power to drive her off on my own. My father's face had gone ashen, but he continued to stare at her. I don't think he was capable of doing anything else.

"Go," I said, putting as much menace into the word as I could.

She laughed and faded slowly, still in my mother's body. "Until next time," she said, the voice and accent all Saorla.

Once she was gone, my father took a long shuddering breath.

"Sorry," he said. "I should have . . . I don't know. I should have done something." He set his plate aside.

I did as well. Neither of us had finished our meals, but my appetite was gone, as was my dad's, I'm sure. I stood, walked a few steps down the path toward the street, to the place where Saorla had stood. Then I turned.

"What happened, Dad?"

I blurted the question, not even bothering to explain what I meant. He knew: my mom's death, and that of Elliott Hesslan. The question had been burning inside me for years, through all the accusations and whispered rumors, through all the dead, silent moments we had spent together. God knew I'd wanted to ask a thousand times, and always I swallowed the words. It was none of my business, I had told myself, though of course it was. He'd tell me when he was ready. But I had known that he wouldn't. Only now, after all that had happened in the past few days, had I finally given voice to that desperate need to know. And again, I had sounded like a little kid, unable to contain myself any longer.

He regarded me from the stairs, his eyes sunken, his shoulders slumped. Already, I regretted asking. No matter how much I wanted to know, he didn't deserve to be put through having to tell me.

I opened my mouth to say as much, but he held up a hand, stopping me. A tear spilled down his cheek and then another.

"I should have told you a long time ago," he said, emotion roughening the words. "But I didn't know how, and I'm not always able to . . . well, you know."

"I do know. You don't have to tell me. I shouldn't have asked."

"Of course you should have. You should have asked me when you were a kid, but I understood that you couldn't. That was my fault. I shouldn't have waited for you. But I was chicken."

He buried his face in his hands, and I thought he was crying. But when he lifted his head again a few seconds later, his eyes were dry.

"She should have left me. The phasings were wearing me down, and I was drinking too much, afraid of what the moon was doing to my brain. She should have left. But she loved me, I guess. And she was nuts about you, and she knew I was as well. 'A boy needs his father.' She said that to me the one time I asked her why she continued to stick around. She wouldn't leave because that would have meant taking you, and she didn't want to do that.

"But she was angry, and hurt, and she needed someone. We'd met the Hesslans a couple of times—mutual friends, I think. It's funny, I don't remember the name of the couple who introduced us. But Elliott and Mary seemed nice enough. I didn't give them much thought. Dara did, though. She was friends with Mary first, but she and Elliott both liked to garden. That was what did it in the end. Tomato patches and marigolds." His laugh tipped over into a sob. But after a moment he went on in a low quaver. "I don't think she was out there searching for someone to replace me. Not really. But like I say, she needed more than I could give her, and he was the one she found.

"Thing was, he was looking for her in particular."

That I hadn't expected. "What?"

Dad nodded. "He was after her. After me, really. But through her. Hesslan was into dark magic, and even then there were beings like that one." He pointed to where the necromancer had been standing.

"Like Saorla?" I said.

"Yeah, like her. For all I know, it was her. He started the affair with your mom and made her believe that he loved her. But then he started asking questions, trying to make her tell him stuff about me and my magic. At least that's what I think happened. I pieced most of it together after the fact. But I'm right. I know I am."

"So he was asking questions," I prompted.

"That's right. And she got suspicious. Smart lady, your mom. She figured out that he was a weremyste, too, and she was pissed. When she worked out that he was using her to get to me, I think she tried to break it off. He must have threatened to expose the affair to everyone, including you, because . . ." He took a long breath. "Because she killed him. And then she killed herself."

"*She* killed *him*," I repeated in a whisper.

Dad nodded. "That much I know for certain. I know how to read a crime scene, and I was the one who found them." His voice had gone flat, and his gaze was unfocused. "They were in a hotel. I'd followed them there a week or so before, and that night I was going to confront them. Never got the chance. She stabbed him in the heart, and then used the same knife to cut her carotid artery. She was dead in minutes.

"I altered the crime scene. Not a lot, but enough to make it less clear who killed whom. I couldn't leave her there like she was, knowing that she'd be thought of as a murderer. That's why so many in the department thought I'd done it, because I was the one who found the bodies, and because the evidence was too hard to read. I didn't care, really. I'd have taken the rap for her if it came to that. Hell, there was a part of me that would have been happy to kill the bastard myself."

He swallowed and faced me. "I'm sorry I didn't—"

"Stop. No apologies. I know now. That's all that matters."

"I'm sorry you know."

"I'm not. I appreciate you telling me."

"Did you ever think that I'd killed her?"

"Not once, not even for a second. I think you know there was a time when I hated you, when I blamed you for every bad thing in my life, stupid as that was. But even then I knew you hadn't killed her."

He nodded, even chanced a smile. Tears streaked his face again.

CHAPTER 25

Later that day I went to see Billie, who was continuing to improve. For once, I didn't need to rush my visit. I had nowhere else I needed to be, and no fear of running into the police. I sat with her, told her about all that had happened in recent days. I even brought lunch with me—fajitas, of course. We were able to spend a few hours together.

After, I went back home, picked up my dad, and drove out to Wofford to assess the damage to his trailer. My first reaction upon seeing the wreckage was that it was far, far worse than I had remembered. But he seemed pretty upbeat and thought that if we could find a way to prop it back up, it would just be a matter of replacing the cinder blocks and windows, as well as whatever items inside had been broken when it fell. He had homeowner's insurance, but I wasn't convinced that it would cover this. The trailer was supposed to be sitting on a foundation, not on blocks. Still, I didn't argue, and I tried to sound as optimistic as he did.

We got back to Chandler well before the moonrise and hunkered down for the night. Like me, Dad preferred to endure the phasing alone, so he retreated to the guest room and I retreated to my bedroom. But to be honest, as the second night of the phasing began, I found something oddly comforting in knowing that he was nearby, going through it with me.

We passed the third day and night of the phasing much the same way—I went to see Billie again, and Dad and I drove back out to Wofford with a new set of cinder blocks and the phone number of a guy who claimed that he could "tow, lift, or dig anything." He joined us on my dad's land and, after assessing the damage and hemming and hawing a bit, said that he could put it back in place. For a couple of thousand dollars. I thought the price was outrageous, but again Dad took it in stride and even talked him down to eighteen hundred. A handshake later we had an appointment for Friday morning.

The following day, the first after the phasing, I was awakened by a call from Jacinto Amaya, who requested that I join him at his home.

I drove to his place and went through the usual security check by his guys, though they were friendlier this time. Rolon met me at the door with a smile and a thump on the back and led me to Jacinto's living room. Amaya greeted me there, shaking my hand and steering me toward the bar.

"I thought I'd hear from you before now," he said. "I believe I owe you money. Drink?"

"No, thanks. And you don't owe me a thing. You gave

me a thousand up front, and I only worked for you for three days. If anything, I owe you a hundred bucks."

He shook his head. "Nonsense." And then he handed me a check drawn on the Chofi account. It was in the amount of ten thousand dollars.

"What's this?" I asked.

"Consider it a bonus. You did good work, Jay. Together, we struck a hard blow against dark magic in the Phoenix area. Sure, Witcombe is still alive, but that's hardly your fault."

I held out the check to him. "I can't take this. You've paid me what I earned. Things are settled between us."

"You're refusing a gift from me?" he asked, an edge to the question. I remembered what Rolon had said about refusing to accept the Glock as a gift. *He'll be insulted, and he's not a man you want to piss off . . .*

That might have been so, but he also wasn't a man to whom I wished to be beholden to the tune of ten thousand dollars.

"I don't work for you, Mister Amaya. I was happy to take you on as a client, and I'll do so again, if you need me. But this . . ."

"You need the money," he said. "I know you do, if not for you then for your father. His place was wrecked the other night. I was there, remember?"

I said nothing.

"No strings attached. I swear it." He smiled, and it appeared genuine. "This is what I do for my friends. Now, don't tell me that you would refuse my friendship."

If refusing a Glock would piss him off, I guessed that refusing his friendship would be a good deal worse.

"No, sir. I wouldn't."

"Good. Then take the check. Fix up your father's place. If there's money left over, buy something nice for Miss Castle."

He knew too much about me, and now that he had equated the check with his friendship, he knew as well that I had no choice but to take it. And regardless of what he said, I had the feeling that this money came with all sorts of strings. I couldn't see yet where they led, but they were there, as fine and strong as spider's silk.

I pulled out my wallet, folded the check with care, and slipped it into the billfold. "Thank you, sir."

"My pleasure," he said with too much enthusiasm for my taste.

"You were right," I said, returning the wallet to my pocket.

"Of course I was. About what?"

I had to grin. "About competition from dark sorcerers. I'm pretty sure that Patty Hesslan-Fine, the woman who lit herself on fire, had every intention of building a criminal empire to rival yours. She was going to hide it within the workings of her real estate business."

His expression had darkened. "What makes you think so?"

"Just something she said. Witcombe won't chance it— you have nothing to fear from her—but Patty would have."

"And now that she's gone, someone else will step forward to take her place."

I nodded. "Probably."

"Then our work isn't done. But we both knew that, didn't we?"

I didn't like the idea of being in a longterm alliance with Jacinto Amaya, but I found it hard to argue with his logic.

"Yes, sir, I guess we did." I turned to go.

"You orchestrated things very well," Amaya said, stopping me.

"I'm sorry?"

"The other night. You brought together my men, your father, the runemystes, not to mention two homicide detectives from the Phoenix Police Department. I wouldn't have thought that was possible. And what's more, you made it work. That was impressive."

I shrugged. "Thank you. But you were the one who hired me in the first place, who enlisted me in a war I hadn't known was going on and had no intention of fighting. You did as much orchestrating as I did."

"True. Clearly we work well together."

"I prefer to work alone." It was probably a foolish thing for me to say, but I couldn't help myself.

Amaya didn't seem to take offense. "So do I. But there may come a time—another one—when we won't have that choice."

I considered this, and decided once more that I couldn't argue the point. We chatted for a few moments more, until at last I managed to leave. I was glad to get away.

I drove next to 620. I parked nearby and walked to the front entrance, running into Kona just as I reached the door.

"Hey there, stranger," she said, a brilliant smile on her face. "You here to see me?"

"Actually, no. I'm here to see Hibbard."

Her entire bearing changed. "He call you in?" she asked, sounding concerned. "Because if he's still trying to pin the Royce murder—"

"No, it's nothing like that. I came here on my own. I want to talk to him."

"And you think that's a good idea."

I grinned. "I think it's something I need to do."

She pursed her lips for a moment. "Well, I'll assume you know what you're doing."

"Right, because that always works out so well."

She didn't laugh, but she opened the door and held it for me.

In truth, I wasn't any more convinced than she that coming to see Hibbard made sense. But now that I knew what had happened to my mother, I wanted him to know as well.

I went to his office, second-guessing myself with every step I took. By the time I knocked on his door, my pulse was racing. He called for me to come in, and I opened the door.

Seeing me, his face reddened. "What the hell do you want?"

"I'd like to talk to you if I may."

"About what?" he demanded, sounding as though there was no answer I could give that would satisfy him.

"About my father."

He hadn't been expecting that. "What about him?"

I pointed at the chair opposite his desk. "May I?"

He hesitated, nodded. "Close the door."

I told him all of it. Everything. I started by admitting

that both of us were weremystes who didn't take blockers.
I tried to explain what that meant, but he stopped me.

"I know more about magic than you think," he said.
"I've been a cop in this town for a long time. Go on."

From there, I told him about this most recent case,
about all that had been done to my dad by the dark
sorcerers. And I concluded by repeating almost word
for word what Dad had told me about my mother's
death.

For a long time after I finished, Hibbard said nothing.
He had shifted his chair so that he could look out his
window without turning his back on me, and he had his
fingers steepled, his index fingers resting lightly against
his lips.

"Why did you tell me that?" he asked, his voice
subdued.

"I thought you should know."

"Did he send you?"

I shook my head. "He doesn't know I'm here. But
once upon a time, you were his best friend. And I know
you cared about my mom, too."

"How is he? The last I heard he was . . ."

"He's in and out," I said. "He has a few good days, but
mostly he's what you'd expect of a burned-out old
weremyste."

He nodded.

We sat in silence for a few minutes. At last I stood and
said, "Well, that was all I came to tell you. Thank you for
seeing me."

I stepped to the door.

"Are you angling to come back to the force?"

I bristled at the question, though his tone had been mild and not at all accusatory.

"No, sir. I miss the job, but I'm doing all right on my own. And I don't expect that anyone in a position of power would take me back."

"Probably not, no." He swiveled so that he was facing me. "Shaw tells me that your input on the Howell murder, and also on the killing in Sweetwater Park, was invaluable."

"I was happy to help."

I expected a snide response, but he just nodded again. "Thanks for telling me this," he said. "I . . . I'm glad the rumors weren't true."

I waited, wondering if he would say more, or if that was as close as he could come to admitting that he had been wrong about my old man. When he didn't say anything else, I let myself out of his office, left 620, and drove back to Chandler.

Namid kept his distance for about a week. When he finally materialized again in my living room, it was late at night. Dad was still staying with me, but he had already gone to sleep.

"Ohanko," the runemyste said. "It has been too long since you trained." He lowered himself to the floor and eyed me with that same annoyingly expectant expression, like a puppy waiting to be walked.

"Not so fast, ghost." I ignored his rumble of protest. "What have you done with Saorla?"

"We have done nothing with her. She remains free to do as she pleases, except that she cannot trouble you or your father, and she is watched at all times. If she attempts to kill more of our kind, we will stop her."

"There'll be others you know." I heard an echo of Amaya's words in my own, but I pressed on. "She can't be the only necromancer who wants all of you destroyed."

"Assuredly she is not. But we know nothing of others, and so for now we can do little about them. We will watch Saorla, and perhaps we will learn of others from her."

It wasn't the most reassuring of strategies, but it wasn't the worst I'd heard, either.

"Now," he said, "sit and clear yourself."

I sat across from him and closed my eyes, summoning the calming image of my Golden Eagle. When I felt that I was cleared, I opened my eyes once more.

He nodded once. "Defend yourself."

I got my dad settled back into his trailer a few days later and the following morning brought Billie back to her home in Tempe. We spent a quiet day together making her house a bit more comfortable and convenient for someone with an arm in a cast. And I stayed with her for a few nights—purely to make sure that she was okay. Right.

The following Tuesday, she and I went out to Wofford for my usual visit with my dad. Even through the phasing—not the nights, of course, but the days—he had been unusually lucid. Maybe it was the relief of no longer having to endure the torment meted out by the necromancers. Whatever the reason, I had started to take the clarity of our conversations for granted.

When we arrived on this day, though, he was hunched

in his chair, mumbling to himself, his T-shirt stained. He wore no socks, and he smelled like he hadn't showered in a few days. Despite Namid's assurances, my first thought was that Saorla had recommenced her attacks on him.

But he wasn't flinching, and his color was good.

"How are you feeling, Dad?" I asked, giving him a quick kiss on the forehead.

"Hot wind blowing," he said. "It's that brown haze on the city. Makes the wind hot, hurts my eyes and my throat. Used to be you could count on the birds to keep it cool, to bring rain and such. Not anymore. Birds are as helpless as we are. More. That wind bothers them—keeps them from flying straight."

On and on he went. A classic Leander Fearsson rant. There was no point to it, no beginning or end. Just the random thoughts of a crazy old runecrafter. It was perfectly normal for him, but still it broke my heart. Billie sat beside me and we both listened. Occasionally we tried to engage him, though it did little good. But she held my hand, and she got me through it. By the time we left he was dressed in a clean T-shirt and was balancing a plate of fresh-cooked steak and roasted potatoes in his lap. I felt that we'd done everything we could. Until next week.

"Come on, Fearsson," Billie said, pulling me gently toward the car. "We'll get some dinner and watch a movie. He'll be fine."

"Yeah, I know." And I did. He was safe, at least for now. But there was no way to change who and what he had become over the years. Or what I would become eventually.

I turned away from him and kissed her. "Thanks for coming out with me."

"Of course. I'm your wife, remember? That's what we wives do."

I had to laugh. But gazing at her in the dying light, I felt my breath catch. I'd come so close to losing her.

Her brow creased. "Fearsson?"

"I'm glad you're all right," I said, my chest tightening. I lifted her good hand to my lips.

"Yeah, well about that."

Uh-oh. I had been waiting for this. She was better off without me. Certainly she'd be safer. Had she finally figured this out as well?

"I think," she went on, "that it's time you started teaching me to defend myself."

I blinked. "Defend yourself? You mean from magic?"

"I was thinking of bombs, guns, knives, stuff like that. But protection from bat-shit crazy magical women would be a good idea, too." We both grinned. "Your life doesn't ever seem to slow down," she said. "And, much to my surprise, I kind of like that. But it would be good to be able to rely on myself a bit more."

"That's not what I expected you to say."

"No?"

I shrugged, looking away. "I thought you were going to tell me that you were leaving me for that good-looking history professor."

"Joel Benfield?"

I would have preferred she not come up with the name quite so quickly. "Yeah, him."

"Fearsson, are you jealous of Joel?"

"Maybe a little."

She shook her head. "Clown." She stepped forward and kissed me lightly on the lips. "I've not leaving you for anyone," she whispered. "It's too late for that. But I've had enough of feeling helpless, and of people using your feelings for me as a weapon."

"Yeah, I don't like that either."

"Teach me then."

"All right, I will. We'll start tomorrow."

We kissed again before I helped her into the Z-ster. I started the car, but then cast one last look at my dad. He still sat with his chair angled toward the hills, the desert wind stirring his hair, the last golden light of day touching his face.

CHAPTER 26

He watches as the boy and girl drive away, red dust rising into the desert twilight. There is so much he wishes he had told them, so much he wanted to say. Already, though, his thoughts are drifting upward with the dirty haze, vanishing into another night like a balloon whose string has slipped through the fingers of a child.

The aroma of cooked meat draws his gaze down. His dinner. Good, he's hungry. He's always hungry. But when he glances up again, she's there.

At first he's frightened, remembering one who used this form to hurt him.

But she smiles her inscrutable smile and spins, making her blue dress swirl and fan like a dancer. This is his Dara, not the other. Honey hair stirs in the breeze; blue eyes lock on his.

He has so much to tell her, too. But he can't bring himself to speak. He watches her, and it is all he can do to inhale and exhale.

It was real, wasn't it? he wants to say. *You loved me once.*

But he doesn't need to ask the question aloud. The smile deepens. She nods, spins again. His heart soars.

It's good that she didn't make him speak. Because they're here, too, keeping an eye on him.

Oh, they don't hurt him anymore. No visions. No burning. Not for days now, not since the boy fought beside him and the myste said that he would protect them both. They're afraid of the myste, and they leave him alone. They don't even speak to him.

But they're watching. That hasn't changed. He senses them, knows they remain near, impatient for their next opportunity. He feels their hunger, their malice, their promise of retribution.

So he smiles back at the woman, and keeps silent, knowing that once he was loved, and that the boy loves him still.

And the dark ones lurk in deepening shadows, keeping their vigil and waiting.

Acknowledgements

● ● ●

Once more, I am grateful to Karen Kontak and Jeri F. of the Phoenix Police Department's Crime Analysis and Research Unit, who gave me valuable information about life in the PPD and in Phoenix's various police precincts and beats, and to Gayle Millette, of the Phoenix Medical Examiner's Office, for her help with details about the OME. Thanks also to Rand Vogelfanger and Bill Kershner for sharing with me their vast knowledge of aviation And finally, I owe a great debt to Michael Prater, for his expertise on firearms, and for his bravery in actually taking me out shooting.

Faith Hunter offered a good deal of feedback on the manuscript and also answered countless questions about hospitals, medical procedures, and the possible effects of myriad injuries on my characters. Thanks to her, this is a better novel, as well as a more realistic one. Once again, I also want to thank all my wonderful friends at Magical Words.

Huge thanks as well as to my agent, Lucienne Diver, for

her close reading of the book, her support and professional advice, and her friendship.

I am deeply grateful to Tony Daniel, for his editorial feedback on the manuscript, as well as his patience with a writer who is sometimes too stuck in his ways. Thanks as well to Toni Weisskopf, Jim Minz, Laura Haywood-Cory, Gray Rinehart, Danielle Turner, Carol Russo, and all the great folks at Baen Books.

Finally, as always, I am grateful to Nancy, Alex, and Erin, for the countless ways in which they fill my world with laughter and love.

—D.B.C.

About the Author

David B. Coe is the Crawford Award-winning author of eighteen novels and the occasional short story. Under his own name he has written three epic fantasy series, as well as the novelization of Ridley Scott's *Robin Hood*. As D. B. Jackson, he is the author of the Thieftaker Chronicles, a historical urban fantasy. *His Father's Eyes* is the second book in the Case Files of Justis Fearsson. The third novel is already in the works. David's books have been translated into a dozen languages. He lives on the Cumberland Plateau with his wife and daughters.

INTRODUCING
THE SEER
AN EPIC FANTASY BY NEWCOMING AUTHOR
SONIA ORIN LYRIS

Everybody Wants Answers. No One Wants the Truth.

The Arunkel Empire has stood a thousand years, forged by
wealth and conquest, but now rebellion is stirring on the bor-
ders and treachery brews in the palace halls. Elsewhere, in a
remote mountain village, a young mother sells the prophesies
of her sister, Amarta, in order to keep them and her infant
child from starving. It's a dangerous game when such revela-
tions draw suspicion and mistrust as often as they earn coin.

Yet Amarta's visions are true. And often not at all what the
seeker wishes to hear.

THE SEER
978-1-4767-8126-6
$15.00 US/$20.00 CAN

"Compelling characters, a fully imagined world, and a gripping narrative: *The Seer* announces Sonia Lyris as a new
and exciting voice in epic fantasy. I highly recommend
this novel, and I look forward to her next."—David B.
Coe, author of best-selling Winds of the Forelands series

"*The Seer* is something extremely rare these days: a fantasy
which is complex, complete, so intricate that you feel the picture goes on far, far beyond the parts of it which are in the book.
There is a wonderful depth to it, and the characters and the setting in which the characters find themselves (both horrific and
fascinating) made it compelling reading."—Dave Freer, author
of the critically acclaimed Dragon's Ring series